D1121861

*A*
*Garland Series*

# VICTORIAN

# FICTION

## *NOVELS OF FAITH AND DOUBT*

*A collection of 121 novels
in 92 volumes, selected by
Professor Robert Lee Wolff,
Harvard University,
with a separate introductory volume
written by him
especially for this series.*

# THE TRIUMPH OF FAILURE

**Patrick Augustine Sheehan**

---

# A FLOWER OF ASIA

**Henry E. Dennehy**

*Garland Publishing, Inc., New York & London*

*1976*

**Library of Congress Cataloging in Publication Data**

Sheehan, Patrick Augustine, 1852-1913.
    The triumph of failure.

    (Victorian fiction : Novels of faith and doubt)
    Reprint of 2 works published in 1899 and 1901,
respectively, by Burns & Oates, London.
    1. English fiction--19th century.  I.  Dennehy, H.E.
A flower of Asia. 1976. II.  Title. III.  Series.
PZ1.S5523Tr    [PR1304]    823'.8'08    75-467
ISBN 0-8240-1545-2

# THE TRIUMPH OF FAILURE

Bibliographical note:

this facsimile has been made from a copy in the British Museum (04410.f.11)

# THE TRIUMPH OF FAILURE

# THE

# TRIUMPH OF FAILURE

### A SEQUEL TO
### "GEOFFREY AUSTIN, STUDENT"

BY THE

## REV. P. A. SHEEHAN
### DONERAILE
#### (DIOCESE OF CLOYNE)

LONDON: BURNS & OATES, LIMITED
NEW YORK, CINCINNATI, CHICAGO: BENZIGER BROTHERS
1899

# CONTENTS

## *BOOK I*

| CHAP. | | PAGE |
|---|---|---|
| I. | A MENTAL AUDIT . | 3 |
| II. | A DUAL LIFE | 18 |
| III. | URSULA . | 25 |
| IV. | AMONGST THE OLYMPIANS . | 35 |
| V. | SIBYLLA MEA. | 45 |
| VI. | LEAVES FROM A DIARY | 60 |
| VII. | NOËL ! NOËL ! | 76 |
| VIII. | TABLEAUX VIVANTS | 89 |
| IX. | IN THE DEPTHS . | 103 |

## *BOOK II*

| | | PAGE |
|---|---|---|
| I. | AMONGST THE MEDICALS | 123 |
| II. | AUF WIEDERSEHEN ! | 138 |
| III. | A DIPSOMANIAC | 150 |
| IV. | ATTIC NIGHTS | 163 |
| V. | ATTIC NIGHTS (*continued*) | 176 |
| VI. | A STERN NOVITIATE | 185 |
| VII. | THE YOUNG REFORMER | 198 |
| VIII. | NIGHT SPECTRES . | 212 |
| IX. | SHADOWED | 222 |
| X. | AT GLASNEVIN | 238 |
| XI. | A BURNING HAND. | 256 |
| XII. | EPHREM OF EDESSA | 271 |
| XIII. | THE YAWNING OF HELL | 287 |

| CHAP. | | PAGE |
|---|---|---|
| XIV. | A MOONLIGHT VISIT | 295 |
| XV. | FROM THE MOUNTAIN OF MYRRH | 308 |
| XVI. | TO THE HILL OF INCENSE | 329 |
| XVII. | ARRESTED | 351 |
| XVIII. | TRIUMPH AND DEATH | 365 |

## BOOK III

| I. | SELF-QUESTIONINGS | 379 |
|---|---|---|
| II. | AT LAST | 388 |
| III. | CONSULTING THE SIBYL | 405 |
| IV. | A WEARY QUEST | 418 |
| V. | FROM MY CELL | 429 |
| VI. | L'ENVOI | 442 |

# BOOK I

# THE

# TRIUMPH OF FAILURE

## *BOOK I*

### CHAPTER I

#### A MENTAL AUDIT

> I am become a name
> For always roaming with a hungry heart ;
> For all experience is an arch, where through
> Gleams the untravelled future.

NOT quite in the suburbs of our city, and yet removed from the odours of the Liffey and the jingling of tramcar bells, is a quiet terrace. The houses are built in couples, and are therefore what is called semi-detached; and they are built in uniform style, three-storeyed, bay-windowed, Venetian-blinded, although, as their aspect is decidedly northern, there seems to be no urgent demand for this latter characteristic. Of course, there is a tiny lawn in front of each house. In some of these, wild weeds, like conquering Vandals, overrun and stifle the poor little fragile mignonette, or geranium, or stunted rose-tree; in others, there is a vague attempt at carpet-gardening, evidently non-professional, evidently the work of the master of the house, who takes his legitimate exercise, smokes his evening pipe, and conscientiously favours the fine arts, in shirt-sleeves, on the long summer evenings after supper. These trim little gardens, with their geranium-beds, and calceolarias, and the sweet little lobelia hedging them in, certainly look with some scorn on their unkempt neighbours. So, too, do their railings, shining in bright buff colours ; so, too, do bell-knob and knocker that glisten every morning like gold ; so, too, do the trim, neat children, and the servants, in all the glory of pronounced and flaring summer blouses ; so, too, but good-naturedly, does the amateur-gardener and recognised master of the establishment ; so, too, above all, does the queen and mistress of the place, who throws back her head, and therefore her bonnet, every inch of which dances in scorn with black, glistening bugles and beads, as she moves down her own well-gravelled, if limited walks, and says, with lips of scorn that never articulate the word " Disgusting ! "

One evening, in the November of the year 187—, just as the lamplighter was touching with his long wand the lamp at the corner of this terrace, and blinds were being pulled down by the housemaids, and pleasant pictures of tea-equipages could be seen through the windows, a solitary figure passed along the path in front and scrutinised these villas closely, as if he were looking for a number that was not yet visible, or some characteristic that remained unseen. Apparently unsatisfied, he passed along the range of houses, and came in front of a detached dwelling that seemed, as if from some higher pretensions, to stand aloof from and contemn its neighbours. It was quite detached. The flower-garden in front had some appearance of elegance—there was a garden-seat, and in the hall, dimly lighted by a crimson lamp that flung a warm colour all around, a few palms threw up their long glistening leaves against the rose-tinted garments of two marble, or, perhaps, plaster goddesses. There was one fatal feature, however, that disillusioned the visitor of any dreams of independence that the surroundings might have suggested. It was a square white placard with the significant legend : *" Furnished apartments to let !"*

With some misgivings, the young stranger pulled the bell. There was a delay, then some hurried shuffling in the drawing-room ; and after an interval a young maid appeared, pinning on a lace apron, and evidently disturbed at such an apparition at such an hour. She ushered the visitor into a room on the left of the hall, took his card, and retired. He had time enough to look around, for he was left alone for half-an-hour at least. During that time he discovered that there was a large, heavy mirror over the mantelpiece, a massive mahogany dining-table in the centre of the room, a massive sideboard at the farther end, six heavy chairs, an oil-painting of some military gentleman looking desperately fierce ; and that was all. Now, he was nervous on entering ; but the nervousness wore away and gave room to impatience as the minutes sped by and no one appeared.

At length, the door noiselessly opened, and a middle-aged lady entered. She threw a swift glance towards her visitor, and sank with an air of wearied dignity into a chair.

" Mr. Austin, I presume ? "

I, Geoffrey Austin, bowed ; for I may begin now to speak in my own person, not as if telling the story of a stranger.

" Take a seat, please ! "

Her awful dignity sent a cold chill through my spinal cord, and out through the back of my head.

" I thought I saw an advertisement in the morning papers to the effect that apartments were to let in the terrace. But I fear I have mistaken the number."

"It is true," she replied with chill dignity, "that we have apartments to let, but—I presume you belong to the gentry?"

"I cannot say I do."

"Ah! . . . Then perhaps you belong to the— the professional class?"

"I am afraid I can hardly presume so much!"

"Ah! indeed," she said. Then after a pause, "Am I wrong in supposing that you are *littery?*"

At this word my nerves drew together and braced themselves, and I felt the firm ground under my feet. As a letter from a superior officer, of whom you stand in wholesome dread, if marked "strictly *privete*," gives the subordinate a feeling of superiority and even contempt for such a blunderer, so this one word revolutionised my feelings and put me on a level with my dignified interviewer.

I rose to depart. My timidity was giving way to a more robust sensation. She made a gesture as if to stay me.

"Well, at least you can give me some reference?"

I boiled over.

"I haven't demanded a reference from you," I said hotly; "I shall pay you in advance, and I am quite sure that it is all the reference you require."

The good lady was stricken dumb by such impudence. She made a tearful appeal to the military gentleman in the picture as if she would like to say, "My poor dear husband, can you stand this?" What she did say was—

"Then perhaps you would like to see your rooms?"

"Not mine, as yet," I murmured. "I shall be pleased to see *your* rooms, madam."

Evidently she thought it better not to quarrel on

such slight acquaintance. She led the way up a broad flight of stairs to the third storey, and then for the first time inquired—

" A suite of apartments, or a single room ? "

" A bedroom," I said decisively, " with a southern aspect " (I regretted the " southern aspect " next day), " and the use of a sitting-room."

She flung open the door of a spacious bedroom, which I examined minutely, and declared myself satisfied.

" Then as to terms ? "

She eyed me narrowly, from which and from other symptoms I had long since concluded that I was not dealing with a lady of reduced rank. I had almost gone so far as to believe that the colonel was a myth.

She demanded something extravagant. We agreed to fifteen shillings a week.

" But your vahlet ? " she queried.

" My valet has been obliged to remain at my father's residence in the country on account of an unexpected influx of visitors."

" Then will you bring your own pleet ? "

" My plate is at my banker's. You can hardly suppose that I would bring plate to Dublin on a hurried visit."

" But," I added, to relieve her apprehensions, " I won't make too large a demand on *your* silver. I shall probably dine out every day, and only trouble you at breakfast and tea-time. And I shall probably do all my writing in my own room."

This was apparently a great relief to my hostess, so we parted on fairly good terms. As I passed through the hall, the sounds of a piano came softly through a half-closed door ; and a voice, low and musical enough, was not singing, but murmuring, some little ballad.

Next evening I entered into residence. I am

quite sure my new friends were first impressed and astonished at the extent of my luggage—then probably disappointed on finding that these heavy cases contained only books.  I unpacked these latter as quickly as I could by the aid of the housemaid, assorted them, placed them on improvised book-shelves, laid out my writing materials, and went down to tea.  My hostess was good enough to invite me to her own drawing-room ; but I had some reason for declining.  After tea I flung myself into an arm-chair, and took a survey of my position and surroundings.  I confess I was somewhat melancholy. The large room, the strong, massive furniture, the absence of anything light or elegant, and above all, the singing of the gas-jets over my head, plunged me into a condition of mental depression.  I wanted to think, but could not.  I went hastily to my room. The little housemaid brought me a lamp.

"What's your name ? " I asked.

She was a bright, saucy little body, with black eyes, like beads ; but I suppose I frightened her.

"My name is Kate," she said, " but they call me Katrine.  I don't know why.  Please, sir, do you know ? "

"Well," said I, "I suppose they are Scotch. There is a lake in Scotland of that name ! "

"Indeed, they aren't Scotch," she returned, " they're Irish enough.  There must be some other reason."

"Well, you know it sounds grand," I said, "and when you are mixing with great people, you must try to do as they."

" H'm, great people indeed——"

Then she stopped suddenly.

"Look here, Katrine," said I, " I'm afraid I shall be an awfully troublesome fellow.  I am the most untidy creature that ever lived.  You mustn't be surprised in the morning to find a slipper here under the wardrobe, and another under the bed: and a smoking cap here, and a pipe there, and the floor littered with scraps of paper——"

"Oh! I don't mind, sir," she said, smiling, "I hate old maids."

"You hate what?" I said.

"I mean I don't like gentlemen that are too particklar," she said with a blush.

"But won't you be angry if I turn everything topsy-turvy?"

"No," she said.

"But if I drop grease on the floor?"

She gave a little shudder.

"No," she said again.

"But if I spatter the bed-clothes with ink?"

"I'm sure you'll do nothing of the kind," she said, "but you are only poking fun at me."

We were friends from that hour.

Now, whenever I reach a fresh point in my queer career through life, I always perform an exercise in geography, and mental bookkeeping. I found that for years my ideas of the ancient Greeks, whom I loved so much, were quite undefined and hazy because I had such nebulous notions of the topography of that wonderful country; and I am quite sure I never read a line of Scripture with profit, because I did not know whether Jerusalem was in the mountains or on the plains; nor did I know if Sechem or Hebron was in Syria or Chaldea. Then, again, my mental accounts get into inextricable confusion, if I do not make a careful audit from time to time, and close my books for transfer. So next morning, I gave a brief moment to a survey of my surroundings, and a long, long reverie to my exact position in this little drama of my life. For the former, I discovered that I was in a back room, a little musty, but quite capable of ventilation, in a remote suburb of the city of Dublin, under the tender, but I guessed, curious and prying supervision of a lady, who was engaged clearly in a laudable desire to keep up appearances and make ends meet; who had a daughter hitherto invisible, who could play, and perhaps sing, and with a little maid who would be more merciful to my shortcomings than her mistress.

The result of my audit was this. To my credit I could place youth and strength, a splendid constitution, a fairly liberal education, a love for learning, and £80, the balance left after my expenses in Mayfield and London, and which my guardian sent me, at my own request, on my return after my failure at the Control Examination. On the debit side could be placed that dismal failure, the cause which led up to it, my utter inexperience of life, and a disposition very prone to extreme and abnormal depression or the reverse. I should add to my credit account a small but select library; to my debit account, alas! a faith and religious feeling, theoretically intact, practically shattered and undermined.

Perhaps this is too harsh an expression. If I were asked then, or at any other time, what was my religious profession, I should say without hesitation, Roman Catholic. If any one in my presence spoke slightingly of any article of faith, I should have resented it; and if any one spoke even in unrespectful terms of priest, or nun, or saint, I should have struck him, and thought myself fully justified. What then? I should rather have said that my faith, unused to exercise, and unsupported by those external aids and practices that are of such supreme importance to Catholics living in the world, had grown to be a negative quality so far as its influence on my daily life was concerned. It had evaporated, and had not even become a cloud-shadow overhanging my life, and containing promise of future fertility. In other words, it had ceased to be a motive power;

and in its place had come a passion for learning, an insatiable curiosity to pry into the crypts and vaults of human beliefs, and a secret, but unavowed, inclination to seek in the pursuit of knowledge, and the principles of the world's thinkers, that happiness which I was already assured was far beyond the grasp of those who sought their elysium here in external and artificial pleasures. It will be seen at once that there was nothing gross, earthy, sensual, or even sensuous, here. In a word, I wanted to lead a life of pure thought : and I dreamed that in the abstraction of my mind from all things temporary or paltry, I should, like the sages of the East, find my Nirvana even here. It may be said that these were at least unusual ideas for a boy of immature years ; but it must be remembered that I have spoken of myself as a highly impressionable being, quick and alive to ideas and sensations that would be absolutely foreign to ordinary students; and it must also be remembered that I had been thrown into the society of two men who had already had experience of the world, and who, despising the factitious advantages which wealth and position give, found their happiness in simple living, and in the company of the kings of thought. It did not occur to me, until after many years of pain, that these two men were also deeply religious, and had learned the grand secret of subordinating earthly wisdom to the wisdom that is from above.

When, a few days before I departed for London, Mr. Dowling said to me that I was only a neophyte in knowledge, that I was only standing as yet in the outer porch or vestibule of the glorious temple which only privileged souls could enter, I was seized with the desire to make myself worthy of taking the inner vows. And when I asked him who should be my guide thither, and he said, "Commence with the Greeks, and come down to the Germans," I determined that this should be the line of my future studies.   In the after years, on one of the few occasions that I met him, and reproached him with having misled me, he opened his eyes widely, and said—

"Imperilled your faith?  You might as well accuse me of having imperilled your life, or infected you with delirium !   You have grossly misunderstood me !   If you took my silver and gold ornaments, and turned them into suicidal weapons against yourself, you have only yourself to blame."

"But your Plato, and your Zeno, and all your sceptics——"

"They are, my friend, but the acolytes of the Church ; you have made them rival priests, and their tenets rival religions."

Meantime, I was beginning to find that my religion, about which I was so indifferent, was a matter of supreme concern to others.

On the Friday morning after I had entered into residence with Mrs. Oliver, Katrine placed my breakfast as usual on the table.   I raised the dish-cover to find the customary rasher and eggs.   Katrine delayed a little.

"What day is this, Katrine ? " I said.

"Friday, sir."

"Then would you be good enough to take away this meat, and bring me two poached eggs."

She blushed with pleasure, and brought me back two eggs, cooked in the highest scientific style. She was accustomed in her usual household work to lighten her labour by singing.   That evening there was an unusual trill in her voice, as if a great sense of restraint had been taken away, and she felt quite sure of her new lodger.   With her mistress, who was also a Catholic, the case was different.   The discovery that I belonged to the common faith lowered me fifty per cent. in her esteem.

It was manifested in this way.   The first evening

that I, in response to repeated invitations, honoured the ladies with my presence at the tea-table, Mrs. Oliver, in an accent that I shall only call indescribable, asked me—

"I was wondering, Mr. Austin, if you belonged to the Austins of Fermanagh?"

Now, I fear, I am not quite polite; but questions of this kind always set my temper on edge.

"No," I said quietly, "I am not aware that any persons of the name can claim property in me. I have no master but myself."

The daughter looked at me in a pained kind of way, as if she would despair of ever getting on terms with so brusque a subject.

"Ah, pardon me," said the mother, with a little laugh, "I was not quite explicit. But it is easy to perceive that you belong to a good family; and I thought, your name being so rare and unusual, that you might claim relationship with my friends."

I was awfully tempted to take the high aristocratic tone again, but I merely said—

"I am afraid I cannot claim the honour even of their acquaintance. I am from the south of Ireland."

"Yes, and I perceive that you are a Roman Catholic, and this branch of the Austins is, ah—Protestant!"

Mrs. Oliver felt she was scoring against me here. I said—

"That circumstance makes it more pleasant to me that I have not the honour of their acquaintance, much less of a family connection with them."

"Oh, how illiberal, Mr. Austin!" she replied. "Now, I consider Protestants highly—well—interesting."

"And, mumma," said Miss Oliver, addressing her mother, "surely we must admit that Protestants are not only better educated than we, but have the monopoly of all the culture and refinement of the country."

This was hard.

"Then, I presume, Miss Oliver," I said, "that most of your acquaintances are Protestants."

"Oh dear, yes!" she said, with a pitying laugh, "there *really* is no other society."

"And you know, Mr. Austin," put in her mother, "we have some blue blood in our veins. My mother was a Protestant; and I frequently heard her say that her ancestors were Huguenots that fled from France at the promulgation of that dreadful edict. What was it, Gwen ? "

"You mean Nongz, mumma, I suppose," said the young lady, with a most pronounced inflection on the French word.

"You have been at a Protestant academy, Miss Oliver ? " I said.

"Oh dear, no!" she replied apologetically; "it was my misfortune to have been educated—shall I call it educated?—at a convent; and I am sure I shall never cease to regret it."

"You see, Mr. Austin," Mrs. Oliver said, "nuns are very good, poor things! but they are not *au courant* with the age. The advanced education of the day has no place in our convents. Fancy, my daughter never heard of Baudelaire, till a professor from the High School spoke of *her*——"

"O mumma!" said Miss Oliver reproachfully.

"Yes, dear, and Dant and Gothy were unknown names. Even our own dear Swinburne was forbidden literature; and Gwendolen actually assures me that parts even of Shakespeare were considered unfit reading for the young ladies."

"How dreadful!" I said; "and I suppose, Miss Oliver, you have made the acquaintance of these distinguished authors since your emancipation ? "

"Oh dear, yes!" that young lady replied with vivacity. "I never tire of reading them."

"You remember that pretty thing, called 'Our Lady of Pain'?"

"Yes, it is quite lovely!"

"And 'In the Garden of Venus'?"

"Yes! it is really charming. Such sentiment, you know, and such rhythm. He can do what he likes with words!"

"There's a passage," I said, throwing my head back meditatively, "in 'Faust'——"

"Oh! we have seen 'Faust' over and over again. Have we not, mumma?"

"I don't mean the opera," I said, "but the masterpiece of Goethe. It runs thus—but am I right in saying it is in 'Faust'? No matter; you'll correct me—

> 'Geheimnissvoll am lichten Tag
> Lasst sich Natur des Schleiers nicht berauben,
> Und was sie deinem Geist nicht offenbaren mag
> Das zwingst du ihr nicht ab mit
> Hebeln und mit Schrauben.'[1]—

Now, Miss Oliver, that is an opinion with which I cannot agree."

The poor girl looked appealingly to her mother. I continued—

"Now, that's a mere parody on the old, old story of the veil of Isis. But is it true?"

I waited a reply. The poor girl looked the picture of misery, but I went on—

"For if so, does it not directly contradict all that we have been taught about the achievements of modern science? Why, the boast of all our scien-

---

[1] Inscrutable in noonday's blaze
Nature lets no one tear the veil away;
And what herself she does not choose
Unasked before your soul to lay,
You shall not wrest from her by levers or by screws.

tific men is, that it is only with hammer and pick they have torn their secrets from Nature—that she has been *obliged* to show them all her secrets—that all the discoveries in botany, geology, and astronomy have been made by doing violence to Nature, and compelling her to yield to the superior wisdom of her master, Man.   Even her Æolian melodies, heard of old in forest and on mountain, have been captured and tamed into the modern sonata, or——"

"Oh, I perceive, Mr. Austin, you are musical too," interjected the mother, whose experience came to her succour here.   "Perhaps you would like to hear Gwen play?   You spoke just now of sonatas.   Try, Gwen, that sonata from Beethoven."

I was defeated, horse, foot, and artillery, and could only say—

"I assure you, nothing could give me greater pleasure."

I opened the piano and set the music for Miss Oliver, and sat down.

The girl played well, with expression and force, and without that mechanical stiffness that is so common with beginners.

She then ran through the mazes of some difficult piece from Chopin, and then a delightful little waltz from Strauss.

I rose to go, and murmured my praises with all sincerity.

"Clearly, Miss Oliver, you are in the hands of some great master!"

"Well, no! curiously enough," replied her mother, "she has had no teacher since she left the convent at——"

"Indeed," I said.   "Then, if defective in their literary training, I must say the nuns have more than made up for it in the extraordinary musical proficiency Miss Oliver has acquired."

"Well, I should say it was her own gift.   Probably Gwen would be able to make music a profession if she had sat under some of the masters here in Dublin."

As I went into the hall and said "Good-night," I asked, " Did you say, Mrs. Oliver, that your ancestors were Huguenots ? "

"Yes ! " she replied, but with a little misgiving, "they were, at least one ! "

" But Oliver is not a French name ? "

" I said *my* ancestors," replied Mrs. Oliver sweetly. " My name is Gascoigne ! "

She gave the word its full French emphasis, and was evidently as proud of that Gascoigne, who was probably a disreputable dragoon, as if he had walked the quarter-deck with Nelson at Trafalgar, or carried the colours under Wellington through the hell-storm of Quatre Bras.

**B**

# CHAPTER II

## A DUAL LIFE

In my breast
Alas ! two souls dwell—all there is unrest ;
Each with the other strives for mastery,
Each from the other struggles to be free.
One to the fleshly joys the coarse earth yields,
With clumsy tendrils clings, and one would rise
In native power and vindicate the fields
Its own by birthright—its ancestral skies.

—*Faust.*

WHICH of the two is the better gift of the gods—
the ignorance of youth, that shuts out from their
mental vision all the dread spectres of the future,
or the experience that helps them to exorcise those
spectres, when, perhaps, they are no longer formid-
able ?   Yet, I think it is the more merciful dispensation, that which lets fall a thick curtain of
obscurity across the years, nay, across every day,
that looms up ominously from the tenebrous gulfs
of the future, and only lets us exercise our fancies
in painting dark shadows on that impenetrable veil,
behind which the Fates are waiting for our footsteps.   And who would take from youth its san-
guine dreams, its buoyancy, its hope and trust,
which, after all, help it to leap lightly over the toils
and snares and pitfalls of life, merely for the sake
of that wisdom which only helps to make men
timorous, dimming their vision with fear, and ener-
vating their lithe activity with a sense of caution
that is no match for the pitiless destinies that await
them ?   I know I often thank Providence in my

better moods for that, when I was fated to descend, it was by easy steps and slow experiences I went down into the deep pit : and that there was no sudden revelation made to me of the yawning chasms and cavernous gloom of the abysses into which I was hurrying. For now my life took on a double aspect of struggle and triumphs, of defeat and victory, of mornings spent in wrestling with men for a pittance, and nights spent in luxurious contests with demigods to drag from them their secrets, and to know whether a satiety of know-ledge meant also the perfection of peace. It was with a sinking heart, after a few dismal failures, that I put on my overcoat one morning, drew up my faded gloves, and stepped into the dripping streets in search of some decent employment that would merely yield me a competence.

I had already met a few rebuffs. This morning I entered a large mercantile establishment in the city, confident that I could secure an honourable position there as clerk or accountant. I passed up the central aisle, stared at unmercifully by the well-polished clerks and the counter girls, and asked the " walker " for the manager.

The manager came bowing and smiling, and rubbing his soft hands together. His manner was deferential and subdued. He expected a large order, or some pleasant message.

" I am in want of a situation ! "

His face fell. His manner became dignified. He put his soft hands in his waistcoat pockets, and looked me all over. His subordinates saw the change and sniggered.

" You have papers ? "

" No."

" But you have had some experience at our business ? "

" I regret to say I have not. But," I interpolated, "I have had a liberal education, know classics well, can keep accounts——"

"What system of book-keeping did you learn?"

"I am sorry to say that I have not learned book-keeping. It did not enter into our curriculum!"

Then he became sarcastic. Leaning forward on a desk, and looking around to secure the attention of an admiring audience, he said—

"I am afraid, young man, you have made a mistake. You have taken this place for Trinity College. They want professors over there badly. Or, if you tried the College of Science, or——"

"I am obliged for your good opinion," I interrupted, "but you don't need my services?"

"If," he said in the same tones, "if this was a collegiate establishment, and these were my pupils" (his subordinates laughed loud at the witty assumption), "I would be glad to take you as an assistant. But as we are only commercial people, we hardly want high college swells like you. Now, do try Trinity. Perhaps you don't know it. Collins, go to the door, and show this young gentlemen the way to Trinity."

I was getting angry, and he saw it.

"Yes, show him the way to Trinity," he continued in a most exasperating tone, when I shot in—

"You are a miserable cad."

He did not lose his temper.

"Collins and Wright, as this young gentleman won't be directed to Trinity, show him—the door!"

The two counter hands advanced, laughing. I lifted my hat in mock courtesy to this despot, and was retiring; but he should have his revenge. He beckoned to his subordinates. They placed their hands on my shoulders, and, laughing and shouting, they pushed me down the long aisle, amidst the giggling and sneers of counter-hands and fringed shop-girls, and flung me into the street. A policeman passing made a gesture of inquiry, as if asking them would he arrest me. One of them said cheerily—

"Never mind the poor devil."

He passed to his work, and I, dazed and blind with passion at such an insult, walked the wet pavement, not knowing whither I was going. I only remember that I strove, by a vigorous effort of my will, to bring back to reason my wild fancies, and that I thought to smother my fury by leaning against the heavy brass railing that defended the plate-glass windows of a bookseller's shop. The crimson and gold on the backs of the books shone before me in a hazy manner; but to this day I do not remember the name or outline of a single volume. They swam before my eyes, distorted by the fierce fires of passion and revenge. I only know that I meditated some swift and terrible retribution, as yet undefined, for the foul insult that had been offered me. I went home, but could not rest there. I took up my favourite philosophers, Seneca and Marcus Aurelius. Their poor platitudes irritated rather than soothed me. I put a small duodecimo copy of the *Enchiridion* of Epictetus in my pocket, determined to seek some hidden spot, and read at my leisure. For I felt very much humbled that all my stoicism should vanish on such small provocation; and I had began to realise that there was some great defect in my education. How was I equipped to front the storms of life, when I reeled and staggered under such a feeble breeze? I walked the streets of Dublin that day, unconscious of the fine, thin rain that soaked through my garments and wet me to the skin, trying to exorcise the demon that possessed me. Oh! for some sedative, some kindly word, some gentle deed to reconcile me with my kind! I was a rebel against society, a raw, full-grown communard, hating everything around me.

I raged against man and God. I hated the people who, rolled up in furs and sealskins, swept by in close carriages; I could have cursed the gentlemen who came out from café and bodega after their mid-day lunch. If an earthquake had suddenly swallowed up all the gay and gaudy population around me, I would have exulted in the ruin, even though it meant my own destruction. I did not read Epictetus that day.

Thoroughly drenched, I returned home, when the gas-lamps shone through a misty halo made by fog and rain. I was chilled, but the fire and fever within prevented my feeling the cold. I went to my room, swallowed hastily two or three cups of tea, which Katrine brought me, without a word, although she had placed some dainty slices of buttered toast on my tray. And then I walked my room like a wild beast caged, until the silence of midnight woke me from my trance of madness, and I went to bed to dream of things over which memory would wish to throw a veil.

I woke next morning with the fever of unforgotten anger still burning in nerve and brain. I ate a meagre breakfast, my mind all the time running on some plan of revenge and satisfaction. I quite agreed with all that my spiritual advisers could urge. There was not one proposition advanced in Seneca's three books on Anger which I did not admit, nor one of the maxims of Aurelius with which I was not in perfect accord. But the thought of those grinning apes that dared lay hands upon me, of that " curled and oiled Assyrian bull " who instigated them, of these sniggering shop-girls, and the cool disdain of that policeman, swept my philosophers into utter oblivion; and I stood up from table, calmed by the determination to seek out that fellow's directors that forenoon, and demand that his insolence should be punished. I dressed myself with more than ordinary care, bore the sympathetic curiosity of Katrine and the supercilious curiosity of her mistress without a word, and walked the streets with a lighter step than I did the day before. I lingered around the thoroughfares of the city until the clock struck twelve, then I plunged into a bye-street where the directors of this particular firm had their offices, knocked, and passed in my card by the office boy. I suppose the card or my name was a sufficient introduction, for I was admitted without a moment's delay. I laid the case briefly before the Board, said that I had called on business the day before at their retail establishment in the city, and had been grossly insulted by their manager. They thought the charge serious enough to send for him, and I was left with all respect and deference to await his coming in an outer office. He was delayed for a little time, and came in through my office, looking anxious and perturbed; but when he saw me the look of anxiety disappeared, and he put on a smirk of satisfaction that was infinitely annoying. We appeared before the Board together. I made my statement, and made a visible impression upon the directors. The manager was not at all disconcerted. Clean and cool, perfumed and unguented from his curls down to his shiny boots, he awaited the end of my statement. Then, without condescending to look at me, he said to the chairman—

"This gentleman says he came on business. Please ask him what was his business."

The chairman looked at me.

"I came to seek a situation."

In a minute I saw the sympathies of the Board turned from me.

"I asked the young gentleman," the fellow continued, coolly looking at his shining finger nails, "what were his qualifications. He said classics.

He admitted his utter ignorance of business, even of book-keeping. I said I thought he might do better in an academy or college. He turned and called me a ' miserable cad.' I have no time, gentlemen, to spare from your business for the purpose of exchanging courtesies with the numberless tramps that come around our place day by day. I had him removed."

"And quite right," said the chairman. "And quite right," said the Board.

" Bob, show this gentleman out," said the chairman.

" You may thank your stars, my fine young fellow," said one of the directors, a magistrate, "that I do not commit you. If ever you come before me, I'll know how to deal with you."

My philosophy had left me so much self-restraint that I did not strike him. I bowed, passed through their offices again, bore the triumphant and supercilious glances of the manager, and passed once more into the street, at war with God and man.

# CHAPTER III

## URSULA

"A little child shall lead them."

By some instinct, for it was not conscious reasoning, I found myself again leaning on the massive brass railing outside the bookseller's shop, where I had found a temporary resting place the day before. Again the books and papers swam before my eyes; again the evil one, with seven spirits worse than himself, had entered in and taken possession of me. "If this was the world," I said to myself, "then am I the sworn enemy of the world and society for ever more. All that I have ever read of communism and socialism is a colossal lie—the fabrication of capitalists and labour-masters." Thus I raged, leaning on one hand my burning forehead, the other hung dead at my side. I heeded not the stream of people that swept by; I saw but my passion and revenge, when something soft and warm stole into my hand, and rested there. I turned round, and saw a little girl, who was not more than four years old, looking wistfully into my face. Her hand still nestled confidently in my own.

"Please, sir," she said, "take me home."

She was a dainty little woman. A small oval face was lighted up by two dark brown eyes, where the peace of Heaven shone; and her black hair, with some curious streaks of red or purple gleaming through it, fell in even curves upon her temples. She was well dressed; and a dainty little sealskin

cap (which I still hold, and which I would not part
with for all the diamonds of Golconda, and which
shall be buried with me wherever it pleases God my
remains shall be laid) rested lightly on her white
forehead.   I know not what she saw in me to seek
my confidence, for I am sure hell was pictured in
my face.   But then angels are not sent to angels.
Even in this, God's eternal law, the law of contrasts,
which is the law of love, was maintained.

But a miracle was wrought in me!   What all the
Pagan philosophy of Greece and Rome could not
bring about, the faith and confidence of that little
child effected.   I once saw a picture in some old
mansion down by one of the sweetest spots on earth.
It was painted by a Cork artist, and called the
" Flight of the Rebel Angels."   At the top of the
canvas, Michael, surrounded by a halo of light, and
numberless conquering spirits, is driving down into
the caverns and precipices of hell a host of dark
angels, tossed hither and thither in their defeat, and
shown in revolting and humiliating attitudes as they
plunge into irretrievable ruin.   Light above, darkness below ; and all foul and hideous things hiding
themselves from the lustre and splendour that shone
from swords, and shields, and helmets—faces and
figures of the conquering hosts.   Even so, the touch
of that little child swept from my soul the foul fiend
that possessed me, and I resumed, in one moment,
a tranquillity and peace to which, for the last two
days, I had been a stranger.   I closed my hand
gently over the soft, warm fingers.

"Come, little one," I said, "we will go home
together : and you shall lead me."

We walked the crowded thoroughfares—I silent
and peaceful, she in her own sweet way prattling
about many things.   She had asked my name, and
translated it into Doff; and it was Doff here, and
Doff there, and "Doff, do you see that ?" whilst we

wandered aimlessly along the pavements of the city.
At last I said—

"You must be tired."

"I'se tired," she replied.

I took her into a confectioner's shop, and placed
her light, dainty figure on the counter, and bought
her some cakes and lemonade.

"Have you seen this child before?" I asked the
attendants.

They had never seen her.

"You have no idea of where she resides?"

"Not the least."

"I live," said the child, "in a gwate big house,
and there are twees, and water all awound, and little
fishes, and old Biddy at the corner."

Whence I concluded that she belonged to some
of our city squares. Then when she had done, I
put out my hands to lift her.

She put me aside for a moment, and said—

"I always bless myself after meals," which she
did, reverently and devoutly.

I lifted her gently from the counter, and placed
her against my shoulder. She nestled there as confidently as if she had known me for years, and I
commenced a quest, which I half hoped would never
be successful. Presently she fell asleep. Her black
hair, stained with purple, fell down on my shoulders,
her soft, warm cheek was against my neck, her tiny
hand clasped me; and I was nearer to Heaven and
its angels than ever I had been before. I suppose
we presented an unwonted spectacle to the passers-
by, for a few women stopped and uttered some
sympathetic sounds, a couple of well-dressed young
ladies looked sideways at me and laughed; and
some well-dressed swells stared at me, and made,
I suppose, some ribald jokes; but I had one of
God's angels nestling in my arms, and I forgave the
world. I think I would have lifted my hat to the

directors who had insulted me that morning; and I would almost have shaken hands with the manager. How long I trudged along the streets aimlessly I do not know. I was hoping that she would never awaken. But she did, rubbed her eyes and drew back staring wonderingly at me. Then as memory reproduced on the tiny tablets of her mind what had occurred, she looked around inquiringly, and said—

"I tink we are near home."

"Will mamma be cross?"

"No! mamma never cross; but Susy will scold."

"I won't let Susy say one word to you," I said.

"Ha," she cried, clapping her hands, "there is Biddy."

My heart sank into my boots. It was true we were nearing home.

"Oh, wish! oh, wish! oh, wish! oh, Miss Ursey, 'twas you gave us the fright. Oh! take her to her mother, sir, for God's sake, and she'll bless you every day of your life!"

"Biddy, dis is Doff. Doff, dis is Biddy," said my little burden, introducing her two royalties.

"Show me the house, like a good woman," said I, "and I'll take the child there."

"Give Doff an apple, Biddy," said our little friend. "He dave me takes."

And the old applewoman, in obedience to her imperial behests, gave me an apple. Then she pointed out the house. It was easy to find it, by reason of the large portico that jutted on the square. I pulled the bell. It was answered; and there was, in a moment, a shout of jubilation throughout the household. Their queen had come back. But the gentle mother, quite a girl she looked, had been so troubled that she had not elasticity enough to share the universal joy. But she showered kisses on the truant, who, all the time, kept telling mother and maids that, "Dis is Doff. It was I finded him."

It appeared then that the nursery governess, in whose charge this little queen was placed, had been distracted by the march past of some soldiers, that the strong current of humanity then rolling by had detached her little charge, and swept it along ; and that some mysterious arrangement had borne the little waif into the haven of a troubled soul, that then, by right of such a presence, had stilled its turbulence into serenity.

I rose to depart, for I had been shown into the drawing-room. Then there was consternation. My young princess wanted to instal me then and there, and for ever more, in the place of honour.

" Perhaps you would come and see the child sometimes ? " said her mother.

" Gladly," said I, " if I should not be intruding."

" Oh, not at all," said her mother; " besides, she will order it, and we must obey her. She has grown so much into all our hearts."

" She has grown very much into mine," said I.

" Say good-bye, dear, to your friend."

Then the child became shy. She put out her hand timidly. But, as if her heart upbraided her for want of generosity, she held up her sweet lips to be kissed.

I bent down reverentially, and touched her soft lips, and swore in my own soul to be loyal to her, and to all the purity and holiness she represented, all the days of my life.

As I turned to depart a thought struck me.

" Might I ask the child's name ? " I said.

" Ursula," replied her mother, " Ursula Deane."

"Quite a fit name for such a child," I said, as I raised my hat and departed.

My first act on reaching home was to take up my Greek and Roman philosophers, and drop them one by one behind the highest rows of books on my shelves. I had no scruple about my Seneca (a

splendid Delphine edition, in three volumes, bound
in diamond calf, and with gilt edges), nor about
Marcus Aurelius ; but I balanced the *Enchiridion*,
a neat little volume, in limp vellum, for some moments in my hands.   After all, he was but a slave.
It would be a great sacrifice to part with him.   But
I was remorseless, and in a pitiless mood towards
humbugs.   I dropped him, too, into the limbo of
despised authors, and closed this page of the
history of my dealings with the ancient sages and
philosophers.

Katrine must have noticed a vast change in my
demeanour, for at tea-time she ventured on a few
commonplace remarks and questions, then suddenly
burst into this gratuitous proposition—

" Oh ! he's such a lovely man, sir ! "

" Katrine," said I, looking at her with pretended
severity, " of whom are you speaking ? "

" And he makes everything so easy, sir," she
continued, not heeding my question ;  " and he
preaches lovely, sir, and if you went to confession,
sir, you would think, sir, that it was he was telling
you your sins, sir, and not you telling him."

She drew a long breath after such a burst of
eloquence, then blushed at her hardihood.

" What is his name, Katrine ? " I said gently,
lest she should be frightened into silence.

" His name is Father Benedick, sir," she said,
resuming courage ;  " and O sir, you feel as light as
a feather when you come out of the box, sir, and
he gives such easy penances, sir, and they are all
running to him, sir, and he's killed from hearing
them——"

" Then I'd have no chance of getting near him,"
I said to this young apostle, "and if I did, I suppose
he'd turn me away."

" Indeed'n he wouldn't, sir ; and he'd hear you
first, sir, and let the others wait."

I turned around, and looked Katrine straight between the eyes.

"Katrine," I said sternly, "how do you know that?"

"Because, sir," she said, with a quaver in her voice, for she knew she had betrayed herself, "because, sir, you are a great scollard."

"That's not the reason, Katrine," I said inquisitorially, "you have been to confession. Don't tell a lie."

She burst into sobs. I pressed for an answer. And it came.

"Well then, sir," said the poor girl, "I did tell him all about you, sir. And I told him all about your books, and how you do be writing all night, and how you do come home troubled, sir, and I was sure you had something on your mind; and O sir, if you would only go to your duty, you'd be so happy, sir, and—and—and—I'm sure you'll forgive a poor servant girl, sir, but after all, who have we but God's ministers to look to?"

"Leave me now, Katrine," I said gently and humbly, "and I'll think the matter over."

She gathered up the tea-things, and had gone as far as the door, when she looked back and said—

"You won't say a word to them downstairs, sir. They do be saying such queer things."

"Queer things, Katrine?"

It was not quite honourable, but my curiosity overcame me.

"Yes, sir," said Katrine, balancing the tea-things at the door, "the young lady says you are a nobleman in disguise; the old lady says something else, and they do be poking among your books, sir; and if I were you, sir, I would not leave any letters about——"

"All right, Katrine," I said, "that will do for the present."

" But you won't forget Father Benedick, sir ? "
" No ! "
" And, please sir, tell him who you are."
" But I thought he knew everything, Katrine ? "
" Oh, he does, sir, he knows all about every one,
when once you tell him what you are.   And you
won't forget, sir ? "
" Katrine, close—that—door ! "

There was a loud thundering at the hall-door ;
and a sound of hurried feet and voices in the hall.

I wheeled my easy-chair to the fire, for it was a
cold November night, and staring at the fire-
pictures, I thought—

" You priests of Ireland ! when will your prophet
arise to tell you what an ocean of faith, and love,
and adoration flows softly and silently, without
break or murmur, around the little islets of your
existence ?   If we except the love of a mother for
her child, earth has no love so pure, so tender, so
spiritual, as the love of the Irish people for their
priests.   Nay, it is more elevated even than maternal
love.   For the mother says, ' Thou art flesh of my
flesh, and  bone  of  my  bone ; '  but this people,
eliminating  even  that  sacred, if  human  affection,
flings around the priest who absolves and sacrifices,
a halo of sanctity that might be given to a guardian
angel, should  he  stand  before  them, visible  and
revealed.   The old regard the priest as a son ; and
their eyes are moist with tenderness and veneration
when they behold, standing at the altar in sacrificial
robes, not an aged patriarch with the mystic words
on his forehead, and all the dignity and majesty of
Aaron's priesthood around him, but a youth, scarcely
passed from his boyhood, yet clothed with an awful
dignity, of which the Jewish priesthood was but a
figure and a type.   And the young look upon the
priest with  fear  and  affection  combined ; for his
presence is  a  revelation  to  them of that unseen

world, of which they have been taught to dream
from their earliest years. And all the fascination,
which a vision of the beloved disciple or a St. Louis
Gonzaga will exercise on religious and emotional
natures is here centred on that white figure at the
altar, which prays for them, blesses them, lifts the
white Host above their heads, absolves them with
words of tenderness, and speaks to them in a voice
of power and pathos of the awful mysteries of their
faith. And yet, what a gulf, yawning and impassable, is between them! No matter how close the
ties of affection may be, the priest moves through
his people, amongst them, but not of them! Consecrated by solemn oaths, dedicated to high and
sacred purposes, with all his thoughts in heaven,
though his interests claim him for earth, every one
recognises that whatever else may occur, he has no
part in those earthly desires that subdue, govern,
subjugate humanity. The living impersonation of
principles and ideas that could never have dawned
upon the human mind, had they not been revealed,
he walks his solitary way through life, bending, like
some sublime and pitying spirit, to the weakness
and wants of humanity, and then soaring aloft into
solitary regions of thought, or disburthening, like
the angels in the Apocalypse, the crystal vase of the
tears of humanity at the foot of the throne of God!
Here, now, is the poor girl, finding all the comfort
of her life in the ineffable solace of the confessional,
and only eager and zealous that I, too, her kinsman
in faith, should know the secret of the King that has
been revealed to her. Verily, 'these things are
hidden from the wise and prudent, and shown to
little ones!' And what arguments and syllogisms,
what deep designs of statecraft, or more subtle plot-
tings of misguided Catholics, could shake that poor
girl's faith—that here was the representative of the
Eternal, the incarnation of every beautiful thing—

C

the promise of every hopeful thing that could enter the domain of her existence? And you, British statesmen! wonder-working, far-seeing, whose fingers are on the pulses of half the nations of the globe, you never devised a more subtle, or a more impossible, measure of statecraft than when you tried to drive a wedge of separation between the Irish priesthood and their flocks. And you, the political marionettes of a false Liberalism; you the pamphleteering, platform-shaking orators of Socialism, when you have taken down the cross from all the churches of Ireland, and dismantled their walls, and razed these stately structures to the ground, when you have paralysed the brains of Irishmen, and torn out the bleeding hearts of her women, putting stones in these sacred places, like the *tricoteuses* of '93, you may dream of expecting that subversion of the supernatural which now you ambition. But until then mingle your regrets with those of your continental brethren, whose success is but partial and inadequate. The day of irreligion and indifference has not yet touched the horizon of your hopes."

But, good heavens! whither are my reveries drifting? This is not philosophy; and, if anything, surely I am a philosopher.

A gentle tap at the door woke me up. I cried "Come in" from my chair. I rose with all deference when I saw Mrs. Oliver enter. She had been weeping. She spoke hesitatingly.

"Might I ask you, Mr. Austin, to give me a month's rent in advance?"

"Certainly, Mrs. Oliver," I said.

"You know it is not from any distrust——"

"Don't speak of it," I replied. I went to my desk and handed her five notes.

She thanked me hurriedly and withdrew. In a few minutes I heard the hall-door closing with a bang, and heavy footsteps crunching the gravel.

"Another skeleton in the closet," I thought.

# CHAPTER IV

## AMONGST THE OLYMPIANS

Let us swear an oath, and keep it with an equal mind,
In the hollow Lotos-land to live and lie reclined,
On the hills like Gods together, careless of mankind.
For they lie beside their nectar, and the bolts are hurled
Far below them in the valleys, and the clouds are lightly
    curled
Round their golden houses, girdled with the gleaming world.
                                        —*The Lotos-Eaters.*

"COME down from the Greeks to the Germans,"
was the advice Mr. Dowling tendered me when I
asked him to tell me the secrets and the secret-
keepers of all high thoughts. And had I not his
advice, I should most probably have drifted in that
direction; for I had found that German philosophy
was a vast mirror in which were focused all the
rays of light or shafts of darkness that streamed
from ancient sages and their writings; and from
which were reflected all the many phases of human
thought with which the modern world is bewildered.

For wherever I went in my searches after, I will
not say Truth, for I knew right well where Truth
was to be found, but after high intellectuality, I
found myself referred instantly to German thinkers.
"The Kantian antinomies," "imbued with the spirit
of Fichte," "at that time Germany stood still under
the spell of Schelling's teaching," "the Hegelian
theory of contradictories has coloured all modern
thought,"—these were phrases continually crossing
and recrossing not only high-toned works on history
and science, but even the ordinary novel that is

thumbed and wept over by the emancipated school-
girl. How much of all this was mere pretence and
superficiality I did not know until riper years and
more mature experience brought the knowledge.
But now, in my search after the loftiest thought, I
was easily led to understand that in Germany was
to be discovered the fountain-head of all wisdom
worth possessing; and thither I went in a search
as fruitless as ever commended itself to the tragic
imagination of ancient or modern dramatist.

Perhaps, if my mode of thought had been that
which commended itself to St. Anselm and others,
and is represented by the expression, *Fides quærens
intellectum;* [1] or, to put it more plainly, if I, safely
anchored in the quiet havens of the Church, had
allowed intellect and imagination to roam freely over
the trackless expanses of human thought, perhaps I
would have sustained no real loss. But, with faith
theoretically unimpaired, I reversed the *dictum*, and
wrote *Intellectus quærens fidem;* and out on the
high seas, with winds moaning around me, and indistinct voices calling to me through the darkness,
my soul went wailing for light and peace, repulsed
at every side where it hoped to find rest, and mocked
by the echoes of its own querulous pain. Perhaps
there is some pleasure in such pain; but assuredly
the chiefest woes that follow and encompass way-

---

[1] The great Saint of Canterbury speaks in his famous treatise,
*Cur Deus Homo*, of those "who desire not to approach to faith by
reason, but to be delighted by the intellectual development and
contemplation of those things which they already believe."

"Non tento, Domine, penetrare altitudinem tuam, quia nulla-
tenus comparo tibi intellectum meum: sed desidero aliquatenus
intelligere veritatem tuam, quam credit et amat cor meum. Neque
enim quæro intelligere, ut credam ; sed credo ut intelligam."

"I do not attempt, O Lord, to penetrate the depths of Thy
wisdom, because I cannot measure my intellect with Thine; but
I desire in some measure to understand Thy truth, which my heart
believes and loves. For I do not try to understand, in order that I
may believe; but I believe, that I may understand"

ward humanity are caused by the self-constituted
Light-bearers of the world, who flash the little lan-
terns of their wisdom before the eyes of a dazed
multitude, and command them to follow into the
quagmires and morasses of doubt and unbelief.
But now, the enthusiasm of youth possessed me,
and I said, I will go up unto the gods in high
Olympus; and there, cloud-curtained and careless,
and wrapped in the intoxication of uninterrupted
thought, I will look down on the sordid cares and
still more sordid pleasures of humanity, and speak
in divine dialects of all the wondrous mysteries of
life and being—and that which makes the essence
of being—intellect exercised in the action of free
and sublime thought. It is not difficult for me now
to perceive where the radical defect in my education
lay. All moral feelings—self-discipline, self-rever-
ence, self-conquest—were an unknown factor in my
training. Proud, passionate, disdainful, I had already
had experience of how little qualified I was to face the
rough difficulties of life. And what was worse, all
the emotional nature within me lay undeveloped and
untouched by one single memory of religious thought
that I could appeal to for succour or sympathy. No
recollection of words, hallowed by sacred lips and
places, came back to support; no memory of choirs,
stained by the reflected lights from noble windows;
no abiding echoes of sacred music heard in the long
twilights of summer; no pictures of stalls thronged
with the awful reverential faces of boys to whom the
mysteries of life were opening out, or of pulpits
with the solitary figure of the man who had passed
through the storms of life and warned us of its
dangers; no strong appeals to a life of virtue because of its own glory; no divine panorama of the
history of the Church, its power, its organisation, its
influence; and no appeal to our strong emotional
natures to lift up our eyes to the Heavenly City,

and emulate the courage, as we hoped to share the glory, of its citizens—none of these things, essential to the spiritual life and growth of boys, came back to me to recall my vagrant thoughts and restore me to the lost loyalties of my youth. When I have read, almost with tears of vexation and envy, of long pilgrimages made from distant climes by bronzed, grey men to that little chapel at Rugby, and seen in imagination those silent figures sitting once more in the carved oak stalls, where as boys they had listened, awed and penetrated by the burning words that fell from their old master's lips; and when I witnessed those stolid Englishmen standing over his grave, and breathing, if not a prayer, at least a word of tender gratitude and reverence to the silent slumberer beneath, I thought, is there any defect in our own systems which fail to evoke such enthusiasm, when, not the natural truths that Arnold preached, but the sublime supernaturalism of the Church is taught; and not by the lips of a secularist, however personally estimable, but by the consecrated ministers of Christ, and to the souls of the most generous, the most sympathetic, perhaps the most intelligent youth, that ever trembled under the magic of a mighty name, or the magnetism of a great personality.

Alas! all that I remember was an appeal to intellect, an exhortation to be first, at any cost, in the honours and emoluments offered by a pagan government as a bribe to Catholic boys. How well I learned the lesson the past pages of this history testify. And this night I plunge into the mysteries of German thought, as I would plunge into an unknown forest, not knowing whether I should meet my princess there, or only hags and witches, singing around a devil's caldron their magic incantations.

I opened the *Critique of Pure Reason*, and lost myself in it. At first it was highly attractive. The sweeping away of all human beliefs and creeds, and the bold Luciferian idea of building up *à priori* a new rational system of religion founded on philosophy, and originated by the human mind alone, was of itself sufficient to arouse some dormant sympathies, the origin of which I cannot to this day ascertain. The heavy, lumbering, pedantic style of Kant rather revolted me, accustomed as I had been to the pure classicism of the ancients. But I persevered, with many a bad headache, in cutting my way through German decasyllables that had no meaning in any mind but Kant's. It was philosophy, and I was satisfied. Looking over my notebook, at that time carefully compiled, I find that the result of most laborious reading was this :—

1. That there is no such thing as congruity in Kant's system, supposed to be derived from first principles; and these first principles were untrue.

2. Kant is as pure an idealist as Berkeley. There is no objective reality in the world, the universe, men, or God. Nothing exists outside the mind and its concepts. Here is the flat scepticism of Pyrrho.

3. Kant does not affirm the existence of God, or the immortality of the soul.

What then have I discovered, after my weary nights and burning headaches ? That nothing exists outside my own mind. That my past history was a dream : that Katrine and Ursula are simply phantoms of a disordered imagination. This is unsatisfactory ; but it is philosophy, and I am content. And what a glorious thing it is, to sit up at midnight, whilst the meaner portion of mankind are sleeping, and dwell upon such propositions as these :—

" Philosophy, as cosmical, is the teleology of reason ; *i.e.*, it gives the ultimate end of reason."

" Philosophy is either propædeutic, *i.e.*, critical and explanatory of pure reason ; or it is metaphysical, including metaphysics of nature and ethics."

" Ethics is philosophy, which is purely *à priori* ; hence it is not based upon anthropological considerations, nor indeed upon any empirical matter."

One such night, late in December, whilst I racked my brains over some such difficult theses, I heard the midnight chimes from some far-off church in the city, and presently, the deep tolling of the other bells, answering each other like sentinels in the darkness. I flung up my window, and looked abroad. The great dark city lay slumbering beneath the cloak of night, and the thousands of silent mortals were watched by the eyes of the thousands of silent suns, that took their places as if marshalled by one supreme power which none dared disobey. Here and there some voice of man or nature, some belated reveller, or the tinkling of a little river afar off, made the silence more profound ; and the cool night breezes played at will over the earth, and crept in at the open window, and played fast and loose with my scattered papers and the open leaves of books.

I had just read this sentence in Kant :—

" Two things fill me with awe—the starry heavens, and a sense of human responsibility."

The latter I cannot understand in your system, O philosopher ! The former is clear and palpable enough. Awe, deep reverential awe, is the only feeling any man can have, looking on these palpitating, yet silent, suns. Who framed them, and when ? Out of what gigantic quarries hidden away in space did the Builder drag His material, and where are the workshops of the Omnipotent ? Who hath framed the unerring laws that guide them, that keep their gigantic masses asunder, lest collisions that would shake the universe might occur ; and over the dark opaque wrecks of shattered worlds, who hath placed a night-watch and a warning-bell lest some gay star, careering along in the exuberance and buoyancy of youth, might dash against them in the darkness and become transmuted into fragments of broken slag? Even now, whilst I, a sleepless mortal, am looking, new suns are leaping forth from the hands of Omnipotence to commence a career that will be yet in its infancy when our solar system shall have disappeared from the universe; and ancient suns, that came forth from the hidden chambers of space millions of years before our solitary sun-star was created, are at this moment bursting with a concussion that might make the immortals tremble on their thrones, and strewing the fields of space with luminous fragments, each one of which is itself a sun. And far through the interstellar spaces dark worlds are moving, feeling their way blindly, yet directed by unerring laws; and vagrant comets, the tramps of the celestial worlds, have yet to obey some unseen power that controls their energies and directs their wanderings through space. And if we, little parasites on this speck in space, could hear the reverberations of those star-choirs, could hear abyss calling to abyss, and spheres shouting to spheres through the thunders of flame-waves that stretch their vibrating tongues through ether, what would be our rendering of the eternal anthem—a chorus of jubilation echoing around the throne of Omnipotence, or the unavailing lamentations of a universe that lifts its voice of impotence before the face of a blind God?

I shut down the window and raised the flame of the lamp. Whatever I had been reading, the first words on which mine eyes now fell were these written by Isaac Barrow on a fly-leaf of Apollonius:—

"Tu autem, Domine, quantus es Geometra! quum enim hæc scientia nullos terminos habeat; cum in sempiternum novorum theorematum inventioni locus relinquatur; etiam penes humanum ingenium, tu uno hæc omnia intuitu perspecta habes absque catenâ consequentiarum, absque tædio demonstrationum. Ad cætera pæne nihil facere potest intellectus noster; in his conspiratur ab omnibus. . . . Te igitur vel ex hâc re amare gaudeo, te suspicor atque illum diem desiderare suspiriis fortibus in quo purgata mente, et claro oculo, non hæc solum omnia absque hac successiva et laboriosa imaginandi curâ, verum multo plura et majora ex tua bonitate et immensissima sanctissimaque benignitate conspicere et scire conceditur." [1]

This was the only prayer I said that night.

But when morning came, I was a philosopher and a Kantian again. If I took up the newspaper, and read of some brilliant speech delivered in the House of Commons the night before, I said "Yes! a great orator, but what does he know of Kant?" When I walked the streets, and a momentary feeling of jealousy possessed me for the flashy equipages and dresses of the rich, I consoled myself by pitying them, and saying, "Now, not one of these butterflies ever heard of Kant." If I read of brilliant successes at University examinations, I thought, "If these young conquerors were examined in the categories of Kant, what could they say?" And when I sat under a pulpit on Sunday morning, and heard the

---

[1] But Thou, Lord, how great a geometrician Thou art! For since this science hath no limits—for some room must for ever be left even to human intelligence for the invention of new theories—Thou alone with one glance beholdest all these things without constructing a chain of consequences and without the slow labour of demonstration. In other things, our intellects can accomplish but little; in these things, it is assisted by all. For this reason, therefore, do I find my joy in loving Thee; to Thee do I lift up mine eyes; and with all earnestness do I desire that day when, with cleansed conscience and clear sight, it may be granted to me, from Thy goodness and most immense and most holy mercy, to see and to understand, without the continuous and laborious effect of imagination, not these things only, but things more manifold and greater.

old familiar truths plainly repeated, I held down my
head, and soliloquised—

"Poor man! he has read some dry-as-dust theology, but what does he know of Kant?"

Sometimes the grotesque absurdity of the whole
thing would strike me, and I would laugh at my
own folly, but the thought that I was a lonely
student, like all the great ones I had ever read of,
consoled me, and brought me back to my studies
from the mocking laughter of self-contempt.

I took up the study of the *Critique of Practical
Reason*. I had not gone far when I found that Kant
had brought back with all the pomp and ceremony
of language that Divine Being, whom he had just
summarily banished from His universe. I read:
"God must be omniscient, that He may penetrate
into all our secret intentions, under all possible
circumstances, and in all times; omnipotent, to
apportion to my conduct the consequences which
it deserves; analogously, eternal, omnipresent, &c.,
&c." I rubbed my eyes. Is this Kant? Kant
of the phantasm and phantoms, the idealist, with
his concepts, outside of which was no reality? But
hark! what's this?

"Here is now a perfect religion (Christianity),
which can be set, in an intelligible and convincing
manner, before all men, by their own reason, and
which, besides, has been illuminated by an example,
the possibility and necessity of which, as our rule,
as far as we are capable of following it, all may see,
without making the truth of these doctrines, or the
dignity and authority of their Teacher, to stand in
need of any other attestation, such as miracles, or
scholarship, which belongs not to all."

And here's the end of all my philosophy—what
I had learned, without any circuitous philosophy or
phraseology, in my penny Catechism; and which
every Catholic child must learn.

Kant and Katrina are one! Kant, I'm disgusted with you! Thou drab old philosopher of Königsberg, with thy weight of ninety years resting on thee, thou too must go into the limbo of discredited humbugs!

But oh! that pitiful cry of the human heart for God! The shriek of the drowning mariner, the sobbing of lone women at night, the tears of little children, the silent weeping of strong men—all the *Misereres* that well up in one unceasing Jeremiad from the bruised heart of humanity are a chorus of "jubilates" and "hallelujahs," compared with this. Stifle it, O ye philosophers! under the cumbrous phraseology of your inconsistent and puerile systems; bury it deep down under the Cyclopean masonry of your definitions and axioms; and you can no more quench that eternal, pitiful cry in the heart of humanity than you can check the action of wind or wave, or quench with your feeble breath the star galaxies of heaven.

# CHAPTER V

## SIBYLLA MEA

Sed revocare gradum, superasque evadere ad auras,
Hoc opus, hic labor est.

But 'tis a long unconquerable pain
To climb to those ethereal realms again.
—*Æneid*, Book vi.

URSULA'S parents, Hubert and Agnes Deane, might
be taken as excellent, and not uncommon types of
Dublin society a quarter of a century ago. Every
great metropolis has its mannerisms; and every
little circle its own peculiarities; and those of the
Dublin of this period were well-marked and defined.
Hubert Deane was a solicitor in large practice. He
rarely appeared in court. His business was done
in his chambers. It consisted largely in convey-
ancing; and was confidential to such an extent,
that he was supposed to possess the family secrets,
not only of the city, but of half the province. He
was a silent man. His opinion was always expressed laconically, and if his clients controverted
that opinion, or probed for deeper explanation, he
looked them all over as if they were curiosities,
whose only business was to spoil time, and turned
away to his office papers. He had married late in
life; and his bald forehead, and mature, but not
aged appearance, were a curious contrast to the
youthful beauty and vivacity of his wife. She in
turn was a noble, and not uncommon specimen of
an Irish girl; full of all kinds of generous ideas and
sympathies, tears and laughter for others running

45

side by side through her happy life; and she was
absolutely free from that affectation which spoils all
that is graceful in women, and had a large and lofty
contempt for what is known as the " upper classes "
of Society.

Perhaps because she had been let behind the veil,
and had seen what no other eye should see,—the
ghastly secrets that filled every cabinet in her
husband's possession,—she thanked God for what
He had done for her.   But, unlike the thin, meagre
specimens of Irish womanhood, who are ever straining after high Society, and whose highest ambition
is to secure a nod of recognition from the rich or
powerful, she concentrated all her ideas of happiness in the heaven of her own home, where she
reigned supreme mistress and queen.   Her husband
never dreamed of interfering with her right divine
to rule there.   He came in from his day's toils and
anxieties, and sitting silent by the fire, found his
recompense or solace in watching the gentle and
gifted girl who had come to him to bless and hallow
his life.   And they had gathered around them one
of those curious little coteries, which were then, and
perhaps are now, a characteristic of Dublin society.
Each consisted at most of a dozen families, selected
from the middle or professional classes ; and once
selected, they became as exclusive as Indian castes.
They generally met two or three times a week at
each other's houses, brought with them their musical
instruments—violins, guitars, &c., spent a few hours
together in happy and innocent amusement, from
which every trace of dissipation was far removed.
Perhaps, some would consider them dull.   There
certainly was a marked absence of that unkind wit,
double-edged, and forked like a serpent's tongue,
that characterises social gatherings in other places.
Quiet, unobtrusive, cheerful, kind, I should say they
formed, if not the most brilliant, at least the most

pleasant society that was to be met with in the Irish
capital. Into such society was I now privileged to
enter, my patroness and chaperon being my little
foundling, Ursula. For these generous, large-minded
people, building their faith in me on her intuitions,
asked no questions, but welcomed me heartily to
the hospitality of their home. And now for the
first time I began to feel the fatal want of a certain
and defined position in life. I was nobody, and my
new friends thought I had at least some recognised
profession. I was a Bohemian, a tramp. If I had
even some recognised gift of genius, that would
compensate for poverty, I should have felt at ease.
No, I was simply a speculator on the shadowy banks
of the future—the most pitiable object, perhaps, in
the world. I had entered this kind and hospitable
home, then, under false pretences; and I shuddered
to think what answer I should give if interrogated
about my past history or present environments. My
philosophical contempt for money and position, for
the first time, received a rude shake. I should have
been glad to have been able to say that I was something. I confess I was surprised at the facility with
which I obtained entrance into such a household.
The strange fancy the young empress, Ursula, took
to me was unquestionably my passport to the confidence of her parents. But after a little time when I
came to know them better, the fact that I was
established with such a respectable family as the
Olivers confirmed my title to respectability. I con-
gratulated myself on having selected such a temporary resting-place. In a word, I had abandoned
my philosophy, and become something very like—
shall I say it, a snob? Do not, dear friend, sneer
ever so politely at such an admission. Of course
you are quite free from all such weakness, of course
you believe that all men are equal; and you are so
much elevated above all such social weakness, that

you would shake hands with a beggar as pleasantly
as with a marquis. But did you never feel just a
little thrill of pleasure when you were invited to
that Vice-regal ball? And was it quite inadvert-
ently you dropped that remark yesterday, "when
Lord S—— called to see you?" And, dear me,
is it not curious how the visiting card of the afore-
said Lord S—— always remains on the very top of
the little Sèvres tray? and those of Mr. and Mrs.
Meekly, of Humble Hall, have dropped, as fruiterers
drop the small berries, to the bottom? Never mind!
We all do it, *Ay de mi!* as old Thomas Carlyle
(and he, too, dyspeptic old Diogenes, dearly loved a
lord) would say.

The Deanes knew the Olivers. Perhaps I should
be more accurate if I said that Agnes Deane knew
at one time Gwendoline Gascoigne Oliver. It was
in the old, happy, convent days. Gay, laughing
girls, they had sat side by side together, were fond
of the same gentle nun, grinned and made faces at
the German music master, drew fancy pictures of life
together, and cried and swore eternal friendship
when the holidays came round, and they were not
to return.

How they exchanged little trinkets, promised to
send their photographs, and to write every week
without fail, called one another back, and embraced
a hundred times, and waved farewells from 'bus or
carriage, Agnes Deane used laughingly to tell.

"And so you are with the Olivers?"

"Yes," I said, "that is my present domicile."

"Poor little Gwenny, and the prince hasn't come
yet."

I guessed the allusion.

"She used to take infinite pleasure," continued
Mrs. Deane, "in writing her name in full, *Gwendoline
Gascoigne Oliver*, and what wonderful romances
about her future she used to weave!"

"I am afraid she thinks," I said, "that her valuable time was wasted at the convent. She regrets that she was not placed under a master, or sent to Milan or Rome."

"No, that is all a little affectation," said Mrs. Deane, continuing her knitting, "she was really fond of the nuns; but she had queer ideas about society. I think her mother was responsible for them."

"Then she belongs to an aristocratic family?" I said.

Mrs. Deane looked at her husband, who was reading placidly.

"Well," she said, with a little smile, when her husband refused to respond to her look of inquiry, "they are quite respectable people, but I hardly think they could be called aristocratic. I know Gwen never dreamt that they could be reduced to keeping lodgers, even such as you."

Mr. Deane appeared to be quite engrossed in his book, but he broke in here with—

"What did you say, Aggie, was the young lady's full name?"

"Gwendoline Gascoigne Oliver," replied his wife. "Are you going to draw a deed in her favour?"

"No," he said calmly, "she is making her own destiny."

"What do you mean, Hubert?" said his wife. "You are dreadfully enigmatic."

"I mean she is changing, or about to change, her name," he said, without lifting his eyes from his book.

"That can mean but one thing," said his wife.

"But one thing," echoed Hubert.

"And that is?" she queried.

"Hell!" said he, in such deep and angry tones that we were both startled.

"Now, Hubert," said his wife, resuming her knitting which she had dropped, "you are shockingly profane, and, what is worse, mysterious. Who is it?"

But Hubert Deane went on reading, reading, and no torture, and Agnes Deane knew how to exercise a little, could induce him to break silence. Of course, in the meantime, my mind was running over all possibilities, and I connected this forthcoming marriage with the visitor of some nights before.

When Agnes Deane, despairing of breaking her husband's silence, and musing thoughtfully over her work, at last gave up the problem as insoluble, she turned to me and said in a whisper—

"I think I have a surprise for you too, Mr. Austin!"

"Indeed?" I replied.

"Would you care to meet an old friend?"

"Yes, certainly," I replied. "Who is he?"

"I'm rather surprised that little chatterbox, Ursula, never spoke to you of her. She thinks almost as much of her as of you."

I was bewildered. Ursula had never spoken to me in our many confidential conversations of any one in whom I could feel interested, except some mysterious Miss Bemmy, whom I had pictured to my mind as red-haired, uncouth, and angular.

"Well, as we are all so secret to-night," she said, looking archly at her husband, "I'll try if we, poor women, cannot keep a secret too. But come to tea on Friday evening, and—" she said, pointing and shaking her finger laughingly at me, "meet your fate."

It had been said often, let me repeat it for the hundredth time, that the best grace a young man can receive in life is the friendship of a good woman. And there is no clearer indication of the depths of vulgarity and degradation into which we have fallen than the universal idea that there can be no such friendship that does not degenerate sooner or later into sensuous affection. The universal presumption that marriage is the be-all and end-all of woman's life tends to enervate natures that are of themselves strong and self-reliant. And thousands of women who, as their labours in hospitals and on battlefields testify, might be the supports and props of weary or broken spirits, become the merest parasites, living in the weak presumption that they must find the oak around which they can cling, and rest, or perish. It is impossible to calculate the aggregate loss to humanity resulting from this false and unnatural view. It is impossible to calculate the heart suffering and martyrdom of women who believe they can have but one vocation in life, and whose views of men are restricted to that one idea. Even the good and kindly Mrs. Deane shared the general belief, and thought that my fate was placed irrevocably in the hands of the unknown friend to whom she was about to introduce me. I gave the matter but little thought. I was even now more interested in the little drama that was being enacted under my own roof—the forthcoming marriage of Miss Oliver and the secret visitor who brought tears to the eyes of my proud and disdainful hostess.

There was a goodly company assembled at Mrs. Deane's at eight o'clock when I was announced. Some lady was at the piano, and there was a hush in the room. I slid quietly into a sofa near the door, not so quietly, however, as not to be seen by the vigilant eyes of Ursula who sat almost under the piano on a hassock. She put up her finger warningly, and then laid it on her lips.

After a few minutes the music ceased, and I heard a lady in front of me say to her companion—

"That is rather rare execution!"

In the midst of the hum and noise Mrs. Deane's kindly eyes lighted on me, and she beckoned me to come near her. But my little lady, Ursula, had already come down, and chiding me for being late, she led me to where her mother and the young lady, who had just left the piano, were sitting. The latter was bending over some music, when Mrs. Deane, her eyes lighted up with fun, said—

"Mr. Austin, Miss Bellamy."

Helen Bellamy gave a little start of surprise, and then in her own grave way held out her hand and made me sit near her. I was so confused that I could think of nothing to say, except indeed what was true, how pleased, infinitely pleased I was to see her again. She was dressed in black and violet, whence I concluded that Hugh Bellamy was yet among the living.

"No," she said, as if interpreting my looks, "Hugh is dead. He did not even reach Algiers. He died at Irun in the north of Spain. You are surprised at my dress, which is not the usual mourning; and perhaps that I was at the piano as you entered. It was all Hugh's wish. You shall read it in his diary, when you come to see us. When shall it be?"

"At any time you please," I replied, "I shall be so glad to see Alfred again."

"He is quite unchanged," she said, "even though our circumstances are better. He is still immersed in the old pursuits."

"And you," I said. "How is it that you are teaching still?"

For I now understood that this was the mysterious Miss Bemmy, whom I had already pictured in my mind as a German governess.

"Well, you see," she replied, "Mrs. Deane is so kind, that I was only too glad to be able to continue my tuitions here. And, well, you know what an attractive young lady Ursula is!"

"Then Mrs. Deane is not the Madame Parvenue,

or Madame la Grande, of whom we used to make such fun ? "

" No, indeed, she is a sister and a friend." Then after a pause, she added—

" I did not know that there could be such attractiveness in a Catholic household, where Catholicity is the predominant feature." Here Mrs. Deane intervened, and called Miss Bellamy away to some other friends. Ursula came and stood at my knee.

" So, *ma petite*, this is your Miss Bemmy ? "

" Yeth," she said seriously. " Do you like her ? "

" Rather," I replied, " we are old friends."

" And she like you," said Ursula. There was a pause. Ursula was pouty about something.

" Doff," she said at last, " will you doe away ? "

"No, mignonne," I said, seeing her quite concerned.

" Doff," she said, her eyes filling with tears, " will you marry Miss Bemmy, and doe away from me ? "

I could hardly keep from laughing. But the little mite looked serious enough.

" No," I said, " I have not the least intention of doing anything of the kind."

" Doff, will you pomise me ? "

"·I will."

" Give me your wite hand and word ! "

" Here's my right hand, and you have already had my word ! "

Her face brightened up, but the tears were on her cheek when her mother came up.

" Come, Ursey, to bed. It is late. Why, you have been crying, little one. Has there been a quarrel between you ? "

" Not a quarrel," I said, looking at Mrs. Deane, " but only mutual explanations."

A few nights after saw me enjoying the coveted privilege of seeing Alfred and Helen Bellamy in their new home.

They had left the old dingy lodgings in the lane off Baggot Street, and had now a tidy, two-storied cottage in Frankfort Avenue. A little garden was in front, with its brown, bare beds; two steps led up to the hall, and this evening there stood on the top of the steps my old tutor, with his hands extended to greet me. He was well-dressed: and when I entered the little parlour, I saw unmistakable traces of the betterment of their condition. The old odour of cigars floated around the room; but instead of the dingy furniture and faded books, all Hugh Bellamy's valuable bookcases, &c., were here —looking a little out of place, but his sister would not part with one single article for its weight in gold.

"These are all poor Hugh's," Helen said, "they are doubly dear to us now since he is dead."

I remembered well the last time I saw them, when the shadows were deepening around the doomed man.

"It is a wonderful selection," I cried, noticing some of my favourites; "Hugh must have read everything."

"There are many books there," she said calmly, "which we would not keep, except that they are such precious souvenirs."

"Why would you not keep them?" I said; "there is not a worthless book amongst them. I never saw such a selection."

"Well," she replied with some diffidence, "there are some books there that should hardly be seen in a Catholic household. This, for example," she cried, handing down a volume from the International Science Series, "is a book which I am always tempted to put in the fire. It is wicked and degrading. But then all science is degrading."

She uttered this alarming proposition with all the calmness of manner that invariably characterised her. I could not help saying—

" Very like Mr. Dowling's teaching, Miss Bellamy ;
but very unlike Alfred's."

" Oh! I don't mean the pure sciences," she said
hastily. " I mean those sciences that are for ever
prying into secrets and will not leave God's works
alone."

I was silent. It was *anathema maranatha* to my
own pursuits.

" You see," she said, calmly pursuing the thread
of her thoughts, " religion and poetry alone dis-
tinguish man from the brutes. Religion and poetry
generalise, and you find God. Science analyses,
and you find dust. You may write lovely things
about a violet : but the violet itself feels nothing
but the nip of the frost, or the warmth of the spring
sun. And your man of science comes on and
crushes the dainty little thing between his fingers
and tells you it is only water and a little fibre. But
your poet etherealises it : and your religious man
argues from the beauty of the flower to the glory of
the artist."

Here Alfred, who was in a neighbouring room,
came in.

" Why, Alfred, Miss Bellamy is abusing your
favourite science. Have you turned your back also
upon it ? "

" Not at all," he laughed. " But, look here, Mr.
Austin, aren't these glorious ? "

He took down several beautiful volumes, opened
them, turned them over again and again with all
the affection of a book lover.

" Did you ever see such binding as that ' Pindar ' ?
look at the calf binding first, then at the edges : and
where would you get a tradesman to-day to work
out that gilt scroll work beneath these labels ? And
look at that Livy! Did you ever see such binding ?
I'm the happiest man in Europe." And then he
added softly—

" Poor Hugh ! poor Hugh !

" But what were you saying about science, Elsie ? What do you know about science, dear, except the science of goodness ? "

"Oh, never mind," she said with a laugh. " It was only a fancy."

" She will always except astronomy for your sake, Alfred ? " I said.

"Indeed, not at all," she cried.

" But does it not open to you the magnificence of creation and of God ? "

"Yes, and it makes us what ?   Atoms, molecules, our very solar system a nebula.   Religion and poetry make us children of God and heirs of immortality !   But let me make this concession.   Science is worship when she shows us what Nature does. Science is sacrilege when she shows us how Nature does it ! "

" Don't argue with a woman," said Alfred, laughing, " you're sure to be beaten ! "

" I accept my defeat willingly," I said.   " It was inevitable."

By-and-by she returned to the subject.

" I hate those books," she said to me, "since I read Hugh's latest diary.   I think they poisoned his life, and made him—well, what we thought him. There is something so cold, so cynical, yet so full of despair, about all that these men write, that it is enough to fill the world with sorrow.   And, after all," she cried, becoming quite vehement—the only time I saw her losing her equanimity—" what right have these men, sitting in their professional chairs, to take away from the working masses of humanity what is more to them than bread, or air ?   I don't know why the world tolerates them.   They seem to me to be worse than murderers or burglars, with their airy dogmatism coolly robbing the human race of their most precious birthright—their faith in a heavenly Father. Why women, above all, tolerate them is a puzzle to me. Yet here we have women following in their footsteps, as the angels followed Lucifer, and putting A.B.'s and M.A.'s to their names, forsooth, because they know all the infidelity and dread doubts and misgivings of such and such a so-called philosopher. And so I hate the very look and odour of these smiling volumes ; and some day I know I shall be tempted to put them leaf by leaf into the fire."

"But you know, Miss Bellamy," I interposed mildly and diffidently, "these men speak in the name of Science, and they maintain that Science is knowledge, and knowledge is truth."

She looked at me inquiringly. I thought she would be angry with me.

"Science is not knowledge," she said calmly, "and knowledge is not truth. Science is for ever contradicting itself and building very big ugly fabrics on very slender foundations. And knowledge may be, very often is, a huge unwieldy bundle of lies."

She paused.

"This leads me to ask you," she cried, "if I am not presuming too much, what are you doing now ? "

She looked at me with her calm eyes. I felt like one guilty and arraigned before the highest tribunal I knew on earth.

"During the day," I blurted out at last, "I seek employment, and meet rebuffs. At night I grope and grope, with insatiable curiosity, to find the end of all things."

"You have failed to secure employment, then ? "

"Yes. I am lodging at present with the Olivers, until my little means shall be exhausted."

She at once changed the subject.

"I met that child at Mrs. Deane's. She is good and kind, but weak."

"She thinks she did not do well under convent tuition."

"Ah! yes, that is the usual affectation of a certain class of Catholics. Anything done in the name and under the protection of the Church (of which they are merely nominal members) comes under their criticism. 'Can anything good come out of Nazareth?' is the cry. Why, there is more talent, nay, genius, locked up in our Irish convents than would suffice to create a new civilisation. There are women there who could sing as bravely as any women from Sappho to Elizabeth Barrett Browning; but they are mute—except to God. There are artists there that could create a new school, as the ragged followers of St. Francis created the Umbrian School, but they paint Agnus Deis for little children, and scapulars for beggar women. There are girls with trained voices who would be smothered with bouquets if they appeared on any stage from London to Naples, and they sing only to God. For Him they compose, for Him they paint, for Him they sing; they have no ambition but to please Him, no consolation but to be near Him, no hope but to sit at His feet for ever. Oh! it is wonderful, especially to me, who was never brought up at a convent school, this army of noble women, passing by in disdain all that the world holds dear, and conquered by the love of Jesus Christ. Tell me, did you ever read the ceremony of reception or profession of a nun?"

"No," said I, "I read of such in the newspapers; and it generally wound up with—'the good sisters entertained their friends at a sumptuous déjeuner'!"

"Precisely," she replied, "everything with us is vulgarised. Well, then, I tell you that whoever composed that ceremonial was a consummate dramatist. There is nothing more sublime in the whole range of human composition."

She was silent for a while.

" By the way, you said you were seeking the end of things. It is a far search."

" I know it," I said, " and I know that I am as far away from it as ever."

"The end of all things to some," she said musingly, " is what the Italians call ' L'Inferno.' "

I started.

" I shouldn't mind going through the *Inferno*," I said, " if I had a Beatrice to conduct me."

" Beatrice did not lead through hell," she replied. " She beckoned from the stars to heaven."

We were both silent with many thoughts. Then she took up a little roll, tied with a silk ribbon. "This is Hugh's diary," she said. "Keep it as long as you please. I am sure you will read it with sympathy."

# CHAPTER VI

## LEAVES FROM A DIARY

*London, July* 11*th.*—Detained here many days in the usual bootless task of consulting specialists. Spent a few days in Brompton Hospital. Can't understand this peculiar treatment—compelled to lie, night and day, under a single sheet, with windows wide open, and every morning to be thumped by students with stethoscopes, as if they were in doubt what was the matter. It appears this dread disease is a fever, and the temperature must be kept under by artificial means. Took up my bed and walked, however, when one day a student, toying with a microscope, asked me would I like to see "the enemy." He ran his little finger along a glazed cloth that was saturated with some disinfectant, and placed the results under his glass. Good God! it was swarming with microbes—little demons, straight and tubular. "You have as many of these in your lungs," he said, "as would infect all London." I left that day.

*July* 12*th.*—Took ticket for Paris by Southampton and Havre, for the sake of sea voyage. Arrived at Southampton late at night. Made my way with difficulty to boat. A mere cockle-shell, dirty and ill-smelling, and with a decidedly dirty lot of passengers on board. All night long I was regaled with filthy language, and such innuendoes about exalted personages as made me sicker than the heaving of the boat. Took refuge in conversation with a seedy-looking gentleman. Found him a Methodist preacher from America, wonderfully well read. Challenged me about Quietism. What the d—— is Quietism? Talked glibly about Bossuet, and Fenelon, and Madame Guyon. "Quietism is condemned by your Church, you know, as savouring of Oriental fatalism and passivism—there's something in it." Tried to get him off religion. No use, he had come over to inquire, and was determined to get at the bottom of matters. Put me lots of questions about Port-Royal, and Nicole, and Arnauld. Never heard of them. Asked him about Emerson— what was thought of him in religious circles in America. Orphic and nebulous in his teachings, but a pure, beautiful personality. This ridiculous old Methodist with his snuffy coat amazed me—such far-advanced ideas and such language! Verily, the schoolmaster is abroad. Was delighted when I heard him step down to his berth at two o'clock in the morning—deadly sick. What right had the fellow to make an ignoramus of me? I could have taught fifty fellows like him—but not religion.

*July* 13*th*.—Rose at 6.45 A.M. Had a cup of tea from steward, who was very kind. Accused by fellow-passengers of coughing. Denied it emphatically. Cool old fellow, Anglicised Italian, dealer in skins in Manchester, cosmopolitan in ideas and habitats, quite at home chatting and joking—clearly a citizen of the world. I wonder has he a home, and a little child to welcome him back, and look forward to meet him!

Boat arrives at Havre at 11 A.M. Went to London Hotel. In a few minutes went in omnibus to train. Had some trouble in getting clerk to understand me. Paid four francs and twelve centimes to be allowed to travel first-class. Anything to escape fellow-travellers of last night. Came to English Hotel, mistaking it for Hotel d'Angleterre.

Went to look for Père C——, to whom I had letters of introduction from my uncle. Had great difficulty. Gave it up in despair. "Monsieur est Protestant?" said old applewoman. Had great pity for my white face. It is horrible—this pity and curiosity everywhere. Am I so ghastly?

*Paris, July* 14*th.*—English Hotel, Rue St. Lazare. Rose about 9 A.M. Went again in search of Père C——. Introduced myself to a priest, who very kindly took me quite across the city, through the Parc Monceaux, out of his way, quite three miles. Not a hat lifted to him the whole way. How was the faith of this people uprooted? O Voltaire, Diderot, Renan, what a hell is yours (even if you were in some heaven) to witness the ruin and wreck you have wrought. I wonder is there anything more terrible than to wreck a human soul? Yet why should I moralise, I who have wrecked two lives or more? Helen, would that thou wert with me to banish this remorse! Abbé Chaulliac gone *en vacance.* Visited Church of St. Augustine. Beautiful. Dined early and started for evening train. Took night mail to Bordeaux. Carriage full. Some people passed by *when they saw my face.* All French passengers but one English lady, baby, and *bonne, en route* to Madrid. She cried bitterly. "This beastly place, this odious smell!" A huge fat Frenchman sat opposite me. Commercial. Hair bristling. Studied me curiously for a few minutes, then dropped asleep, and slept sitting during that long night. I was wide awake all night, cough, cough, especially in the chill hours of the morning. My little lady, who was also sleepless, looked sometimes annoyed, sometimes compassionate. Thus we passed in the hideous blackness Tours, Orleans, Angoulême. Then there was a glorious sunburst, and wondrous revelations of vineyards, &c., as we slowed into Bordeaux. My lady made a little toilette with eau de Cologne, and looked wonderfully freshened. I looked a mummy in a bundle of rags.

*Biarritz, July* 18th.—Remained a long time on the pier to-day watching the white spray dash over the rough masonry. It was no place for an invalid, especially as the day was rough, a strong wind beating inshore from the bay, and the pier deluged with the foam, and hidden in the smoke of the breakers. Yet I was well. I couldn't bear the loneliness of my hotel, and that infernal compassion that appears to be on the lips of every man, woman, and child that sees me. What is it to them if I am dying? One more atom lost in the universe—one more poor little microbe crushed by the thumb of the relentless One! Yet is it so? The fire has gone down in my brazier, and my room is cold. Those tiles under my feet are freezing. But I cannot sleep if I go to bed. Let me wrap myself up here and think it out. There is the one fact— the eternal destruction that is going on in nature. From the invisible bacillus that is born but to die, to the vastest sidereal system, that is for ever crumbling into atoms and weaving its constituents into new forms of fire and life—the same eternal system is working—matter pitched into the crucible of nature to come forth in new forms! But what am I saying? Why, all this argues immortality. And, after all, is there not the inextinguishable Ego, hoping, dreaming, longing, never satisfied, quench-less in its aspirations, insatiable in its loves, sub-limely dissatisfied with its noblest achievements, never able to make its work correspond with the Ideal? And where then shall all this aftermath of life be reaped, and the insatiable be satisfied? Surely, if nature be not one vast lie, there must be a home for wandering spirits; one workshop where the querulous artist will find, perhaps with its face

turned to the wall, the long-sought ideal of his
youth and manhood.   But my life has been such a
failure, I have been such a spendthrift of talent—I
have been such a prodigal of priceless love.   Ay,
let there be an eternity, dear God, if for me alone,
to prove to *my* wronged loves, Isabel and Marcella,
that I am not the hopeless profligate I seemed to
them.   Twelve o'clock!   Why do they send us,
poor devils of consumptives, abroad to perish amidst
the cheerlessness of these continental hotels?   What
a night is before me!   Cough, cough, and that
odious perspiration oozing from every pore, and
wetting my hair as if it were sponged!   And the
chills, oh!   Come, poor soul, face thy ordeal.   "Our
Father, who art in heaven!"   Why art thou in
heaven, and not on earth, where we want Thee,
Father?   Well, but there *is* a heaven; and my
spirit will spurn and kick from me this wretched
little globule.   "There aloft the fogs of our days
must one day be resolved into stars, even as the
mist of the Milky Way parts into suns.   Farewell.
We shall never go out.   Farewell, a thousand times,
we shall meet again.   By my soul, we shall not utterly
go out.   Farewell!"   God bless thee, Jean Paul!

*Biarritz, July* 31*st.*—I have been very unwell.
To-day is my first day out of bed for a fortnight.
Am I sinking?   I suppose so.   And I must die
here, here in a foreign land amongst strangers.   But
have I not read somewhere that wherever a Catholic
Church is, there is home?   Perhaps so.   But these
demons of freethinkers have swept this, with all the
other consolations of life, into the limbo of forgotten
and dismembered beliefs.   My hot curse, the curse
of a dying and desolate man, on them!   Am I late?
Listen, my soul!   Thou art a beggar and an in-
solvent, with "Failure" written in capital letters
over thy life.   But there may be an equilibrium in
thy life, hither and forward; perhaps perfection

stoops not to perfection but to the imperfect—that there is an antinomy here as in all things. Well, I'll give myself a chance at least.

*Biarritz, August 2nd.*—He came and is gone. His presence has left me deeper and darker than ever. Is there no presentment of Catholicity except what he has offered? He questioned me as if I were a criminal, argued with me as if I were an infidel, would have everything or nothing, and a general plea of " *Guilty* " all along the line, before he would assure me of pardon. Perhaps he is right, but it sounds hard. I am no infidel, because I am not a fool; I have been a criminal towards the gentlest and best of God's creatures. I admit that fire alone can purge me of my iniquity. But I prefer to be judged by thee, Isabel, by thee, Marcella, by thee, Helen, by Thee—their Supreme Master and Lover, than by men. Yes, I will tell my sin at the public square, if necessary, but however dark I make the pages of my own life, I don't like others to spill ink over them.

*Biarritz, August 3rd.*—It strikes me this clergy-man is one of those who walk to Heaven on a chalked line. If you are within reach of his hand, he may bless you; but he does not know that human nature is like nature in general—a crooked, irregular thing, full of all kinds of cavities and nodes; and that if you wish not to leave an ugly hiatus between this wilful thing and religion, you must bend with every bend of it, and fit in your principles to every cavity in the heart of it, and make, by gentle, humble yielding, a union with it that will be harmonious and eternal. A straight, perfectly moulded syllogism never made a saint; which is only another way of saying that " the heart has its reasons of which reason knows nothing." Heigh-ho! I am philoso-phising again, as if I had not something better to do during these few days that are left me.

E

How lonely and solemn is this evening here by the sea! Nature has its fingers on its lips, musing. The air is heavy with scents, and a canopy of purple overhangs the sleeping sea. Helen, would thou wert here! I think we two understood each other best of all. But what a spendthrift and contemner of good I have been! Never mind. I can dismiss that remorse too. After all, what is remorse but a sensation to be suppressed? But the night is very lovely. How beautiful is the world as it narrows in the perspective and is ringed in the frame of Death!

*Biarritz, August* 10*th.*—When I woke this morning a gentle face was bending over me—the face of an old man, but rosy and healthy, and with a corona of white hair brushed back from his forehead and falling down over his collar. He kissed my two eyes, and chafed my hands within his own soft palms; and although we Northerners abominate these marks of affection, they touched me deeply, for I was sore in spirit and in body. " *Mon enfant!* " he said, " *mon pauvre enfant !* " There was a crucifix in his cincture. We became great friends. I asked him to remain for breakfast; and before we had finished the good old priest had arranged with me that we were to go to Lourdes together.

*Lourdes, August* 11*th.*—Started for Lourdes by mid-day, with my new chaplain, who reminded me so much of my uncle. Fellow passengers, two French ladies, two Frenchmen, an English lady, reading "Orley Farm," and an English gentleman —not Catholics evidently. Passed through a vast wood from Bordeaux to Argenteuil, planted by the late emperor. Came to Pau. Beautiful city perched on the hill, with one of Turner's sun-canopies floating around it. Magnificent view of the Pyrenees! One mountain especially crested with sun-gilt snow. View of Lourdes from train—the Church of the

Apparition. The grotto, with its crowd of worshippers, and its candles red in the sunlight. Lost
my luggage, but very soon found it. Came with
Père F—— to Hotel du Nord. Very kind people.
Washed off the dust by inches, and shaved by half-
inches. Two Irish ladies, connected with high
officials, very solicitous, until they discovered that I
was Irish, when they dropped me. Bought *Journal
de Lourdes*. Came to grotto. Everything as de-
picted in photographs. Presented a candle to our
Blessed Lady. What's coming over me? Prayed
for a little time. Took some water, beautiful and
cool. Visited church. Basilica closed. Saw the
new statue, down in the valley, that was lately
crowned. Visited crypt, where Masses are said.
Dark, but dry and nice. Returned to hotel with
my new chaplain, who is infinitely kind. Dined
at eight.

*Lourdes, August 12th.*—Rose at six o'clock.
Went to basilica. Entered crypt and heard Mass,
said by Père F——. Returned early, breakfasted on
coffee and omelette. French priest, stranger, break-
fasting on salmon and claret. Remained all day
near grotto, in the little wood, dreaming, half-asleep,
and wondering at the green rapid waters of the
Gave. It is a lovely spot, apart from its religious associations. Pyrenees snow-clad high over our heads,
broken ravines and valleys everywhere, a tropical
sun. I breathe more freely, but I entertain no hopes.
" You will gain something," says Père F——. Perhaps so. I thought the eyes of the Madonna bent
downwards towards me to-day as I passed under the
grotto. But what an undisciplined spirit am I?
I went home quite irritated, because some old village
gossips, sitting at their doors, as you would see in
an Irish hamlet, whispered to each other, " *Pour
sa santé.*"

*Lourdes, August 15th.*—Our Lady's Assumption.

Went to Holy Communion this morning. Then wrote a long letter to dear Helen and Alf. A gentler, more loving feeling is creeping over me ; and that hideous skeleton phantom is putting on flesh and an angel's wings. I no longer dread him. I should like to die here and be buried under that grotto. To-day I spent mostly in my dear wood overhanging the Gave. A little book, "Abandonment," was my companion. What a wonderful thing is Catholic philosophy! You are God's property. He can do what He pleases with you. It is all *His* affair, not yours. This removal of all responsibility as to the good or evil things of life is infinitely consoling. It removes all remorse about mistakes and failures. What profound philosophers our Catholic religious are! They give up nothing to gain everything. Even if there were no immortality, they are the wisest of mortals. Away from the jostling of the world, from the rudeness which it calls ambition, from its lust which it calls love, from its terror which it calls progress, from its hate, and from its love which is worse than hate, they pass into the secluded valleys of peace, and walk in its gardens of spice, the wings of angels outstretched over them, and the shadow of the broad hand of the Omnipotent protecting them. Compared with their poverty, which is in want of nothing, what is that restless wealth that craves everything ? Compared with their seclusion and retirement, what is that noisy fame that puts you on a pedestal to be pelted with the world's offal ? Returning at 2 P.M., met a priest who took me back with him to sermon and benediction in crypt. Order of services—Magnificat, Sermon on our Lady of Mount Carmel, and the giving of the scapular to St. Simon Stock. " Qu'il est respectable ! qu'il est avantageux ! Recommandé par le Pape, les Cardinaux, les prêtres, les princes et les princesses ! "

Strong gesticulations. " O Marie ! Mère Immacu-
lée ! Sainte Vierge ! " I thought the " Je vous
salue " very sweet—not so sweet as " Ave ! "
What's coming over me ? Six months ago an
" Ave " would have died on my lips !

*Lourdes, August* 17*th.*—Father F——, my dear
old chaplain, departed to-day, tears in his eyes, and
in mine. Ay, Christ is not dead, but liveth in
these Christlike men. Where have I seen this
thought—You, Kant, where are your children who
call themselves by your name, preach your doctrines,
follow in practice your life ? You, Fichte, Schelling,
Spinoza, whose schemes and systems come up,
angry and impotent, mounting over and levelling
each other like waves of an angry sea, and breaking
in vapour on the sands of time, where are your
followers, your disciples, who would swear by your
doctrines, and give their lives for their truth ? But
the gentle Christ, what awful power He exercises,
as the magnetism of His example and the magic
of His words stretch down along the centuries and
fill to-day the world's convents as they filled the
lauras of Nitria a hundred years after his death.
Good-bye, Père F——, I don't know what secret
influence caused your path to cross mine, but you
judged me in your love, and revealed your Master.

To-day is dark and gloomy—there is thunder
booming in the mountains. The Bordeaux procession comes in to-night.

*Lourdes, August* 18*th.*—The procession from
Bordeaux arrived at eleven o'clock last night. Went
to train to meet them. An immense crowd of very
poor people with bands and banners, and about
sixty priests. They moved down in solemn pro-
cessional order to grotto, carrying lighted candles,
and singing, but badly. All grouped themselves
around an improvised pulpit, whence a bishop
addressed them on the " Ave Maria." It was a

grand exhibition of faith ; but I should have pre-
ferred to see a sprinkling of the better classes—the
old Adam still, no doubt, within me.   On going to
my usual perch this morning, under the pines to the
left of the grotto, I saw an unusual sight.   Clearly,
the pilgrims had slept last night in the open air.
They were seated now, two by two, generally with
a priest between them, and sharing their frugal
breakfast—the long white loaf and the bottle of *vin
ordinaire*.   I was a little—just a little, shocked—the
old Adam again.   But, I thought, this would never
do in Ireland.   It was not the breaking of bread
with the poor that offended me.   God forbid !   But
there was a want of dignity about these good priests
in their dress and attitude, that an Irishman with
his lofty ideas about the Catholic priesthood could
never condone.   After all, deep down in the hearts
of us poor wandering devils of Irishmen, there is an
abiding instinct of reverence for the sacrosanct
dignity of those who minister at our altars.   The
dignity of our priests, and the sanctity of our women,
are the two points where we must not be touched.
I confess, too, I was shocked to see one of the Bordeaux bands filling the sanctuary at High Mass,
the conductor coolly standing on the predella, with
his back to the officiating priest, and swinging his
baton like a fury.   The deacon and sub-deacon,
even the master of ceremonies, were nowhere.   I
didn't like it.   I slipped into one of the private
chapels where a dear old priest, fully vested, had
been waiting half-an-hour for some one to serve his
Mass.   The congregation looked at him coolly.
I imagined an Irish labourer rising up and searching all Lourdes with lamps for a Mass-server, and
dragging him, probably with a good deal of profanity, to minister to the priest.   I proffered my
services, which were gratefully accepted.   I wonder
what my boys at Mayfield would say if they saw

Hugh Bellamy, M.A., serving Mass for an old French priest!

*Lourdes, August 20th.*—Had a violent hemor-rhage last night. Feared I was choking. What a dreadful thing is blood! But your life-blood, flowing away in strong currents, bearing your life with it! But, after all, cannot this be said of time and its swift-rolling sands sweeping away the longest life? I wish I were home again. And yet, leaving here is like leaving a mother's protection.

*Cauteretz, August 30th.*—Came up here from the valleys *en route* to Spain. Find the air in high mountain altitudes clearer and colder than in the lowlands. Spend my days mule-riding and making little explorations. Here Tennyson wrote some of his short poems. How does that run?—

> " All along the valley, where the waters flow,'
> I walked with one I loved two-and-thirty years ago.
> All along the valley, while I walked to-day,
> The two-and-thirty years were a mist that rolls away."

"Mist that rolls away!" The eternal cry of humanity, that notwithstanding sets such value on Time! What is that faculty, inferior to our judgment, which is always contradicting our judg-ment? It is not passion—there is no question of passion in our clinging to life. Yet men will tell you life is a vapour—a dream; and in the same breath they will speak of the value of human life— inestimable blessing of health—the all-important work of prolonging human life, &c., &c. What contradictory beings we are! It is not every one that is remembered so long as Tennyson's friend:—

> " For all along the valley, down the rocky bed,
> Thy living voice to me was as the voice of the dead;
> And all along the valley, by rock and cave and tree,
> The voice of the dead was a living voice to me."

Happy they whose memories are kept so green!
I wondered how long shall I be remembered?
Helen and Alf will remember me, I know.  And
my pupils?  Yes; to blaspheme my memory if I
gave a misdirection to their lives.  May the finger
of Omnipotence erase my name from their minds!
Can any wish be more terrible?

*Cauteretz, August* 31*st.*—I must go down again
into the warm valleys.  Those torn, bleeding lungs
cannot stand the cold air.

*En route, September* 1*st.*—Two fellows (French),
with their legs rolled up under them, discussed with
much animation to-day the mystery of the Trinity
and Incarnation.  It was infinitely amusing.  "Comment?  Il n'est pas possible.  Les termes se con-
tredisent," &c., &c.  Imagine two ants discussing
with their antennæ the mind of Shakespeare.  I
wonder when will this very finite creature, called
man, cease measuring himself with the Infinite!
Is there not something in the cry of the heart which
said: "Happy the sailor of the faith whom the
storms of controversy have landed in the harbour
of silence!  Happy he who is mute when men are
discussing Thy generation, but ringing as a trumpet
when they adore it.  Happy they who know how
difficult it is to understand, how sweet it is to praise
Thee!  Happy he who has not tasted the wisdom
of the Greeks nor lost the simplicity of the apostles!"
Ah me! how far have I drifted under the rays of
the star of the sea?  Twelve months ago, what would
have been my comment if any one had quoted these
words to me?

*San Sebastian, September* 3*rd.*—Burning skies,
white sierras, black eyes, the mantilla, silent days,
music-laden nights—assuredly I am in Spain.  Do
I like them?  No.  These Spaniards are clearly
the descendants of those old savage Romans whose
cry was *Panem et circenses.*  There is some latent

brutality in their natures. They treat their servants badly. To-day I saw my landlady drive her bodkin into the bare arm of a poor girl. Just what you'd read of the Roman matron. They are strong children of the sun. Unquestionable dignity in their bearing —they walk like kings of the earth. I can imagine how they have fallen. All those things that make modern greatness they despise—commerce, science, shipbuilding, railway-making, they have neither taste nor toleration for these things. But the spirit that conquered Mexico and Peru is still living. After all, it was in Spain Napoleon received his worst checks. But what could chivalry do against artillery? And the world won't go back.

*San Sebastian, September 5th.*—I feel very much better. This wonderful air is a luxury in itself. But the craving for home is growing upon me daily. I am losing flesh, but gaining wonderfully in spirits. What utter idiots those foreign doctors are! One fellow wanted to bleed me to-day, as if I had not lost quite enough blood already. Picked up to-day and read for the first time Renan's "Souvenirs." Good heavens! what a pitiful book. It would make a fervent Catholic of a Parisian even. I am beginning to believe that man's mind is a wolf that must be fed at the expense of every other faculty of body and soul. Listen to this!

"O maman, ma petite chambre, mes livres, mes études calmes et douces, mes promenades à côté de ma mere, adieu pour toujours. Plus pour moi du bonheur pur!" Was there ever such a threnody? or so wise a prophecy as this?—"Mais pourtant je sentais bien qu'au premier jour où le cœur cesserait de battre si fort, la tête recommencerait a crier famine!"

*Irun, September 12th.*—A hot, dusty oven, in which I am baked night and day. No sleep. No rest by day. Memory tortures me. How it passes the stinging-focus of the burning-glass, cut from the ice of my cold heart, slowly over every wound of my soul! Isabel, Marcella, shall I see you and be forgiven? To-day I have abandoned hope, if ever I entertained it. My days are numbered. To-morrow, perhaps to-night, my soul, the immortal part of me, shall be poised above these distant and tranquil suns. Is there peace there? They look so calm. But so does earth—silent and still, but oh! so turbulent with the beatings of broken hearts. Yet, when my body, a worn and gaping skeleton after this death in life, shall sleep in the eternal dormitories of Nature—sleep and be still—surely the higher part of me shall also attain rest—by absorption into the Infinite. Stop! That sounds Pagan and Pantheistic. Had I better say, I shall rest in the bosom of Abraham—better still in the bosom of Thee, O Christ. 'I have wandered, like a sheep that perisheth: seek Thy servant.'

> " He is out as of old in the city,
>     He is walking abroad in the street,
> He tendeth the poor in His pity,
>     The leper that crawls to your feet."

Ring down the curtain, O Death! and let the audience go to supper. The little drama is over! Thank God, I have no biographer. For this is the saddest fate of man, to live again, created not by the Supreme Artist, but by some miserable botch, who places your simulacrum on the high-roads of the world, like a beggar with outstretched hands and labelled 'Dumb and Blind!'

*Irun, September* 13*th.*—I am so much better to-night I think I shall face for home to-morrow. Home! Have I a home? Helen! Helen! I see thee draped in hideous black for me. No! no! No black! I hate it. The Church's mourning, if you like. And your piano is locked. No! no! But think of me in the soft summer twilights, as your fingers stray over the keys, and the silence and all the faces that come out of the silence speak. O Helen! Helen! what I have lost, and —gained!

HUGH BELLAMY.

# CHAPTER VII

## NOËL! NOËL!

We should see the spirits ringing
  Round Thee, were the clouds away;
'Tis the child-heart draws them, singing
  In the silent-seeming clay.
Singing! Stars that seem the mutest
  Go in magic all the way.

As the moths around a taper,
  As the bees around a rose,
As the gnats around a vapour,
  So the spirits group and close
Round about a holy childhood,
  As if drinking its repose.
                              —E. B. BROWNING.

THE great solemn day had again come round when, beside the crib of a little Babe, men, otherwise forgetful of God and humanity, allow their better feelings once more to resume dominion, before being subjected again to the harder sentiments that dominate their hearts and rule their actions throughout the year. It was a bright, frosty morning, with cold, crisp air, through which the joy-bells pealed their glad tidings. Two Christmas cards lay upon my breakfast-table, one from Ursula, one from Alfred Bellamy. I had a warm greeting from my poor little domestic, Katrine, who had placed a little holly bunch in the glass epergne, and I got a constrained salutation from Mrs. Oliver, who all these gloomy winter days was sad and *distraite* enough. I had heard an early morning Mass, and to break the day, perhaps from some higher motive which I could but dimly acknowledge, I went to last Mass at our little church. It was beautiful and solemn enough. The dim church, lighted by the blazing candles, which in turn made the holly leaves glisten, and the red berries more brilliant in the contrast; the happy looks on all faces, the solemn silence of the Mass, broken only by the tender music of the "Adeste"— (ah! that wonderful "Adeste!" who composed it? or was it written, as pictures have been painted, by some hidden saint, who wrote for God and His angels, and only cared for their praise?)—all was very sacred, and tender, and solemn; but I was a stranger, and alone in my Father's house.

I took luncheon about two o'clock, buried myself in my books all the afternoon, and at half-past six dressed myself with extreme care. Katrine hardly knew me in evening dress; Mrs. Oliver wished me a pleasant evening—I am afraid she hardly expected such herself—and I went out for a night of adventure. I held a small bag in my hand, supposed to contain a change of shoes. Katrine took it for granted that I was going to dine with the Lord-Lieutenant. She would not have been surprised if I had told her I would dance with a duchess before morning.

I strolled along quietly; the winter night was long. The streets were almost deserted; Christmas night meant home for all. A few birds of ill omen passed me from time to time, and a pair of revellers, holding together for mutual support, tried to sing in unison—

> " I swear, my love, to the stars above,
>   I will be true to you."

The doggerel and the refrain are in my ears to-day.

About nine o'clock I came just opposite the Deanes'. The whole house was brilliantly lighted, and I could hear the children's voices from within. I knew I had been expected, and that Ursula would

have been looking for me all the evening.   But some
foolish, old-fashioned sentiment that I should not intrude upon the sacredness of the family circle on
such a night withheld me, and touching my lips with
my hand I passed along the streets, sick and lonely
at heart.   Involuntarily, or at least without clear consciousness of where I was going, I found myself on
the way to Sandy Cove.   I was in no hurry—the
winter night was long.   The salt breath of the sea
came up across withered gardens and desolate
beaches, and very soon I could see the black-blue
waters heaving and tossing wearily in the starlight.
The tide was out, and I walked in the darkness down
along the little path that led to our old perch over
the channel in the rock, where so many times I had
seen the angry waters swishing and swirling at my
feet.   I sat down, lit a cigar, and tried to conjure
up all the times Herr Messing and I had sat there,
the many things we talked over, our little philosophies, our conjectures about the future, our estimate of this queer world and its little denizens.
Then I began to reflect what a fool I was not to be
at that moment sitting in an easy-chair, before a
comfortable fire, with kind faces around me, instead of this cold pinnacle and that black and irresponsive sea.   Sentiment was getting the mastery
of me, I thought, and I should try to be more practical.   Just then a hand was laid lightly on my
shoulder.   I started, and saw in the dim starlight a
figure standing over me, whose approach had been
noiseless, and a voice in the darkness said—

" Beg par'n, guv'nor, but would ye help a poor
thraveller ? "

At another time I would have started up and
angrily refused him ; but the sense of my own loneliness weighed upon me, and I smoked in silence
without answering him.   And the winter night was
long.

"I haven't eaten bread for forty-eight hours," continued the apparition. "I have walked from Wicklow here. I'm starving, s'help me God, and this is Christmas night!"

I never replied, but smoked on placidly as if I were in a billiard room.

"You had your Christmas dinner," he continued, "soup, and roast beef, and plum-puddin' and—and brandy-sauce, and you have come out in the night air to cool yer head. Dat champagne is hatin', you know."

The spectre was getting sarcastic.

"And I, God help me! have asked for a crust, and didn't get it. For why? Because I am a tramp, and in rags; and wummin runs away from me, and childher cry, and men set dogs at me."

This was getting interesting. I stood up and looked at my companion. In the starlight I could see that he told the truth. He was an ugly specimen of humanity. Unkempt, unshorn, and with his rags flapping in the night wind, he looked the personification of human misery, and to a weak person he would certainly be an object of not unreasonable terror.

"Yes," he continued, as he saw my white front glistening in the starlight, "you will go in now to your drawin'-room, and you will dance with your intended till morning. What do swell folks like you know of us poor divils, who have never a bed to lie on, and who see more of the stars than of the sun? But I'm detaining you," he continued. "Go in now, and forget that you ever saw such a scarecrow as me."

I handed him a shilling. He looked at it contemptuously.

"You'll win, or lose, a hundred times as much to-night," he said, "at nap or loo. Never mind; it manes a bit and a sup, whatever, for me."

"I say," I exclaimed, at last breaking silence, "what brought you out of your road down here this bye-path?"

"Nothin' perticklar," he exclaimed; "perhaps that was my luck to meet such a howling swell as you. Besides," he said, with exquisite sarcasm, "I likes the say. There's a lot of poetry about it, you know, perticklarly if you're in love."

"I'll walk along with you," I said, throwing away the stump of my cigar, "I daresay our roads lie together."

"Not at all, with many thanks for the compliment. You don't catch an old tramp so aisy. I don't want to be braceleted by a cop to-night."

So saying he shuffled away, with a parting shot—

"I'll drink your helt in Guinness. You can drink mine in shampain. But don't come out from the hated drawin'-room again. You'll catch cold mebbe, and your intended will be crying over you. Good-night and good luck, me patent shoes."

The whole scene was delightful in its exquisite sarcasm. I was as hungry and as homeless as the tramp. I wonder are such contrasts, or seeming contrasts, rare in life? or do the great ones of the earth, looked up to with envy and jealousy, sometimes smile at the ignorance that knows not its own felicity? I have always maintained that there is, contrary to all appearances, an absolute equilibrium of happiness amongst all classes in this life, and that there is no need of waiting for the General Judgment to justify the marvellous ways of Divine Providence. "Envy no man" is the logical conclusion from the old sad formula—"Call no man happy, till he dies."

Again I proceeded on my rounds that wonderful winter night. And by a natural instinct I found my way to Alfred Bellamy's. Here again I could have had a comfortable Christmas, a warm welcome, and the delightful society of Alfred and Helen Bellamy; but again, the thought came back, they will wish to be alone this Christmas night, especially as it is the first since Hugh died—I cannot intrude. Two or three times my hand was on the brass knocker, but I withdrew it, and I watched the dimly lighted window from a dark recess near the limestone steps. It was now after eleven o'clock, and the night was very chill. I was cold and hungry, and would have given a good deal for a cup of tea, but my shyness or pride prevented my asking hospitality where I was most certain of receiving it. After a little time the lamp was lowered, the blind raised, and brother and sister came to the bay-window beneath whose dark shadow I was hiding. They stood there a long time together, his arm round her neck, and her arms entwining him. Now and again he would lift his hand and point upwards to the skies as if showing her some particular wonder of the firmament, then they would look out in the silence across the black earth, and, I suppose, their thoughts went down to that land of sun and song where their sad brother lay in a peace to which he was a stranger during life. What my own thoughts were it would not be difficult to conjecture; but the blinds were drawn, the figures faded from the window, and I set out on my midnight quest again.

It was chiming twelve o'clock from church tower and public building when I entered the city. I looked around for a restaurant where I might have a cup of tea or coffee to keep out the night chill, for now I had determined to spend that Christmas night on the streets. But all the cafés and restaurants were closed. I went out from the broad streets into the slums, there was more animation there. Groups of women in dirty lanes congregated under the light of street-lamps, and talked as gaily as if it were noon day. Songs of bacchanals resounded from

F

the recesses of tenement-houses and wretched lodgings ; here and there men were locked in a drunken embrace ; and hideous women, from whose faces everything not only feminine, but human, was obliterated, stood arms akimbo, and indulged in that sarcasm on their neighbours, which is such a delightful entertainment to those not immediately concerned.

I was turning a corner to escape some pleasant comments that were just then being made on my own personal appearance, when a man in a frightful hurry ran full tilt against me.

"What the devil—" I was just saying, when he stopped me.

"I most humbly beg your pardon, sir," he said, "if I have hurt you."

When a man humbly begs your pardon, he puts you at once kneeling at his feet.

"Never mind, my poor fellow," I said, as I saw him wipe the blood from his nose ; "but you were in a mighty hurry.   What's up ? "

"It's my wife that's dying, sir," he said, "and I was flying for the priest and doctor."

He could not go much farther now.   He was bleeding profusely.

"Look here," said I, with a sudden impulse, "let me know where you live, and I'll do all in my power for her until you return."

"You, sir," he cried, looking me all over ; "what would the likes of you be doing in such a place ? "

"Never mind," I said, "I suppose there are some women with her.   And I may be of some assistance."

"There's no one with her, sir," he said, "but the great God."

"Then all the more necessity," I cried, "for some one to keep her company till you return. Now, come along, and show me the way."

He led me through narrow streets, dimly lighted, then turned suddenly through an archway into a yard. We entered a dark stable together, and climbing a rough ladder, we found ourselves in a room, with open rafters across the roof, and absolutely devoid of all furniture, if we except the straw on which the young dying mother lay. Close beside her, and covered only with a piece of torn flannel, was the dead child, a waxen Bambino, sent from God that night to symbolise to this wretched pair some lofty mystery, beyond their comprehension, but not beyond their faith. There it lay, a puny little thing, its features coloured like wax, and even with the gloss of wax upon them. The little hands were clasped together, purple at their extremities. It never opened its eyes to the blackness of this wretched world. Filled with the effulgence that streams from the great white throne, it had closed its eyes to all lesser lights, until it sought and found its home in the bosom of God.

All around the floor was wet. I pointed it out.

" Yes," the poor fellow answered, " the mother insisted that I should baptize the child ; and she gave me directions."

The young mother lay back on the straw pallet, wondering, dreaming who the stranger was.

" The doctor ? " she faintly whispered.

" No. He is coming."

Her face was very white ; her lips still whiter. The Angel of Death hung over her. I knelt down and put water to her lips.

" Is the priest coming ? "

" Yes, he'll be here soon."

" Pray, pray, sir, that God may not take me in my sins."

I did. Nay, I went farther. I took up her beads and whispered the Rosary, bead by bead in her ear. I ransacked my memory, and thought of every sweet

prayer that had ever softened my heart in the days
when——well, never mind; and I repeated, I
suppose twenty times, that marvellous prayer of
St. Bernard, known as the *Memorare*. I sang
through the glorious Litanies, and sent acts of
charity throbbing through her ears. And when the
priest arrived, and I retired to make way for him,
she murmured—

"May God bless you, sir, and never forget this
night's work for you!"

Was I rewarded? Yes, a hundred-fold. I
went down into the darkness of the stable and
thought—

"Now, Goff, supposing that you had poured into
that dying woman's ears all that you ever read from
your Greek poets and philosophers; supposing that
you had told her all those wonderful things that you
have been reading in your very discursive and not
altogether vagrant researches through the tangled
mazes of human thought, what consolation would it
have brought to her? what a mockery, wicked and
inhuman, would your unintelligible jargon have
appeared to her! Nay, something whispered, but
she is illiterate, uncultured, unrefined! Yes, but
suppose that she belonged to the upper classes,
suppose that she was the very highest amalgam
from the *crême de la crême* of society, would it have
made any difference? None whatever. Which
proves, here in this dark, ill-smelling stable, with
the hoofs of horses prancing impatiently near me,
and the murmur of a dying woman overhead, that
philosophy, culture, whatever else you call it, is all
very well for the easy-chair and the warm slippers
of a man who is at peace with the world, and has
a good digestion; but for the sorrow-stricken and
the afflicted—in a word, for the vast, heaving masses
of humanity, with all the cark and care of life upon
them, one "our Father" is a million times better

than all the heavy, undiluted speculations of academical loungers and cloistered *dilettanti !* "

The priest came slowly down the rough ladder,
the husband of the dying woman holding the lantern
over his head. He looked strangely at me. No
wonder. To see a young fellow dressed in white
front and swallow-tails on a Christmas morning,
in a foul-smelling stable, and know that he had
spent half his Christmas night by the bedside of
a dying woman, was a mild surprise. He was not
for a moment, however, off his guard. Buttoning
his overcoat around him, and pulling on his warm
gloves, he said, as if in soliloquy—

" If I had a hundred young fellows like you in my
district, I would soon stamp out vice and misery.
Imagine, I have a population of five thousand souls
in my district to look after. Why, the thing is an
impossibility. And no help, no succour, no assistance of any kind. I am helpless, powerless ! And
people have no idea of what we have to contend
against. Everything is against us ! Human nature,
organised vice, ignorance, the public hells, music
halls—pah ! I am often tempted to fling up the
whole thing in despair. But give me a hundred
young fellows like you, full of faith and piety (the
poor woman told me how you prayed for her), I
would revolutionise this city in twelve months.
But—but—there's no use in talking. I do not
know who or what you are, sir," he continued,
turning to me, " but God will bless you for this
night's work."

He held out his hand and passed into the lane.

I lingered a few moments longer, and then came
out into the streets. Already the wren-boys were
on their rounds.

> " Mr. —— is a noble man,
> And to his house we brought the wran ;
> And if his honour be so great,
> He'll give the wran a noble thrate."

I gave the little beggars a mite, and thought what a number of undeserved compliments, culminating in an attribution of nobility, had been showered on me this night.   I made my way hastily to a certain restaurant in Sackville Street, ordered a cup of coffee and some meat, leaned my head on the table, and fell fast asleep.   It was fully ten o'clock when I awoke.   The waiter was standing over me.   He looked seedy enough after the night.   Yet I shrank from his eye, which plainly said—

"Christmasing too freely, young man! you'll pay for it to-day!"

Then I breakfasted greedily.   And carefully concealing my evening dress, I made my way homeward.

"I hope you had a pleasant Christmas, Katrine?" I said to my young attendant.

"I can't say I had, sir," with a pout.   "I hope you had!"

"Delightful," I answered, "but what occurred to mar the festivities here?"

"Oh! the usual thing, of course.   *He* came in and demanded whisky, and was half drunk, and they had a dreadful time downstairs; and—and —it's the last Christmas I'll spend here whatever."

"But who is this mysterious individual, Katrine, that is constantly upsetting all your nerves?"

"I'm sure I don't know, sir," she replied.   "He comes here always at night: he never comes in the daytime.   And he must have some power over them, for Mrs. Oliver, though she tells me not to let him in, is afraid of him.   He kep' us up all night last night, and went away before dawn this morning."

"Surely," said I, "it can't be the gentleman to whom Miss Oliver is to be married."

"No," said Katrine, who knew all about the matter.   "And what they are most afraid of is, that

that gentleman will come here when the other gentleman is here, and then there will be trouble."

" Do you know the gentleman to whom Miss Oliver is to be married ? "

" Just by appearance," said Katrine. " He is a judge, or something in the law, and very rich. And the other fellow hates him."

" And so you had a poor Christmas, Katrine ? "

" Indeed'n I had, sir."

" Well, may you have a happier New Year."

" Thank you, sir."

She went away and presently returned.

" Mrs. Oliver would like to see you, sir."

" Tell her I shall be down in a moment."

I changed my dress rapidly, had a good wash, and went down.

Mrs. Oliver looked fagged. Gwendoline looked cross and pettish.

But with that marvellous power of transformation which Nature has given women, and which may be considered hypocritical by us, who never by any chance conceal our feelings, both ladies brightened up, assumed a gaiety which they were far from feeling, and asked me, with effusiveness, if I had had a happy Christmas.

I said yes. I hoped they had a similar experience.

" Yes, indeed it had been a very happy time. Yet, every one is glad when Christmas is over."

" You have heard, I suppose, Mr. Austin, of Gwennie's engagement ? "

Yes, I had heard it from their good friends the Deanes. It was the gossip of all the legal circles in Dublin. I took the opportunity of congratulating Miss Oliver on such a brilliant engagement.

I thought of that awful exclamation of Hubert Deane's.

" I understand that Mr. Leviston is magistrate for some city division ? "

Mrs. Oliver winced.

" Yes, he is Q.C., you know, and obliged to do disagreeable things sometimes."

" Well," I said, " I am quite sure that in future the unpleasantness of professional work will be more than mitigated by his domestic felicity."

Gwendoline smiled incredulously.

" We shall have a little dance for a few chosen friends on New Year's night," said Mrs. Oliver. " May we have the pleasure of seeing you ? "

" Nothing could give me greater pleasure," I replied, " especially as I am to have the privilege of meeting Miss Oliver's fiancé."

# CHAPTER VIII

## TABLEAUX VIVANTS

SCENE.—MRS. OLIVER'S *house, decorated and prepared for an evening party, viz., dining-room, the supper-hall ; the drawing-room turned into a ball-room ; an extemporised conservatory outside the French windows.*

TIME.—10.30 *p.m.*

PERSONÆ.—MRS. OLIVER, MISS OLIVER, MR. LEVISTON, Q.C., HUBERT *and* AGNES DEANE, *one or two half-pay officers, who knew the deceased paymaster, some school friends of* MISS OLIVER'S, *some elderly spinsters, &c., &c.*

1st ELDERLY SPINSTER (*fanning herself*). And so it is to come off. What a fool to marry a penniless girl !

2nd E. S. No accounting for tastes, dear. They say she caught his fancy at some ball.

1st E. S. By what peculiar attraction ?

2nd E. S. I'm sure I don't know. But sometimes these middle-aged men, *blasés* and *ennuyés,* are taken with a baby face.

1st E. S. He has a history, then ?

2nd E. S. Yes, dear, what man has not, or woman either ? But it would be well for him to have a *modern* historian to record it !

1st E. S. I think I understand.

*A pause.*

1st E. S. It was clever angling on the part of Mrs. O.

2nd E. S. I should hardly give her credit for so much ability.   But where everything is at stake people will develop extraordinary talents, dear.

1st E. S. And there were not many rivals in the field ?

2nd E. S. No!   (*Significantly.*)

Mrs. OLIVER *approaches.*

1st E. S. Allow me to congratulate you again, dear, on the extraordinary success of this evening, and on dear Gwennie's approaching marriage.

2nd E. S. And what a delightful man Mr. Leviston seems !

Mrs. OLIVER (*moved to tears*). Thank you *so* much.   But it will be *so* hard to part with the dear child !   You know, she has grown into my life, and has been a companion rather than a child since poor Captain Oliver died.

1st E. S. Well, she ought to be happy, if we are to judge by appearances.   But he is rather young, is he not.

Mrs. O. (*with a glance of suspicion*). Well, not so young as to be unable to follow his own opinion !

2nd E. S. (*changing a dangerous subject*). Who might that tall young man be, leaning over there against the piano ?

Mrs. O.   A Mr. Austin—one of the Austins of Fermanagh.   Just come up to the city on a brief visit !

1st E. S. Oh ! indeed.   They are reputed to be fabulously wealthy.   You are happy in every way, Mrs. Oliver !

Mrs. O. Well, yes, I am particularly happy in my friends.   Will you dance, Miss C. . . . I shall have great pleasure in securing a partner for you ?

1st E. S. No, thanks.

Mrs. OLIVER *retires triumphant.*

SCENE.—*Dining-room.* Mr. LEVISTON, Q.C., *and some officers stand at a side table. It is still early, but there is an unpleasant odour of whisky in the air.*

LEVISTON (*sotto voce, aside*). D——d stupid, the whole affair! Why couldn't the old leviathan let well alone? Bringing all those old harridans and roués around us. (*To the officers.*) You are enjoying yourselves, of course?

1st OFFICER. Yes, just now. (*Sipping brandy and soda.*)

2nd OFFICER. You ought be very happy, old man! Every one envies you!

LEV. (*gloomily*). So I am. My days of freedom are coming to an end. I suspended the freedom of many in my time. My own turn comes now.

1st OF. Ay, but your chains are of roses. The manacles of your prisoners are of harder stuff.

LEV. (*musingly*). There was one chap, I remember—why do I recall him to-night? something in little Gwennie's eyes, I suppose—he was up before me for swindling or cheating—a bad lot. I was in bad humour—liver out of order, I suppose. I gave him two years' hard labour! Why does he come up to-night?

*Officers look at each other and lift their eyebrows.*

1st OF. Come out and have a cigar!


SCENE. — GEOFFREY AUSTIN, *leaning against piano.* Mrs. OLIVER *approaches softly, alarm in her eyes.*

TIME.—11 *p.m.*

Mrs. OLIVER. Don't look alarmed, Mr. Austin, but pray help me! I am in great trouble.

G. A. I assure you, Mrs. Oliver, anything I can do I shall be most happy, &c.

Mrs. O. I fear an unpleasant visitor. He may come at any moment. I have received a note. If he meet Mr. Leviston, he will strike him and cause a scene. Can you help me?

G. A. Well, really, Mrs. Oliver, I cannot well see how. I have no right to interfere with a gentleman visitor. He would resent it, and justly——

Mrs. O. Quite true! Oh my! what shall I do? what shall I do? I must tell. It is—Mr. Austin, I must tell you, but in the most sacred confidence— it is my son, and he has already got into conflict with Mr. Leviston.

G. A. I'm so sorry. Would you depute me to see him and—and reason with him?

Mrs. O. Oh! certainly. Many thanks, indeed. But—don't reason with him, but get him away. He may ask for drink.

G. A. And then?

Mrs. O. Give it him, but, for God's sake, get him away!

Mrs. OLIVER *retires and puts on the regulation smile.*

1st E. SPINSTER. Mrs. Oliver is in trouble, my dear.

2nd E. S. She doesn't look it.

1st E. S. Nevertheless she is! That young fellow has been keeping the wolf from the door for her. The Austins of Fermanagh! Well, well, how some people can play a part!

2nd E. S. I wonder where she got these palms?

1st E. S. You wonder? Have you the least doubt?

2nd E. S. Who?

1st E. S. Either of two persons—Leviston or Austin—the first by preference.

2nd E. S. Happy child, to get away from all this poverty and pretence.

1st E. S. And to get into wealth and position
and——

2nd E. S. And what?

1st E. S. The arms of a debauchee.

2nd E. S. Oh! my dear, you are not charitable
to-night. What's that.

*A tremendous knock is heard at the outer door; all
start; Mrs. OLIVER whispers GWENNIE, who
is at the piano, to continue her fortissimos, looks
concerned for a moment, then smiles off her
anxiety. In the hall, GEOFFREY AUSTIN
meets FRED OLIVER.*

FRED O. What the deuce is all this row about?
Full dress, too, regulation white choker, and swallow-
tail. Turn round, my buck, and let's have a look at
you. Why, you are fit for a vice-regal party. And
palms, and flowers, but blow me, where's the
liquor?

G. A. Come in here, old man, and you'll have
plenty of it. It's a little supper party given in
honour of your sister's approaching marriage!

F. O. And if your royal highness don't object,
would you tell me who the deuce are you, and
what the deuce brought you here, and what right
have you to dictate to me in my mother's house?

G. A. Your mother? Then you are Fred Oliver?
Dearest old fellow, how are you after all these
years? (*Shakes his hand effusively.*)

F. O. I'm all right, thank you; (*dubiously*) but I
am not aware I had the honour of your acquaintance
before!

G. A. Come in, come in, Fred, and we'll talk it
over a glass of wine!

F. O. No objection to the glass of wine, I'm sure,
but (*aside*) who the devil is he?

*Enters dining-room and looks around bewildered.*

G. A. And so we meet again. Don't smoke, the ladies are coming in to supper.

F. O. Will you prevent me ?

G. A. Never mind. But—don't—smoke.

F. O. (*aside*). Where the deuce did I meet him ?

G. A. And so you don't remember me ?

F. O. (*coolly*). I told you already I had not that honour.

G. A. (*coming close and whispering*). You don't remember that little affair of the Long Firm ?

F. O. *starts, and the cigar falls from his hands.*

G. A. Do you remember Mr. Rose and the little plot about the prisoners coming up to Mountjoy, and how you peached——

F. O. For God's sake, who are you ?

G. A. Never mind, old man, you'll know me soon. Which are you most afraid of—a detective or a pal ?

F. O. *stares.*

G. A. You can take your choice. Copeland is in the conservatory. Markham is in the kitchen.

F. O. Good God ! Look here, how can I get out of this infernal place ?

G. A. If you promise never again to set foot inside these doors. It was not kind of you to go back upon your pals when they could have escaped but for you——

F. O. I told old Rose in confidence——

G. A. Well, never mind now. Will you go, or stay ?

F. O. Another drink, and I'll go. What the deuce of a trap I walked into.

G. A. Come now, there is no time. I may not be able to see you through.

*Voices in the hall.*

G. A. This way ! If Leviston sees you, all's up.

F. O. Yet I'd do five years to get a blow at him. And he's going to marry little Gwen. I *won't* go.

G. A. Come quick, I tell you, or you're nabbed. Come, come!

*Exit* GEOFFREY AUSTIN, *dragging the unwilling* FRED OLIVER *after him.*

SCENE.—*The extemporised conservatory.* AGNES DEANE *and* GWENDOLINE OLIVER *in close conversation.*

TIME.—*Midnight.*

A. D. You happy little minx! And so the prince has come?

G. O. Yes, dear Aggie. Isn't it all delightful?

A. D. Delightful! But you won't recognise any of your old friends when you get into this new circle. I am expecting to be cut by you any day that I shall meet you in Grafton Street.

G. O. O Aggie, how can you say so? You know, dear, that is not my way. I am sure Mr. Leviston is very kind, and will let me see any one I please; and mamma will live with us——

A. D. And you'll have the handsomest house in the city, and the finest horses, and the entrée to the castle! Why, where did you find the fairies' ring?

G. O. But, surely, people ought not to be envious of me; and you have no idea of the looks I got this evening.

A. D. Never mind, dear. But won't Sister Angela be delighted!

G. O. (*a little startled*). I'm sure she will. Oh, why did you say that, Aggie? (*Bursting into a paroxysm of tears.*) O Aggie, Aggie, I'm the most wretched, miserable girl in the world. Oh! could you save me at all?

A. D. (*surprised at this outburst of emotion*). Save you, dear? Save you from what?

G. O. Oh, will you never understand? I hate him, I hate him.

A. D. (*shocked*). You don't mean Mr. Leviston, child?

G. O. Yes, I do, I do, I do. (*Wringing her hands.*) Oh, what have I done to deserve such a fate? He's simply horrid, Aggie. You don't know him. And I *must* marry him. Oh, why did you mention Sister Angela?

A. D. Now, dear, this won't do. You are betrothed to the man, you will soon be his wife (*Gwennie shudders*), and you must respect and love him. What do you see objectionable in him?

G. O. I don't know. He looks horrid sometimes. His face quite red; and when I danced with him a little time ago he smelt dreadfully of—of——

A. D. Of what, child?—patchouli?

G. O. Oh no! no! something worse (*whispering*), spirits—whisky!

A. D. Well, it was rather early, I admit. But you know, dear, men do take drink freely at these meetings.

G. O. And he said such nasty things. Oh! (*covering up her face*), who'd ever think I could hear such things?

A. D. Never mind, little one, it will all come right. When you roll away from Marlborough Street in your carriage, you'll forget it all!

G. O. But it isn't Marlborough Street at all. Oh! there again—what a horrid business!

A. D. And where will you be married?

G. O. (*whispering*). At the registrar's. Now, I knew I'd shock you. But (*defiantly*) I don't care. The archbishop refused a dispensation, and we're to be married at the registrar's. It is all right, you know.

A. D. (*shocked*). All right! It's all wrong, child!

G. O. I shall shock you more!

A. D. You cannot !

G. O. I can. Mr. Leviston is——

A. D. Is what ?

G. O. (*whispering*). A Freemason !

A. D. Good heavens !

G. O. Now congratulate me, won't you ?

A. D. Poor little Gwen ! And is this the end of all our dreams ? Do you remember the old walks we had at the Abbey, down where the lilac and laburnum used to twine their blossoms together in May, and how we used to race down the walk toge- ther when we saw the white guimpe of Sister Angela through the trees ; and the long summer evenings, and our hymns to our Blessed Lady at the Grotto, and our little theatricals—you were always Galatea (do you remember the day when you nearly fell from the window where you were posing ?). Ah ! it was all a valley of peace, did we know it.

G. O. O Aggie, you'll kill me, you'll kill me !

A. D. And here we are out on the high seas, in storm and tumult. Do you remember Sister Schol- astica, Gwen ?

G. O. Oh, I do ! I do !

A. D. Do you remember what we used to say ? We didn't like her, you know, she was so grave and solemn. Don't you remember her big brown eyes, and how you used to say " What white hands you have ! " and she used to fold them up in her long sleeves. I wonder do they ever think of us ?

G. O. I suppose they do, Aggie. But I wonder what would Sister Scholastica *say* if she saw me now ?

GWENDOLINE *looks down on her bare arms, flashing with jewellery, and puts out her little slippers, and sighs.*

A. D. (*with a start*). Here comes that br——— your betrothed—Mr. Leviston ! Rub your eyes, child, with this cologne.  It would never do to let him see you cry. •

LEVISTON *approaches rather unsteadily, and puts on an inane smile.*

Mr. LEVISTON.  Sho glad t' find you.  Old shtory—mis'toe bough !  Will you dansh, Miss Deane ?  No !  Ah, Deane, clev' fellow, up to date (*leans heavily against a flower stand, and knocks down stand and a splendid cineraria*).  Damn unshteady things.  All broke.  (GWENDOLINE *and* AGNES DEANE *escape.* Mrs. OLIVER *comes up, angry, but smiling*).

Mrs. O.  Hope you haven't hurt yourself, Mr. Leviston ?

Mr. LEVISTON.  Not 'tall!  Everything sheems drunk here.  All shwims 'bout.  Jolly ole muzzer'n law, won't you dansh ?

Mrs. O.  Not now, thank you.  Allow me to take you to the sofa.  There !  Rest awhile.

Mrs. OLIVER *departs ; so does company, leaving drawing-room deserted.*

Mr. LEVISTON *rises, and looks around.  Spies bust of Duke of Wellington.  Goes up and affectionately embraces it.*

Thought I knew you, ole fel'.  But you're drunk, too (*pedestal and bust reel*), drunk and dis'orly.  Two monsh ! !—hard labour, ha ! ha !

*Looks around, and sees room empty.  Smiles inanely.  Then says—*

I feelsh like one that threadsh 'lone
Shome bang' hall desherted,
Whose lightsh are fled, whose garlands dead
And all but him dep—ar—ted.

*Sinks into a chair, and falls asleep. Enter figure stealthily. Approaches the sleeping man and stands over him.*

FRED OLIVER. And this is you, you brute! (*kicks him*). You, that sent me to black bread and breaking stones for two years! You sot, you beast, at last I have my revenge!

*Draws over chair and sits opposite* LEVISTON.

How often in the black pauses of the night did I dream of my revenge! How often, when I went down upon my knees on the flags of my cell, and gathered up the black crumbs of bread and ate them, gritty as they were, for I was starving, did I think I should one day come even with you! How often, when my knees were breaking on the accursed treadmill, did I remember you with a curse! And how often, when shivering on the hard boards by night, did I pray to God to prolong my life that I might have satisfaction on you! And to-night, despised, hated as I am, you are even more hated and despised. Men avoid you, and women fly the contamination of your presence. And even my wretched mother, who is selling my baby sister for your gold, even she despises and loathes you!

*Strikes him with his open hand on the face.* LEVISTON *starts and mumbles* " whash that? "

Poor little Gwennie! And this is your fate! But if ever this brute attempts to hurt you, or even frighten you, so help me God, I'll——

*Lifts his hand to strike him, but is immediately pinioned from behind by the two detectives who had glided into the room.*

MARKHAM. So this is your little game! Assaulting and threatening to murder a magistrate  You

had not enough yet of the stone-breaking.    Copeland, fit on these bracelets.    This is an old hand.

F. O.  All right !    But I was near it, nearer
to-night than I shall ever be again.    Lead on.

FRED OLIVER *led out handcuffed.*

SCENE.— *The hall.*  HUBERT DEANE *and* AGNES
*leave the supper-room, and prepare for home.*
HUBERT *arranges his wife's furs, and* GWEN-
NIE *steals out.*

G. O.  One word, Aggie !    What shall I do ?
Tell me for God's sake.    He—is lying in there—
drunk !

A. D.  Run away, child.    Back to the Abbey, anywhere from such contamination.

G. O.  Oh ! how can I ?    Mother would seek me
out ; and things would be worse than ever.

A. D.  Then go speak to your parish priest, or
some priest, and throw yourself on their protection.

G. O.  Oh ! how could I, how could I ?    I do not
know them.

A. D.  Do not know them !    Then go, child, and
make their acquaintance, and insist on their protecting you.

G. O.  But I have never—have never——

A. D.  Never what ?

G. O.  Never been introduced to them, you know ;
and mother says we should never speak to gentlemen without being introduced.

A. D.  Well, well !  How I wish I was a man so that
I could swear.    Never mind, Gwen, dear, I suppose
it will all come right.    Good-night, poor child !

SCENE.—HUBERT *and* AGNES DEANE, *in their
close carriage, rolling home under the stars.*

A. D.  Poor little Galatea !    And this is her Pyg—
malion !

H. D. Agnes! Agnes! How dreadful!

A. D. What's dreadful, you cynic? the pun or the pig?

H. D. Oh dear! Women are so uncharitable.

A. D. I know now, Hub, what you meant when you muttered "hell" in the stage tones that night.

H. D. Was I right?

A. D. Yes, Hub, but now you are uncharitable.

*A pause.*

A. D. I wonder how is little Ursey to-night? She will be looking out for us.

H. D. I don't know, Aggie; but I have horrible presentiments. Did you tell Austin?

A. D. No, I was afraid. When you tell him anything, he puts such an awful look in his eyes. The iris, isn't that what they call it, disappears, and his eyes are all pupils and dark light.

H. D. A very Hibernian remark, my dear.

A. D. And then, he remained but a short time at the dance. I saw Mrs. Oliver speak to him, and he went out and did not return.

*A pause.*

A. D. Do you know, dear, I think he is very poor.

H. D. Very likely.

A. D. Could we do anything for him?

H. D. Perhaps not. He'll kill himself if anything happens to Ursula.

A. D. Poor Ursey! and poor Mr. Austin! and poor little Galatea! We are all poor, Hub!

H. D. Yes, dear, but I'm very rich in you. Here we are!

The soul of man is to the soul of woman what the plectrum is to the lyre. You can evoke soft celestial harmonies from the strings, or tear them in pieces, and make them discordant or dumb for ever!

## Two Paragraphs.

LEVISTON—OLIVER.—On Monday, 7th January, William Henry Leviston, Q.C., to Gwendoline Gascoigne Oliver, only daughter of the late Captain Frederick James Oliver, retired paymaster.    No cards.

On Monday, Frederick Hales, *alias* Hutton, *alias* Oliver, was sent back to penal servitude for a brutal and unprovoked assault on one of the city magistrates.    He is an old offender, and received his sentence with that swaggering air that denotes the hardy criminal.

# CHAPTER IX

## IN THE DEPTHS

When sorrows come, they come not single spies,
But in battalions.

IF the darkest hour is that which precedes the dawn, is it not also true that very bright moments are but the preliminary to dark and saddened hours? On the whole, things were looking very bright with me just now. And if, as they say, men who are very much inclined to be superstitious, rarely feel presentiments of coming evils, and to them only such harbingers of future misfortunes come who are least prone to believe them, or be affected by them, let me be ranked in the former class, for assuredly no idea of anything but ordinary trouble crossed my mind during these happy days of Spring.

I had, after great labour, secured a small position as maker of catalogues, in a second-hand bookstall in the city. The work was light, and to my taste. The remuneration was little; but I was placed above immediate want. I had made some new friends and renewed an old and valued acquaintance. Things were not rose-coloured; but neither were they very dark.

One day, when I was very busy, working at names, and dates, and bindings of books, my hands blackened and my face begrimed with dust, I heard a well-known voice asking for a Foulis Euripides. I at once recognised Mr. Dowling, but would gladly have hidden myself from him.

"Mr. Austin, kindly hand down that octavo edition of Euripides," said the proprietor.

I took it down, and, with eyes bent to the ground, I handed it to Mr. Dowling.

He did not look at the book.   He looked at me.

"Austin," said he, "is that you?"

"Yes, sir," I said, with an affectation of gaiety I was far from feeling, "I am true to the old love still."

"Yes," said he, balancing the volumes, but looking keenly and pityingly at me.   "I heard you failed in that examination.   Was it in classics you failed?"

"No, sir," I said, "thanks to you there, I got highest marks in Latin and Greek.   I failed in mathematics."

"Probably," he said to himself musingly, "yet perhaps I was to blame in concentrating your thoughts so exclusively on classics!"

"Oh! I don't think so, sir," I said airily.   "I believe I lost courage, and had too much diffidence in myself.   That was the cause of the failure."

"And this is your present work," he said, looking around the dusty shop.   "It is rather an anti-climax to a Government sinecure of £600 a year.   Yet, perhaps you are happier here."

"It is quite possible, sir," I replied, "at least I have had a few glimpses of happiness lately; but I do not know how long they will last.   I have not grasped the secret yet."

He looked at me keenly.

"You will never grasp the secret until you cease to seek it."   Then after a pause—"Are you reading anything just now?"

"Yes," I said with some bitterness, "I have been probing and searching in forbidden places, thinking that I should find in the masters of human thought the secret of human happiness—which is content."

" And have you found it ? "

" No."

" Who directed you thither ? "

I paused, for I was embarrassed. At last I blurted out, " You ! "

He started as if accused of a crime.

" Yes," I said, now more firmly, though I knew I was arraigning him, for whom I had always had such respect, " you told me to search the Greek philosophers, and then come down to the Germans."

He looked puzzled. Then knitting his brows, he said—

" For what purpose ? "

" I presume," I said, " to seek wisdom, the only wisdom to be found."

" And have you found it ? "

" No," I said bitterly, " but your advice has imperilled my faith."

" Imperilled your faith ? " he cried,[1] " you might as well accuse me of having imperilled your life, or infected you with delirium ! You have grossly misunderstood me ! If you took my silver and gold and turned them into suicidal weapons against yourself, you have no one but yourself to blame ! "

" But your Plato and your Zeno, your Kant and Fichte, and all your other sceptics ? "

" They are," he interrupted angrily, " but the acolytes of the Church ; you have made them rival priests, and their teachings rival religions."

It was my turn now to be angry. " Why was not all this taught us ? " I cried. " The whole tenor of modern liberal education is to glorify these men and to decry Christianity. I want to ask you a question."

" Go on," he said wonderingly.

" What is your opinion on the very much

[1] I have quoted his words in a former chapter, but they are necessary to the context here.

debated question—Is art independent of religion or morality?"

"My opinion is," he said with his old emphatic deliberation, "that art is but the handmaid of higher things, and must never be made their mistress!"

"Then art or science of any kind that tends to injure religion or morality must be sternly laid aside?"

"Certainly."

"Then why hold up to the admiration of youth the art—the literary art—of Pagans, whose teachings and suggestions are diametrically opposed to Christian dogmas and morals; and who create in the minds of the young the idea that the Christian dispensation was unnecessary, because Pagan morality and Pagan ethics were already perfect?"

"I don't understand you," he said. "Do you mean to say that Socratic wisdom was superior to that lofty revelation which has come to us?"

"I am very far from saying such things," I replied. "I have already had bitter experience of how worthless the whole tribe of cultured heathens are when you come to test them. But if their morality is deficient, why cultivate the art that conceals such ragged poverty? Yet, I can understand an admiration for these glorious old heathens. But why profess admiration for these new Pagans, whose works, when they are intelligible, are simply a farrago of idle dreams about subjects that are beyond human reason, and a tangled mass of contradictions and absurdities, hidden under the glittering web of philosophical names and definitions?"

"Perhaps there is something in what you are saying," he said musingly. "Fortunately, the vast masses of students are more tempted to curse their learned obscurity than to be fascinated by their learned speculations. But, you see, Austin, you always push things to extremes. I don't care a hang for Cicero as an individual (he was a vain poltroon), nor for his philosophy, which is cheap and second-hand; but I shall always admire his wonderful rhetoric, his power of placing words just where they have most effect, which is the definition of poetry or oratory."

He was somewhat annoyed, as if he had been caught napping. But, on reflection, he saw his way out of the difficulty. He was very straight-forward.

"You have betrayed me into saying things that I hardly admit. But see, Austin, you are confounding two things—art, which I always admire—science, which I always detest. Now, when I gave you that advice (which I really forget, but you must be right), I intended only that you should read the poetry of the ancients and moderns. Their sciences, philosophical and metaphysical, I never recommended. You remember I would never read Plato, nor any other dreamer for their ideas, and only Virgil amongst the Latins. And I never intended you to worry your brains and disturb your reason with writers who did not understand themselves. Why, the cause of Kant's popularity was that not twenty in Germany understood his speculations. If he is spoken of to-day in academical circles, it is because not five in the British Isles outside Scotland could follow his abstruse and complicated reasoning. What then did I teach you? That Art is always true—that Science, which boasts to be the harbinger of light, is nearly always false. And the grand mistake you have made is, to have forsaken the immortals of Greece and Germany for the twaddle called science —for the worst of all sciences, because it is the most nebulous—metaphysics. Go back to the poets—they never lead astray."

"Ay, but, Mr. Dowling, the poets dabble, too, in metaphysics."

" So much the worse for the poets and their poetry. This accounts for the awful decadence of poetry in the Victorian age."

" But Goethe is the worst of all, for ever touching —and with a profane and sacrilegious hand—the highest mysteries."

" Go back then to the immortal Greeks. Take up your Sophocles and Æschylus, and study there human nature, presented in the highest forms of dramatic art."

"And find," said I, in a parting shot, "what Lucian describes as beautiful books, with golden knobs and purple morocco outside, and within a Thyestes devouring his children, or Œdipus marrying his mother."

" You are degenerating, Mr. Austin," he said, smiling. " Good-day ! "

I was turning aside to my work with a certain sense of complacency, such as only an irresponsible Bohemian can feel, when, to my surprise, my employer accosted me. He was an illiterate man, but making money fast by literature.

" I beg your pardon," he said, " but I overheard your conversation with that gentleman. Did I understand you to say that you were a freethinker ? "

"Certainly not," said I, in amazement.

"Did I understand yer to say," he continued in a magisterial tone, " that you were reading bad books ? "

"I don't know what you call bad," I replied angrily.

"Bad books," he said, " is the ruination of the world."

"Then why do you sell them ? " I said hotly.

"Me sell bad books?" he said, quite shocked. " I'd burn my hand before I'd pass out a bad book to the public."

" What do you call this, then," I replied, handing

down Boccaccio's " Decameron," "and this, and this, and this ? "

I took down the " Mysteries of Paris," "Ovid's Art of Love," and the "Heptameron of Queen Margaret of Navarre," and placed them before him. He was stupefied.

"Why," said I, "if you were to clear out all the bad books in this shop, you'd have nothing but spider's webs remaining. Look at these illustrations," I cried, opening up some art journals. " Are these the kind of figures before which you'd like to say your prayers ? Take this Psyche, and this Venus rising from the bath, and show them to your daughters. It is all high art, you know. Wouldn't this lady, with her scanty drapery, look well framed, and what a delightful lesson in high morality is this Caliban and Ariel ! "

"Good God ! " the poor man cried, sinking into a chair, and mopping his forehead with a handkerchief. " I bought them for a job lot, and I thought they were all right. Leave them there," he cried, as he saw me about to remove them, " leave them there for a moment ! "

He recovered his senses presently, and took out a pocket-knife. He slit open carefully the bindings of some books, and then deliberately cut the strings, and tore the books leaf from leaf. He piled up the leaves in a disused stove, and set a match to them. In a few minutes there was nothing left but a fluffy mass of charred paper. I made one or two feeble protests, particularly in one case, where a valuable and exquisitely bound book, an antique, was going to the holocaust.

"Stop ! " I cried, "that's worth thirty shillings at least."

" If it was worth thirty thousand pounds, it must go." And it did.

That evening at six o'clock, as I put on my hat

and greatcoat previous to my departure, he accosted me—

"At what letter in the catalogue are you working now ? " he said.

"The letter S."

"What number ? "

"871."

"When do you expect to finish ? "

"To-morrow evening."

"Because I shall not need your services any longer."

This was a great blow to me. Again my flippant tongue had spat the bread from my mouth. My funds were now very low, barely enough to pay rent for a month or two. I stood at the door, look-ing on the quays irresolutely. Blank, black despair came down upon me. I was a fated, doomed mor-tal! And surely, if the world has any superfluous pity to spare, there is no worthier object than a young man, facing life without friends or prospects, not knowing where to-morrow he shall lay his head or get his daily crust. It is very easy, when the prize has been won, and the golden ease and luxury acquired, to take a hopeful view of life and its issues. From the depths of your armchair, O my prosperous friend, in the calm luxuriance of your drawing-room, with all the appurtenances of modern comfort around you, you can look out with complacency on the storm and stress of that battle, where you played such an easy part. But if ever you have known the sinking of a young man's heart, who is disposed neither to beg nor 'list, but who looks in despair on the dismal vista of life that stretches before him, seeing nought but the gaunt walls of the workhouse at the end, perhaps you will understand this feeling that there is not one of all God's suffering creatures so much to be pitied. He goes down in the fierce struggle for existence, and does not know where to look for a pitying voice, or a strong hand to help him.

I suppose my employer read something of this kind in my face, for he came to the door and touched me on the shoulder.

"Hold on here," he said, "till you get a better place."

It was human, and I was thankful; but I declined.

It was eight o'clock before I reached my lodgings. As I hung up my greatcoat and hat in the hall, I saw sitting on a hall-chair a young girl, whom I had noticed in the same place a week before. She nodded at me and smiled. I did not recognise her.

As I passed upstairs to my bedroom, Miss Oliver was coming down. She was dressed for a dance. Her long train swept up the stairs for several steps behind her. She drew back into a corner to let me pass. Usually she had a smile or a cheerful "Good-night" for me. To-night she was silent. I looked up. She was dressed to perfection. A white camellia with a spray of maidenhair was on her shoulder. Something very bright gleamed in her hair. There was a subtle odour of some sweet perfume in the air. She did not look at me. Her eyes were cast down, not shyly and diffidently, but proudly and defiantly. She drew back with one sweep of her hand her long train. I passed upstairs, wondering and sick at heart.

A small note was on my plate when I came down to tea, and apparently Katrine was full of some important subject.

"It was that minx in the hall that told them," she said.

"Told whom, Katrine, and what?"

"Told the missus, sir, that you was—was— poor."

"And how did that young lady know that interesting fact?" I asked. "I have never seen her face before."

"She said that you came into their shop some time ago, and that the manager, a perfect gentleman, got you thrown out."

I had the letter opened, and was reading—

"DEAR MR. AUSTIN,—Your little friend Ursula is seriously ill. She is asking for you. Would you say a prayer for her recovery? You know how dear she is to us.—Yours, &c.,

"AGNES DEANE."

I was blind and deaf to my new troubles. "Never mind, Katrine," I said, "I have now a more serious matter to think of. I am poor, God knows, very poor to-night. But if ever you prayed—and you do, good girl that you are—pray God and His Blessed Mother to spare a little child to-night!"

"I will, sir," she said, looking gravely concerned. I took my hat and went out into the night. And as I went I prayed and prayed that God would spare that little child to me. And as I prayed I was ashamed before God. And I spoke to Him with a stammer and a blush. For—I was now a Fichtean. I had had a little fit of Hegel. But he was an unattractive character; yet, like Heine, my silly vanity was flattered by his teaching that the true God was not the God who lives in heaven, but myself here on earth—a Pantheistic idea that was perpetually haunting me. But he was a rough, uncouth philosopher, and his remark that, "The stars, hum! hum! the stars are but a brilliant leprosy on the face of the heavens," was so grotesque and repulsive that I said I should have nothing to say to such a painful realist.

But, disgusted with the father of German philo-

sophy for his inconsistency, and his sacrilegious
interference with sacred things, and disgusted, most
of all, by his inhumanity to poor Fichte, who, starving at the time, wrote him such pitiful, proud
letters, I turned to the latter—I was told he was
one of the loftiest minds of Germany. I was attracted to him by his romantic fidelity to Johanna
Rahm, who became his wife; by his resemblance to
myself, a starving student; by one or two aphorisms,
by his prayer to the impersonal God, whom he
affected to worship—his philosophy I did not and
could not understand.

"Gave a lesson in Greek to a young man between
eleven and twelve o'clock; spent the rest of the day
in study and starvation." Here was his history.

"Upon the whole, gold appears to me to be a very
insignificant commodity. I believe that a man with
any intellect may always provide for his wants; and
for more than this gold is useless; hence I have
always despised it. Unhappily it is here bound up
with a part of the respect which our fellowmen
entertain for us, and this has never been a matter
of indifference to me. Perhaps I may by-and-by
free myself from this weakness also; it does not
contribute to our peace."

"I desire to lay aside all vanities. With some the
desire for literary fame, &c.—I have in a certain
degree succeeded; but the desire to be beloved,
beloved by simple true hearts, is no vanity, and
I will not lay it aside."

"I am also firmly convinced that this is no land
of enjoyment here below, but a land of labour and
toil, and that every joy should be nothing more than
a refreshment and an incentive to greater exertion;
that the ordering of our fortune is not demanded of
us, but only the cultivation of ourselves."

"My ambition thou canst understand. It is to
purchase my place in the human race with deeds,

to bind up with my existence eternal consequences for humanity and the whole spiritual world ; no one need know that I do it, if it be only done."

These are a few of his ethical maxims that attracted me, side by side with the superior attraction that came from his simple, studious, secluded existence. But when I came to his speculative philosophy I was hopelessly bewildered. All that I could ascertain was that there was an Ego, and a non-Ego, of which I could predicate nothing. That there was a finite Ego, which one day would pass into an infinite Ego ; and that there was a God—it would be madness to deny it—but He was impersonal, unsubstantial, of whose attributes we knew nothing, and could declare nothing. What then ? His ethics I reduce to a level, even to a lower level than those of

> " That halting slave who in Nicopolis
>    Taught Arrian, when Vespasian's brutal son
>    Cleared Rome of what most shamed him,"

and his theology, what is it but that of the Athenians whom St. Paul rebuked, and who built their altars to " the unknown God ? "

But Fichte was the fashion with me just then, as his brother Agnostics are the fashion nowadays, they who tear to rags the ravelled garments of their predecessors to weave new warp and woof with the same lurid lights of falseness and lies shot through them. It is the old and new story ever repeated. " They understand Fichte even less than they did his predecessor," writes a contemporary, Forberg, " but they believe all the more obstinately on that account. *Ego and non-Ego* are now the symbols of the philosophers of yesterday, as *substance* and *form* were formerly." And " all the truth which J—— has written is not worth a tenth part of the false which Fichte may have written."

It is singular what a fascination all this nebulous and mystic philosophy has for unformed minds. It is the old, old story of Greek incredulity repeated in involved phrases and pretended erudition, but leaving on analysis but a very poor precipitate of sense or truth. And yet compelled by some secret but inexorable necessity, these men, whilst denying the necessity of a special revelation to mankind, are for ever driven back on that Divine Personality which they would fain eliminate from their speculations, or reduce to the level of a Zeno or Apollonius. Clear and luminous as the handwriting on the walls of the palace of the Babylonian King, vivid as forked lightning on the black bosom of the storm, and with every line quivering with fire, stands out against the dark background of a reason obscured by vain philosophy, the eternal legend—JESUS CHRIST! From the lips of little children, from the tongue of illiterate servant maid, from the ponderous literature of the study or the academy, that sacred Name comes to smite me with remorse. And here opening the very title-page of this memoir of Fichte, I see a medallion portrait of Christ, under which is written :— ·

" The whole material world, with all its adaptations and ends, and, in particular, the life of man in this world, are by no means, in themselves and in deed and truth, that which they seem to be to the uncultivated and natural sense of man ; but there is something higher which lies concealed under natural appearance. This concealed foundation of all appearance may, in its greatest universality, be aptly named the ' DIVINE IDEA.' "—FICHTE, *The Nature of the Scholar.*

What effect on me had these sudden apparitions of my Divine Pursuer in the most unexpected places ? The same as if I had met a dear friend in a savage and unfriendly country. To see that sacred name flashing across the inhospitable pages of an alien philosophy made my heart leap with joy.

And this night, threading my way through the labyrinths of this city, I spoke to Him of whom I was so much ashamed, and as if I were begging a favour from the enemy. But His time had not come; and it was all blackness and despair for me!

When I entered Ursula's house, I found that hush upon all things that means sickness or death. Voices were lowered and steps muffled—the Angel of Sorrow was there. Mrs. Deane told me, with red eyes, that the child had been ill for a week. It was pronounced scarlatina, with diphtheric complications. Did the doctor consider it grave? Yes. Did he give—give a hope of recovery? Very slight.

Mrs. Deane wept, and my heart was bursting. We went upstairs. The room was darkened but for a night light, and it was warm and close. The nurse, a professional sister, sat by the bedside; and my little idol was wrapped up hands and all, and muffled, lest the tiniest stream of cold should touch her.

" Here is Goff," said Mrs. Deane in a whisper.

The child looked at me steadfastly with all the serious absorption that you read only in child-eyes. I knelt down and touched her forehead and lips. They were hot and dry. The nurse made a little gesture of warning; but I did not heed it.

" Don't you know me, mignonne?" I said, " don't you remember Doff?"

She heaved a great sigh, and again stared at me. The tears burst from my eyes.

" Don't try, Doff," she murmured with a stifled and pained voice, and with many intervals, " Don't try! I am doe-ing away! But I'll tum back to you, Doff, and det into your arms, and I'll tell you all about Dod, and the Blessey Ursin. And you'll tum out to see me, Doff, where I am buried; and

you'll put the little flowers on my drave, and I'll
hear you, Doff, and tum out to talk with you. And
mamma," she said, making her last will, " you'll dive
Doff my—my prayer-book and my beads; and—
and——"

The little mind was wandering now, and my heart
was tugging away, like a wild beast in his cage.
Good God! what a load of sorrow lies on this weary
world!

Presently she made a little gesture. I bent down
again.

" And Doff, you may—may—marry Miss Bemmy
now!"

This was a cruel stroke from the child. But she
was too young and pure for revenge. It was only
the child-mind in its sweet unconscious innocence.

I remained in the house that night. There was
no sleep for them or me. When morning came,
Ursula was better; and I went to work with a light
heart. But all day long, as I bent over that weary
catalogue and marshalled those dreary, ill-smelling
books, the thought of the little child, choking to
death, overcame me, and my tears fell fast and free
on the page. My employer, a good, kind man,
misunderstanding my emotion, again begged me to
remain. Again I declined. And at six o'clock I
was scudding across the city, with hope fighting in
my heart against desperate forebodings of evil.
There was a deeper hush on the house when I
entered—the indefinable silence that means but one
thing. The Angel of Death had come and stood by
the side of the Angel of Sorrow. Yes! I needed
not the tears of the sorrow-stricken mother, nor the
blank white face of Hubert Deane, to know that the
child who had rescued me from sin, and who had
been sent from heaven to teach me some of the
deeper meanings of life, was now resting on a safer
and sweeter bosom than mine. I saw her (and if I

am not profane, I envied my God His treasure) on the bosom of Him who had said, " Suffer little children to come to Me." The little face was waxen, and showed no trace of the agony which my pet had suffered. The waxen petals of her fingers were intertwined, and her rosary, my rosary now, was woven between them. Some one had put a white narcissus on her breast. I knelt down. Would the sweet brown eyes ever open on me again ? Would I ever feel again the touch of those warm fingers ? Would the child-voice ever whisper to me its love and its truth ? I blessed from my heart every good man that ever wrote a kindly word on immortality, and I am afraid I uttered no blessings on those cloistered iconoclasts, who, to show their pedantry and pride, rifle every little chamber of the human heart, that holds its cherished idol ; and like Death the remorseless, and unlike Death the beneficent, break and destroy before our faces the little images of God that He has lent us, to lead us to Himself.

I went home. In the hall I was met by Mrs. Oliver. She looked nervous, but determined.

" Mr. Austin, could you kindly let me have your rooms before this day week ? "

" By all means. Might I ask why you disturb me ? "

" Well—ah—you came to me under false pretences ! "

" What were these ? "

She was silent for a moment.

" You pretended to be a gentleman."

" And I am—what ? "

She did not reply to the question, but said again, " I want my rooms, sir."

" You can have them with pleasure. If your distinguished son-in-law, or still more distinguished son, should occupy them, I shall have reason to congratulate you on the happy exchange."

She bit her lip, and said nothing.

I went to my room. My head was reeling, the solid earth was giving way under my feet. I tried to gather comfort from my books. Pah! It was like the gibing of jesters, the ribaldry of mummers in the presence of Death! I thought of every text in ancient and modern literature, every line of prose, every jingle of verse—the pithy aphorisms of great philosophers, the grave thoughts of lay teachers, the couplet or distich that enshrined some pearl of thought, that, like the amulets of old, might exorcise the evil spirit of darkness and despair.

Poverty faced me—in a week I should be on the streets; worst of all, my guardian angel had gone back to her place in the skies. I cried to my gods, as the priests of Baal shouted around their idol. But deep down in the abysses into which I was falling, I only heard the plummet-line of reason searching in vain for rest, and my own voice reverberating through the rocky caverns, and flung back to me in mocking tones from the recesses, where the sheeted ghosts of dead gods were hiding. For, when I cried in my agony, "Father, Friend, where art Thou?" the echoes of vain philosophies travestying my cries, and mimicking my anguish, cried, "Thou, and Thou, and Thou!"

.     .     .     .     .     .

Two days later, the arrows of the north wind piercing through us, Hubert Deane and I stood, bereft and forlorn, over a tiny grave in Glasnevin. And when that awful sound, the first thud of the heavy earth on the hollow coffin, struck my ears, I saw no hope for me in heaven or on earth. But just as Ursula came to me in my passion and wrath to soothe me into reason, so now, too, I felt a soft hand in mine, and a gentle voice whispered, "Come home." It was Helen Bellamy. Her sisterly kindness, her simplicity, the word "Home" struck upon the hard soil of my heart, and Hubert Deane said, "Go, Austin, it is better; you look ill!"

One week after, the very night I had engaged to yield up my rooms to my landlady, I lay, tossing, agonised, delirious, under a complicated attack of pneumonia and diphtheria.

Waking out of delirious dreams, in which Ursula came to me, I was conscious now and again of angry voices in my room. Once I overheard this dialogue, as it came to my mind, blurred and indistinct in my fever—

"The van is at the door—he *must* be removed immediately. I shall *not* keep a fever patient in my house!"

"The van—what van?"

"The van for the workhouse hospital. Come, my good girl, this won't do. He must go!"

"Do you mean to say you'd send a gentleman to the workhouse hospital?"

"A gentleman! a tramp, you mean!"

"Wisha, bad luck to you—a tramp from the likes of you——"

"Katrine! Katrine!" I shouted faintly; then passed out into unknown regions of madness and delirium.

# BOOK II

I fled Him down the nights and down the days ;
I fled Him down the arches of the years ;
I fled Him down the labyrinthine ways
Of my own soul ; and in the mist of tears
I hid from Him ; and under running laughter.
—FRANCIS THOMPSON.

# BOOK II

## CHAPTER I

### AMONGST THE MEDICALS

As when a sick man very near to Death
Seems dead indeed, and feels begin and end
The tears, and takes the farewell of each friend,
And hears one bid the others go, draw breath
Freelier outside (since " all is o'er," he saith,
" And the blow fallen no grieving can amend ");
While some discuss if near the other graves
Be room enough for this, and when a day
Suits best for carrying the corpse away,
With care about the banners, scarves, and staves ;
And still the man hears all, and only craves
He may not shame such tender love, and stay.
—R. BROWNING.

FIVE years had rolled by, and had wrought but
little change in me. The old dual life continued, a
continual struggle during the day with men for a
subsistence, a continual struggle with God at night
for light. I had been in turn law-clerk (secured
through the intervention of Hubert Deane, for we
had become fast friends), tutor in a small family,
from which pride and bad temper procured my dismissal, copyist to an author until I got tired of his
banalities, framer of catalogues once more, and in
one or two other professions too humble to be mentioned. On the night of my illness at Mrs. Oliver's,
Katrine took me to her mother's house, a very
humble cabin in the outskirts of the city. There I
was nursed by tender hearts, moving rough hands,

towards convalescence. I woke up one morning, weak, and with a badly blistered chest, in a little room, that was as clean as an officer's cabin on a man-of-war. I realised gradually that I was resting on a small wire-woven mattress, that the floor was newly carpeted, that there was an odour of violets in the room; and, looking around, I saw piled up against the opposite wall, in neat bookshelves, all my treasures. A glance at the mantelpiece told me that I had been a bad invalid; and when I tried to rise and fell back exhausted, I understood that I was not yet out of the doctor's hands. A stronger, all-pervading odour of soap-suds and heated irons told me that I was now the boarder of a washer-woman. I was wondering and wondering and wondering where I was when the door opened ever so softly, and I saw Katrine's ruddy face and black eyes looking inquisitively towards me. I° shut my eyes. She came over and looked with infinite anxiety at me. I opened my eyes and whispered, " Katrine."

I know right well that if half the diamonds of Golconda had been laid that moment at Katrine's feet, she would not have been half so overjoyed as at the thought that she had nursed me back to convalescence. For it was in her mother's humble house I was now an inmate and an invalid, and it was her mother's care and her own that had brought me back from delirium and the grave. She told me during the days of my convalescence that she had had a pitched battle with Mrs. Oliver that night, which closed my business relations with that amiable lady; that she had called her son a jailbird, for which she had been sternly reprimanded by her friend, Father Benedict; that she and the workhouse officials had taken me downstairs between them, Mrs. Oliver superintending with a bottle to her nose; that when I was placed in the van, she

ordered the men to take me to her own home; and
here I was, and the doctor was awfully kind, and
that I'd soon be well, please God, &c. I did not
know in what words I could shape my thoughts to
thank the poor, generous-hearted girl. She did not
need them; she was satisfied, with the self-sacrific-
ing affection of all noble women, to see me well, and
it was enough.

Katrine had now procured a better place in the
city, and was permitted to come home every Sunday
to see her mother. The latter was still in the prime
of life, a strong, hale, vigorous, hard-working
woman, who never "took a drop of medicine in her
life, and never would, please God." She toiled all
day long at her washing tub, sometimes singing
snatches of old nursery songs, sometimes whispering her prayers. I used often watch her at her
patient toil, scrubbing away, whilst the steam rose
in clouds around her; or trundling along the heavy,
stone-weighted waggon that was called the mangle.
Sometimes, wrapped up in blankets by the fire, with
a book in my lap, I caught her eye fixed upon me
with that curious, suspicious, but not ill-natured
stare that betokens interest and curiosity combined.
But with that marvellous delicacy so characteristic
of our people, she never by the slightest word or
question intimated that she regarded me otherwise
than as a distinguished lodger, whose very presence
was ample compensation for expense or trouble.
But, like her daughter, Katrine, she could not resist
the temptation of a little sermon now and again, but
couched in language so delicate that no one, but
some conceited fool, could take umbrage at it.
There was a photograph on the mantelpiece of a
young soldier, dressed in the uniform of the hussars.
This, I ascertained, was her son, Katrine's only
brother, who had run away from his home and left
a good situation to fight for the "widder." Many a

little sermon preached at that photograph found its
subject nearer home.

"He'll come home a sergeant some day, Mrs.
Gallagher," I would say, "and when you see him
coming in with his gold-laced cap and a slashed
uniform, all yellow and gold, and his sword clanking
behind him, won't you be proud?"

Her eye would kindle for a moment at the
thought, then its fires would die down into ashes,
and she would say—

"Aisy to say so, sir, but, manetime, he might be
lying out there amongst the savages wid a bullet in
him, and not a priest widin a tousand miles."

"Ay, but look at the glory of it. Dying for his
country and his Queen!"

"For his country, inagh, God help his poor
country. And as for the Queen, well I have nothin'
to say against her. She is a good woman, they
say. But his soul! his soul!"

"But he was a good lad, you tell me. What fear
can there be of him?"

"Good? So he was. But the best want the priest
at the last hour. Ah, sure, we never think of it till
it comes."

She would say a "Hail Mary" softly.

"I put the scafflers round his neck, when he was
going away—my own scafflers. May God and His
Blessed Mother forgive me if I done wrong. And
I gave him my own bades, blessed at the last
Mission; and, sure, if he thinks of them, it will be
all right, but boys will be boys."

Did all this goodness bring me nearer to God?
Well, it humbled me exceedingly; and the first step
down, in our own estimation, is the first step upwards towards God.

But one day, when the tramps of butterflies were
rifling every little flower in the garden outside, and
the air was humming the song of spring in prepa-

ration for the grand oratorios of summer, I slipped
away quietly, and took lodgings in a remote part of
the city. I left a letter (and an enclosure) to the
effect that I was infinitely grateful for their kindness, but I could not bear to think that I was a
burden to them. After the first disappointment and
chagrin were over, I visited there again; and have
kept up a steady acquaintance with as good and
true women as are encircled within the Irish seas.

Then commenced my five years' misery—such
vicissitudes of want and plenty, wild joys and sombre
distresses, such contact with the noble, where nobility is least expected, and with the vile, whose vile-
ness only close contact can reveal; such mornings of
despair and nights under the stars, such cold and
hunger, such mean shifts for food and shelter, such
humiliation and exaltation as only Bohemians know.
All that weary time I never broke with my friends.
The Deanes and Bellamys showed me the most
unobtrusive kindness. Their homes were the only
brief glimpses of gladness I saw. My Sunday afternoons were always spent with my little Ursula in
Glasnevin; and, say what you will, O my most
incredulous friends, my little saint kept her promise
sacredly.

" I will come out and speak to you, Doff, and tell
you all about God."

Once I passed Mrs. Oliver and Gwendoline as
they rolled along in a glorious brougham. I was
standing at the gate of Trinity. Mrs. Oliver stared
at me and turned away. Gwendoline looked and
blushed crimson. She had a weary, wasted appearance. She had had Oriental experiences, and was
as haggard as the children of the East.

I cannot now determine what was the particular
attraction that took me into Heytesbury Street one
bright evening in the early autumn five years after
my illness and Ursula's death. I had some dim

idea that it was the happy hunting-ground of the
medical students of Dublin; and as I had always
a hankering after students, particularly impecunious
ones like myself, I suppose I wanted to see whether
Fate dealt as hardly with them as with me. I was
conscious, as I passed down the street, of windows
open on either side, of young faces, half clouded
in tobacco smoke, of some skulls and bones that
took the place usually occupied by mignonette or
geraniums in the science of window-gardening, of
some thick books with black covers and gilt letters
on the back. Then the street began to swim around
me, and the students' faces paled away into revolv-
ing shadows, and I knew that something fell; and
then I woke up to half consciousness, but not to
speech, to see myself surrounded by a body of
students, who were busy in trying to determine my
ailment. One stood at the end of a bed—a tall,
handsome fellow, with quiet searching eyes. I heard
him say—

"You, Forrester?"

"I think 'tis *paresis*, cap."

Cap shook his head.

"You, Meldon?"

"It looks like *aphasia*," said Meldon.

"What do you think, Synan?"

Synan was puzzled, and took off his cap to assume
greater freedom of meditation.

"If it isn't *locomotor-ataxy*, I'm——"

"Locomotor, your grandmother," shouted all, and
Synan put on his cap.

"Gallwey, you're watching closely; what is it?"

"I don't know that we have any right to hold
a clinical discussion on our friend," said Gallwey,
"but I think 'tis—*fames!*"

"And you're right," said the captain. "Now,
lads, to work! You, Synan, run over to Devlin's
for some brandy. And you, Meldon, run down to

Supple's for a pound of beef. Unloose that belt; 'tis hurting him!"

"My dear cap," cut in Synan, "Devlin would not give me credit for a thimbleful of the lees of his porter."

"And I am afraid," said Meldon, "my account for beef, never very great, is rather overdrawn."

"Then chip in, all you fellows," said the captain. "Roche, what have you? Stokes, look here, Gallwey——"

"I've a set of bones," said Stokes; at which there was a general and profane laugh.

"I have 'Quain,'" said Roche.

"Take them over to Uncle," cried the captain.

"Uncle has as many sets of bones," cries a young medico, "as would set up a Roman catacomb."

"And as many 'Quains' as would reach to heaven. Think of something else."

The captain lifted his heavy watch-chain, took out his gold repeater, unhooked it, and handed it to Stokes.

"No," said Stokes, drawing back, "I'm damned if I will, cap!"

"Your profession tells you, sir," said the captain, with all the airs and solemnity of a professor at the College of Science, "that the preservation of human life is above every other consideration. Raise a pound on this—this bauble, and make haste."

The bauble was a birthday present from his mother. I saw the inscription afterwards.

And there I lay, eyes and mouth open, but unable to articulate a single word. Whilst the messengers of mercy were gone, some fresh students came in. One curly-headed fellow inquired what was up.

"Some poor devil of a scholar, like ourselves," said one, handing up a tattered volume which I kept in my pocket.

"H'm! like ourselves?" said the curls. "Poor

I

devils? yes.    Scholars? doubtful.    Gi' me a look
at him."

He came over and bent down to see me in the
gathering twilight.    Then he called for a light, and
made my eyes blink.    He stood up and whistled.

"Goff! by all the saints in the calendar!"

"Why, do you know him, Sutton?    Who is he?
What is he?" came from all the room.

But Cal, for it was he, could only mutter, "By
Jove!"

He came over and shook me, looked into my eyes,
felt my pulse, threw back my hair, and asked—

"Goff! old fellow, don't you know me?"

I only stared.

"Is there any danger?" he whispered the captain.    The captain said "No," and the brandy and
beef came in.

They gave both in very small doses at first.    Then
as the warmth began to tell, and the mills of life
took up their work one by one, reluctantly it appeared; but they had to obey, and the streams of life
ran down their channels once more, and each moved
its own tiny world of nerve and muscle, I began
to think and wonder.    But the imperial brain would
not surrender at once.    Only gradually each cell
woke up to its duty; and I thought that long, very
long ago, in mediæval, or perhaps prc-Adamite ages,
I was walking through a street and saw faces, and
they danced around in a kind of phantasmagoria, and
all things faded away from me.    After a little time
a clearer consciousness came, and I wondered where
was I.    I had never seen that room nor those faces
before.    Then I recognised Cal, and concluded I
was in Mayfield.    Until at last the whole adventure
spread itself in every corner and fissure of my brain,
and at the same time my tongue loosened, and I
could ask—"Where am I?"

Cal whistled with joy.    The captain put on the

look of a great surgeon, who had successfully per-
formed a most difficult operation.

"Where are you, Goff?" repeated Cal. "You
are now surrounded by the élite of the medical
profession in Dublin. You have become resident
patient and pupil in an academy that is destined to
revolutionise medical science. You have the honour
of being the first patient in the hands of the future
torchbearers——"

"Stop that nonsense, Sutton, and let the poor
fellow rest!" said the captain.

I looked around wonderingly at the circle of
faces that gleamed down upon me. It was my introduction to the bravest, most chivalrous, most
childlike band, that ever broke new ground, carrying
aloft the banners of their noble science. I was at
once admitted to their comradeship and love; and
had plenty of opportunity of witnessing how devoted,
how enthusiastic, and how innocent of real evil our
students can be, until the world steals in with its
poisoned precepts, and changes as with a Circe's
wand all that is most attractive into all that is most
repulsive and undesirable. What wonderful things
I saw amongst the medicos! Such loyalty to each
other, such contempt for wealth or position! such
absorption in their studies, yet never a whisper of
the degradation of the mere animality of man! such
chivalry, Quixotic, if you like, as when Hughes
married his landlady's daughter, because the little
minx chose to cry whenever he could not take her
to the theatre! such awful metamorphoses of raw,
red-handed, dowdy peasant lads into mashers, who
spurned the pavement of Grafton Street! such a
splendid parade at the Trinity sports, purchased
by wonderful abstemiousness that the tailor might
be satisfied—such glorious running in debt, yet
never a failure to meet the ultimate demand, such
rashness and devilry, such honour and chivalry, I

suppose I shall not meet again.  Poor fellows, some of
you are dead, struck by the awful arrows of the sun
in India ; some are epauletted, lace-bedizened officers
on the quarter decks of Her Majesty's fleet ; some
are in the Colonies, with big reputations and big
balances ; a few, least fortunate, are chasing "red-
runners" in some obscure Irish village, and cursing
the grocers that drag you out of bed on frosty nights,
because you won't buy their sugar—but wherever
you are located on this little planet, I am quite sure
the same honour and loyalty to your profession, the
same regard for the sacredness of human life, the
same spirit of *camaraderie* distinguishes you!   At
least, I am grateful for having met you, although
my introduction was informal and abrupt.   For from
that day, I was admitted within the sacred circle,
and I owe a great deal of instruction, and not a little
happiness, to my medical friends.

It was unanimously agreed upon after solemn
consultation, that I was a fit subject for the M——
Hospital : and thither next morning I was conveyed
with the warning that I should not be surprised
if "Old Noakes," the senior physician, addressed
me as "My Lord," or recommended me to "Hunt
with the Kildares."

"'Tis a way he has," explained Synan ; "he
assumes that every patient that consults him is a
lord or a millionaire."   And so I was installed in a
cosy ward ; and placed under the eye of the senior
physician, and Sister Philippa.   These were pleasant
days in which I was nursed back to convalescence ;
and again had I the opportunity of witnessing how
much Christlike charity there is in the world—only
the world will not admit it.   "Old Noakes" did not
address me as "My Lord," but after I was able to
sit up, he recommended me very strongly to take my
yacht, and make a six months' cruise, first to Norway,
then to the Mediterranean, then to the Cape.   He

was very kind and gentle. But often in the wakeful pauses of sleepless nights, when nothing was heard but the laboured breathing of invalids, did I from my pillow watch with interest that gentle sister, who was placed by God's mercy and her own benevolence over our ward. In the thick blackness of the night, a solitary lamp shone clear and steady, and there sat by it that gentle woman, reading and working alternately, but ever on the alert, if a restless sleeper threw off the bed-clothes, or some feverish person cried for a drink. Often in the dreary pauses of silence, from speech to speech of the sleepless clock, the word "sister" would be whispered from some corner of the ward, and Sister Philippa would arise, and gliding over the floor, bend over the sufferer to relieve him. And I confess, when the morning came, and we were all done up for the doctor's parade, and the long line of students came in, and we and our condition were critically examined, I could have flung my medicine bottle at the head of some pompous fool, who in the interest of science, of course, would turn angrily on the unfortunate nurse, and abuse her before us all.

"Come here, do you call that bandaging? Where is the record of his temperature? This patient has not got his medicine during the night. If he had had the bottle I prescribed, the febrile symptoms would have disappeared. My God! here he is again at 103. There's the grossest neglect here!"

This was a frequent and fertile subject of argument between Cal and myself. Cal was the Ariel that came down, winged and beautiful and cheerful, on these dismal scenes. He was grave as Solon during professional hours, followed the doctor meekly, listening to his clinical lectures; but the moment the doctor had left, Cal waltzed up between the rows of beds, caught up Sister Philippa, who was generally in tears after the morning's ordeal, snapped his fingers,

sang out his favourite " Zitti ! Zitti !" or " Figaro giù,
Figaro sù, Figaro lá, Figaro qua !" and brought sunshine into eyes that were craving for light and mirth.
He was .immensely popular; but he had one fault
(perhaps it was a great virtue)—he stood by his profession through thick and thin, and his faith was—
Science.

"My dear Goff," he used to say, in answer to
some objections of mine, "you don't understand.
That's science!"

"But where the —— is the use of tearing the
coverlet off that poor consumptive, and pounding
him with these stethoscopes? Every man of you
seem to think he will hear his fortune foretold from
that poor devil's lungs, the way you all listen!"

"But it is science, my dear fellow. You don't
understand. We know nothing but science. We
have no pity, no sympathy, we are not tired, nor
disgusted at all we see and have to do. A patient
is a subject and no more!"

"But you do the most abominable things," I said.
"Look at that fellow this morning taking off the
*Sputa* of that poor devil, as if he had a prize, that
some one was going to take from him."

"But that's science!" Cal would protest.  "How
are we to learn if we don't examine?"

"I saw a chap yesterday," I continued, "he had
a phial containing some abomination, which he called
'Pus'; and no little girl was ever so proud of her
first doll as he was of that filthy liquid."

"Science again," cried the self-satisfied Cal.

"Then you take a poor devil and you turn him
upside down, and inside out; you examine every
inch of him, as if he were a machine, and a very
dirty one. You have no more respect for the poor
body of man than a watchmaker has for an uncleaned
watch."

"Of course,"-Cal would rejoin.  "My dear fellow,

if we were all as fastidious as you, science would be yet in its infancy, and mankind the loser."

"It's a d——d irreverent thing, at any rate. But why don't ye spare the feelings of these ladies? Why do you compel them to witness, and to do such abominable things?"

"Look here, Goff," Cal would say, "you were always an idealist. Now, we are realists of the most advanced school. We may not be always right. We may not be always reverent. We may not be always fastidious or nice. But we are always scientific. Nay, we may do absurd things, and make absurd statements, but it is always science and that's enough."

"Well, I hope you pay the poor ladies well. God knows they deserve it."

"They are not paid at all," said Cal.

"And I suppose that is science too," I could not help saying.

"No," replied the imperturbable, "they learn their profession, and then take up cases as they occur."

"And what are they paid then?"

"One pound a week, half of which goes to the establishment under whose patronage they work."

"H'm! for sickness and old age what provision?"

"None whatever. Look here, Goff, you are nearly as big a fool as Verling!"

"In what does his folly consist?"

"Well, you see, he is what I call a 'Philosopher of the Unconscious.'"

"What's that?"

"He never knows when he is making a fool of himself. He believes himself Hyperion: he says his father was an archangel, his mother a seraph, his little brothers and sisters are the cherubim. All his goats are sheep, all his geese swans. He says the most absurd things, and despises us all for our stupidity; he makes the most egregious ass of

himself, and smiles at our imbecility. Everything
he has is the most superior thing in that line in the
world. He talks about 'my tailor,' 'my hatter,'
'my haberdasher,' as if he owned the Vice-regal
Lodge; and I suspect 'my tailor' and 'my hatter'
have some fun with him, especially in making out
his bill. He is a born idiot, he is a prize imbecile, a
mattoid, a degenerate, and he thinks that Solomon
in all his glory was a child to him. He is delightful.
It is a daily comedy. But he is happy."

"And where are exactly the points of resemblance
between this genius and my humble self?" I said,
not a little nettled.

"Did I compare you together?" said the innocent
Cal. "My wits are wandering. Cheer up, Goff,
you have no idea what we were going to do for
you."

"Indeed! what new honour were you about to
confer—in the name of science?"

"Now," said Cal, "you are sarcastic. I assure
you we were very kindly disposed. If you had died
on our hands——"

"You'd have held a *post-mortem*, and divided
every inch of my body between you?"

"No! honour bright! *experimentum fiat in cor-
pore vili!* No, we were going to take a delicious
revenge."

"You are keeping me in suspense."

"Well, we found by the only letter you possessed, and which we discovered in a particularly
vacuous pocket-book, that you were under the juris-
diction of a she-dragon, who had the unpardonable
presumption to dun you for rent. We'd have given
her a lesson for life—if only for the future good of
the profession. We were going to take your body
on a shutter, covered with a snow-white sheet, bear
it in solemn procession through the city, place it at
the door of your present hospitable hostess, sing the

'Dead March in Saul,' with kettle accompaniment, and place your mortal remains in her hall for decent, and, let us hope, expensive interment. You fell amongst Samaritans, Goff. But here comes old Noakes!"

Old Noakes and I were soon the fastest friends. Like most general practitioners he had a speciality, and that was bacteria. He would travel Ireland to see a new species of microbe, just as Huber, Réaumur, Leauwenhock would have travelled the world to see a new kind of ant or moth. I drew him out, for I confess he made me deeply interested in this matter, and he would go on for hours, forgetting urgent calls to rich patients, and dilating in a Christian, philosophical spirit on the infinitely great and the infinitely little, and man the centre from which both radiate. He was a good man, a great scientist, a sworn foe to materialism.

"Don't tell me," he used to say, "that soul and mind are one. There is a will, an Ego, floating over all the faculties of mind and touching them as you would touch the strings of a harp. For thought is only nerve-tension, just as a harp-string vibrates into music when you stretch it. But the imperial soul is over all—mind and memory, intellect and understanding. It has no master but God."

He surprised me one day when I had grown quite strong by asking me what prospects I had before me. "None," I replied.

"Would you take charge of a patient?"

"Certainly."

"An alcoholic patient?"

"Yes."

"Sister Philippa is going too."

"Is she!" I cried eagerly.

The venerable doctor smiled.

# CHAPTER II

AUF WIEDERSEHEN !

But thou and I are one in kind
　As moulded like in Nature's mint ;
　And hill and wood and field did print
The same sweet forms in either mind.
　　　　　　　　*—In Memoriam.*

I SHOULD tell here how I resumed another old acquaintance in quite as singular a way. It was in the month of March in the spring-time of this same year, in which I was thrown amongst the students, and commenced a new epoch in life. I was strolling along one of the quays of the city— dinnerless, cold, except for the angry fires of passion, that would come blazing up, as I remembered every taunt and bitter word which had been flung at me by the genteel beldame, with whom at that time I was lodging. I think I had reached the extremity of despair, as I walked along, gathering my poor threadbare coat more closely about me, to keep out the icy needles that shot through its threads and pierced me. I held a cigarette between my lips, but the ancient comforter for once failed me. There was a choking sensation in my throat, as I thought of the reception I would meet on my return to the wretched place I called home. The dark river flowed sluggishly along on my right, lapping against the quays, and gay lamps flashed from the shops on my left, where many as wretched as I were trying to forget in luscious poison that life to them, too, was misery. I stood for a moment in the door of a

public-house and looked. Then I lifted my hat to
my Maker that I had not gone down so deep into
hell, and passed along. I came to a shop dimly
lighted after the flare of the gaslights in the hells.
The windows were choked with brushes, and the
panels of the doors lined with them, and the shop
littered with them. There was a young girl behind
the counter knitting, who lifted her eyes quietly to
my white face as I passed, and then went on knitting
again. I looked at the sign over the fanlight, and
my heart leaped as I read, *"Messing."* Poor old
professor! Thy name over a brush shop on a
Dublin quay, and thou in thy Vaterland, talking
thy guttural Teutonic, and pouring out the love of
thy strong heart to all who come within sight of
thy homely face! I wondered would it be any
harm to inquire of this Irish girl, for Irish she
certainly was, with dark flashing eyes and a ruddy
face, who this Messing was. Wondering I stepped
in. She laid down her knitting and said—

" What can I do for you, sir?"

" It is not on business I have come," I said, "but
the name over the door caught my eye. It is the
name of an old friend of mine, a professor of German,
to whom I am under great obligations——"

"When did you know him, sir?" said she, looking
rather depreciatingly at my worn gloves and faded
hat.

" In a college called 'Mayfield,' " I said, "and——"

She threw down her knitting, rushed to the glass
door that led to the little parlour off the shop, and
said in a whisper—

" Henry, a gentleman wants to see you." The
door opened wider, and there, little changed by time
or trouble, with the familiar spectacles beaming upon
me, and clothed, like the magic hand that held
Excalibur, in spotless white, was my dear old friend,
Herr Messing. He came up to me shading his

eyes from the light, and looking rather irresolutely at me.

" Has the world changed me so much, Herr Professor," said I, " that you don't recognise your old friend, the Astronomer Royal ? "

" Goot Gott in Himmel," he cried in an ecstasy of joy, " id is he ! Id is the Asdronomer Rol ! Vhere did you goom vrom ?   Vhat are you doing ? Vellkoom ! vellkoom ! goom in ! goom in ! "

And he dragged me into the parlour to the astonishment of his wife, whom he had completely forgotten, and of a crowd of small *sans culottes* who had gathered around the door.   Inside the parlour, his joy bubbled over in a kind of childish merriment which was very pleasant to see.   His dear old face beamed and shone with pleasure ;   fifty times he rubbed his spectacles that were wet with moisture ; he held me from him at arm's length, and surveyed me from head to foot, all the time venting the love of his grand old heart.

" Who would haf tought id ?   De last man on earth I egspected to zee, and de one I most wish to zee !   De Asdronomer Rol !   Grown so great and grandt, living up in Merrion or Mountjoy Square, and goom do zee his oldt brofessor !   Wond't we haf dinner ?   Wond't we valk togeder again ?   Haf you forgodden your Zherman ? " and he rattled out a string of Teutonic deca-syllables that took his breath away.

" No, mein Herr ! " I said, answering him in German ; and stretching out my hand, I recited his favourite passage from Schiller.

" Goot poy !   Goot poy !   I thought you would not forged me ! "

" But, mein Herr," I said, " who is that distinguished lady outside ?   I always thought you were a celibate."

" Dot's my vife," said he, suddenly remembering

his marital relations. "Aleese! Edelweiss!" he shouted, "Goom in! goom in! and I will introdoose you to my old friend, the Asdronomer. We do be talking about you sometime," he said, as if to prepare me for the ceremony.

So Alice came in, her face suffused with blushes. "She was very happy to see a friend of Henry's," she said simply. "But he lives more in the past than in the present. He is always talking of his 'Tear old poys,' as he calls them," she said with irresistible Irish fun. Then she slipped out quietly again, and left me to the professor. He seemed quite unable, dear old soul, to control his ecstasy. He rose from his chair fifty times to show me this book and that, and his piano, and his working tools, and the portrait of Goethe which I gave him, enshrined in the place of honour over the mantelpiece. At last he drew out his big pipe from a drawer, saying "Do you remember?" and he settled down to a quiet smoke.

"Mein Herr," said I, "before we commence allow me to congratulate you on the admirable taste you have displayed in the choice of a companion. If I am to judge by appearances, and if love is the bread of life, you are the happiest man on this planet at this moment."

He looked very solemn for a moment; then, taking his pipe from his mouth, and blowing a cloud of smoke up the chimney, he bent over to me, and whispered, "She is *ber*fection."

"But how in the name of all the gods of Greece," said I, "did you come here? and how have you exchanged your employment of brushing cobwebs off our dusty minds by brushing dust off our floors?"

"Lisden!" said he, "lisden! I left the school. Where was I to go? To Zhermany? No! To Ameriga? No! I hadn't enough to pay for de voyage. I dook up what you call—tuitions. Den I dook the room in this house. Dey were zelling prushes here, but how pad! No prush at all! The pristles all come out the moment you but the prush on the door. Dey were zell out. I gommence. I take up the prush-making. I make goot prush. Vhell! I sugzeed. The pig vharehouses employ me. I sugzeed more. I go out in evenings to teach Zherman and music. But it vhas all girls! Pah! I give dem up! I notize leedle girl come to my shop for prush. I like her. She vhas modest and glean. ' Vhill you marry me?' I say. She laugh, but goom again. ' Vhill you marry me?' I say again. She laugh more, and run away. I could not put her image oudt of my mind. I go to her parendts. I dell dem who I vhas; vhat I vhas doing. Dey look zerious. She cry. ' Vhill you haf him?' says her mother. ' Vhatefer you like,' she say. And we vhos married, and she is *ber*fection!"

"And, without flattering you, mein Herr," said I, stretching out my hand to grasp his across the table, "she has got as good a husband as there is between the Irish seas."

"Dank you! dank you!" he said, and was silent. After a little time he roused himself, and looking at me earnestly across the table, he asked—

"But, mein vrendt, how is the world going mit you?"

He evidently had some idea that the world had not placed me exactly in that zenith of bliss which is betokened by residence in Merrion Square.

"Badly, mein Herr," I said, "badly, I am what the papers call a Bohemian; what I call," I shot out the word, "a beggar!"

"Don't say dot! don't say dot!" he cried, coming over and laying his hands on my shoulder, "you are not a beggar!"

"And I suppose," said I, "that like the rest of

the world, you will turn me out in the street when
you know what I am."

"Vhot for you say so?" he cried indignantly,
"vhot for you say so? Nein! nein! I lofe you all
the petter because you are not rich. I am boor;
you are boor. Zhake hands!"

I could hardly keep back a tear at this profession
of charity from one who would be quite justified in
keeping himself a perfect stranger from me. With
infinite tact he changed the subject.

"But we must not dalk about yourself now," he
said, "what became of C—— ?"

"Came to nothing," said I, "raved and dreamed
until his people got tired of him, and sent him to
Australia. He is now a sheep-driver in the Bush."

"And poor little F—— ?" he inquired.

"Became a solicitor in the south of Ireland, and
after a couple of years he died."

"Boor fellow! boor fellow!" said the professor.
"And Charlie Travers? I'm sure he sugzeeded."

"No, mein Herr! Unless, indeed, in a higher
sense than I can imagine. He failed at one or two
examinations, then remained at home meditating by
the sea for some years, and is now here in Dublin,
engaged ostensibly as a solicitor, but in reality
carrying on a singular propaganda. Have you not
heard of the young enthusiast who is setting all the
young men of Dublin wild with excitement about
religious profession and reformation?"

The professor jumped from his seat.

"Mein Gott! you don't zay zo? I have been
reading all about him, and he vhas my pupil. Poor
fair-haired poy! Ve vhill go hear him, you and I.
Ve vhill join him, and vhork mit him!"

I didn't share the professor's enthusiasm. He
saw it, and changed the subject.

"But, dell me, dell me, what became of dot idiot,
dot imbecile—Evans?"

"Oh, the lad that used to break your heart at the German!" And here I mimicked the professor, flying wildly up stairs into his room, gesticulating, raving at his Bœotian stupidity.

"Well, you'll be glad to hear that he and another dunce are the only pupils of Mayfield who have succeeded in life. He passed into the navy as a surgeon, how, I don't know, for he couldn't translate Cæsar even, without a crib. He was sent on the Indian service, became a mighty swell, in Allahabad or Hyderabad, and married a Maharajah or a Begum, or some other kind of negro, with as many lacs of rupees as there are brushes in your shop. Mein Herr," said I, standing up and facing him, and speaking bitterly, "the prizes of this world are carried off by its fools and imbeciles!"

"Berhaps so, berhaps so," said he, in a kind of reverie.

"Now," said I, bridling up, "how many professors are over there in Trinity without a tithe of your ability or knowledge, yet drawing princely salaries? How many perfumed idiots in Government offices who can spend from £200 to £800 a year for merely biting the ends of their penhandles three or four hours a day? How many professional men, looking as wise as owls, and just as stupid, are defrauding the public by pretensions to knowledge they do not possess? How many members of Parliament that have glib tongues to lick the public into good humour whilst they push their way to fame and wealth. Pah! the world, of course, is but a stage, but it is a sad thing that the artists are kept in the green-room and the blockheads sent before the lights!"

"Go easy! go easy!" said the professor in that calm, measured tone which I remembered so well in our many discussions at Sandycove, "I do not vollow you dere! But, subbose you are right, mein

vrendt, zhall I vret pecause vhools strut? No! I
look avhay vrom the stage mit regret, and I look at
the auzhience and the zenery. Who are dey? De
immortal zpirits of the past and the anzhels of de
living Gott!" He lifted his little skull-cap, placed
it reverently on the table, and went on. "I zhee in
boxes and stalls de edearealized spirits of dose who
were lifted by their genius apove other men, and to
whom, as to the zaint in Patmos, it vhas given to
zee de things dat no other man may zee, and
to shpeak to de ears of de vorld, unto all time,
divine vhords of wisdom and high gomments on life
and its izzues. Dere vhords gome to us in zorrow
to soothe, dey gome to us in zickness of mind or
body to heal. Dey are the recognised zaints of our
race, ganonized by de voice of humanity. But
vhere did dey zpend dere mortal span? In de
balace? No! In vealth? No! In luxury?
No! But in de attick, in de garrit, in de byelane,
scorned, despised, in cold and hunger, in fasting and
nakedness, dey vhalked de rough vhays of life, and
drough sorrow dey learned vhisdom. Vhere are dey
now? Mit de anzhels, upborne by dere vhings,
lifted on dere broad zhoulders, no zorrow, except
when they drop a dear for poor humanity, when
men's dricks are more vantastic than usual. And
the zenery! painted by the great Artist! Glory of
day, mit its golden dawns and white splendours of
noon, and the meek gentle beauty of sunsets, and
the burple dwilight. De earth mit its tender beauty
of vlowers and vields, and zolemn mountains and
zee; de night mit its velvet darkness sown mit the
blazing ztars! Do you dink," continued he, quite
angrily, "dot I vhill turn avhay from the var-vlash-
ing glories of the heavens—from Orion, mit his
jewelled belt, from Sirius that comes leaping and
curvetting dowards us, vrom the glittering nebulæ
and de colossal suns, do envy de shpark on the

K

vhinger of a vhool? To-day carriages roll by my
door mit grandt dames and zhentlemens. Do-
morrow vhere are they? Yesterday the Lord
Chancellor died. In a month who vhill think of
him? Yet the zame ztars goom oudt at night in de
heavens and look down mit eyes of pity on us, poor
barasites of this little globe. And the zee gooms in
at Sandycove, just as it game in the mornings of our
youth, crystal-clear, foam-whitened, health-bearing
to the zons of our race. And here haf I all that
man may dezire. My vife—Alice—Edelweiss—
mein leetle Alpine vlower, and Vritz—but you haf
not seen Vritz—my leetle poy,"—here he forgot his
apologue, and cried—

"Vreetz! Vreetz!"

But Alice came running in from the shop in alarm,
and said in a whisper—

"Why will you wake the child, Henry? He has
been in bed these two hours!"

"What for childrens go to ped at such small
hour," said the professor in a tone of disappointment. "However, don't mind, all right." He evidently thought it better to leave Fritz in his mother's
hands.

Presently, however, when Alice had returned to
her shop, we heard the falling of two small feet on
the floor above our heads, and the professor rubbed
his hands, and chuckled softly, as the two small
feet came pattering downstairs; and a curly head
was visible over the balustrade, and a child-whisper
came down—

"Pap!"

"All right, my leetle zon!" said the professor in
huge delight, "sdeal down! sdeal down!" and then
turning to me—

"I knew he'd goom to me!"

So Fritz appeared, a wee creature of three years,
with great blonde curls on his forehead, and his

mother's eyes round and wondering, and half-filled
with delight, half with fear of his mother. The little
lad was simply clothed in his night-dress, opened at
the neck, and falling just to his knees.

"Goom to me! goom to me! my leetle mans," said
the professor, and the child came and curled himself
under his father's coat, and fixed his big eyes wonderingly on me. So we made friends, and Alice
was won over to condone this breach of domestic
discipline, when she saw how much I admired her
boy. And we clothed him, and of course fed him;
and then the professor planted his little image firmly
on the table.

"Now, Vritz, ve vhill go through our Cadichism!"
And the professor with closed eyes, and reverent
bent head, and the little child with clasped hands
repeated the universal prayer of mankind, which
calls the Great Maker by the name of "Father," on
the grounds that we are all brethren.

"Now, my little mans, what gountryman are
you?"

"I'm an Irishman," shouted Fritz.

"I grandt dot to the mother," said the professor
in explanation to me; "but dot is all."

"Vhat are the two best vhords in the Gherman
dongue?"

"Gott und Vaterland," said the child as gutturally
as if he had been born on the banks of the Elbe.

"Now vhee vhill zing the zword-song together.
Where is your zword, Vreetz?"

The sword—a small, bright blade, with gilt handle,
was found; and the professor drew his own old
Spanish blade, which I knew so well, from its leather
scabbard; but I slipped forward and said—

"Allow me, professor; but Fritz and I will sing
the song, and you shall accompany us on the
piano."

"Bravo! bravo!" said the professor; and sitting

down he touched the notes of Körner's brave song :
and Fritz and I clasped our blades at hurrah !

"One song more, my little mans, and then you'll
say good-night.   Vhat shall it be ? "

"Hab und Leben," said the child.

"Goot poy! goot poy!" cried the professor,
and the child sang in his light treble, yet with
extraordinary vigour the song of the University
students :—

> " Hab und Leben
> Dir zu geben
> Sind wir allesammt bereit ;
> Sterben gern zu jeder Stunde,
> Achten nicht des Todes Wunde,
> Wenn das Vaterland gebeut."

It was a beautiful sight.   The professor, with the
grey sprinkled plentifully through his hair, bending
over the piano, and touching the notes with as much
care as if he were playing at a concert for a *prima
donna ;* the mother diligently knitting, and with a
half smile of pride and amusement playing around
her mouth, and the fair boy, looking aloft, and singing his soul into the words—assuredly, mein Herr,
our happiness is mostly of our own making in this
world.

I rose to say "Good-night!" kissed little Fritz,
who went away beaming in his mother's arms, and,
turning to the professor, I said—

"Herr Messing! I told your wife, when entering
the house two hours ago, that I was under grave
obligations to you.   But to-night you have added
the greatest of all; for you have taught me more
than I have ever learned from books or men, or
even, God forgive me! from the Spirit of Wisdom
Himself.   When I passed along the quay a few
hours ago, it was a question with me, whether I
should walk into your house or into the river.   For
I undervalued the meaning and blessing of life,

and I have failed and fretted because its lights and shadows have fallen unequally on me. Your words have sustained me, and given me fresh vigour; and the sight of your little home with all its sweetness, has destroyed the foolish thoughts on which my heart was set. Professor, make me your friend once more, and God will bless you!"

"You are my vrendt!" said Herr Messing, "and Aleese and little Vreetz will lofe you, and you vhill gome to us, and be of ourselfes. And somedime you vhill haf your own house and wife and child, and vhee vhill go do Zandycove togeder, and read my Schillare and Goethe, and let the damn vhorld go ids own vhay. Don't vret! don't vret! goom, Aleese, and say Good-nicht!"

She did, and the professor accompanied me to the door and held me by the hand, as if he would never part with me, and said, "Don't vret! don't vret!" a hundred times. And as I passed down the quays, now brightened to my eyes, I heard his voice through the darkness: "*Auf wiedersehen.*"

# CHAPTER III

## A DIPSOMANIAC

A dreadful sound is in his ears: in prosperity the destroyer shall come upon him. Trouble and anguish shall make him afraid.—JOB xv. 21–24.

"A LITTLE—a—brandy, please."

"No, no; impossible!"

The clock ticked furiously on the mantelpiece, and showed the hour, 1.30 A.M. There was a moan in the room overhead, and the shuffling of felt slippers. Leviston lay back on his pillow, and picked the strands of the coverlet with trembling fingers.

"A little brandy—one spoonful, please!"

"Quite impossible. You know the doctor's directions. Try and compose yourself to sleep."

"I can't sleep. My brain is all alive, and alive with such hideous things. Phew! Get away!"

He made a gesture of grabbing something hideous and flinging it on the floor.

"A little sherry and bitters, for God's sake! It can't hurt. Why, sherry would not hurt a babe!"

"But it would hurt you. Try and sleep."

It was pitiable. The poor, flushed, congested face, and the white hair, thin and wispy, and the shaking hands. Tick, tick, went the clock, and knelled out 2 A.M. I went to the window. A grey fog had crept in from the sea, and was shrouding all things, even if the starlight tried to dissipate the darkness. The window panes were wet with the dews of the night; and a few long tendrils of the

150

Virginia creeper stretched their ghostly fingers and
swayed in the faint night-breeze.

"Mr. Austin."

"Yes, sir. What can I do?"

"Just lift the pillow. Do you see that bloated
spider with red eyes glaring at me? Take the thing
away. I thought we could have a little cleanliness
at least."

"Mr. Austin."

"Yes."

"A little Pilsener, please."

"No, no; take a little soda and milk, and try and
rest."

The weak hands fumbled with the counterpane,
and the watery eyes went wandering after the
hideous distortions of the brain.

"I must get up and see Gwennie."

"Not for the world. She is very unwell."

"Why, unwell! Who made her so? Was
it I? Good God! have I been a brute? Mr.
Austin!"

"Yes, sir."

"A little eau de Cologne, please!"

I put a teaspoonful of Cologne in a wine-glass,
filled the glass with water, and gave it to him. He
swallowed it at one gulp. This appeared to compose him.

"I cannot sleep. Will you read or talk?"

"I shall read if you like; talking will only worry
you."

"Anything, anything to soothe these dreadful
nerves."

"What shall it be?"

"I don't care. The Bible, if you like, though it's
the last thing I care for."

I took up the big Bible and laid it on the counterpane.

"Where shall I begin?"

"Anywhere. Try the *Sortes Virgilianæ*, and read the first line you open."

The sacred book opened at Job, and I read—"A dreadful sound is in his ears: in prosperity the destroyer shall come upon him. Trouble and anguish shall make him afraid——"

"Stop that, d——n you," he cried; "you did this to insult me."

He was trembling with fear. The spirits of the perfume were vanishing.

"Mr. Austin."

"Yes."

"I beg your pardon most humbly. Will you forgive me?"

"Certainly."

"Then, in token of forgiveness, give me one teaspoonful of brandy?"

"Impossible, Mr. Leviston; you know it is impossible."

"Then I swear that I must have it. Who the devil are you, you tramp, to keep from me what belongs to me? Pull that bell there, you, sir! No, then, by heaven, I must get up. It is an infernal shame that a gentleman can be browbeaten in his own house."

He tried in his paroxysm of fury to rise, but I put him back gently. He glared at me, and shouted—

"Ho, there, Rawlins! ho, there, Ellen! Come here and help me. This fellow wants to choke me!"

There was no answer in the solemn night but the echo of the awful voice. And the clock ticked furiously. There was a moan and some whispering overhead. I had brought a few books and magazines to while away the time; but I could no more read, face to face with that ghastly spectre on the bed, than if I were in a theatre with *Macbeth* upon the boards. I was still dallying—God help me, and all poor fools who put trust in human wisdom—with such poor presentments of philosophy as a verse of Goethe or an aphorism of Novalis could advance. I remember that on these memorable nights, when I kept watch and ward over Leviston, one phrase of the latter sage was continually recurring to me— "*You touch heaven when you lay your hand on a human body.*" There was something in it that appealed to me. It was the antithesis of all that horrible irreverence which is the root of our modern civilisation. I did not know that St. Paul had said the same thing in far better terms. But I looked at the wrecked body on the bed, the shattered brain, the broken nerves, the congested veins, and all the horrors that were coming up like sheeted ghosts from the sepulchres of the past and ranging themselves around the deathbed of that poor profligate. I laid my hand on his wet forehead and asked myself, " Is this heaven ? " And yet I could not answer no.

" Austin, why do you stare at me ? Why don't you turn these women away ? "

" They won't hurt you ; try and rest ! "

" Austin—Mr. Austin, I beg your pardon—one spoonful of champagne."

" You know, Mr. Leviston, I should be most happy to help you, but my orders are most positive—that under no circumstances were you to be allowed to touch alcoholic drinks ! "

" But, my dear Austin—Mr. Austin, I mean—you don't mean to say that there is alcohol in Pilsener— or a spoonful of sherry ? "

" There is no use in arguing the question, sir, but I cannot give you any. Try and sleep ; or if you cannot (it is now near four o'clock in the morning), let me give you a slight injection of morphia."

" Morphia," he laughed, "a slight injection. You

can give me as much as would kill six men and it
wouldn't compose me.   Look here ! "

He bared his right arm to the shoulder, and
surely enough it was speckled as thickly as with
measles.

And so the dreary night wore onward to the
dawn ; and never dawn broke over a sleeping earth
so happily, or at least so welcome, as that dawn for
me.   Leviston had a slight doze just about six
o'clock in the morning, and I was able, without
leaving the room, to watch the first faint ripple of
light that stole, as lightly as footfall of mother, over
the cradle of the slumbering earth.   The very mist
that hung low its curtains over tree and field felt
the awakening, and began to fold its white tents for
departure.   Sleepy little birds, close by in the thick
creeper that shrouded the front of the house, began
to wake up and chirp feebly to each other, as if
asking, where are we ?   A gardener's cart lumbered
along the high road ; cattle lowed from the lawns ;
and then the great scene-shifter rolled back mist
and fog and curtained cloud and showed the tender
morning landscape with all its mellow autumn
colouring, shaded darkly against the purple pencil-
ling of the mountain haze, over which rose the white
splendour of the dawn.   The light fell on the face
of the sleeping man and made it ghastly.   I cried
for the close of my night-watch and a breath of air.
At eight o'clock the nurse came in, bright and
smiling, and handed me a cup of tea.   I resigned
my charge and ran into the open air.   There, face
to face with God and His beautiful world, which we
mar so foully, I threw up my hands, and drew in
deep, deep draughts of the morning air.   It was
such a delight after the close, unwholesome smells
of the sick-room—odours of morphia and brandy,
and cologne, and heavy perfume, and—shall I say
it ?—the rank, sepulchral odour of decomposition

that was going on in the living body of that poor
profligate, that I whistled and sang with the birds
that were pouring out their matin hymns on the
morning air. It is well for us sometimes to be
deprived of God's cheap but inestimable blessings,
that we may know better how to appreciate them.

I was humming gaily, as I walked rapidly up
and down under a thick beech-hedge, the old child-
rhymes :—

> " Up, up, in the morning's cheerful light,
>   Up, up, in the morning early,
> The sun is shining warm and bright,
>   And the birds are singing cheerily ! "—

when I heard the refrain taken up on the other
side :—

> " For now the dew is on the grass,
>   The birds are singing cheerily :
> Up, up, in the morning's cheerful light,
>   Up, up, in the morning early."

It was not hard to recognise the voice of Sister
Philippa. I passed out under an arch of beeches,
and joined her in her morning walk.

" This is delightful after such a night's experience," I exclaimed. " But you're used to these
things."

" I enjoy it all the same," she said. " Now, let
us take a Mark Tapley view of the situation. How
many thousands of young ladies, and young gentlemen, too, will rise this morning about twelve o'clock,
and yawn, and dawdle over breakfast, and take up
a novel, and never enjoy the delicious air of this
morning ? "

" By Jove, you're right," I said; " it is my old
theory confirmed—that there is a perfect equilibrium
in the world. But how is your little patient ? "

" Poorly, I am afraid a perfect wreck in body and
mind. I do not know what your night's experiences

were, but I had rather attend fifty hospital patients than witness the mental agony of this poor girl. It was awful. One long protracted wail of self-reproach, and one long cry for the consolations of religion. I tried to do my best to soothe her, but there is something about your religion that we can never understand."

I was silent. It was another of these ghostly lessons that were now preached at me from all sides, and from such unexpected lips.

"Now," she continued, slowing down into a quiet walk, " I did all I could. I spoke of the Redeemer, His mercy, His love, His compassion. She knew it all, but yet there was no consolation. I quoted the sweetest and strongest texts from sacred Scripture — texts that breathed all the infinite charity of God—but there was no alleviation of her remorse and despair. I told her that all would come right yet, if only she had faith, but I cannot persuade her into that belief; she continues calling, and calling, and calling for a priest. What is the secret of it all ? I feel it myself sometimes. Often after a weary night I have envied your nursing sisters, who go calmly into their chapels for morning service, and come out smiling and happy, like children. I would give the world to hold your secret. I know it would make life pleasanter, and the burdens of this weary world more tolerable."

"You never, sister," said I, "spoke to a poor fellow less qualified to tell you the secret of the King than I. For I have been fleeing all my life long from that very source of strength which you seek, and I have been burying under such awful lumber the very secret which you are so anxious to possess. That's the way we Catholics fling aside God's most matchless graces. But God bless you for all your kindness to that poor soul. And why shouldn't she have a priest to console her ? "

"Well, you see, her mother doesn't like it. She is afraid Mr. Leviston would be displeased."

"And what the dev——the mischief does she care about the old reprobate now ? "

"Hush!" said Sister Philippa, "I don't think you should speak so unkindly. We don't know all. And there is but One who has a right to judge."

I was shamed.

"Probably," she continued, "you have thought all kinds of hard things about this poor invalid."

"I have thought worse of myself," I interrupted.

"That's right," she said, "that's the beginning of all good. But to return. Did you ever hear of the doctrine of heredity ? Well, I have seen it manifested in marvellous ways. If a child inherits its mother's eyes, or hair, or even her complexion, what shall we say of the deeper emotions and passions that are part of her nature ? Yes. Without destroying human responsibility the doctrine of heredity will revolutionise our whole penal code : it may even abolish capital punishment. 'The fathers have eaten sour grapes, and the teeth of the children are set on edge.' 'Who hath sinned,' asked the Jews, 'this man or his father, that this thing has happened to him ?' Then consider his early education. Probably he was petted and spoiled, and taught to indulge every whim and caprice ; and when he grew to manhood he got such a presentment of religious truth as most men get, and then came the world and the flesh and——"

"Yes," I interrupted, knowing that she would not for the world utter that last word, "but, sister dear, where did you learn all this philosophy ?"

She laughed.

"Nurses and doctors," she said, "are for ever examining the consciences of men, when they seem to be probing for diseases. Did you ever dread the doctor's keen scrutinising glance ?"

"Yes," I replied, "the only two classes of men I am afraid of are doctors and waiters."

"How you do reduce everything to the absurd. Then you are not afraid of us?"

"I did not say so," I replied seriously, "in fact, were it not for one woman, a girl like yourself, I should be now probably at the bottom of the Grand Canal!"

"The old, old story," she said, picking a leaf to pieces.

"Not at all. I'd as soon think of falling in love with a saint in a stained glass window. Not one minute, microscopical particle of love in our relations. But she has been my guardian angel. She says 'come!' and I go. A few words with her, just like you, and I am quite toned up. Do you know Cal is afraid of her."

"Impossible," said Sister Philippa, "he is afraid of no one."

"I assure you he is," said I. "It's the greatest fun to see him flushing up when she talks to him——"

"Doesn't he sing *Figaro sù, Figaro là?*—"

"Not for the world. But I must be going——"

"One moment. You know all about these people?"

"A good deal. Once on a time I was under the patronage of Mrs. Oliver, in fact, I was her lodger."

"Well, be careful what you say in your relations to the family. There is a little tragedy going on there."

I began to think, but could make nothing of the remark beyond what I was hourly witnessing. Sister Philippa passed down under the trees. A sudden thought came to me.

"Sister! Sister Philippa!" I cried.

She was down under the shade of the high elms, and didn't come at my call. I went to seek her.

She came out of the recesses of the trees, and I saw, at a glance, she had been weeping.

"Sister," I said, "forgive me if I have been flippant."

"Oh dear, it is not that," she said. "You called me?"

"Yes," I replied, my eyes on the ground. "I want to tell you the secret of the King."

She brightened up.

"If ever," I said, "you pass by a Catholic church, be it a cathedral, or a convent chapel, or some poor thatched dwelling-place on the hills; be it in India or in China, in London, or in Dunedin, if you see a red lamp swinging like a burning heart, inside the sanctuary rails, enter in; you will find yourself in the King's chamber, and He will tell you the rest."

She didn't expect so much solemnity from me, and she looked at me seriously. Then she held out her hand.

"Thank you very much," she said.

Mrs. Oliver was walking in front of her house. She had dark circles under her eyes, and her mouth was white and drawn.

"You have had a weary night," she said.

"Well, I expected it."

"Was Mr. Leviston troublesome?"

"Not very."

"He seems now quite rational and composed. He talks quite sensibly."

"Oh yes," I said, "he is quite as rational as you or I."

"This is Wednesday, or Thursday, I am beginning to lose memory of time, through grief."

"It is Wednesday, the 26th of September," I said.

"Wednesday, the—26th—of—September," she repeated, pausing at every word. "Go in, and have breakfast, it·is ready. Where is Sister Philippa?"

" I don't know."

I had breakfast, tried to snatch a few hours' sleep, woke up unrefreshed, had a hasty dinner, and at six o'clock I was speeding down the lighted streets to Herr Messing. My old professor was sitting by the fire, several books and manuscripts before him, and his head was wrapped round with a wet cloth, that did not add at all to his appearance. Fritz was on his own little stool, and as mute as a mouse. Alice smiled, and whispered—

" He is quite cross to-night over these old books. But he'll see you."

He jumped up the moment I entered, and grasped my two hands—

" De very man I vhant joost now."

" What's up, professor, are you studying for a degree ? "

" No. Lisden ! Vhee are going to have a great night to-night at Miss Bellamy's. You are gooming, of course ? "

" Well, I may drop in, if I can be spared. What's up ? "

" Vhell, I don't know. Dot's the puzzle. If I knew how the gonversation would turn, I should be all right. I vhant to shine. I vhant to appear great in Miss Bellamy's eyes. I vhant to quote Richter, to devend all dot she does zay. But how am I to do it ? I do try to lead the gonversation around to dot point ; but den, dot dom Gallwey, or Vorrester, he do but in a vhord, and presto ! we are all off again. Now, you vhill gome to-night ; und you vhill lead the gonversation, and you vhill know how to pring out mine ideas, and den I vhill strike in and I vhill shine ! "

He rubbed his hands with delight at the prospect.

" Now," he continued, " let us zuppose de gonversation turns on money—dot is a favourite topic. I vhill zay—

" ' Id iz de metal vheel-vhork of human agtivity—
de dial-plate of our value !'   Is not dot good ? "

" First rate !" I said.

" Zuppose it turns on poverty, I vhill zay, ' Id iz
eazier to pear poverty, like Epictetus, than to choose
id like Antoninus !'   Iz not dot good ?   Won't Mees
Bellamy be pleased ? "

" Delighted !" I said.

" Zuppose id turns on friendship.   I vhill zay
nothing for a long time.   Den I vhill break in, ' De
dithyrambic moments of vriendship !'   Vhill your
boys understand dot ? "

" Oh yes," I replied, " they have all got a classical
education."

" Very goot !   I vhill shine to-night.   Let me
zce.   You vhill pring de gonversation around to
zenery.   Dot is your strong point.   Mees Bellamy
vhill be delighted.   Den I vhill break in, ' De
grystal, light-reflecting grotto of an August night
spread its illuminated vault over de tark green
earth.   Night trew up ofer de earth, and down
beneath id, de gurtains of heafen, vhull of zilent
zuns.'   Iz not dot grand ?   But you vhill be jealous?"

" Never, mein Herr, your glory will be mine.'
And Helston, and Forrester, and Gallwey will all
be asking together, ' Who the devil is that clever
man ? ' "

" Dot is goot ! you, let me zee !   Dis vhill blease
Alfred, und, therefore, Mees Bellamy, ' De man
of de vhorld often possesses an upright carriage
und a grooked zoul ; de scholare ovten possesses
neider de one nor de oder.'   Isen't dot glefer ? "

" Sublime is the word, mein Herr.   But look
here, you'll annihilate us all.   We shall be pigmies
before a giant."

The professor laughed, took off the wet towel,
lighted his pipe, and winked at little Fritz, who,
understanding his father's gestures, jumped up

astride of the professor's legs, and pulled his beard.

"I am galm, now," said the professor. "I am satisfied. After all, id dakes uz Zhermans to understand you here. Won't these poys open dere eyes do-night ? Won't they ztare ? Won't dey zay, what learning ! ah, if we had been his pupils ! But, mein Gott," he cried, as a sudden thought struck him, " berhaps dey have read Richter, and I should be laughed at ! "

" Never fear, mein Herr," I said, " that time has not yet come, if it ever will come. You are as safe in quoting your poets as if you quoted the Veda, or Zendavesta. We know lots of things in Ireland, but not such sweet and serious things as Richter has said. Do you know what we would call Richter ? "

He stared at me, holding his pipe poised.

" We would call him a rhapsodist, an enthusiast, or that most contemptible of all things—a poet. We, in our present humour, are a practical people, and we call all that high sentiment nonsense."

" May Gott help you, den ! " said the professor, " dere is no chance for you. Goom ! "

But I did not go that night, for there was a swift, urgent message, which I had to obey. But I must say a word about these wondrous gatherings.

# CHAPTER IV

## ATTIC NIGHTS

"From scholars they passed on to learning; and then all the clouds of life melted away, and in the kingdom of knowledge the head that was bowed down with care and wrapt in the mantle of hunger was once more lifted up and free. The spirit inhales the mountain air of its home, and looks down from the lofty Alps of Pindus, and see, there below lies its sorely-wounded corpse, a burden which it had to bear with sighs, like a nightmare."—RICHTER.

HOW it was brought about I do not know. It was one of those silent movements that gradually takes form, without any apparent collusion or any attempt to formalise. But, insensibly, Helen and Alfred Bellamy's little home became the centre of gatherings, that differed somewhat from the tamer and more prosaic meetings of other houses. Subjects of novel interest were discussed there. The peril that faces every one in Ireland who attempts to lift the plane of conversation above its ordinary low level, was unknown. All subjects—literary, artistic, religious—were freely discussed. And there was no embarrassment or constraint, for there was no contempt or conceit. I feel quite sure that the spirit which animated this little circle radiated from its central figure ; and this was its secret charm, for every one felt a distinct and individual relation to Helen Bellamy. It was rather an interesting study to myself, particularly as I was partly the originator of the little scheme, to see grouped around Helen Bellamy in her drawing-room a little circle of men, diverse in thought, in aspiration, in feeling, yet all drawn irresistibly by that magnetic attraction that belongs to a personality, whose ideas and principles we recognise to be cast on a far loftier level of thought than our own. And we were all, more or less, Bohemians. A few young artists and law students, one or two professional men, who had not as yet taken silk, a foreign professor from a neighbouring college, a couple of French *émigrés*, who were teaching in public academies—that was all. Herr Messing, of course, after I had renewed his acquaintance, came as an old friend, and the avowed admirer of Helen. "She vhas fit to be the vife of Goethe," that was his canonisation. Then the Deanes, as dear valued friends, would occasionally drop in, and by degrees the little circle expanded; and I had the intense pleasure of seeing there the grave, pale face of the captain, and the quick, earnest Gallwey, and Synan, and Cal. And on the winter nights there was quite a corona of faces around the tea-table, at which my Sybil presided with all her own grace and dignity. My own visits were very rare. And just now I had a little tragedy on hand, which I should see to its close.

If I were to form an opinion from the few nights in which I had had experience of that little home gathering, I should say there were many very solemn questions discussed there, and many high and lofty principles advanced, perhaps controverted, perhaps denied, finally admitted, and sent to form part of that curious admixture of sentiment and truth that go to build up the moral fibre of men. Cal hated these discussions. Sometimes he would fall asleep; sometimes he would appeal to Mrs. Deane, for they had become fast friends, to stop the Parliamentary debate and let Miss Bellamy play. Mrs. Deane, who treated him as an overgrown boy, would laugh, and appeal to Helen. And Helen, in the midst of her most brilliant remarks on men and things, would rise up and go over humbly and ask Cal what she would play for him; and Cal, the unabashed before every one else, would blush and stammer before this girl, laying up for himself the Nemesis of many a quip and jest at the hands of companions who were merciless, for he had no mercy upon them.

Herr Messing always occupied the place of honour on these occasions. He monopolised the right to sit at her feet, and punctuate Miss Bellamy's remarks with some saying from his German masters. And he beamed from his spectacles at the little group, as a showman who had a prodigy to exhibit, and expected the audience to be appreciative. One evening, during the brief hour that I could steal from my present duties as warden over a drunkard, the conversation drifted, as it often did, to the eternal question of our national and racial talents and possibilities. No people in the world are so fond of self-introspection as we. That is what makes us so unhappy.

Gallwey, who was a born controversialist, though shy as a girl, had been saying something of utter despair about the country. Herr Messing took him up.

"I do not despair of you," he cried, "because I do lofe you all."

There was a laugh.

"You are shildren, babes. You can vight—like de teevil! You can lofe like vhomen! You can drust, like de leetle shildren! You gannot tink like men! I do not know vhere you game vrom, but id vhas an awful fate that angored you to the zide of England. You should have made one of the Cyclades, or been put between Chios and Samos!"

He looked around with a smile. He knew he had been complimentary.

"I think Herr Messing is right," said Helen Bellamy (the professor was ecstatic), "we are *Orientals*, placed here in the mists and the rain by some mysterious power.  Our place is under burning skies, under tents of skins, the desert or some Persian paradise throbbing around us by day, our cattle lowing around our tents by night.  We are Orientals from the hair on our heads to our feet, which, with true Oriental freedom, we hate to have covered.  In our love of freedom and freshness, in our contempt for eating, in our passion for narcotics, in our love of colour, in the heavy muffled dress of our peasant women (which is but a relic of the weighty southern infula or the Arab's burnoos), in our music, with its semitones and minor chords, in our language, which has every one of the sounds of the ancient Hebrew, in our very religion, which is Oriental in origin, in concept, in ceremonies—in all these things we are a race cut away from our country and people, by some inexorable fate that has given us but a pitiable exchange, yet a glorious destiny."

"And what might that destiny be, Miss Bellamy?" said Gallwey.

"This," she replied.  "To quicken with all the enthusiasm and emotional energy of our race the dull cloddish materialism of the heavy-footed races with whom we come in contact.  And here is the grand mistake of our rulers, whether they are made so by conquest or by our own choice.  The whole process of educating us, whether with books, the plank bed, the bullet, or the gibbet, is directed towards bringing us down from our own lofty position and assimilating us to all the coarse virtues, or coarser vices, of our masters.  They would make a nation of artists' artisans.  They would clip our wings, and bring us grovelling to the earth.  They would create uniformity out of natural and picturesque irregularity.  They would use us as their beasts of burden, and feed us for our work.  We have built up their empire with our blood, and they laugh at us. We have given them back the glorious heritage of faith which they sacrificed, and they scorn us for it. And we, and our elect leaders, go on co-operating with them, swallowing their little baits, and handling their little bribes, and trying all the time to eliminate from our national character all that is hereditary and glorious, and make it all that is commonplace and hideous! Mind, I do not want to extenuate our faults. I know well what we can never be. I know, for example, that there is no literary instinct just now in Ireland. I know we lack imagination. I know we shall never, for example, produce a great poet. We cannot. Our enthusiasm is not imagination. It is not the dream-ecstasies of a Teuton in his black mountains and forests. It is the very antithesis of poetic imagination! We ought to be the greatest dramatists or critics of the world. We never can be great poets. Here again is our Orientalism."

"Miss Bellamy," said Gallwey, looking very white under the eyes, "I gather from what you are saying that if your religion is of the very essence of the Irish nature, and Protestantism thoroughly Saxon and Teutonic, you would be disposed to think a paternal and theocratic form of government best for us?"

"Dot is goot now," said the professor approvingly.

"I think," said Miss Bellamy slowly, "that under other conditions such a system of government as that of which you speak would unquestionably be best for Ireland, and for the world. I am not at all sure but that the world will, of its own accord, seek a theocracy yet——"

"And put a Hildebrand over it to drag our kings to Canossa?"

"Now, Mr. Gallwey, you have dragged me before the two-faced statue of history, and asked me to worship," said Helen Bellamy sweetly.

" I thought," said Gallwey, with hesitation, "that there never was but one opinion on that matter."

" And that opinion was—— ? " said Miss Bellamy.

" That Hildebrand was the perfection of an ecclesiastical despot; and that his ultimate fate was richly deserved."

" Then you do not believe that Henry was a tyrant and a profligate; and that Gregory it was who rescued not only Germany but Europe from a condition of vassalage, that, but for his genius, might be one of the existing conditions of the present day ? "

" I never heard or read so," said Gallwey firmly.

" Perhaps," said Miss Bellamy, " I as an Oriental have more sympathy with priests than with kings. But, to show you that there may be another view, different from that wherein you have been instructed, Alfred," she said, " would you hand me that volume of ' Ecclesiastical Biographies ' ? "

She opened the volume and read in her clear, firm voice: " Yet the Papal dynasty was the triumphant antagonist of another despotism the most galling, the most debasing, and otherwise the most irremediable under which Europe had ever groaned. The centralisation of ecclesiastical power more than balanced the isolating spirit of the feudal oligarchies. The vassal of Western and the serf of Eastern Europe might otherwise at this day have been in the same social state, and military autocracies might now be occupying the place of our constitutional or paternal governments. Hildebrand's despotism, with whatever inconsistency, sought to guide mankind by moral impulses to a more than human sanctity. The feudal despotism with which he waged war sought with a stern consistency to degrade them into beasts of prey or beasts of burden. It was the conflict of mental with physical power, of literature with ignor-

ance, of religion with injustice and debauchery. To
the Popes of the Middle Ages"—["The Middle Ages,"
she cried, "the Dark Ages!"]—"To the Popes of the
Middle Ages was assigned a province their abandonment of which would have plunged the Church and
the world into the same hopeless slavery. To Pope
Gregory the Seventh was first given the genius and
the courage to raise himself and his successors to the
level of that high vocation."

"You are quoting, of course, Miss Bellamy," said
Gallwey humbly, "from some Catholic apologist?"

"No," said Helen Bellamy, handing him the
volume, "you see it is the work of an Edinburgh
reviewer, Sir James Stephen, K.C.B."

"I am beginning to see there are two sides to
most questions," said Gallwey.

I slipped out quietly to go back to my dreary work
of controlling a drink-lunatic. Agnes Deane followed me.

"How is that poor child?"

"Poorly, I am sorry to say. Sister Philippa is
a great help."

"You have disagreeable work, I daresay?"

"Very. The whole thing is tragic enough."

"Mr. Deane tells me that young Oliver is out
again."

"That means more trouble to the family. He is
sure to come around and persecute them."

"And Mrs. Oliver, how is she bearing up?"

"Damn Mrs. Oliver! I beg your pardon, Mrs.
Deane, but I hate that woman."

"Well, but how is she?"

"Very lively; making wonderful efforts to discover if there be a will, or to have one manufactured
if there be none."

"Oh dear! oh dear! men are so uncharitable.
Do you know, these are nice young lads, wherever
you picked them up. That tall handsome fellow

who is always pulling his moustache with both
hands will propose some fine day for Helen."

" And be accepted ? "

" Well, you're concerned there.  You know best."

" How little, after all, you omniscient women
know !  Some day you'll be surprised."

" I am not surprised now, but I am awfully
puzzled."

" I thought so," I said, and went away laughing.

Helston, Synan, Cal, Forrester, and Gallwey
strolled home together.

" Well, Gallwey, you've won the Victoria Cross,"
said Cal, " I'd as soon face a battery of artillery."

" She's a wonderfully clever girl," said Gallwey
reflectively.  " Are there many of that sort amongst
you Papists ? "

" Tens of thousands," said Cal airily.    " But
where the mischief did you come to all this knowledge about Middle Ages, and Gregory, and Otho,
and Matilda, and all these other celebrities ? "

" Well, we used to be taught them in our Sunday
School.  And then, instead of novels and newspapers, we had to read such things at home.  I
thought, though, that you Papists knew little of
these things."

" My dear fellow, never make that mistake again.
We know everything.  I now, for example, could
pass an examination in theology where I have failed,
oh so many times, in anatomy.  And don't tackle
me in Ecclesiastical History or Hebrew.  Helston,
you're pulling that cigar to bits.  Is it to be to-
morrow ? "

" What, you little beggar ? "

" Because I'd like to be there to see.  You'll take
her out to India, of course, and won't she shine at
Simla or Peshawur ?  By Jove !  you'll have a hundred duels on your hands, old fellow ! "

" Say what you like here, Sutton.  You're dreadfully afraid of Miss Bellamy yourself. Only for your mamma "—(this was Mrs. Deane)—" you couldn't hold that cup of tea she gave you."

"That's true, by Jove!" said the unabashed. "Do you know I'd give—what? Well, my chances at the next exam., to introduce Bryce. I wonder would she mesmerize him?"

"Hullo! Bryce," he cried, as they entered the cap's room and saw Ned Bryce in his favourite posture, legs stretched out before the fire, hands deeply sunk in his pockets, and in a half-maudlin sleep. "We have discovered another brand."

"Have you?" he cried, starting up, "where?"

Then, as there was a laugh, he subsided with a grunt, and said, "Jameson's good enough for me; but I prefer de Cork Distillery. There is a tang, a taste of de peat about it," he continued critically, "dat no other possesses. It is quite enough for me, you fellows, if there is plenty of it."

"Ah, but," said Cal, "this is quite a new thing; adopted at the Bar, and recommended, ahem! by the medical profession."

"What's de name of it?" said Bryce dreamily.

"Hildebrand," said Cal; "invented by a man called Gregory."

"Anything to Gregory of the powders?"

"First cousins only. Don't you remember reading about him in your catechism?"

"Never learnt catechism," said Bryce. "Tried to get over the third chapter, and bolted. Know all about Samson, though."

"Well, go ahead."

"Well, you see, Samson was a powerful man, with a forceps like—like—like——"

"Never mind comparisons," said Cal; "they are not your strong point."

"Well, we'll say like de divil. Well, he had a wife called Deborah, the deuce of a scold; and one day dat he wanted a drink, she refused him, and he went out in a fit of bad temper, and pulled down the timple of Zama—dat place, you know, where Scipio defeated the Carthaginians. It must have been a mighty small timple, like our little chapel at Coolgaragh, where the neighbours used shake hands on Sunday morning from one gallery to anoder, across de altar, and poor Father James (the Lord be merciful to his soul, 'twas he kept the good drop) would call out, 'Step down here, Jim Deluchery, and serve Mass for me.' Well, I must be going. Give us a lift, Sutton, across de road. De legs are unsteady, dough de head is clear."

With many a quip and crank, taken good-humouredly by the tipsy giant, for he loved Cal, although frequently annoyed by him, Cal convoyed his heavy burden across the road, and returned, after he had settled Bryce comfortably in bed, and made him say his prayers, for Cal was scrupulous on the point, to find the other students disappeared, and the cap. gloved and hatted for a night-stroll.

"You'd rather be alone, cap?" said Cal insinuatingly.

"Well, no! Come along, you imp."

They strolled along the lighted streets, passing some favourite haunts without entering, though Cal hinted plainly that he would like to see some old friends again.

"Let us drop in, and have a game of pool at Davis's."

"No," from the captain, laconically. "Later on."

"Won't you come see little 'Fan'?"

"You can go if you like. I won't."

"Look here, cap, did you bring me out for a lesson in astronomy? for I'm blessed if I know what else you have in view."

"Let us take a look at the 'Royal,'" replied the cap.

"All right, that's something definite," said Cal with alacrity.

They mixed with a crowd of loafers around the Theatre Royal, for it was the hour when boxes and stalls and pits disburthened themselves, and the oyster saloons were opened, and the drivers looked after their horses' heads.

Suddenly a thought flashed across Cal's ever-active brain.

"I'll tell him," he said decisively. "Would you care to hear a story, cap?"

"All right. Is it a true one or a make-believe?"

"True as gospel! One night, I don't know how many years ago, there was a crowd here, as there is now, and the people were coming out, as they are now, and there was a girl singing a ballad just there under that gas-lamp. She was poor, pinched, starved, hungry, shivering. Two tremendous swells came down these steps, very sweet on each other— they were just married. Their carriage drew up here. Just as the bridegroom held open the door, and was ushering his bride, with her silks and furs, into the carriage, the singing-girl fainted. The lady stepped over, and bent over the girl. Then she ordered her to be taken to a neighbouring house, and followed her. So did the bridegroom, proud of his wife's charity. When the poor girl awoke, she recognised this gorgeous gentleman as her brother, and was foolish enough to say so. He let out a long lasso of an oath, and fled the scene."

"Is that all?"

"Yes. But I was near forgetting—that girl was Helen Bellamy!"

"Very good; a pretty little fiction indeed. When you, Sutton, and your friend, Austin, concoct a story again *for your own purposes*, let it be more reasonable and less dramatic."

He was buried in deep thought. Cal saw that

he had made a fool of himself. The crowds were pouring down the stairs, laughing, talking, and with all that appearance of splendour, and all those little reciprocal attentions that make heavy the hearts of young men, who have not as yet attained their majority in wealth and position before the world.

The well-dressed golden youth of the city were indulging in their usual minute criticisms: "What eyes!"  "Did you ever see such a dazzling complexion?"  "Pah, all rouge and paste!"  "Who's she?"  "Don't you know?"  "That is Sylvia, the daughter of Dawson, the distiller; just come out!"  "By Jove, she'll be soon snatched up!"  "I say, Jack, here's a fresh toast!"  "By all the saints, I am tempted to put my coat under her feet!"  "Don't. 'Tisn't your own, and what would Moses say?"

Helston woke up.  "What beastly animalism! Come, Sutton, and have a liquor just to wash down that lie."

Little Mimi, poor little spectacular Mimi, brightened up her sleepy eyes when she saw Helston. He was one of her favourites, because, as she said, he always treated her as a gentleman.

He appeared cool enough, but his hand trembled as he tossed off two glasses of drink in rapid succession.  Cal whistled softly to himself the first bar of a popular song—

> "For when a young man is off his feed,
>     And bolts his liquor, sez I,
> I tell you there isn't so very much need
>     To question the reason why."

They went home at midnight. And little Mimi filled her big eyes with foolish tears as she rubbed her glasses and decanters, because her "perfit gentleman" did not say "Good-night!"

Cal was in the habit of making a nightly examination of conscience in this wise. He threw off his coat and vest, and, crowned with a gorgeous smoking-cap, faced his own image in his dressing-glass. This evening the soliloquy ran thus :—

"Cal, old fellow, you and I are pretty old acquaintances; but if ever I was disposed to hire a Chinaman to curse, or an iron-shod mule to kick, it is to-night. Cal, you are not a success in life. You have been plucked three times, because you studied everything but your *materia medica* and your *anatomy*. You have got yourself into several bad scrapes by minding every one's business but your own. Cal, it is an old adage or maxim or something, 'Mind your own business.' Sometimes the advice is given rather abruptly, but it is always wholesome. You have studiously neglected it ; and some day you will be principal at a coroner's inquest, but probably the least interested in the proceedings. Keep your clappers quiet, Cal, for is there not something in Scripture about a man who has a wise fool for a friend ? But Helen Bellamy does not even dream of such a thing. She never will leave her brother. And Goff ? Well, it's all interesting enough; but what is that to you ? Mind—your—own—business ! "

He shook his curls at the glass, and went to sleep —the sleep of the just.

The captain did not propose for Helen Bellamy.

# CHAPTER V

## ATTIC NIGHTS

*(Continued)*.

For to be wroth with those we love
Doth work like madness in the brain.
—COLERIDGE.

I DID not know whether during all these years my
good friends suspected the awful depths of poverty
to which I was reduced, though later revelations led
me to believe that with the keen instinct of kindness
my pitiable condition was half suspected. But never
by word or deed was there the least allusion to my
worldly position or prospects; or the smallest hint
that it would make any difference in their acceptance
of me as a friend. The Bellamys themselves had
seen trouble enough to make them sympathetic, if
it were not their natural disposition; whilst with
the Deanes there was a strong feeling of that splendid independence that heeds neither caste nor circumstances in the selection of a friend. Yet, I
confess, there were times when my heart sank within
me, when I thought, as I sat in their luxurious
drawing-room, of the awful slums where I had
made a temporary home; or of the makeshifts to
which I was obliged to have recourse to keep up
even the appearance of respectability. I had a feeling that the whole thing was not quite honourable;
and it was the greatest relief to me when my student
friends were admitted within the sacred circles of
my acquaintants. It brought me from the sordid
level of a tramp or beggar to the romantic elevation

of a Bohemian. I was a student, and if irresponsible and impecunious, well—so have students always been. Yet, I had such a shrinking reverence for these dear people, that I seldom intruded, except when driven by the absolute necessity for human companionship, other than that of night-birds and scavengers. Then I sunned myself for a moment in the warm light of men I loved, and women I worshipped, only to plunge down in deeper, darker abysses of experiences that even memory shudders to reproduce. Ah me! how very near to each other are the two extremes of human life; and how often do fluttering rags touch rustling silks which never dream of such contamination!

On those nights, therefore, when either at Agnes Deane's or Helen Bellamy's, the little coteries of professional men or students met and talked over the subjects of yesterday or to-day, but always of perennial interest to the educated, I looked in, as somewhere I have read [1] of the lost Iscariot staring

---

[1] A friend supplies the verses. It appears they are taken from a poem by Robert Buchanan :—

> " 'Twas the soul of Judas Iscariot
>     Crawled to the distant gleam,
> And the rain came down, and the rain was beat
>     Against him with a scream.
> For days and nights he wandered on,
>     Pushed on by hands behind ;
> And the days went by, like black, black rain,
>     And the nights like rushing wind.
>
> 'Twas the soul of Judas Iscariot
>     Strange, and sad, and tall,
> Stood all alone at dead of night
>     Before a lighted hall.
> And the world was white with snow,
>     And his footmarks black and damp,
> And the ghost of the silvern moon arose
>     Holding her yellow lamp.
>
> And the icicles were on the eaves,
>     And the walls were deep with white,
> And the shadows of the guests within
>     Passed on the window light."

M

through the closed windows at the Supper Table of his Master. But I was always restless and uneasy in society, and I used to fly, with such pleasure, to the little den on the left side of the hall, where dear old Alf, surrounded by gleaming brasses, badly-bound books, lines and circles and figures, that might content the heart of a Pythagorean, smoked and dreamed at his leisure. Here on the long winter evenings Alf and I would smoke in silence, listening to the rain pattering without, or the voices from the drawing-room, or the laugh at some solecism of Herr Messing, or the rich, wonderful voice of Helen Bellamy, when in her royal charity she broke through the forms of debate, and sang for Cal or some other who cared more for music than for metaphysics. Sometimes Alf and I would hold a little debate between ourselves, always on the subject—his love for science and my contempt for it. And sometimes Hubert Deane would come in and join us, with the remark—

"You two fellows know how to enjoy life—that is, by holding your tongue, and letting the world talk for your amusement."

One evening, whilst Hubert Deane and Alf and I were together, and quite a concert was going on in the drawing-room, where a Spanish lady, who had just introduced the mandoline into the city, was the great centre of attraction, Hubert, who was usually as taciturn as a statue, suddenly broke in with—

"I wonder how long do these Platonic friendships last without a rupture!"

We wondered what "these" meant; but he gave no explanation. But went on—

"Because it seems to me—a soured and crabbed old lawyer, who sees in his business hours only the seamy side of human nature—that the 'ignotum pro magnifico' principle very often applies here, or rather the 'notum pro parvo.' Hence I should say,

if you desire to maintain a Platonic friendship, keep
your thoughts wrapped up from your dearest friend.
There is only one eye that is never scandalised at
what it sees."

We were mystified; but I ventured to say—

"Your good wife, Deane, complains that you are
always oracular, and that you utter your opinions as
if always sitting on a tripod. But you are particularly obscure this evening."

He went on smoking, but after a while continued—

"By the way, Plato is put down for a lot of mis-
demeanours of which he was never guilty. You
know every young professor quotes Plato. He may
not know much about that philosopher; but somehow
it savours of much knowledge. Every young miss
that has just given up pinafores and tea-aprons, and
bread and butter for caramels, talks of this Platonic
friendship. Every fool that meditates suicide is supposed to hold a soliloquy, ending, 'Plato, thou rea-
sonest well.' I wonder what did the unfortunate
man do to merit this awful immortality?"

"Look here, Hubert," said Alfred, "come down
from the clouds and tell us what is it all about?"

"Mind you," said Hubert, as if not heeding these
interruptions, but as if arguing against some unseen
antagonist, "I don't believe in these things at all.
An old lawyer, who has been mixed up in ten or
twelve divorce cases, comes to have a poor opinion
of philosophical resolutions."

I don't know how long this curious soliloquy
lasted; but just then Cal's sweet high tenor was
heard singing out some favourite operatic air (for
Cal was, above all things, classical in his tastes, and
would not touch vulgar melodies), in the drawing-
room. We, or rather Hubert Deane, paused to
listen. The song ceased, there was a gentle murmur
of applause, and Alfred said—

" I suppose he'll come in now to get the alms of our congratulations."

So he did. In his own easy, nonchalant way, Cal strolled in after a little time. We affected to be pre-occupied in some debate and took no notice of him, except that Alfred offered him a pipe. Poor Cal began to feel uneasy. He smoked, but evidently was in very uncongenial society. We talked of everything but music.

"Any singing going on in the drawing-room?" asked Hubert Deane at length.

It was impossible not to laugh. Cal bridled up; but immediately resumed his quiet tone and manner.

"Look here, Deane," he said, "there was some little time ago in England a profound artist and student of human nature. He knew everything from dukes and duchesses down to servant-maids and crossing-sweepers. He made many most profound observations on human life and character, and I am not aware that his judgments have been questioned."

We were becoming interested. Hubert Deane took the pipe from his mouth, and poised it between his fingers as he looked at Cal and listened.

"But," said the latter slowly, and with emphasis, "he made one profound and pregnant remark that contains more wisdom—more practical wisdom—than anything else he has said."

"Out with it," said Hubert Deane, "you are keeping us in suspense."

"You won't be offended?"

"Certainly not!"

"The philosopher and sage was Dickens. And he said: 'The law was a—hass.'"

We hardly knew whether to laugh or be serious. Deane looked angry for a moment, and seemed inclined to resent the insult. He said nothing, however, but resumed smoking. Lights began to dawn upon me, ugly, alarming lights as I looked from Cal to Deane. Cal, after an interval, shook the ashes from his pipe, and without a word passed into the drawing-room.

"To resume," said Hubert Deane, "the thread of what I had been saying when this—this—*persifleur*, interrupted us. I had a strange consultation to-day. You both remember that curious case that excited so much notice a few months ago, when a young fellow of good station in the city was arrested on his own confession, and convicted of forgery of a bank-book to the amount of about two hundred pounds?"

We nodded. The case was a notorious one.

"The poor fellow was a chamber-lawyer just getting into a little practice. I was interested in him, as we had some business dealings with each other. He was a truthful, honourable fellow, but a fool. He had all kinds of sentimental ideas chasing each other through his little brain; and every new fad he took up and made his own, and thus of course became extravagant and a spendthrift. Art and science, blue china and old pictures, ancient coins and postage stamps—nothing was strange to him; and especially, where a woman was concerned, who had some mad fancy of her own, he was a perfect fool. Well, he became infatuated about a certain lady, who, in her own way was a faddist. She used him, without caring for him, to carry out all her little whims and oddities which she knew her husband would not tolerate. He was simply a tool in her hands; and he spent money like water to humour her. You know these imbeciles are very much flattered by the notice of married ladies. The usual three-volume novel, which is responsible for so much of the wickedness of the world, teaches that the conquest of a married woman is the only victory worth achieving. Well, the poor fellow ran heavily into debt. The husband's bank-book was forged, and on his own confession Lothario was arrested, and is enjoying life in Mountjoy. Pardon the pun. I have picked up the habit from—from—Agnes." He choked at the name. "Well, a week ago I had a letter and affidavit from a solicitor in Texas to the effect that this innocent is really innocent. The affidavit is made and signed by the lady's brother, who was employed in her husband's office, and was a bad lot. Whether this poor fellow with the broad arrows on his grey jacket, deliberately sacrificed himself for this woman's sake, and to save her pride, or whether she cajoled him into doing so, may not be known. But here comes the cream of the joke. I called on him to-day; saw him in the governor's presence, showed him the affidavit, told him I thought we could effect his release if he would only co-operate. He looked at me wildly for a moment, then, with a silly oath, to show, of course, his manhood, he swore the affidavit was a lie, and that he himself was the culprit. I was dazed. I told the governor afterwards what I thought. He agreed with me, 'Such things are possible,' he said."

When Hubert had stopped, I said—

"But all this only confirms and does not contradict the theory of Platonic affections. Why, you are disproving, very unlike a lawyer, your own case."

Deane gave a little sardonic laugh and said—

"No, my dear fellow. It proves what I have said that there is no such thing as Platonic love. That is only a euphemism for crime or insanity."

He spoke so unlike himself—so bitterly, that again alarming lights began to flit and flicker before my eyes. And I remembered how he spoke the name of his dear wife with a gulp and an effort. Surely, no evil spirit is going to bring the poison of distrust and dissension into that sacred household, doubly-consecrated to me by the memory of my little saint. The thought was appalling. Yet, clearly, there was no love lost between Hubert Deane and Cal. I wished the Attic nights were over. You cannot bring men and women together, but the Evil One will poison the atmosphere with the sirocco of his breath.

We went into the drawing-room about nine o'clock. Helen Bellamy was at the piano, Helston arranging her music. He was looking down dreamily at her, whilst she, unconscious and careless of admiration, passed her eyes slowly over the pages. Groups of ladies were chatting here and there; Herr Messing was pouring out some of his platitudes (may he forgive me if he sees these pages) to a number of school girls, who apparently did not know whether to laugh or be edified; and in a corner, where a lamp, shaded in salmon-coloured silk, threw a dim light on the little table, Agnes Deane was turning over the leaves of an album, and Cal, bending down, was making some of his usual witty and sarcastic remarks on the pictures. I saw Hubert Deane give one rapid look at them, then flush suddenly. He passed over to chat with some ladies, and Alf and I went to the piano. Helston looked annoyed, and after a few moments, walked away.

" By Jove !" I said to myself, " I am getting into hot water. There appears to be a lot of misunderstanding floating about."

Helen lifted her head and said to me—

" I am wishing for the long summer evenings !"

"Why ?" I said. "These long winter evenings are so much pleasanter. I know the evenings of summer make me always lonely and miserable."

" I wish this evening were over," she said more straightly. " I am beginning to feel frightened."

" At what ?" I asked.

" At people and their ways. There appears to be

always a little tragedy brewing when men and women get together.    Alf, dear, what do you think of the old days ? "

" They were very pleasant," he said ; but, guileless and unsuspicious always, he continued—" but I like these little gatherings too, if not too often repeated. After all, Helen, we need a little brightening now and again—at least I, a confirmed old bachelor, do."

Hubert Deane had gone out alone, and Agnes came over to where we were standing.    She asked—

" Where is Hubert gone ? "

We did not know.    I passed quietly into the hall. Hubert was outside the door in greatcoat and muffler.    The odour of his cigar filled the hall.

" Where are you going ? " I said.

" Home," he said huskily.

" Agnes—Mrs. Deane is inquiring and is anxious."

" Is she ? " he cried.

" Yes," I said, " she cannot understand your prolonged absence from the room."

He said nothing, but threw off his greatcoat and came back.

An hour after, I had the intense pleasure of seeing him wrapping his wife up in furs in the hall, and smiling and jesting as usual, as he handed her to his carriage.

" Good-night, Austin," he said.

" Good-night, Mr. Austin, good-night.    Helen, dear ! don't come out in the cold."

I stood for a moment at the open door, as the carriage rolled away.    Then I heard a hearty " Thank God ! " from some one near me.    It was Helen.    She, too, had been looking after them into the darkness.

" Why do you thank God so fervently, Helen ? "

" Why do you stand there looking at the blackness ? " she replied.    We said no more but passed into the drawing-room together.

# CHAPTER VI

## A STERN NOVITIATE

*"The character of the true philosopher is to hope all things not impossible; and to believe all things not unreasonable."*—SIR J. HERSCHEL.

MEANWHILE that beautiful soul, that had been associated with me in the singular vicissitudes of College life, was undergoing an austere and stern novitiate for a high and exalted purpose. I have already spoken of Father Aidan; and, perhaps, I have impressed on some minds the idea of a character, strong, self-reliant, self-contained. Let me now throw in a few dashes of the brush, and bring out this singular being more clearly on my canvas. Father Aidan, if he had lived amongst the apostles, would have been a Baptist and an Evangelist combined—with all the fierce zeal of the former, and all the tender love of the latter. Had he lived two hundred years later, he would have gone into the Libyan desert with Macarius, and stifled the fierce, passionate eagerness of his soul amongst the penitential sands. Had he lived in mediæval times he would have been a Francis Assisi, or a Xavier. But as he was fated to be cast into the nineteenth century, he was, and would remain, a country curate on the coast of Clare. The Church now is so well organised, concentred, and compacted, that there is no room for guerilla warfare. Her machinery now moves with all the smoothness, silence, precision of the piston that plunges into the cylinder, and withdraws, to set vast, unwieldy machinery in motion. Perhaps the world is not aware of, very likely hundreds of churchmen do not advert to, the perfection and symmetry of this superb organisation that works in unerring obedience to a discipline and order, that have no equal in any other organism, secular or religious, in the world. Of course, all this is but saying that the Church is abreast of the wants and idiosyncrasies of the age. If the spirit of the world is a spirit of concentrated energies, controlled and directed by one central power, and all harmonised into obedience and unswerving fidelity, the spirit of the Church is the spirit of a vast and complex world, controlled, directed, subdued, and guided by one principle, or by one mind. Hence, we can see that that spirit will tolerate no irregularity; if there are fiery spirits they must not attempt to guide the chariot of the sun, but be harnessed like ordinary workers, otherwise—well, think of Lamennais, and be silent! Hence, for the turbulent, fiery spirit of Father Aidan there was no vast theatre to disport itself, no masses of humanity on which to exercise itself. And this strange, weird, but noble character spent its energies in some easy task of sanctifying a simple and religious people, and then—eat itself up in fruitless dreams and barren imaginings of what might be. Now, the catastrophe of Charlie's rejection, and his subsequent humiliation, came to this great soul as a heaven-sent benediction. Calculating with the utmost nicety the exact depth and calibre of his soul, Father Aidan determined to do, through Charlie's agency, what ecclesiastical discipline forbade himself to accomplish. He would make Charlie a lay-missionary; and having drilled him according to his own views in the spiritual zeal and endurance, that would be requisite, he would send the young soul abroad into the multitudes of men,

itself a living flame, and destined to enkindle into
living flames the hearts and souls of the young men
of Ireland. It was a glorious, if daring ambition ;
and it afforded rest to that restless spirit, and a free
scope for all the latent energies that consumed his
hidden life. But he had to count with Charlie's
friends. He did not expose to them his entire plan
of action. He simply put his project before them ;
the means he kept shrewdly to himself. The mother
demurred, the sister wept, the father consented.
He would have consented to test Charlie's vocation
by an ordeal of fire, if Father Aidan had demanded
it. And now commenced a long, stern novitiate of
five years under an uncompromising master. He
began by studiously excluding from Charlie's mental
vision everything that could win him back to a
worldly career, or seduce him from the royal road
on which he was entering. As brave invaders burn
their ships and thus cut off all hope of return, and
must conquer or perish, so Father Aidan literally
burned to ashes in the fire of his own humble
parlour every one of Charlie's books that savoured
aught of worldliness. A similar sacrifice, yet a
greater one, he himself had made many years ago.
Like all great thinkers he had written much. Fascinated and imbued with the scholastic philosophy,
after he had been a rabid Platonist, he had sought
to reconcile Greek philosophy with the teachings
of Christianity—to reconcile Plato with Augustine.
It was a noble idea ; and he laboured hard for many
years to perfect it. But, after fruitless labours, the
impossibility of such an attempt forced itself on his
acquiescence. He saw that philosophy might teach
God, but could not reach Him ; that it enlightened
the understanding without strengthening the will ;
and that the revelation of the Word Incarnate alone
could bridge the chasm between man and God.
Then, deliberately, he put the labours of years in

the fire. Leaf by leaf he placed his beloved manuscript on the burning coals. Sometimes he drew
back, when some page of special interest and
workmanship was to be sacrificed. Then, that,
too, touched the blaze, curled into sparks, and
became blackened dust. And when the final leaf
was burned he felt that now he had broken with the
world, and was a free man unto God. A similar
sacrifice he demanded of Charlie. Every dainty
volume, carefully annotated and marked, was cal-
cined into dust; and then Father Aidan placed
in Charlie's hands the *New Testament* and
the *Imitation of Christ*. For twelve months no
secular book or newspaper met Charlie's eyes. He
was wrapped up in the abstractions of sacred
science. His feet were not permitted to touch the
earth. In the meantime, Father Aidan inducted him
into all the sweet and sacred mysteries of the Divine
Office; and when the little chapel door was closed
at seven o'clock, prior to the evening devotions, the
two figures might be seen in the sanctuary of the
little chapel, chanting by the blear light of two
candles the solemn psalmody of David. But the
one eternal thought which this stern preceptor
dinned into the willing ear of his ductile pupil
was, to see the awful figure of Christ everywhere
—flitting through the psalms, personified by David,
hiding in the recesses of the tabernacle, gliding
amongst the masses of men; always with the same
Divine ministry and mission—the saving of the
souls of men; always with the same Divine agency
—that of love. That sacred and awful presence was
realised by this great priest, and after a time, by his
pupil, to such an extent that they saw *the Christus*
as really and tangibly as if He had appeared to
them in the flesh. If on Christmas night, when
Father Aidan bent lovingly over the Bambino which
he had purchased (he was too poor to purchase a

crib), and if the Sacred Infant put its arms around his neck, as we read in the lives of saints, Charlie would not have been surprised. For one such night, just before Christmas, as they were chanting Vespers together, and Father Aidan, his whole soul filled with exultation, flung out his arms into a crucifixion, and chanted the Antiphon—

"O Orient! splendour of light eternal, and sun of justice; come and enlighten those who sit in darkness and the shadow of death!"

There was a pause, and high up in the fretted roof, one voice of entrancing melody intoned the Magnificat, and a whole choir of celestial melodists took up the immortal Canticle, and sang it alternately to the end. From that moment Charlie gave himself up, body and soul, to Father Aidan. Heaven had spoken, and he had but to obey.

As a consequence of this, Father Aidan strove to develop all that was bright and holy in this young soul; and to harden and anneal, as by fire, all that was weak and sensitive. For the two things that had to be accomplished before Charlie was fit for his great apostolate were the enkindling of an enthusiasm that should never flag, and the implanting of a courage and fortitude that should never know a moment's weakness. For the former, Father Aidan supplied the motive by instilling into this young soul the ardour that supported the martyrs for three hundred years against all the cruelty and power of Imperial Rome—that is, a personal love for Christ so strong that the flames of blazing pyres were as a breath of a summer breeze, and the teeth of wild beasts and the rack were but as the pressure of loving fingers. For the latter, there was but one principle and practice—a contempt, not bitter and acrid, but lofty and charitable, for human opinion. Given these two things, and the favour of heaven, and Father Aidan hoped to see the dream of his life

realised—the world once more at the feet of Christ.
It was a long and terrible probation for Charlie.
This constant gazing from the cliffs of time into the
ocean of eternity, and the contemplation of the unspeakable and unfathomed mysteries that are hidden
there, sometimes unnerved him.  Then came some
great sentence from the lips of his preceptor that
pulled together the quivering nerves, and gave new
life to the listless spirit.  Sometimes there was a
cry for human sympathy, that was immediately
stilled by the soft voice beside him, that cooed like
a mother over a sleeping child.  Sometimes there
was a fretfulness and impatience under such discipline.  Then Father Aidan, his own heart quivering with emotion, would remind Charlie of his past
great sin, and the big, big D would start up, an
angry reminder of the past, and a revelation of
present weakness.  On one such occasion, when
Charlie chafed more than usual under such control,
Father Aidan forgot himself for a moment, and said,
but kindly—

"But you remember, Charlie, that house in
Queenstown."

Then, when the tears welled up in Charlie's eyes,
the heart of his stern teacher was smitten, and he
went home, and with the discipline cut his own flesh
into ribbons.  But these were rare accidents.  During these first twelve months the long tenure of
enthusiasm was rarely broken by such depression.
The teacher and his pupil walked together on the
crests of the everlasting hills.

After the first year had elapsed a new course of
instruction commenced.  Father Aidan put into the
hands of his pupil simultaneously a small hand-book
of Catholic philosophy, and the writings of Tertullian.  His object was to give him an idea of the
Church's teaching, and at the same time an idea
of how the Divine Presence always animated His

Church from the beginning. Thence he passed to
St. Augustine, with a view of more completely de-
veloping the central idea of philosophy as ancillary
to religion, and heresy serving in the hands of an
overruling Providence for the Divine development
of doctrine. Then he led him hand in hand down
through the centuries, pausing at the disruption of
the Roman Empire, the enthronement of the Popes
in the palace of the Cæsars, the Divine mission of
Constantine; and whilst he kept his pupil's attention fixed on these vast and momentous changes,
he never failed to rivet his mind on the great
characters that stand out in bold relief in the pages
of Church history. Ambrose, standing at the door
of his cathedral, and sternly forbidding Theodosius
to enter because of his great sin ; the stern rebuke
of Polycarp to Marcion : "I know thee, thou first-
born of the devil"; the penitent Henry shivering
for four days at Canossa at the doors of the inexorable Hildebrand—such tableaux from Church history
as these were ever presented to the wondering eyes
of the sensitive pupil, to imbue him with the idea
that God, and not man, was to be feared. Then the
glorious example of the Church's heroes appealed
to his enthusiasm. The Saint of Assisi, in rapture
with his poverty and humiliation, and for these, lifted
into the third heavens—Xavier, dying in a tattered
cassock on the yellow Indian sands—Ignatius, forming from his sick bed at Pampeluna his idea of that
glorious *landwehr* that have been to the Church
what the Old Guard was to Napoleon—anchorites
and recluses, hermits and denizens of cities, missionaries and students, preachers and Cistercians, all
the myriad powers which the Church, with infinite
variety, summons to her aid, meeting every want of
humanity with some new solace or help—all passed
before the wondering eyes of Charlie and stimulated
him, as they have stimulated thousands of others,

to join the devoted ranks, and consecrate themselves
to a noble service.  But most of all was his soul fed
by the examples of the early martyrs, and by the
sweet enthusiasm for Christ that breathes through
the writings of the early Fathers.  Many and many
a time did Charlie weep at the thought of these
children that went forth to die for Christ with the
calm longing of friend about to meet friend.  He
saw, as in a picture, Perpetua torn from her babe
and tossed by the angry bull in the Roman amphi-
theatre, and each time that she touched the ground,
wounded and bleeding, gently lifting up her hair
and weaving it again with calm dignity for the
struggle ; he saw the blind girl, standing unabashed
before her captor, till the whispered admiration of
the crowd sent the blushes into her face, and she
sank dead from modesty.  The child Agnes and the
brawny executioner quivering before her ; Agatha
and her bleeding bosom ; the boy Pancratius with
the panther sucking at his throat—all these passed
before his enraptured vision and questioned him—
Why cannot you, too, leap into the arena like these
fearless athletes of Christ, and brave what is even
worse than the rack and the fire—the scorn and
laughter of men ?  Will you, too, not be supported
by the same Divine vision that hovered over their
quivering bodies, and shone before their enraptured
eyes ?  And here, in the old beloved Greek, with its
strong sonorous syllables, breathing of the East, its
magic and its mysticism, were the burning thoughts
of men, some of whom had seen Christ—all of whom
were intoxicated with that rapture that fills the soul
when the body and senses are annihilated.  Better
far than the old poets, with their legends and their
lies, their impure gods and goddesses, and their lust
and blood, were the sweet divine thoughts of saints,
couched in the old divine language, and the *Logos*
shining on every page.  Charlie plunged into this

ocean of beatitude, and came forth braced and strengthened with holy ideals and immaculate sensations. And he lived in spirit with the ancient fathers, and in imitation of them, crushed the body that the spirit might arise chastened and strong. And so, for five years, up and down through the centuries, to-day with some noble philosophical passage from the fathers—to-morrow with some noble example of heroic fortitude and endurance, our young apostle went, until at last he had grasped in all its fulness the idea of the living Church of God, and saw in all its height and breadth and depth the massive proportions, the splendid cohesion and uniformity of this great Divine organisation. Here were no feeble, hesitating phrases or enunciations of truth; no temporising with the world, its enemy; no pusillanimity in the face of danger; but with unbounded reliance in the Divine promises, an apostolate of doctrinal truth and discipline—uniform, consistent, perseverant. Such was the vision that now opened itself to the wondering eyes of Charlie and stimulated his enthusiasm and zeal. In a word, he was brought face to face with the City of God on earth—with its shining walls, its turreted battlements, its numberless niches for saints and heroes, and the Spirit brooding over all; and he thirsted for the lofty vocation to be one of the chosen band who was to stand up and defend that Imperial City, and after the martyrdom or the triumph to be entitled to some place of honour in its beadroll of heroes and saints.

But all this time his teacher, reliant as he was on the eternal promises and the supernatural aid he invoked, did not neglect the natural means that are quite necessary even for such spiritual projects. If he preached that doctrine that no greatness or success was ever achieved save by austerities and conquests of the flesh, he at the same time watched over Charlie's physical health with more than maternal solicitude. He prescribed his dietary, took him on long walks or long sea trips to harden his muscles and nerves ; and he put him through a regular course of training to help him to pitch his voice, in all its varied intonations, to the farthest capacities of an audience. On wild and gusty days Father Aidan would take his pupil to one of those rugged amphitheatres which the sea has cut out of the slate beds on this most picturesque coast, and, placing him on the highest rock, would train him by arduous but persevering work to conquer the tumult of wind and wave by the shrill intonations of his voice. On calm days Charlie would launch out into the deep, like the Master he was preparing to follow, and deliver from the prow of some frail coracle one of the long, impassioned orations which he had composed and written carefully, his sole audience being the critical master on the rocks, and the penguins and gulls that, startled from their nests, made a shrill accompaniment to the voice of the youthful orator. On one such day, in the early spring, they both were tempted far from the land, probably allowing their frail boat to drift with the current. They had been talking as usual of divine things—of the slender thread that tied them to life —of the almost transparent veil that concealed eternities. It was the closest view Charlie had yet received of the vast abysses over which our little lives are poised : and he was unusually silent. So was Father Aidan. They had not noticed a curious copper-coloured mist, thin at the edges, dark and black and ominous in the centre, that was creeping up from the west, pushed along by a faint sultry wind. The sun-shadows on the water were darkened before Father Aidan noticed this threatening visitant. When he did, he cast one swift glance around and pulled with all his might for shore. Charlie sat in the high stern, pale and concerned. They had drifted down along the coast, half a mile or more from the little bay where they had always found shelter, and from which they had embarked; and as they came close to shore they could see only huge ramparts of cliff above them, and the jagged, angry teeth of black rocks beneath. To land on such a coast meant instant destruction. They looked out to sea. Already the black cloud had come down upon its bosom, and the waters began to chafe at the angry pressure. The horizon was whitened by huge breaking billows, and the expanses nearer shore were black and sullen. The weight of the approaching storm made itself felt inshore, and the teeth of the black rocks were whitened by the spray that washed up their sides and fell back in ineffectual rage. After a little time Father Aidan desisted from rowing, as if half-ashamed of his momentary weakness in depending on human help in such a crisis. And with a little smile he shipped the oars, and said to Charlie—

"We must trust in Providence now, Charlie, but it is probable that we are very near to the end we were foreshadowing a little time ago. Let us make all the preparation that we may."

He bent down his head reverently and appeared lost in prayer. The light boat, made of tarred canvas, rocked and plunged on the rising waves. Suddenly a squall swept down on the deep, flattening the waves only to render them more furious, and whitening the face of the waters under the black, frowning sky. It struck the little coracle, and sent it flying towards the shore. Its occupants were helpless. Nearer and nearer it came, until it shot under a huge needle of rock that pierced the sky a hundred feet over their heads, and was engrailed, as by the blows of a thousand hammers, into shelves, where the white gulls were screaming. A few huge billows lifted the coracle high on their crests, and passed it as in play from one to another, until the last, with gathered strength, took it up and flung it contemptuously on the rough slaty shingle. It was torn, as if cut by a knife, from end to end. Father Aidan and Charlie were uninjured : and when some rough fishermen from the Arran islands came down the narrow path, treading cautiously with their rough cowskin boots the paths which the goats had worn, they found the two kneeling on the shingle and lifting their eyes in thanksgiving to God. Thus, and in other ways, the five years rolled by ; and the time had come to commence the mighty work for which this rough novitiate was intended.

The two things Father Aidan desired to effect through Charlie's agency were: The establishment of a system of lay co-operation throughout the Irish Church, under the control of the Irish hierarchy, and extending to all works of charity and religion. And secondly, the revival of the monastic spirit, such as at that time was taking place in Catholic countries on the continent. The idea was a bold one, it might have seemed an impracticable one. But what reason could there be for doubting that in the ranks of the Irish Catholic laity could be found volunteers, whose zeal and intelligence might at least be equal to that displayed by the members of Protestant communions ? And what was there in our age to prevent the spread of sanctity, such as that which filled our Irish valleys with the monasteries, whose crumbling ruins still testify to their beauty ? And Father Aidan was fully of opinion that there are to-day in Irish hearts germs of sanctity which, if developed, would blossom into flowers as fair as those which made our island in the past a garden of God : and, well, why say more ? the experiment was worth tying, even if it was doomed to partial failure.

Mrs. Travers, whose hopes were to see her only boy distinguished in the world, openly opposed the scheme when it was placed before her. The sister trembled and doubted. Mr. Travers, with all his faith in Father Aidan, demurred when the time came.

"I know," said Father Aidan, "that, like most parents, your ambition is to see your son a Q.C. or on the Woolsack. I want this to be said of him"—he put his finger on a line in his breviary, and Mr. Travers read: "Et tu, puer, propheta Altissimi vocaberis; præibis enim ante faciem Domini parare vias ejus."

# CHAPTER VII

## THE YOUNG REFORMER

. . . . .
> And Power was with him in the night,
> Which makes the darkness and the light,
> And dwells not in the night alone ;
>
> But in the darkness and the cloud,
>   As o'er Sinai's peaks of old,
>   While Israel made her gods of gold,
> Altho' the trumpet blew so loud.
>                    —*In Memoriam.*

IN the spring of the year of which I am writing
there were some faint rumours of a great religious
revival that was quietly showing itself in the city.
An occasional short paragraph in the papers, a
poster on the dead walls, a brief word of comment
from business commercial men, as they met in rail
or tram on their way to work—these were the indi-
cations, and they were few and faint of the revolution that was being quietly, but effectively, put in
motion.   Men are so engrossed about their own
affairs, that it is only a passing glance they can
vouchsafe to matters of supreme interest to the
Church and the toiling thousands who find in religion the only solace of life.   Most things in our
days of rapid movements are but of transient interest; and religious topics, always excepting a
controversy or a scandal, are uninteresting to that
class who enjoy the slippered ease of competence or
wealth.   Very faint, therefore, were the rumours of
the new revolution; but down in the blackness of

the slums, in the hideous squalor of tenement houses, in the hearts of sad women, a new light was dawning.   And there was an awakening from the sordid cares and ambitions of life in the hearts of the young, who for the first time were taught to realise that life is neither a game of May-poles and wreathed flowers, to be enjoyed with dance or song until the grim watchman comes and closes the revel ; nor yet a dreary alternation of hopes that disappoint when realised, and ambitions that disgust when satisfied ; but a solemn and sacred probation of work and worship for a destiny that transcends in majesty and sublimity the loftiest dreams of the human mind, or the intensest yearnings of the human heart.   The visible manifestations of the change were thronged churches, deserted public-houses, a quieter and calmer demeanour amongst the people, and a look in the eyes of the young men of the city, as if a new spirit were awakened, very different from the pride and frivolity of the past.   And yet there was no interference with the rights of others, no street calling, no amateur preaching, no forcing of opinions; but a quiet, serious spirit, that seemed to actuate all into a sacred conspiracy for the doing of good, and the restriction of evil.   And, curiously enough, the chief agent remained all the time practically unknown.   He gave the inspiration and vanished.   He gave the impetus to thought, and retired.   Sometimes, indeed, one might read on a modest poster that Mr. Charles Travers would that evening address the Young Men's Society, of Clarendon Street, on the important question of the "Church and Society"; or one might read in some obscure advertisement that Mr. Charles Travers would address the St. Andrew's Conference of the Vincent de Paul Society on the "Sacredness of Poverty," or the "Divine Vocation of the Poor"; but people looked and passed on — they passed, like the Levite in the gospel, the wounded and stricken world of the poor, without deigning a word of sympathy, or extending the hand of succour.

The minds of men are very slow to move, or at least, they are slow to acknowledge that they are set in motion by some superior spirit. And it was only late in the autumn of the year that a faint rumour, as I have already indicated, came to my ears of a young advocate in the city, who, by reason of his marvellous eloquence, and the novelty of the subject he was teaching, was stirring unknown depths in the public mind, and directing men's thoughts into channels that never were known before. It appeared, too, there was a fearlessness and a holy audacity in his teachings that made men angry at first, and then, in their honest moments, willing converts to his principles. He inveighed against all the modern vices of society, its love for ease, its mad passion for wealth and distinction, its godless education, its dread of trial, its hatred of sickness or poverty, its want of charity towards the fallen or afflicted. He pointed out, that between the well-to-do city merchant, who picks his teeth after his luncheon, and poises his heavy seals in his hands, and goes to his Turkish bath in the afternoon, and sits down to a stately dinner, and stares at half-naked women from his opera box—and the cultured Pagan, who, wrapping his toga around him, strolled down to the baths of Vespasian, and supped with Lucullus, and frequented the circus in the days of ancient Rome, there was not a hair's-breadth of difference. It is true the latter laughed at his gods, and jested about the augurs; but the city man, too, would not spare a clever *mot* about a priest, and would send his women and children to church on Sunday. Where exactly does Christianity come in ? Not in our personal habits—they are sensuous and voluptuous; not in the splendour of our churches—

they are vile and contemptible compared to a Roman or Grecian temple; not in the well-being of the working-classes—they were never so poor, ill-educated, comfortless; not in the extirpation of vice, as our streets testify; not in the checking of drunkenness, as our distilleries testify. Surely that Divine Man of Judæa had some message for the world besides the platitudes of philosophers or the divination of augurs. Yet, where is it visible or audible in the world?

Meanwhile, the new paganism, called modern civilisation, is working out its own destruction and solving its own problems. There are subterranean mutterings of a future upheaval, that will change the map of the world as effectually as did an irruption of Vandals or Visigoths. In the self-degradation of women, in the angry disputes between labour and capital, in the dreams of Socialists, and the sanguinary ambitions of Nihilists, in the attitude of the great Powers towards each other, snarling and afraid to bite, in the irreverence and flippancy of the age manifested towards the most sacred and solemn subjects, in the destructive attempts of philosophers, in the elimination of the supernatural, in the concentration of all human thought upon the fleeting concerns of this life, and the covert, yet hardly concealed denial of a life to come, in the rage for wealth, in the almost insane dread of poverty— and all these evil things permeating and penetrating into every class—there is visible to the most ordinary mortal a disintegration of society that can only eventuate in such ruin, as have made Babylon and Nineveh almost historical myths, and has made a proverb and byword even of Imperial Rome. Where is the remedy? Clearly Christianity; and still more clearly the only Christianity that is possible, and that can bear the solvent influences of the new civilisation. Nothing but the poverty

of Christ, manifested in the self-abandonment of
our religious communities; the awful purity of
Christ, continued in a celibate priesthood, and the
white sanctity of our nuns; the self-denial and
immolation of Christ, shown again wherever the
sacrificial instinct is manifested as in our martyrs
and missionaries; the love of Christ, as exhibited
in our charge of the orphaned, the abandoned, the
profligate, the diseased, the leprous, and the insane;
can lead back the vast masses of erring humanity
to the condition not only of stability, but of the
fruition of perfect peace.    For what is the great
political maxim of government but "the greatest
good of the greatest number"—in other words the
voluntary sacrifice of the individual for the welfare
of the Commonwealth ?    And where is that seen
but in the ranks of the obscure and hidden, the
unknown and despised (unknown and despised by
themselves above all) members of the Catholic
Church ?

If, then, this Church is the bulwark of modern
society, can there be a more ignoble destiny than to
sit still and let her, unaided and single-handed, con-
front the vast and terrific forces that are arrayed
against her.    On the other hand, can there be a
more sublime destiny, or a more noble undertaking,
than to stand by her side and throw in such little
forces as are placed at our disposal in her support,
and for the confusion of her enemies ?    Yet, hitherto
the entire struggle has been tacitly left by laymen
in the hands of the captains of the King's hosts.
Against all the natural and supernatural agencies at
work in the world opposed to God and His Christ—
heresy and infidelity, with their tremendous intellectual forces; irreligious governments, with all
state appliances, treasuries, armies and navies at
their disposal; the press, with its far-reaching
power; literature, that derives its supreme attrac-

tion from its unchristian or immoral teachings; art, that is the workshop of Satan; politics, that would exile the Church from the world; the drink syndicates, that are becoming omnipotent through human impotency—the social evil that has forced itself to be State-recognised—schools, from which God is banished; family circles, where religion is never mentioned; society, that would take offence at God's name—in a word, against all the professed badness of the world, and all the unconfessed indifference marshalled in hostile array, as Lucifer marshalled his unthroned hosts before Michael, stand timidly on the side of Christ a handful of priests, a few weak women, a literature that is saved from ridicule barely by its good intentions, and a few saints, who lift their hands like Moses from the mountain, whilst the armies of Israel are hard pressed in the valleys of humiliation and defeat. All this time what are Catholic laymen doing? Absolutely nothing, either defensive or aggressive. With the exception of a few Vincent de Paul societies, there is absolutely no organisation that would combine in one solid body all the zeal and talent of thousands of young men, who would dare and do a great deal for Jesus Christ, but who are now kept back from want of an inspiring voice, that would tell them, Go and take your place under the red banner, and throw in all your resources of mind and body to destroy the empire of Belial and extend the empire of Christ.

This, then, was the mode of argument, the reasoning, and the appeal addressed by this young advocate (for Charlie was a student for the Bar) to vast masses of young men, who, constrained by his vivid eloquence, and overmastered by the strength and directness of his appeals, felt stirring within their souls emotions and desires that transcended all the experiences of their lives. It was whispered that vast and important changes would result from the mission of this young apostle; and grave priests, whose hearts were broken by the daily contemplation of evils they were unable to master or even oppose, began to whisper amongst themselves something about "a man sent from God, whose name was John."

But this grand apostolate did not want that most significant sign of Divine approval which comes from the opposition of the elect. Men shrugged their shoulders, and asked that question that never yet won a battle, Is it wise? Wasn't there danger here and wasn't there danger there? Above all, wasn't there novelty in these teachings, and wasn't everything novel, untrue? Leave us to the dear old platitudes, the balancing between Christ and the world, the steering the even keel between God and Satan? Above all, wasn't this a young man—a very young man—and what could you expect? And "Leave well alone" shook hands with "Just as well as we are," and both combined with "What's good enough for us is good enough for our children"; and all declared that the authorities, whom they never assisted or supported, should step down and stop the preaching of these revolutionary doctrines, and leave good Catholics to the exalted sanctity that demands short Masses and shorter sermons, and pays for the accommodation by the regular discharge of Christmas and Easter obligations. Even zealous people, who were keeping alive in their hearts the sacred love of God, as the Hebrews kept the sacred fire hidden during the Captivity, began to think it was going too far. Was it wise to array against the Church such stupendous power as the liquor interest of the country? Was it wise to send down young men into slums and rat-holes even with the crucifix in their hands? Wasn't there a hostile government to be conciliated; and, above all, was not this return to mediæval ideas directly in antagonism to the advanced thought and culture of the present day? How can you reconcile Baudelaire with the Gospel of St. John, or Paul Verlaine with the *Imitation* ?

It was in meeting these objections that Charlie surpassed himself. It roused his indignation, and a good fit of anger is the best inspiration. "What!" he used to say; "talk to me of your modern culture, the thinnest veneering for a so-called civilisation, which is as pagan as that which drew down the angry scorn of Tertullian, and the fierce invective of St. Jerome. I know well what it means. A superficial acquaintance with a few Greek or Roman authors, a more intimate acquaintance with their mythologies; a knowledge of science deep enough to create unbelief, not deep enough to discover the eternal operations of Omnipotence; a knowledge of philosophy, that is, of its shallow watchwords and shallower professors, and a profound ignorance of the only philosophy worthy of the name, that which is the warp and woof of Catholic theology; an acquaintance with literature, that is, a memory to hold all the erotism of our poets, and all the blasphemy of our essayists, and a profound and abysmal ignorance of the vast and exalted regions where saintly scholars disport themselves, sunned by the effulgence that streams from the source of all light and knowledge. And for this ephemeral and superficial culture what are you sacrificing? All the divine ideas of saints and prophets, all the sweet and true and mystic interpretations of sacred Scripture, all the art that has made Michael Angelo, Raphael, Guido, Correggio, Murillo, Rubens immortal; all that vast world of sacred and solemn melody, through which, as through an atmosphere of light, the spirits of Palestrina, Mozart, Haydn, Handel, Gounod for ever float. Ay!" he cried, "your cheap culture is the culture of oleographs and the buffo song, broken French and ungrammatical German; but from all that high and lofty culture, where saints and geniuses found a home, you are as far removed, for you have drifted as far, as a pavement artist in London, or some poor *cantatrice* of the boulevards."

All this excited comment and criticism; and that cheap sarcasm, which is now our modern substitute for Irish wit, was levelled at the new movement. Clever things were said to level it down to a mercenary, or at best, an ephemeral movement, which rather puzzled me, accustomed as I was to believe that the public conscience was well-nigh unerring in its estimate of men and things. For now, in some mysterious way, which I could neither define nor explain, a curious undercurrent of sympathy with Charlie's ideas began to stir and move within me. From hostility I had passed to sympathy; and the fierce attacks that were levelled against the apostle of the slums and gutters roused all my apathy into an active and warm desire to co-operate. Not that I could yet enter into all Charlie's ideas and projects. A living body lay upon the dead. My intellectual convictions were all enlisted on his side; but the virtue of faith was yet dormant, and needed reawakening; and nothing but faith, active and intense, could take up the laborious and thankless work my old comrade was now pushing to success. But I was puzzled at the opposition of the good, and—I consulted my Mentor.

Herr Messing was not in excellent humour when I met him; but his pettishness was that of a child. It evaporated the moment his mind was distracted. He was annoyed with me for not helping him to carry out his little programme at Miss Bellamy's. It appeared the conversation did not at all flow in the channels where he was prepared to enliven it, and all his careful preparation went for nothing.

"Dot Helston," he said, " began do dalk about

boating and vishing; and Gallwey vanted to know eif Mees Bellamy efer vhent do de Opera, for he had vree dickets (vhere did he get dem) to a box-stall; and deh began do dalk apout Norma, and vhat a Norma Titiens did make; und dey asked my opeenion, und I did zay—'Do not dalk do me of Titiens und your tingle-tingle museec. Go hear Wagner und you vhill hear a master-singer."

" How did they take it ? "

" How did dey take it ?   How do de vrogs dake it vhen de leetle poys do throw de stone ?   Dey began do croak, ' Wagner, de Zherman brass band,' ' Wagner, de rumbling of railway vhaggons,' ' Wagner, dot makes you put wool in your ear,' ' Wagner, dot emptees de theatre,' until I got mad, and I did zay, Yees, Wagner, dot teach you something better dan de ' Wearing of the Green,' played upon a union pipes und a wheezy goncertina.   Go away, ye are zhildren ! "

" How did Miss Bellamy take it all ? "

" Zhee did zmile; but she vhas dot evening *distraite*.   Zhee had been reading apout our young vrendt, Zharlie.   But, I forgot, he is not your vrendt now ! "

" What particular mode of reasoning, mein Herr, leads you to that conclusion ? "

" Nodings," the professor replied with indifference, " but vhen I mentioned his name, und zaid, vhee vhill hear him sometime, you lifted you eyeprows, and dot means a great deal."

" All right, mein Herr.   Now, I want your advice."

The professor brightened up.

" What is the reason that, when a fellow like Charlie takes up a great question and a great apostolate, and faces the world with it, a whole crowd of respectable people begin to yelp and bark at him as if he had done them a personal injury ? "

The professor saddened. " I vhill dell you."

The professor held down his head, and began to think.

" Dere are two elements at war in de whole vhorld —and dey are more at war in Ireland don anyvhere else—Apollyon, de destroyer, und Christ, de Healer, de Restorer. Dot it is liderally true. As a symbol id is also true. De gonstructive spirit, dot builds in hope, and goes on zmiling mit its vhork in face of awful diffigulties, is met by the spirit of destruction, dot, unable to do unyding of itself, seeks to anni- hilate de labours of oders. On de zide ov de goot spirit—dot of Christ—is zeal, learning, charity, labour, humility ; on the zide of Apollyon iz envy, jealousy, sarcasm, pride, nefer zo exultant az when it drags down to its own level of do-nodingness the vhork that promises to zoar on high like the turrets of a mighty demple. Dot is specially drue of Ire- land. In politics, for one man dat builds up dere are a hundred dot gast down ; vor one dhinker dere are a tousand gritics ; vor one great gonstructive genius dere are a hundred who revel in ruin. In lideradure id iz ze zame ; hence all your writers und dhinkers fly to London de moment dey gan get a vhoothold dere. Und there is no remedy. Men vhill gover, are forced to gover, de rags of their own intellectual nakedness mit de cloak ov sargasm ; und de great und gentle spirits vlee away az you would run from a zarcastic dough picturesque beggar. But Zharlie vhill go on, on, und he vhill fail, und he vhill sugseed. Dot is, he vhill go down in de fight, but the mustard-seed he is planting vhill burst into a mighty dree ! I hof zeen him ! "

" Have you ? " I cried eagerly.

" Yes, und Mees Bellamy. Vhee did go to hear him."

" Is he changed ? "

" No ! de zame gentle, enthusiastic poy we did

know. But you should zee de young men—id iz a pigture. Dey gome out, az if an angel had touched dem. Dere iz great good in Ireland, but id vhants to be awakened."

"What does Miss Bellamy think of Charlie?"

"Dot he iz zent from Gott. She says dey are her own ideas put into vhords und made eloquent. Zhee says——"

"What, mein Herr?"

"Dot—you—ought—to—be—by—his—side!"

"H'm! But does she think he is quite right or prudent in his crusade against culture and education?"

"Dere is no grusade against gulture," said Herr Messing, with indignation; "dot iz a galumny. What he condemns iz unchristian and superficial gulture—de gulture of de modern drawing-room, not de gulture of de monastery or de study! Do you understand, or shall I egsplain more?"

"I understand," I replied, "but the world won't. Am I right in interpreting Charlie's teaching thus— Catholic education should aim at raising its members to that height of cultivation that will enable them to despise mere culture?"

"You hof zed it," said the professor, which, with other things, led me to believe that there was a new dawn rising over the mists and darkness of my soul. And Helen Bellamy *did* say, "He ought to be side by side with Charlie." That presumption bespeaking her good opinion, and a deeper knowledge of me than I possessed, woke up emotions that had not surged through my heart for many years. Evidently good people thought better things of me than I could conceive of myself. Alas! we do not break with old habits and old prepossessions in a day, and the old refrain came to my lips, "Not yet; not yet."

Yet, the picture of these young men, bringing back from these evening conferences new lights in their eyes, new aspirations in their hearts, made me jealous and bitter. For, of all the ambitions of life, I had always thought the most honourable to be the power of swaying the hearts of young men and kindling in them a passionate reverence for the things that are holy and sublime, and a passionate zeal for the things that are honourable to God and profitable to men. For, under every kind of flippancy and foolishness, under the more hideous mask of dishonour and degradation, there are features in these souls that need but little furbishing to be recognised as the lineaments of the Divine. And it needs but little zeal, but a great deal of love, to remove the ugly and hideous painting of vice and folly, and show under its ugly palimpsest the hand-writing of the Eternal. Oh for one hour with Charlie, one quiet walk under the limes, one uplift-ing of this dead soul of mine by his inspiration, and, perhaps—who knows ?

But this grand crusade of his against vice, this magnificent propaganda of Christian science, will be a test, keen and searching, of our much vaunted faith and fidelity. The deep bell of Irish faith tolls solemnly and slowly through the world. What is its pitch, what the resonance of its metal ?

> " How will you know the pitch of that great bell,
>   Too large for you to stir ? Let but a flute
>   Play 'neath the fine-mixed metal ; listen close
>   Till the right note flows forth, a silvery rill ;
>   Then shall the huge bell tremble—then the mass
>   With myriad waves concurrent shall respond
>   In low soft unison."

Shall this be so ? Will the soft flute of Charlie's voice awaken echoes far and wide, wherever the humming of the deep bell has penetrated ? Shall we see new life in the Irish Church, not mere good-ness, but sanctity ; not only fidelity, but activity ? Will Charlie's dream ever be realised, of a youth strong and resolute in their faith, and with an intelligence that must command the unwilling attention of a world that would gladly forget that there was such a word as Religion? And will the old hopes of Mayfield ever reach fruition in the spectacle of a great race returning from the desert, as the Jews from the Captivity, to build up, on the ruins of the past, stately shrines where, segregated from the world, our grand old race will once more take up the broken psalmodies of the past, and make the whole island once more resonant with prayer and praise unto God?

It was a grand thought, and it was neither reactionary nor ill-timed. The condition of the Church demanded it; the world's sad destiny required it. The men, the time, the place, the circumstances were propitious to it. But Apollyon! Apollyon!

# CHAPTER VIII

## NIGHT SPECTRES

Nicht hoffe, wer des Drachen Zähne sät,
Erfreuliches zu ernten.

—SCHILLER.

Who sows the serpent's teeth, let him not hope
To reap a joyous harvest.

WHEN I returned to Leviston's house in response to the sudden and peremptory summons that took me from the Bellamys, it was not the voice of man but the howl of a wild beast that accosted me. "He has got drink again, and is a madman," I thought.

He was. His bedroom was a mass of confusion and filth. The mattress was on the floor, and he knelt on it in his night-shirt with a naked razor in his hand. He had been seeking for some tormentor, and he had found him in a hard knot of hair in the corner. The calico was hacked and hewn in a hundred places. The floor was covered with the *débris* of a plaster cast, which he had smashed into a hundred fragments, I understood to the accompaniment of "Croppies, lie down!" It was not the soul of man but the savagery of a hunted animal that glared at me through the windows of his eyes. He cowered in a corner, facing me in rage and terror. I did not know from one moment to another but that he would spring on me. I was unnerved. And as a nervous man gets a paroxysm of courage, I diverted his attention for a moment, then knocked the razor from his hands, and in a moment his madness ceased, and he became only a maudlin idiot. We got him back to bed, and I called the nurse.

"Mr. Leviston has been supplied with drink. You have neglected your charge, and I must report you to the doctor in the morning."

"He had no drink whilst I was with him, but——"

"Your hours are from 8 A.M. to 10 P.M. You are responsible for him during that time."

"I was called away," she said deprecatingly.

"By whom?"

"I dispute your right to catechise me. You are not my superior."

"Quite right," I said. "But, all the same, I shall report to the doctor."

Another weary, desperate night rolled on to the dawn. Sleepless, nervous, haunted by spectres of his own imagination, Leviston had a dreadful night. Every five minutes he pleaded piteously for brandy, which I had to refuse. He asked me to leave the room. I refused. I suspected he had drink concealed, and I found I was right. On the top of a high wardrobe I found two bottles of brandy. I brought with me some books and magazines, but, as on the previous night, there was no sleep for him, no peace for me. He was a ghastly, miserable spectacle, shaking all over with terror, the mind conjuring up all kinds of hideous things, the feeble fingers picking at the coverlet, the odour of increasing decomposition filling the room as if with a thick vapour. I was so accustomed to his seeing visions of women, spirits, demons, and being asked by him to drive them away, that I was quite unconcerned when he asked me whose were those faces at the window. I should have said that his bedroom was on the ground floor, with French windows opening into the garden, and that partly to relieve the tediousness of the night by looking up at the living and active heavens, or on the dead and slumbering earth, partly for some kind of companionship with Nature in my dreary and solitary watch, I never drew down the blinds or closed the shutters. And as the house was far in from the roadway, and sheltered not only by fir plantations but by a thick shrubbery of laurels and rhododendrons, there was little danger from the curiosity of prying eyes. Three or four times Leviston asked me whose were those faces at the window, before I began to realise that it was no longer the fantasy of delirium, for I just caught the glimpse of white faces fading into the night; and then I watched. Surely enough, in a little time, three faces peered out of the darkness, and it was easy to see that they were men, and very ugly specimens of their kind. This time, instead of vanishing quickly, they pressed their faces to the window, and stared steadily into the apartment. Leviston was in an agony of terror; I was unnerved and trembling.

"For God's sake, Austin, send them away, and get me a little brandy."

As if they were past masters in the art of keeping our feelings on the rack, the faces came, looked, and vanished with steady persistence every quarter of an hour, until at last the bright idea dawned on me that I should have drawn down the blinds when first they appeared. This I did now noiselessly. Leviston was not reassured.

"They'll come in now!" he said. They tried to force the door open, and if they persevered they would have succeeded. But, dreading the effect of violence on the poor creature upstairs, I went quietly to the door, turned the key in the lock, and when they came around next time, I flung the door open, and said blandly—

"Come in, gentlemen!"

Fred Oliver, with two rough-looking fellows, in

the dress of mechanics, stepped into the room, after some hesitation and careful scrutiny as if they dreaded some trap. Oliver did not recognise me, although he looked keenly at me. The others awaited his orders.

"I have let you in," said I, "although I cannot conjecture what business you have with this poor invalid. But I beg that you will cause no disturbance, for there is a sick lady upstairs."

"You mean his wife, Gwen—Mrs. Leviston?"

"I do. She has been ailing for some time, and is now in charge of a nurse. I am the only man in the house."

"And a pretty specimen of a man you are to open the door at two o'clock to three—well—anything."

All this time Leviston was moving and muttering in his bed, looking in abject terror at the three visitors. He did not know what to expect; but his mind was haunted with untold terrors of the secret societies.

"Ask them to go away, Austin," he said, "and leave me in peace."

Oliver went over and leaned his arms deliberately on the brass railings of the bed, looking intently at the wretched man, who, by a peculiar fascination, kept his eyes fixed on his tormentor. They continued thus gazing at one another for a long time. Then Oliver drew deliberately a bottle from his pocket. He held it up against the light, shook it, uncorked it, poured its contents into a wineglass, and held the glass mockingly towards Leviston. Leviston's eyes glistened, and he held out his hand.

"I thought so," said Oliver, and he threw off the contents of the glass. He filled another. Leviston's eyes shone like those of an enraged tiger. Oliver held the glass towards him, drew near, put the glass to Leviston's lips, and spilled it to the last drop on the counterpane. The poor wretch dipped his fingers in the fluid, and sucked them with avidity.

" If I thought I would have given you that gratification," said Oliver, " I would have thrown the liquor out of the window."

Leviston had the corner of the counterpane in his mouth and was sucking it eagerly. His terror had departed.

Oliver filled another glass. " Let the poor devil alone," muttered one of the men; " let him die in peace ! "

Oliver held up the glass steadily between his fingers.

"Leviston," said he, " you are going down to hell slowly, too slowly for my taste. A speech and a toast before you go ! For five long years I have been dreaming of to-night. I have thought of it amongst all the nameless horrors of penal servitude. Revenge—on—you has been the mainstay of my life. For you have made me what I am—a returned convict——"

" Hush, Oliver ! " said one of his companions hastily, " you are going too far ! "

"Yes," said Oliver, unheeding, " you have made me what I am. Little did you think when you sentenced poor devils like myself to imprisonment what you were doing—that you were changing men into fiends to pursue you, and torment society. When I got up with aching limbs from my straw bed in the morning, I thought of you. When I dragged, yoked like a beast, the heavy granite from the quarries, I sang out curses of you. When my fingers bled from the oakum, I flung the blood into your face. I choked down every insult offered by brutal warders, that my time might be shortened wherein I could face you. When I was locked in, like a tiger or a leopard, into my cage at five o'clock on a summer evening, and saw the long streamers of yellow light shining on my bars, and thought of all the pleasant things the sun was shining upon —green fields, laughing waters, children at play in the meadows—you, about to dress for your sumptuous dinner, I swallowed my despair in hope of once seeing you again. And here you are, and here am I—the convict face to face with the roué and the profligate. Which has got the best of the bargain? You brute, I would face another five years rather than be reduced to such a condition as you are in! Why, you stink of the grave——"

"Look here, Oliver," said one of the men, "you are going too far. Let the poor devil alone. You've had your revenge!"

"Have I?" said Oliver. "Well, true, I won't break my word. But the toast. Fill his glass, you fellow!" he said, turning to me.

"No," said I, "do it yourself: but I may tell you you're a coward and a bully to torment the poor man."

"Hello! my fine fellow," said he, "who are you?"

He came over, and at once recognised me.

"Ah!" said he contemptuously, "I should have known you—the valet and hanger-on of the Oliver family. I'll deal with you another time."

"Any time you please," I said. "Were it not for your poor sister, it should be now."

He paused, as if the allusion to his sister had touched him. But it was only for a moment. He filled a glass of brandy, and put it in Leviston's trembling hands, who had to put the glass on the coverlet and hold it with both hands.

"Here's the toast! In a few days you will be in hell. When there, may the thirst of Dives burn your tongue, and may there never be a drop of water in heaven or earth to quench it! Drink!"

The poor wretch held the glass to his lips, but spilled the whole of it on the counterpane, and Oliver, holding his own glass steadily, lightly touched it with his lips, and shot the remainder, like a stream of fire, between the eyes of Leviston. The latter shrieked, and the men left the room. When outside Oliver turned to me and said—

"Not a word of to-night's visit to any one. We shall be lingering around, for we have business to do. Where is my sister's room?"

I pointed overhead. He took off his hat, showing a cropped head, kissed his hand lightly to his sister, and vanished into the darkness. I closed the door firmly and went back to Leviston. His eyes were red and inflamed, and must have been torturing him. But he was trying to squeeze some drops of liquor out of his soiled night-shirt. It was pitiful.

I told Sister Philippa, when we met in the morning, that Leviston had got drink again.

"You're bound to mention it to the doctor," she said, "but I think I understand."

When the doctor came and found Leviston so bad, he was furious. The nurse was summoned. She admitted she had been called away from duty by Mrs. Oliver, who took her place. What happened then she knew not. But a dark suspicion crossed my mind: and I remembered that Sister Philippa had foretold a tragedy.

I think it was about twelve o'clock the same day that I was again suddenly summoned. The doctor had gone for some time; and when the nurse, alarmed enough now, called me, she told me that Mr. Leviston had escaped. Mrs. Oliver had had a swoon that morning, had summoned the nurse hastily, and when the latter returned Leviston had fled. He had not gone far. He was standing on the gravelled walk outside the rhododendron hedge; he had a battered silk hat on his head, his boots were hanging open over unstockinged feet, his clothes were all tossed and unbuttoned, the sleeves of his night-shirt, not particularly clean, were hanging down over his very dirty hands. And with all the manners of an accomplished and courtly gentleman he was speaking to three young ladies and a rather elderly gentleman, who looked like their father. The ladies were crimson with shame and agony, there was a scarcely perceptible smile around their father's mouth, for the more than Chesterfield manners of Leviston made his appearance all the more comical. In a few minutes Mrs. Oliver appeared, looking remarkably well after her swoon. Even that hardened woman was shocked at the sight.

"Good God!" she said, "the Annerleys! We are for ever disgraced!"

Whilst she spoke, we saw Mr. Annerley take out his purse and hand some coins to Leviston. The visitors took their leave, Leviston accompanying them to the gate. He lifted his dingy hat with the air of a prince. The Annerleys departed; but when I strolled leisurely down to the garden gate to bring back my prisoner, he was nowhere to be seen.

I searched every public-house in the suburbs that day, and it was only in the evening I discovered him, perfectly unconscious, in some tavern called the "Sailor's Rest." He had come there early in the day, the barmaid said, with three men, they had called for pen and paper, there was a great deal of drink, the men departed a little after mid-day, leaving Leviston to command unlimited quantities of brandy. I had but little doubt that these three men were our nocturnal visitors of the previous night, but for many reasons I kept my counsel. Sister Philippa would have been my confidant, but she had been summoned back to hospital.

I ran down for an hour's chat with the medicos.

I entered the captain's room as usual. He was unusually grave and silent.

After some pauses, which were exceedingly embarrassing, he said—

"That was rather a shabby trick, Austin, you and Sutton played me."

"I am quite unconscious," I replied, "of anything that could bear that interpretation."

"You can pretend so," he said, "but it was clumsy, besides being dishonourable."

"Look here, Helston," I said, "I am under tremendous obligations to you, and therefore I cannot resent what you are saying, as I would in another. Once more, what are you referring to?"

"I refer," he said warmly, "to a put-up job between you and Sutton to prevent me from——"

"From what?" I said anxiously.

"Well, from expressing my feelings towards Miss Bellamy," he blurted out. "And I did not think that any man could force me into a confession of that kind."

"Now," I said, "would you kindly tell me particulars?"

He was choking, poor fellow, with excitement, but after a few moments he composed himself and said—

"I shouldn't mind myself, but it was an infernal shame to concoct the vile story about Miss Bellamy, that she had been a ballad-singer."

I saw what Cal had done.

"Do you know what I shall do, Austin?" Helston continued. "I shall tell the whole story to Miss Bellamy, and let her know who her friends are."

"All this time," I said with commiseration for him, for I saw he was deeply affected, "you are quietly forgetting to tell how I am implicated in the matter."

" Why," he said indignantly, " how can you deny it ? It's as clear as noonday that you are attached to Miss Bellamy. I am afraid it is also clear that I have not successfully concealed my feelings. What more reasonable than to suppose that you and Sutton concocted that story to turn me away, and have the field clear to yourself ? "

" It is not a very honourable suggestion, Helston," I said, " and coming from any one else I think it would mean a permanent rupture of all our friendship. But I am very sorry for you. As for myself, a thought of Miss Bellamy, except as a very noble woman, whose friendship was an honour to me, never crossed my mind."

He looked at me incredulously. " Listen," I said, " and I'll tell you the whole history of our relations."

He listened patiently as I detailed all that happened since I knew the Grinder and his sister. He was much affected. He continued pacing up and down the room.

" Then," he said at last, " there is no obstacle in the way. I may address Miss Bellamy ? "

" Assuredly," I said, " so far as I am concerned. And if I can say a good word for you I will. But be prepared for disappointment—Helen Bellamy will never leave her brother."

He shook hands with me warmly, asked pardon for his suspicions, and I went back to my weary work pitying him.

# CHAPTER IX

## SHADOWED

Show his eyes, and grieve his heart ;
Come like shadows, so depart.
                                        —MACBETH.

THE attention of the doctor, and the steady abstin-
ence from drink, brought Leviston back from delirium
and the grave.  But the seeds of death were in him.
He recovered his intellect, and became once more
interested in life, and although he never resumed his
professional duties, he went about his garden in-
valided but comparatively happy.  He begged of
me to remain with him.  " I won't call you my
warder," he said, " but my amanuensis."  And
partly because he had asked me, and the good old
doctor pressed me earnestly, and partly because
I had no chance of getting a more easy or lucrative
position, I gladly remained.  We had slipped into
October, and it was a lovely month.  Not wet and
slushy and making an ugly mess of the harvest of
the leaves, but dry, calm, solemn, letting all the
dying beauty of the year show itself without hind-
rance.  I found that Leviston, after he had recovered
his senses, was a man of much refinement and
culture, keenly alive to the aspects of Nature, and
gifted with a very shrewd discernment of the world,
and the many little tragedies and comedies that
passed under his eyes.  And now his illness and his
weakness made him very charitable and tender of
thought to men and questions on which he was wont

to hold decided opinions. There is no better teacher than affliction, if we except, perhaps, sin. And it appeared as if all the violent antagonisms and prejudices in which he had been educated had vanished during his affliction and left a more sober and tolerant cast of thought behind them. Very often during these mild October days, as we sat under the thick hedges and watched the deepening of the colours on shrub and tree, and caught at a stray wrinkled leaf that was fluttering to the ground, we spoke of many of those solemn questions that alas ! as yet are subjects of controversy amongst us. He had a wonderfully keen appreciation of the points of a debate—would turn and twist and torture sayings and admissions into appearances that were never intended. This, it appears, was an old habit, caught up during the years when he was the keenest debater in the College Historical Society, and was more deeply interested than in later years in questions of religion or those that touched on religion. From these conversations I understood that amongst the younger generations of Trinity students there had always been a strong inquisitive spirit, as of young travellers who, landing in an unknown country, have eyes and ears open to events and persons whose interest fades on closer acquaintance.

" It would surprise you," he used to say, " the things we used to talk of there. There is an idea abroad that Trinity men are occupied solely in preparation for College sports and cricket, and use their leisure time in making flour balls to be used on civilians at Vice-regal processions. That's not the case. At least, a knot of fellows in my time used to thresh out every question, social, religious, and political, that turned up in the history of the day. And we had to read, and we did read harder for these debates than for our degree. Why, you'll hardly believe it of an old battered roué, like myself, but I actually grew immersed in your theology: I was led into it by reading all about that Tractarian movement in England. The fellows used to call me a 'Puseyite.' And as I went on, I used to feel your religion striking me, as with strong blows, revelation after revelation rising up before me and smiting me with surprise and sometimes with terror; but this all passed away when we had to face the world; and let me say, your own men prevented my ever becoming a Catholic, even if my interests did not prevent me. For when I asked some of them about these awful questions, they laughed, and said they had no time to trouble about such things, that one religion was as good as another, &c.; and they were no more interested about their faith than about Buddha or Confucius. I remember well one day speaking to a leading Catholic about the Tractarian movement. You know it had an inexpressible fascination for me—those men, some of them exalted dignitaries, with fine titles and fine livings, reading themselves onward to what they believed to be the light; and then deliberately breaking up their homes—and, mind you, an English rectory is the highest achievement of civilisation, the most perfect centre of culture and refinement in the world—and casting themselves and their families into a condition of abject poverty—all this seemed to me the perfection of heroism, and I used to ask myself whether, after all, there was not something in your Church that could exercise such irresistible fascination. But, to return, this day I spoke to my Catholic friend about these things; and, like all young fools, I was quite enthusiastic, and I said, if I had the courage, I would face the scorn of the world and become a Catholic myself. He listened as if I were talking an unknown language; and then he told me he had never heard of Tractarians, he knew that Newman had been in Dublin, and had written some books; but beyond that he could not follow. His indifference cooled my enthusiasm. And here I was placed in a dilemma. My Protestant friends, like myself, agitated and anxious, and restless in their inquiries about faith; my Catholic friends cool and indifferent, and absolutely uninterested in their Church or faith. Whither was I to turn? Then I said, it's all the same, and I flung the trouble by. Then I found that with us religion is a question, not of dogmas or beliefs, but of caste. We are opposed to you Papists, not because of your faith, but because you are the helots, and we the masters—you are Irish, we Cromwellians; you, the conquered, we, the conquerors; and nothing on earth can change our relations to each other, except the extirpation of one class or another."

"That's a hard saying," I replied. "Why cannot we get on together?"

"Because we cannot lose our traditions or change our natures. Because you are helots, and you bear the brand in every movement, physical or spiritual. Because, though we are sometimes attracted to you by many excellent qualities, your servility always repels us. And we hold you in the palms of our hands. Every office in the country worth holding is with us. Sometimes we give you a tide-waiter-ship, or some obscure railway station, as a 'sop to Cerberus'; but the control of the army, the banks, the postal and telegraph services, the railway interests are with us: and you cannot take them from us. But to return, I never yet met a Protestant who was not anxious to talk religion, nor a Catholic who was not anxious to avoid it. Why?"

"Because we are so secure of our religion, it does not interest us. You know there must be doubt in order to create interest."

He laughed. "I don't agree with you there. But there is something in what you say. We are

P

perpetually tortured by misgivings: you are at rest.
But why should you not be interested about us?"

"Well, to tell the truth, we are too delicate to
broach such questions. For notwithstanding all that
you have said, we are a thousand times more tolerant
of you, than you of us."

"Of course. *Odisse quem læseris.* We cannot
help it. But you could often help us—nay, I will
go farther, you could often convert us, if you cared.
Your indifference makes us unbelievers. Why, only
that I have been a brute, that little wife of mine
would have made me a Papist long ago. I married
her because she was innocent, and I—too experienced; she was an *ingenue*, and I, alas! knew good
from evil. But here she comes to seek me."

I rose from the seat as Gwendoline approached.
I had not seen her since her marriage. This was
her first day, since her grave illness, in the open air.
She was white as marble, moved languidly and with
difficulty, and when she came near, I noticed that
pathetic little mark of trouble or of age—a few gray
hairs. Leviston also rose and went to meet her,
and conducted her to the seat with the deference he
would have paid a princess. I would have gone
away, but she motioned me to be seated.

"I am so glad to see you downstairs once more,
dearest," Leviston said.

She laid one white, transparent hand on his, and
leaned her head against his shoulder.

The little confiding gesture touched him deeply,
and I saw his eyes fill with tears.

On the pretext of finding some rugs and shawls,
I went away.

Now, during the latter days of September, and
the opening days of October, I was haunted by a
curious sensation. I felt wherever I went I was
followed, "shadowed," as detectives would call it.
If I entered the city, I was painfully conscious that

somewhere in the distance, a figure was stealthily watching me. When I looked, no one was to be seen. I argued boldly against the sensation. I attributed it to the fright I received the night Fred Oliver and his companions visited the house. The threats which he held out, the sinister hints he gave, the evil looks of his comrades, the suspicion that some secret society was behind them, perhaps created this delusion, as I regarded it. But I could not shake it off. A few times I detected some ill-visaged fellow following me, and sneaking down a back street if I turned to face him. Once, a young Dublin *gamin*, with a bundle of newspapers slung over his shoulder, stopped me and asked, " Please, sir, are you called Geoffrey Austin ?" and when I would have detained him for further inquiries he fled. I thought one or two old applewomen, whom I chanced to know, used to look curiously at me as I passed. And altogether I was very miserable, although for the first time I had a comfortable situation, and a prospect of being lifted above poverty. One day, the very last day of September I think, as I turned a corner into Sackville Street, I thought I recognised a familiar figure standing before one of the bookshops. It was a figure of an old priest, the shoulders bent and head stooped. A few gray hairs straggled down over the collar of a coat that was becoming rapidly green. I stood near. The figure passed on to a tobacconist's shop, and continued gazing there with the same unconscious scrutiny. After a little time he left off gazing there, and unheeding the stream of people that swept by him, and who smiled or jested as they saw him, he lingered before a photographer's shop, and bent the same unconscious gaze on portraits of professional beauties, actresses, and the like. He seemed to be looking for some face which he would be glad to recognise, and to be absorbed in the pursuit of it.  After a long interval he turned, and, his back still towards me, he passed with a slow and weary gait along the crowded streets.  I dismissed the idea that it was my old guardian, and passed on to my usual work ; but the feeling of being haunted and pursued never quite left me until the gloom of Christmas had come and gone, and the purple and yellow crocuses were peeping under the hedgerows, and the larch was hanging its silver tassels, and the primulas were starring the gardens ; and from the dark recesses of some thick-set hedge, or from the topmost spray of ash and elm, the thrushes were tolling out their joy-bells, and telling the world that spring had come, and that the time for nesting and mating was at hand.  Then, too, the gloom lifted from my soul, and life took a new aspect, for nature and we are close akin, and she puts her moods upon us, and touches quite different chords when she sends the drip, drip of her rain, or the keen arrows of her sunshine.

But my employer (I was about to call him patron) was fading visibly.  Swollen feet and puffy eyes told their own tale, even to unprofessional eyes, and he, too, knew that his days were to be as the cloud that vanisheth, or the flax that is consumed by the fire.  He made no spiritual preparation, except by asking me to read for him occasionally all those texts of Scripture whose burden is that all flesh is as grass.  It was a consolation to the dying man to know that humanity was dying with him, and that he was but one of that melancholy procession that is moving on, with songs or sighs, to the same grim portals of death.  But he had some thought for his wife, and he said to me more than once, and once, to my intense chagrin, in Mrs. Oliver's hearing, that he was disposed to change his will.  " Of course," he said, " I have left her a jointure that will place her in comparative comfort ; but I should

like to do more to make reparation for the past."
However, the days came and went. Gwendoline
grew somewhat better, as if the dying strength of
her husband had passed with new life into her.
And she was unspeakably tender to him, all her
beautiful, girlish, compassionate nature wasting and
exhausting itself in feeble attempts to save him,
which only resulted in making him happy. And he
was very happy those soft spring days, and he
thought that, after all, God's world was very beautiful, only that men mar it so foully. His better
nature came upwards and dominated him, and he
was once again the happy student, troubled only
with the abstractions, or stimulated by the inspiration of great ideas ; and his troubled manhood fell
away from him, as a garment is flung aside by the
wearer, who seeks not notice but rest. Once or
twice she delicately broached the subject of religion
to him. But he only shook his head, and said with
a smile—"Too late ! too late ! I must sport the
acacia to the end."

"It is curious," he said to me another day, "on
what little threads of circumstances our destinies
hang. One word would have placed me on the
right track when I was going wrong. But, at the
parting of the ways, I took my own course, and got
derailed, and my life and soul have been wrecked."

We used to put him out into the sunshine of an
exceedingly mild February. He would sit for hours,
wrapped in shawls and rugs, and holding pitifully
his swollen hands to the light and heat. Sometimes
his wife, sometimes I, would read for him. He was
very grateful. All the best of his nature came up-
ward as the physical frame sank into decay, and the
hitherto ugly lineaments of his character became
moulded and softened into accents of beauty and
light. Mrs. Oliver never came near him.

The attitude of this woman was remarkable during

these days of trial. The master passion of her life
had been to get into society, to be noticed by the
high and honourable. She would have made any
sacrifice to be able to show certain visiting cards, or
to be seen in any public assemblage in certain distinguished company. I dare say she was not an
intrinsically bad woman, but her ruling passion so
dominated her entire character as to make her minor
virtues invisible. The sacrifices she was prepared
to make to gratify her ambition may be judged by
the fact that she had brought about the marriage of
her only daughter with one of the most notorious
profligates of Dublin. She was not successful, even
after her Iphigenia had been offered up. The gods
were against her. The society into which she had
hoped to enter shut their doors remorselessly against
her. A few people, of more or less distinction, left
their cards, carefully handed in by their footmen ;
but no feet ever crossed the threshold of her door,
or ruffled the soft plush of her carpets, except, indeed, those feet which had long since cast off their
dust against the world, for the world repudiated and
rejected them. Many a weary evening did Mrs.
Oliver dress herself carefully, drill her servants, put
every article of dainty furniture into perfect order,
and place her silver tea equipage where she could
easily reach it from her couch by the fire, waiting
for the knock that never came, and straining her
ears for the step on the gravel that never reached
them. It was infinite fun to her servants, who
hated her, to watch and mimic her every gesture ;
and sometimes, I am afraid, they used to ply that
knocker for the purpose of seeing how quickly Mrs.
Oliver would start up from her lounger where she
was enjoying a quiet siesta, to don the habit of pro-
priety, and put on the dignity that beseemed a lady
whose son-in-law sat on the magisterial bench.

" Who was that, Sarah ? " she would ask, when,

as her heart sank, she heard the servant's step going back to the kitchen without a message for her.

" The butcher's boy, mum."

" Oh ! I thought it was Lady Sypher. I expected her to-day. Mind, Sarah, if her Ladyship calls there must be no delay in answering."

" Yes, mum."

And Sarah, stuffing her apron into her mouth, would play the little comedy for her sisters down-stairs. Alas ! and we all think we can deceive those private detectives, who read our very thoughts, and have the whole panorama of our lives and actions open before their keen eyes, when we imagine we have rolled it up and put it away even from our own vision.

It is not difficult to imagine how these repeated disappointments soured her character and embittered her relations towards her daughter and Leviston. The former paid the penalty of her sin in listening all day to the reproaches of her mother, and all night to the maudlin madness of her husband. In the beginning tears came to her relief, but after a little while that safety-valve of overwrought nerves failed her, and she had to bear the rack and the screw of reproach and profanity without external relief. Even the slight consolation of her very limited friendships was denied her. With all the vulgar pride of her class, Mrs. Oliver declined to return the call of Agnes and Hubert Deane, thus cutting off one source of comfort for the young wife. No one else came. And often poor Gwendoline had to lay her weary head on the shoulder of some poor servant, and pour into her sympathetic ear the facts of her sorrows ; but the causes she had to keep locked up in the secret cabinets of her own soul. And the consolations of religion were denied her. She thought she dared not approach the Sacra-ments, so great was her sin ; even after a little

while, when her health began to give way, she was
easily persuaded by her mother to remain away from
Mass on Sundays.   And all the time her conscience,
never stifled, but gifted apparently with infinite
powers of torture, upbraided her, and the memory
of her school days, and of the dear old Abbey, came
to smite her almost to the verge of despair.   Little
wonder that under the terrible torture from without
—the withering sarcasms of her mother, her young
tender innocence brought into daily contact with
loathsome vice, openly revealed in her husband's
character, and the self-accusations of conscience—
that her health should give way, and she should
become what Sister Philippa found her—a physical
and mental wreck.   The approaching death of Leviston awakened a new interest in her soul, for a
woman's tenderness, if not love, lasts under the
most searching influences; the secret visit of a
priest brought balm to a wounded soul, and she
revived so far as to move about and make easy the
downward steps of her husband.   But the mother
never came near them, never spoke to them, but
moved around with a certain light of triumph in
her eyes that was to me quite inexplicable.   It is
hardly necessary to say that during my attendance
on Leviston her attitude to me was one of secret
hostility, thinly disguised by the faintest veil of
politeness.   She regarded me as an interloper, a
secret agent of the doctor, a spy on her own actions.
As for me, I carefully avoided her, and when I met
her, without abating one jot my own independence,
I treated her with a courtesy from which all deference was carefully extracted, and for the rest, bore
her scarcely concealed dislike with perfect equanimity.   Why she should triumph I do not know.
She would suffer, I thought, a rude awakening when
she found her son-in-law had left a mere jointure to
her daughter and absolutely nothing to herself.

But she went on smiling as Leviston neared the end. It came more suddenly than we thought.

I had been down to Helston's in the afternoon, especially for the purpose of reading Cal a lecture on his chronic laziness. The exam. was coming on; he was quite unprepared, and Helston asked me down to pitch into him in his presence. This was no easy task. Cal's imperturbable good-humour put aside easily the volleys of abuse and entreaty which Helston and I fired at him. He sat coolly on the bed, alternately twisting and smoking cigarettes, his eyes twinkling, his mouth twitching with suppressed fun. When we had grown tired of abusing him, he said—

"Look here, you two fellows. You have wasted valuable eloquence on a worthless subject. Goff, you have spoken to me like a father; Helston, you have spoken to me as a sister." Helston looked daggers at him, but he continued imperturbably, "Now, what do you complain of? That I am not abandoning my sphere of usefulness and honour here to become a money-grubbing physician. You take low views of life. Now, look at me here. I am leading a useful and honourable existence. I keep these fellows in perpetual good humour. I am secretary to Helston. I am 'guide, philosopher, and friend' to Bryce. I put him to bed when he is hopelessly drunk. I bring him his soda in the morning. I am useful to Forrester, Gallwey, &c., in other ways. I am the only solvent student here; and that's well known at 'Uncle's.' I am the confidant of all their love affairs. I write their love-letters. If anything is up, it is at once: 'Where's Sutton? Where's that damned Sutton? Did any one see Sutton?' I am not too vain or proud of all this. It is honourable, and as such I am satisfied. Now, again, I am the special favourite at the hospitals. The patients would rather see me than

fifty doctors. They admit that I am better than
Fellows' or Easton's for toning up. Why, I got a
fellow the other day to break an internal abscess by
laughing. Noakes could never get at it. I am the
favourite of the nurses. When they get an awful
wigging in the morning from the doctors, especially
from that masher, Esmonde, because some bandage
is crooked, I sing for them, and we have a waltz up
and down the ward, and, presto! the poor things
are all right again. I am not boasting, and am
not proud. But what do you fellows want me to
become? Take out my degrees? And then? go
down and hunt for a dispensary! That is, try and
cut out some poor devil with a wife and family who
wants £120 a year to buy bread for them, and a
decent bonnet for his wife; plot and scheme, and
cajole a lot of county gentry and farmers to get the
wretched thing. Then, curse at every poor woman
who has a pain in her back, and who drags me out
of bed at four o'clock in the morning, and spend the
rest of my existence in spitting over the bridge,
smoking bad cigars, and reading French novels.
No! gentlemen, thank you for your eloquence.
You may become 'successes' in life if you like,
I'd rather become, by Jove! I would, like Charlie,
a preacher!"

"There's no use, Austin," said Helston, turning
to me, "he's incorrigible. Some day the gov. will
strike, and then Sutton will go down to Bally-
hilane, or Toorenadrimm, to become an apothe-
cary's assistant, and help in poisoning half the
country."

"Poor old Helston!" said Cal commiseratingly.
"No, if all comes to all, Bryce and I will open a
liquor shop, and call it the 'Student's Home.' By
the way, what have you got for all your pounding,
and, Goff, my fine philosopher, what has the world
given you for all your learning?"

"I see it is no use," said I; "Helston, Cal was always dreaming of a lunatic asylum, and he'll wind up there."

"Ah," said the imperturbable, "you touched me now on my weak point. I have no interest in the lower animalisms. I look higher to the imperial seat of thought, where the soul of man sits enthroned. I *am* studying—and studying not bones, nor tissues, nor muscles, but the brain. I am deep in psychology and cerebral anatomy. Don't talk to me of dispensaries, or hospitals, or such like. Give me the place where men cease to reason, and are happy; where they cease to desire and are content. I want to meet the Emperor of Mexico, and the Queen of Sheba, and the man who has something hanging to his nose, and the man who has a watch ticking in his brain. I leave the lower animal to you, Helston, aud your comrades. I shall never rest content until I shall issue the standard classic on mental operations, and see the name of Sutton immortalised."

"You are an attractive little jackass," said Helston. "Go out, I want to say a word to Austin."

Cal winked, first with his right eye, then with his left, and departed.

Helston walked up and down the narrow room.

"Have you spoken of that matter, Austin?" he said rather tremulously.

"Not yet," I replied, "I had no opportunity."

"I suppose," he said, "I am a fool. But who can help being a fool under such circumstances? Now, I know I have nothing to offer Miss Bellamy, and the whole thing looks hazy enough. But if I thought she would condescend to think kindly of me, and to wait, just to wait for a year or two, until I had cut my way to something, why, I'd have an object to work for, and I would work."

I was silent.

"You think unfavourably of the matter, Austin," he said nervously.

"At the grave risk of offending you," I replied, "I think, as I told you, that Miss Bellamy's ideas do not run at all in the direction of marriage.  She is deeply attached to her brother, and will not leave him."

"Look here, Austin," he said, "I look upon you as a friend and you won't deceive me.  Now, I cannot face a direct refusal from Miss Bellamy; but if I could be assured positively that there was no chance there, I would try to get away, and distract myself."

"Well, perhaps," I said in dismay, "I can ascertain something for you; but, you know, my dear Helston, you are placing me in a deucedly awkward position."

"I know, I know," he said hastily, "but I depend implicitly on your honour."

"I'll get some information immediately," I said, "but will you promise me one thing?"

"I will.  What is it?"

"Well, look here," I replied, "I have had few friends, and I cannot afford to lose even one.  Will you promise me that whatever is the result, it will not terminate my friendship with you?"

He grasped my hand warmly.  "I promise," he said.

It was late when I got back to Leviston's.  I was now relieved from night duty since Leviston had grown so much better.  But I made it a duty always to see him before retiring.  The lights were still burning in hall and kitchen.  The servants had not retired.  I went straight to his room.  A lamp was burning on the table.  By its light I saw that a change had taken place.  His head lay back upon the pillow, his eyes were open, his arm hung down by the side of the bed. I ran over hastily, shook him violently, flung water upon him. All in vain. He was dead. I rang the bell violently. The servants flocked in.

"Call Mrs. Oliver," I said.

She came in her dressing gown, apparently angry for being disturbed. She looked slightly shocked. A servant was looking at a phial. I took it from her hands. It was marked—*Chloral.* I bent down. The lips of the dead man exhaled the unmistakable odour.

"Some one will have to explain how this came here," I said, looking at Mrs. Oliver.

# CHAPTER X

## AT GLASNEVIN

Thus he delivered his message, this dexterous writer of letters,
Did not embellish the theme, nor array it in beautiful phrases :
But came straight to the point, and blurted it out like a school-boy :
Even the captain himself could hardly have said it more bluntly.
—MILES STANDISH.

I WAS now in a desperate fix.  I was experiencing
the painful sensation of having made a foolish
engagement, and of realising too late the vast difficulties that loom up in the process of fulfilment.  I
should now either act dishonourably and break my
promise to Helston, or face the possible displeasure
of Helen Bellamy.  It might be more.  Perhaps she
would dismiss me in contempt.  This I could not
bear to think of.  Since the first moment I saw her
at Alfred's, when she came in to us, wild, young
students, and looked so grand and queenly, but then
thawed out into friendship towards us, down to this
day, when I had learned to esteem her and reverence
her more intelligently, I saw only the gradual and
uniform unfolding of nature, made beautiful by its
intelligence and charity.  I often wondered which
did I admire most—her marvellous, well-developed,
well-fed intellect, touching and subliming every
subject of human interest, or the gracious way in
which she would step down from her lofty place
and make the vision of her beauty and intellect less
seraphic, but more beloved, in its familiarity with
the commonplaces of our poor lives.  She was so
solemn, yet so gentle : so austere, yet so kind : so

great, and yet so lowly: that I could not determine whether she would let the hidden fires of anger flash out and scorch me, or whether she would take me pityingly and smile away my awkwardness and presumption. And Alfred, how will he take it? Will he be insulted and refuse to see me again, or will he laugh in his own quiet way at our folly? Yet it was a terrible risk. If I were to be expelled from that sacred place, that had been more than home to me, I should indeed be houseless and a wanderer. I should not have faced the risk. A hundred times I was going back to Helston to withdraw from my engagement: but I dreaded meeting him and exciting his worst suspicions. I must go forward, and may the gods help me.

It was the night, I think, after Leviston's funeral that, with a heavy heart and much misgivings, I touched the bell at Alfred Bellamy's. Alfred himself opened the door and took me into his den. We talked about Leviston, his death, his funeral, and many other indifferent topics. I was hoping that some expression of his would give me an opening to explain my mission; but after some remarks he noticed that I was unusually silent and distracted, and said, in his own kind way—

"You must see Helen; she would be displeased if you went away without seeing her. Mrs. Deane is here."

We went into the drawing-room, where the ladies were sitting, and no criminal ever went to execution with more forebodings of despair than those which now weighed on me like a grievous load. I tried to assume a manner and a tone, which at once were recognised as quite foreign to me: and I think I made a few irrelevant remarks which made the uncharitable Mrs. Deane bend her brows and look at me suspiciously. At last, heaven inspired the remark—

" I hope all your medical friends are doing well, and not over-working themselves for examination."

I stammered something about Cal.

" He looks like a student who would be fond of desultory reading, but unable to bend his mind to one task."

This opened the subject : and I launched forth eloquently in praise of Helston.

" I never knew a better friend : all the fellows look up to him, he is so sensible, and far-thinking, and true. A silent, self-contained man, who does not allow his words to run away with him : but is always ready at a pinch. And he has such splendid resources. He thinks and acts together, not hastily, you know, but so firmly that the one follows the other quite naturally and fits in infallibly. I never saw any one like him. So strong and tender. Why, he nursed a sick boy all through last winter, bringing him into his own room, and supplying all necessaries from his own purse. And he has a splendid future before him. You know, he belongs to one of the County L—— families; and he has taken up the study of medicine just because he happens to have scientific tastes. Possibly he will go down and take up his position as a landed proprietor ; or, as so many young fellows do, he will go into the army or navy for a few years ; and then, when he has seen the world, he will return and take up his ancestral property. But, whatever he does, he is a noble fellow : and I am quite thankful for the illness which brought me to make his acquaintance."

I put myself quite out of breath with this eulogium of my friend. But the ladies looked puzzled. Mrs. Deane was leaning both arms on the back of a chair and looking at me curiously.

" H'm," she said at last, " I did not know that young Sutton was such a paragon of perfection.

He always struck me as a good-natured, wild young fellow."

I stared at her with open mouth.

" I have not been talking of Sutton," I said, "'twas Helston I was talking about. I am very fond of poor Cal, but I would not think of comparing the two men."

Then a great light broke in on Mrs. Deane's mind, and her eyes fairly sparkled with laughter. Helen was silent and grave.

" Go on," said Mrs. Deane cruelly.

" I was saying," I stammered, " that you know Cal is not equal to Helston at all. Helston is head and shoulders above us all. He understands everything, you know. He is the only fellow that takes an intelligent interest in our little gatherings here, and I have heard him speak with great enthusiasm of all that we fellows owe to Miss Bellamy."

" Very good, Mr. Austin," said Agnes Deane, "go on. I am following you with interest."

Helen was looking from one to the other, as if puzzled at our strange conversation. She could not help noticing my embarrassment and the suppressed fun in Agnes Deane's eyes.

" Yes," I continued, " he thinks we are under an everlasting debt of gratitude to Miss Bellamy. He went even farther: but perhaps I should not say it?"

"Oh dear, don't be bashful, Mr. Austin. I know it is something complimentary to Miss Bellamy, and, like all ladies, she will accept a compliment gracefully."

Helen looked pained and uncomfortable.

" Well," I blurted out, " he said it was a rare privilege for us, that when Hypatia came to Dublin we should have the good fortune to be her pupils."

Helen stood up, and, saying quietly, " Pardon me," she left the room.

Agnes Deane smiled, and nodded her head sadly at me.

Q

"My God," I said, "I fear I have made an awful mess of it."

"You have," she said with emphasis. "When you bring a message of that kind again, take lessons from some woman who knows the heart of woman. But why 'didn't you speak for yourself, John'?"

I took no notice of the allusion, for I was dreadfully troubled.

"I suppose," I said, "Miss Bellamy will never speak to me again."

"It is quite probable," said my tormentor, "you have been—well, not too wise; and he—that is, Mr. Helston, not too courageous."

"I told him," I said, "that it was hopeless, that Miss Bellamy would never marry, that she would never part from her brother. He suspected that all that was a ruse, and that I, God help me, had some designs in that direction. Why, I'd as soon think of proposing to St. Teresa. I have been an awful fool. What am I to do?"

"Well, the first thing is to let matters rest just where they are. Possibly Helen did not understand the drift of your argument——"

"God bless you," said I.

"But I think she did. She looked awfully solemn."

"I did not notice that," I said in despair.

"Well, perhaps not. And of course, like myself, she thought it was of Sutton that you were speaking, and this did not excite suspicion."

"I hope so," I said eagerly.

"But then that unfortunate allusion to—what do you call her?"

"Hypatia," I said in dismay.

"Who was she? A classical goddess?"

"You know right well," I replied, "you are tormenting me."

"But was not this Hypatia a pagan?"

" Certainly."

" And supposed to be a sorceress ? "

" That was the assumption of an ignorant crowd."

" And wasn't there an apostate monk running after her ? "

" Yes, but——"

" Helen will never forgive you. What a dreadful and most unfortunate comparison ! "

By this time my hands were clammy with perspiration, and my forehead wet with the agony of the whole thing. I stood up to depart, shamefaced and remorseful. I took out a handkerchief and mopped my forehead. The little movement touched Agnes Deane, and she came over and said gently—

" You should have known I was but jesting. Helen will come all right in a day or so. But see Alfred before you go. But there's another matter —that will of Leviston's will be contested to the end, and you will be an important witness."

" I can only tell the truth," I said.

" Yes," she replied, " but where will the truth lead ? "

I was reckless and said " I don't care."

" Well, it will be a *cause célèbre*, and I sincerely hope that old dragon will get the worst of it."

" But what am I to say to Helston ? " I cried, thinking only of my present trouble.

" Ah, ridiculous," she replied, " you are making a mountain out of an ant heap. Don't you know this boyish fancy will pass ? "

" That's all right, Mrs. Deane, but I have to face a jealous, passionate fellow, and to tell him that my mission on his behalf has been a signal failure. How am I to do it, and bear all his unjust suspicions ? "

" The whole thing is a comical absurdity ; go, and tell the truth, however, and bear the consequences."

" I suppose it puts an end to our Attic nights ? "

" Yes, I fear so.   One of Helen's little Platonic ideas has been knocked to bits.   She thought— well, no matter.   Good-night, see Alfred, and look out for the Probate Court."

I am quite sure the judge of that court would have promptly committed me for contempt if he had heard my profane exclamation.   I closed the door ruefully on Mrs. Deane, and went in to Alfred's den. The dear fellow was as usual immersed in his favourite study.   Big star-maps lined the walls, there were two handsome globes near the fireplace, and one or two highly polished brass instruments with cogs, and screws, and wheels enough to puzzle Edison.   Alfred was smoking at perfect ease, and I found it no small trouble to bring him down from the stars.

" Look here, Alf," I said, " I'm in a tremendous fix.   Come down from the Zodiac for a moment, and try could you help me ? "

" Is it anything in a business line ? " said Alfred hesitatingly, " you know I am a child there."

" No and yes," I replied, " I have made a tremendous fool of myself; and I fear I have offended, in an unpardonable manner, Miss Bellamy."

" 'Twould take considerable proofs to convince me of that," he said.

Then I went into the whole thing, telling him all about Helston's infatuation, my foolish promise, my awkward intervention, &c.; and how I was never so sorry for anything in my life, for no power on earth could make me do anything that would be even remotely disagreeable to Miss Bellamy or himself.   He listened patiently, smoking in silence.

" It is possible," he said at last, " that the offence is not so great as you suppose.   If Helen thought that you came to make an offer of marriage on behalf of Helston, I am pretty sure she would be very angry. The thing is too absurd. And it would be especially humiliating to her. Perhaps we have been too unconventional. It is not usual to throw open a drawing-room to a number of medical or other students with whom we have had no previous acquaintance. We drifted into it, chiefly on your initiative." I winced. It was dreadfully unlike Alfred. What would Helen be?

"But it is quite possible that Helen did not understand the drift of your remarks. The flattery, and you know it was rather broad, probably annoyed her; and the comparison was not a happy one."

"It was intended to be complimentary," I said deprecatingly.

"I am quite sure. But apart from its inappropriateness, it was somewhat extravagant, and therefore offensive."

"Well," I said, "I am suffering for my benevolence and folly. But Alf, dear fellow, will you say a word for me?"

"Make your mind easy," he said, "about Helen. She is not one to remember such things very long. But we shall have to be more careful."

"But you won't cut me off, will you?"

"Oh dear no. Don't dream of such things."

"And you'll let me know when I may come again?"

"Certainly, we are not going to sacrifice the friendship of a life for a hasty word."

"God bless you," I said fervently, as I wrung his hand.

From all this it may be gleaned that I had come down from high places, and that my pedestal of pride and self-sufficiency was just now vacant. I had been learning many things lately; and my most fruitful lesson had been a certain diffidence in self, and a certain reverence for others which had hitherto been foreign to me. In a word, I was becoming humble, and therefore clear-sighted. Many things were dawning on me that I had never been able to see through the mists of pride.

With a heavy heart I went back to the house of mourning. My trunks, already packed, were in the hall. The servant handed me a letter. It was a curt dismissal from Mrs. Oliver, and a cheque. Whilst reading it, Gwendoline came into the hall and said simply—

" Mr. Austin, you are not to go. I want you to remain and put my husband's papers in order."

I showed her her mother's letter.

" Never mind," she said with some firmness, " I am mistress here. I wish you to stay."

I stayed. My work for a couple of weeks was pleasant and congenial enough. I was sole master of Leviston's library and his papers. I had plenty of leisure; and curiosity enough for the mysteries of books and the mysteries of the human heart to be engrossed almost entirely in the volumes and letters that came under my notice. It is quite true, that so far as literature was concerned, Leviston's library could hardly be called rich. There were, of course, some old classics, souvenirs and relics of college days, a few Church of England divines, such as Hooker and Taylor; but the rest of the collection consisted of French novels, ranging all the way down from the Dumases to Paul de Kock and Guy de Maupassant. There were also a few shady English novels, and that was all. The letters were more interesting. Invitations to secret Masonic meetings, crested with awful symbols, letters from high places appealing for clemency for high-class criminals, letters from rich parvenus, asking for invitations to Castle balls; and a large number of little square perfumed billets, the contents couched in most mysterious language, which only one possessing the key could decipher. These I carefully destroyed. There was one other letter which I read carefully, and which was an affirmative answer from Hubert Deane to a request for a favour.

And now, for the first time dabbling in these little historical fragments of a vanished life, I began to solve a riddle that had been puzzling me for many years. For I had often wondered, and found no answer to my wonder, why students who had consecrated the best part of their lives to the service of the Muses, or the higher service of thought itself, could at last tear themselves away from the holy seclusion of their libraries, and from the fascinations of literature and philosophy to descend from Olympian heights into the noisy and vulgar arena of political life. When I read that such a distinguished writer, whose name appeared under the highest philosophical speculations in *Mind*, or some of the Quarterlies, and whose opinion was deferred to by some of the professors of Paris or Berlin, actually appeared as a candidate for Riverstowe or Cokevalle, and saw by the daily papers that he addressed a vulgar mob, and was hissed by them, or, worse still, was applauded by the brainless followers of some parrot-cry or dishonest Shibboleth, I wondered what had made him disgusted with his books, or what had made him the victim of a momentary frenzy. And when, upborne on the shoulders of the senseless mob, he took his oath and his place in "the mother of parliaments," the same question arose, What does he see in these green benches to seduce him from his library armchair? and what does he hear in these noisy and vulgar debates to keep him away from the silence and solemnity of the world's picked and canonized sages? For, after all, there is a difference between the platitudes of Parliament and the lofty dreams of Plato; and the question of sewerage in Stoke-upon-Avon is hardly so exalted as the question of the immortality of the soul. Well, there must be some explanation of the phenomenon, and I was beginning in a very small humble way to understand it. The high regions of speculative thought are, like Alpine altitudes, too thin for man to breathe in for long periods of time. There is a craving of the heart for human fellowship, as well as a thirst of the mind for knowledge; and what is said of solitude is true of study—that but an angel or a beast can tolerate its continuance. I confess life was taking on new lights and colours since I became interested in the little drama of human feelings and passions; and, whilst I thirsted for the unattainable heaven of pure thought, I felt that the very pricks and stings of human passions gave life a zest, to which my solitary life had as yet been a stranger. I believe now that the best of all existences here below is a compound of action and thought, a steady practical interest in the welfare of the race, and occasional breathing moments of silent conference with the Eternal. But during those spring days I was able to put down the time pleasantly enough by wading through the interesting correspondence of Leviston, and trying to invent some means of regaining the lost confidence of the Bellamys, and coming to a satisfactory understanding with Helston. One good thing I did immediately. I got Agnes Deane to call at once on Mrs. Leviston, and she brought about an introduction between Gwendoline and Helen Bellamy.

It was on the Sunday week after Leviston's death I found myself at my old post at the foot of Ursula's grave in Glasnevin. I had hardly missed a Sunday since her death. I used to stand there leaning on the adjoining railings, and dream that her pure spirit would come floating down from her throne amongst the cherubim and take up its old place on my shoulder, and whisper "Doff" in the old, beloved accents. A long cross of crocuses, like the cross of the Holy Trinity, yellow and purple, lay on the ridge of the little grave ; and just now a cluster of lilies of the valley at the head, and a thicker cluster of violets at the foot, were scenting the still air. I saw as in a dream groups of people wandering about in the streets of this city of the dead. One group, a man, his wife and child, were not far off, going from grave to grave, and spelling the names of the departed ones. A rather thick willow tree, its arms just then gemmed with green buds, was on my left, and effectually screened me when they came up to the little grave and began to read the inscription. They were Herr Messing, Alice, and little Fritz. I heard the deep boom of the professor's voice—

### URSULA DEANE.

#### AGED FOUR YEARS AND FOUR MONTHS.

(" *Suffare leetle shildrens do goom unto Me.*")

"Come away!" said Alice sharply, dragging little Fritz by the hand. "Come away. I hate to see children's graves." She went away. But the professor lingered, and after steadily gazing at the little grave and the white cross that surmounted it, he began to murmur an improvisation, which came to something like this :—

> " Poor little babe ! they do not say 'She died,'
>     But ' Come to Me !'
> The Lamb has called His little bride,
>     And said, ' Come, come to Me !'
> There's not one word of gruesome death—
> Closed eyes, hands folded, faded breath—
> But welcome sweet from Him who saith,
>     ' Ursula, come to Me !'
>
> There's not one word of portals grim,
>     But ' Come to Me !'
> No cadenced woe, no stammered hymn,
>     But ' Come to Me !'

O Death ! where is thy sheathed sting ?
O Grave, thy victories I sing !
What art thou but a second spring,
   Heralded, ' Come to Me ! '

Sing it in accents gay and blithe,
   ' Come, come to Me ! '
Thou, warden of the glass and scythe,
   Dost hear it, ' Come to Me ! '
Ah ! thou didst cut my lily white,
And thou, an angel of the light,
Shedding thy garments of the night,
Didst plant it where His flowerets bright
Their lily sisterling invite—
   ' Ursula, come to Me ! ' ' "

I listened in utter amazement, partly at the tenderness of the professor, partly at the nature of his
strange soliloquy.    Fifty times I was about to come
out from my shelter and reveal myself to him, but I
held back.    Then I saw him baring his head after a
little pause, stoop down, take one little violet leaf
from the grass, put it to his lips, place it in his
prayer-book, and depart.    I cannot put in words
how much I loved that man.

That same evening, a little toned up and strengthened, I sought out Helston.    He was not at home
when I called.    I remained in his room, poring
listlessly over medical works and some tattered
novels until he returned.    He greeted me warmly.

" I won't sit down, Helston," I said, " until you
hear all that I have to say, and then decide whether
we shall remain friends."

He knew then that all was over.    But he took it
well.    I told him simply what had happened, laying
particular stress upon Alfred Bellamy's words.    He
listened patiently, his head resting on one hand.
When I was done he stood up, and coming up to
where I stood he shook me warmly by the hand, and
said—

" Let us dismiss the subject.    I confess I dis-

honoured myself by my foolish suspicions of you.
You have acted like a man. We must not speak of
the matter again."

So had Ursula blessed me.

Meanwhile, injunctions were sent to Mrs. Oliver
not to attempt to take up the office of executor until
the courts gave permission. But her lawyers at-
tended every day and remained for hours, receiving
instructions, ferreting out information, and laying
elaborate plans for the maintenance of the will.
Gwendoline was indifferent. I think she had her
suspicions that all was not right. But she never
spoke of the matter. On the Sunday night that I
returned from Helston's, Fred Oliver called, and,
after remaining a very long time, asked to see me.
After considerable hesitation I consented to see him.
He had lost a good deal of his flippancy, and looked
serious enough, as if some weighty business was on
hand. His hair had grown, he was well dressed,
and altogether looked well and spruce, like a naval
officer who has doffed the gold lace and had just
come from the hands of his tailor.

"Austin," he said, "you know as much, I dare
say, about my poor brother-in-law's affairs as any
one else. There's going to be trouble. You and
mother, you know, have not been very good friends,
but I hope you will act honourably."

"Your first assumption," said I, "is quite wrong.
I was Mr. Leviston's servant, not his confidant. I
know nothing of his business affairs. Your second
assumption is quite as wrong. I am no enemy of
your mother's. She, like yourself, has not chosen to
treat me very courteously, but we must not quarrel
with ladies' wishes or whims. Thirdly, I cannot see
what I have got to say to your affairs at all, or why
I should be interested."

"You will be summoned as an important witness,"
he replied, "and I hope you'll act on the square."

He was losing his assumed manner, and dropping into the slang of the gaol.

"By your side?" I said.

"D——n you," said he, "why do you say 'my side'? What have I got to do with the infernal business?"

"Oh, I beg your pardon," I replied, "I thought your interests and your mother's were identical."

He looked at me suspiciously. "Look here, Austin, old fellow," he said, coming over and assuming an air of familiarity. "You and I are men of the world. We understand one another. Now, it will be your interest to act square in this matter."

"I don't understand you," I replied.

"Ha!" he said, with a laugh, "you want to draw me out. Playing at detective, eh?"

"I did not send for you," I said quietly.

"You don't catch an old bird with chaff, Austin. You won't draw me out; but if you act honourably you'll hear of something to your advantage."

His manner, more than his words, was disgusting.

"Honourable is the word," he said, "to act honourable, particularly where ladies are concerned. After all, what is the world without honour? It is the salt of society. I'll tell Langdon that you'll act honourably, Austin."

"You may tell him so," I said, "but I shall put my own interpretation on the word."

He burst into a perfect fury.

"D——n you," he said, "you don't mean to peach, do you? If you do, the day you come off the chair will be your last. We're not going to be thwarted by tramps and beggars like you. I should think not."

"You're giving yourself away considerably," I said quietly. "You are hinting at dark deeds, of which hitherto I had not the slightest suspicion."

He saw his mistake.

"I was only trying you, Austin," he said in a friendly way. "Forget all that I said. I left my wits in the gaol, and—be true to my mother. Why, she has the greatest respect for you, Austin."

He went away; and my next few days were days of torture, for Oliver and his mother tried to make themselves agreeable, thrusting themselves on me at all times, trying to ply me with liquor, offering little dainty souvenirs of poor Leviston—all of which was infinitely disgusting, but so do people of the world blind themselves. There are none so short-sighted as the wicked.

At last, at the end of the fortnight, I had put all Leviston's papers in order, and was free to depart. Oliver and his mother were absolutely obsequious. When I had parted with them, Mrs. Leviston walked down to the gate with me. All my old prejudices against her had been diminished and softened by her sorrows, for she too had been changed and strengthened by suffering, and a naturally amiable and gentle character had asserted itself after the fierce, scorching agonies to which it had been subjected. She now rose up fortified and purified by nearly six years of trials, mental and spiritual, and the old slavery to her mother's will was conquered, even when nature was at its weakest. A certain strong womanhood had engrafted itself on the rather feeble character of the girl; and I looked for the blossoming and fruiting of this frail plant that to all appearances had been scorched and withered almost unto death.

"I am under grave obligations to you, Mr. Austin," she said, nervously pulling some leaves to pieces; "and you have not been treated too well."

"I have nothing to complain of, Mrs. Leviston," I said. "I have done all in my power for your poor husband and yourself, and my time here has not been altogether unpleasant."

How different, I thought, had we both grown from that time when I quoted Goethe in lofty sarcasm at her, and she, poor girl, wilted and faded at every little breath.    I was now humbled, and she had grown strong.

"There is some trouble, and, I believe, litigation before you," I continued, "but there have been grave mistakes in the past.    I would take the liberty of saying to you that it would not be well to repeat those mistakes through foolish pride.    You have suffered much from loneliness and want of sympathy. You have now two fast friends in Agnes Deane and Helen Bellamy.    Do not cast them off under any provocation."

"You know," she said very humbly, "that it was not my fault that Agnes, my dearest school companion, was not invited here.    Oh, it has been all such a mistake, and such a tragic one.    I wonder what I did to deserve such a fate."

"Don't wonder," I replied truly, and yet wishing to give her every help.    "Most lives are as full of mistakes, and perhaps more tragic mistakes than yours. If one so material as I might say it, the imperial soul has an education as well as mind and body, and all the more keen and terrible because of its lofty and regal position."

"If I could think," she said, "that mine was not an exceptionally hard case, I think I could be content.    It is something at least to know that we are not singled out for affliction, but that it is the common lot.    How I used envy Sister Philippa, always so serene and happy."

"I saw Sister Philippa," said I, "weeping bitterly under these elms."

"Then," she said, with a sudden impulse, "I'll send for her, and she shall stay with me."

"A blessed thought," I replied, "you cannot have a better friend in your trouble.    Good-bye."

"We may, I hope, see you sometimes, Mr. Austin," she said, as her hand lingered in mine. "You have not the baronet's crest I used to dream of," she said with a little smile, "but you have become one of us, and we should miss you very much."

"You are very kind," I replied; "there are happy days before us all, I hope."

She went back wearily to her home. And I faced the world for the hundredth time.

But all my experiences were building up a new character within me that fortified me. The very contact with humanity was melting down gradually the cold ice-peaks of intellectual conceit. I was beginning to have an interest in life. The very fact that I was useful to one or two persons created a new spirit within me. It is God-like, I said, thus to straighten and strengthen the bruised reed. One act of kindness is better than all the speculations of Plato. After all, here in this little planet of ours is work enough for a lifetime. I revelled in the thought. Not that I had as yet abandoned my gods. Night after night I dreamed and dreamed over my beloved books, passing from Æschylus to Milton, from Cicero to Richter. A Greek text, seen by accident, would excite as much pleasurable curiosity as a shattered Etruscan vase to the archæologist, or a rare cameo to a virtuoso. A sentence from Goethe or Novalis, happily applied, would make me happy for a day. Yet, I saw that there was something deeper and diviner than high thought and artistic expression, and that man, and not merely man's work, was the highest achievement under heaven. And thus insensibly my thoughts were moving towards Charlie's, as our lives were converging together under heaven's high auspices. Meanwhile, I had to battle with the world again, and ascend the mountains of myrrh and drink of the waters of Marah before our souls merged into one.

# CHAPTER XI

## A BURNING HAND

I will go forth 'mongst men, not mailed in scorn,
But clad i' the armour of a pure intent.
Great duties are before me, and great aims;
And whether crowned or crownless, when I fall,
No matter, so that God's work is done.

A FEW weeks rolled by. And now it had come to
this: that I, the philosopher and student (with all
the corpses of my dead gods hanging around me,
like an Indian fakir weighed down with the leaden
amulets of Vishnu and Siva), was door-keeper and
ticket-collector at the public hall where Charlie
Travers this evening was to be the hero and the
idol. It was a dismal thought enough; and, as I
looked out from my office on the glistening pavements, wet with the weeping of April skies, I had
food for reflection enough to fill a library of every-
day maxims.

"A bad day," said the fellow who cleaned the hall,
and who had just come in from dinner.

"Yes," I replied, "it looks bad enough for to-
night's meeting."

"Pity there shouldn't be a full house," he continued, pulling at a damp pipe; "there's going to be
a jolly row."

"Indeed," I said, trying to look indifferent, "and
what's up now?"

"Well, you see," said the fellow, a rough habitué
of the public-house and police court, "this young
chap is going just a bit too far. He isn't got no

sinse. He can't let well alone. He's stuffing religion down people's throats; and that's business enough for the black coats. Thin, he's destroying trade. I knows one or two pubs that's a'most closed; and other businesses is not thriving. But," here he winked knowingly, taking the pipe from his mouth, and whispering close to my ear, "this is his last night. You'll see a jolly row; and he may get hurted."

This last was suggestive; and intended to be so.

"But it's no business of ours," he continued, "sez I, it's our profession to be neutral. So I sez at Casey's last night. We'll be strictly neutral. Won't we, pal?"

Good heavens! to be called "pal" by this savage!

"We'll be strictly neutral," he continued, smoking placidly, "but if this young swell get's a lick, we'll —be looking the other way."

He winked knowingly again.

"'Tis a wet day; and we'll have a wet?" he said after a pause. "Will it be a short one or a long one, pal?"

Words cannot describe my rage and disgust; but it was necessary to keep quiet.

"I'm off the liquor," I said gaily. "Some other time, old man."

"One of Travers' gang," he muttered contemptuously. I put on my greatcoat, and sped like lightning through the streets. I knew where I was going, and I knew I should not be disappointed.

I found the captain at home. There was no fire in the old, familiar room; but the captain, arrayed in a gay smoking-cap, a dressing-gown, with the Oriental tassels, and with his feet encased in a pair of warm blankets, was smoking an enormous meerschaum, and trying to fathom the mysteries of Quain's Anatomy.

I rushed in breathless. He turned his eyes slowly around ; then went on reading.

" I'm in the deuce of a fix, cap," I said, " there's going to be a big row at our hall to-night, and I'm afraid Charlie will be attacked."

He said nothing ; but handing me a boatswain's whistle, pointed to the window. I flung up the sash, and sent a rattling peal along the street. In a moment, windows were flung up on every side, and hatless heads, heads covered with smoking-caps, with furry caps, and every conceivable form of head-gear, blocked the windows. Cal came in as secretary, took brief orders, and summoned a council of the elders.

When they had all assembled under the silent presidency of the captain, the secretary said—

" You have no engagements this evening ? "

They protested unanimously.

" I dine at the Vice-regal Lodge at eight."

" I take the part of Don Cæsar de Bazan with Albani at the Gaiety."

" I am delivering a course of evening lectures at All Saints."

" I have to meet Wilde about a case of cataract at Stevens'."

" I have a pile of correspondence with Quain and Charcot."

" You are all like the guests in the gospel," said Cal. Then with the air of a judge delivering sentence—" I am beginning to have grave doubts about your immortal souls."

" Go on ! Sutton, what's up ? " they cried in chorus.

" A big row at the L——! "

" Hip ! hip ! hurrah ! " was the response.

" Travers is lecturing there to - night," continued Cal, " and is going to be attacked by hired roughs."

Their faces fell.

"I know," said Cal, with all the humility of a lead-ing counsel who wishes to cajole the jury, "that you have no sympathy with Travers. Neither have I. I dare say he is a good kind of fellow enough, if—you only knew him——"

O Cal, you traitor!

"But he should leave preaching to the clergy."

"Hear! hear!" from all.

"But, after all," continued this special pleader, "they say he is fighting for the working man against monopolists and millionaires, and they say he has saved many a poor fellow who, like ourselves, was going down hill. And, hang it! boys," cried Cal, seeing he was making but a faint impression, "he has a right to fairplay, and who'll get it for him but us?"

"Quite right! quite right!" was the response.

"And then," continued Cal, "our old friend here, and your former patient, Austin, knows all about him, and will stand sponsor for him."

"Will you, Austin? Do you say it is all right?"

"I pledge you my word of honour, gentlemen, it is all right. I'll guarantee that you won't regret defending Charlie Travers to-night."

"Gentlemen," said the chairman, "resolution—duly proposed and seconded. Passed unanimously. Call Bryce!"

"Bryce is rather balmy, I fear," said Gallwey.

"Never mind," said the chairman, "he'll sober up."

Bryce was sent for and came. His blinking, lack-lustre eyes brightened up when he heard there was going to be a row. But when Charlie's name was mentioned as the probable martyr and victim, he sat down, thrust his hands into his pockets, and said sulkily—

"I wo'not."

"Not quite grammatical, but rather emphatic," said Cal. "You won't what?"

"I won't fight."

"What's up, Bryce?"

"That fellow is agin the dwink!"

It took infinite pains and persuasions to convince this protagonist that he would not suffer in reputation by fighting for such a disreputable cause as temperance, and such a milk-and-water hero as Charlie; and it was only when several fellows said, *sotto voce*, but loud enough to be heard, "Bryce's showing the white feather at last," that he shook his unwieldy bulk together, and, after offering to fight any three of his tormentors with his left hand tied behind his back, he engaged to be in the hall that evening and to do some damage.

"So far all right," said the secretary, when Bryce had gone home, accompanied by two subalterns who had strict injunctions from the captain to let him lie still for an hour, then give him a cold-water douche, and lastly two cups of strong coffee in rapid succession.

"Now, who's to be Master of the Ceremonies?"

The captain intimated by a nod that he would assume that responsibility.

"Who shall be the surgeon of the expedition?"

Gallwey was chosen. He promptly went to the captain's drawers, drew out two sheets of sticking plaster, a roll of lint, and taking out a case of surgical instruments, he selected two or three scissors and a forceps, and rolling them in the lint, put the whole surgical equipment in his pocket. I looked on in amazement, not unmixed with terror, at these alarming preparations.

"Never mind, Austin," said the captain, "but clear off, and manage our entrance into the hall."

It was a time of no small suspense and agitation that evening, whilst great crowds gathered around the building, and small bodies of roughs, low-browed, evil-eyed, and smelling strongly of bad whisky, filtered slowly into the hall. They took their places, and were carefully marshalled by a young fellow, sallow-featured, dark-eyed, whom I had seen somewhere before. His face was flitting backwards and forwards across the curtains of my memory, but I could not for a long time remember where I had seen it. Then it suddenly flashed on me that he was one of the night visitors when I kept watch and ward over poor Leviston; and I knew that, if not thwarted, this foreboded ill for Charlie and his cause. When the hall was nearly filled, some score or more of very rough customers appeared, and as there was no trace of my students, my heart fell, when I heard a whisper—

" Goff, is Charlie come ? "

I wheeled round and saw a figure, small as to stature, but heavily moustached, and clad in pea-jacket, with a huge muffler, and I recognised Cal.

" By Jove ! is that you ? "

" Hist ! " he said, " the other fellows are going in. You'll see some science to-night."

" There is no danger of Charlie ? "

" Not the least. But why has he taken to this business ? "

" I don't know," I said gloomily; " but it was in his mind at Mayfield."

" It's a curious kind of insanity," said Cal ; " but we'll wait and see."

" There is a dangerous customer amongst those fellows," I said in a whisper ; " a Yankee-looking fellow ; look out for him ! "

" All right," and Cal passed in, disguised as a mariner from the high seas.

In less than a quarter of an hour a roar from the multitude outside presaged the arrival of the chief actors in the little drama of the night ; and in a few moments a number of priests, accompanied by a much larger number of representative laymen, passed rapidly into the hall; and then, accompanied by two venerable priests, whose names were well known and reverenced in the city, Charlie Travers, my old idol and companion, whom I had not seen for seven years, leaped from a cab and passed within a foot of me. Of course, he did not recognise me, for my face was turned from the light, but I had ample opportunities of observing him.

Very little changed he was from the old Charlie of Mayfield, but his face was grave and pale, and there was the old look of exhaustion about his movements which had so often pained me. But a flush deepened on his cheeks when, passing up the centre aisle of the vast hall, the whole assemblage stood up and greeted him with a royal welcome. If he valued such things, he would have been amply recompensed that night for all his labours; for assuredly there is no reward on earth fit to compare with the honest love and enthusiasm of young men.

The chair was taken; resolutions were proposed and passed; a few priests spoke kindly and feelingly about their "brave young confrère," as they called him; and then Charlie, flinging off a blue overcoat, and appearing in full evening dress, advanced to the edge of the platform. The whole audience rose and thundered their applause into his ears, and he stood humbly before them, with the old gesture I knew so well, running his fingers lightly through his hair, and lifting the curls over his coat collar.

When the applause had subsided, there was a loud, long, protracted hiss from the end of the hall, which made Charlie flush up, and several gentlemen on the platform cried "Order!" angrily. The hissing was repeated; there was some scuffle at the end of the hall, and immediately that attention was directed thither there was a rush of roughs up the centre aisle, and with a shout to his men to follow him, the leader dashed up the platform, and brandishing a stick, made straight for Charlie. I thought it was all over with my old friend, when suddenly a door to the left of the platform swung open, and my brave students, disguised in every conceivable manner, swept onwards towards the centre of the platform. At first the assailants thought they were allies, for with a great whoop of triumph they leaped up the stairs that led to the platform.

They were speedily undeceived. I saw the long form of the captain leap across the boards; I saw his great forearm stretch out, and catching the leader with an awful blow, lift him bodily over the footlights and send him crashing to the floor. At the same time Bryce, standing at the head of the stairs, sent out his terrible clenched hand, and one by one his assailants were sent sprawling amongst the chairs. The others, irresolutely thronging the passage, and seeing new champions coming through the doorway, turned and fled. They passed me in full flight, and I heard them mutter, "Who the devil are they?" "We're split upon!" &c., &c., as they made for the open door.

The fallen men were lifted up by students and brought into the outer hall. Gallwey, rapidly doffing his disguise and rolling up his sleeves, tended them. The leader was badly cut over the eye. Gallwey cut and pared and plastered him, and I think he must have enjoyed his groans. Two of the others had arms badly broken. They were placed in splints. A cab was called, and under the care of Stokes they were driven to hospital.

"Wasn't it nice and clean?" Cal whispered to me.

"'Twas first-class," I said; "they're noble fellows."

Meanwhile a half-hour had elapsed, and when we re-entered the hall Charlie was winding up his speech. I was surprised to see my students, now forming a strong bodyguard around him, listening in reverential silence. Bryce, his mouth wide open, was staring at Charlie as if he saw a ghost and was paralysed. The first words that struck on my ear were these, pronounced in the old gentle, solemn intonation. I almost could imagine that we were walking under the limes at Mayfield.

"Come down from your high places, O ye dwellers on the hills, and look into the darkness of the valleys —valleys cowled in the fogs of unbelief, and seamed by the torrents of desolation! Leave behind your high thinking, and do a little work for God. Forget for a moment your dreams of a Utopia, and make your world a little less like hell. For here in the valleys are your flesh and blood, crushed under a weight of torture that has not even Ethiopic or Hindu mysticism to consecrate it; and here are souls that our faith tells us came from the hands of Omnipotence, but Omniscience itself cannot trace one lingering feature that might recall heaven, nor one lineament that would betray the handiwork of God! For the world has gone astray from Him who made it, and has forsaken His Christ. Mark you, it is no figure of speech that makes this world the battleground of spirits, whose intelligence would appal us could we even imagine it, and whose puissance can only be expressed in human language by saying that it sweeps beyond all natural sources, and passes towards the Infinite! And what is the prize? Human souls. And who are the combatants? Christ and Belial. And alas! that I should say it, the despairing cry of the blasphemous emperor, 'Thou hast conquered,

O Galilean!' can hardly be said to-day. And why? Because we, who have been sworn to fight under the banner of the King, have deserted His standard and gone over to His enemy. We carry His enemy's colours, we speak his language, we whisper his watchwords, we use his weapons; and when we are called cowards and traitors we apologise for our betrayal of Christ by giving the lie to His own words—that there's no serving Him and the world that hates Him. And we point to our Captains and say, 'For you is the warfare and the wounds; for us the rest and the reward.' For lo! Satan has but to utter his watchword, and a thousand agencies leap up to aid him. But the cry for the wounded Christ falls heedless on a generation that has grown enervated by feeding on the lilies and lying in the roses of life. Our Captain calls to us that all along the line the black standards are waving amongst our forces; that sin, and its dread accompaniments, heresy and infidelity, contempt for holiness, a passion for wealth and pleasure, sensuality culminating in the unbelief that actually denies God, are making deadly havoc amongst the children of the army of God, and we sit still, saying, 'The day is far spent, and wounds are for fools; for us the comfort and rest even of the fool who promised himself the morrow that never came.' Here in your own city, surrounded by forces that might make the strongest heart amongst His heroes quail, a handful of priests are warring against vice, colossal in its malice, protean in its forms. A thousand agencies for evil are steadily at work amongst them; and with the motto of a fallen divinity, *ohne hast aber ohne rast*, they pursue with unabated activity and unrelenting zeal the awful work of compassing the destruction of human souls. What pity fills the hearts of those few heroes of Christ, and what despair! what sadness at night when the day's work is done, and but little remains! what sinking of heart in the morning when they go forth to failure and defeat, which they see to be inevitable, God's pitying angels know. And we stand by with folded arms, and talk glibly of progress and of science, the wonder-working of the modern world, the future that lies before our race. And Satan, a living, personal, immaterial, but terrible power, blinds us with the dust of gold, and wraps us in the mists of pride, and goes his way rejoicing to hear his own watchwords on the lips of the sons of God! For if *we* are not sons of the Most High, where on this dismal earth can God look for children that will know their Father's face? Do you know anything of the Presence that wraps your island round like a prophet's cloak—of the cloud by day, and the fire by night, that have ever gone before your race? A cloud of sorrow it might have been, and a fire of martyrdom; but the unspeakable One was hidden there. Have you ever heard that the sea that washes your shore was the choir stall of your Irish monks: and that every sod of earth that is turned by the ploughshare of the hind holds the relics of some Irish saint? Do you know that for six hundred years your forefathers lived a life of sanctity so austere and terrible that when their rule was introduced on the continent of Europe, the weaker races rebelled against its severity, and cried out against its awful heroism? And do you know that the history of the Church holds no parallel to the martyrdom of your race, except what is told in the vaults of the catacombs, and the sands of the Coliseum? nor is there any record of an apostleship like yours, if we except alone the mission of the fishermen of Galilee? The poverty and ignorance of Ireland have gone forth and spoken the living word; and lo! high intellects have bowed down under the magic of their preaching, and empires, far beyond anything we lost in the Satanic conquests of the Reformation, have been gathered into the fold of Christ ?

"With the splendid insolence of souls that having lost everything, dread nothing, your consecrated beggars went forth, and the halls of Oxford echoed with their teaching, and all the architectural wonders of the New World sprang as if by magic from the opulence of their sublime destitution. Half a century has sufficed to evangelise England and America. Another half century may see cathedrals on the shores of Lake Nyanza, and Christian monks in the vast convents of the East. In that sublime revolution which is yet before the world, what part shall be ours ? The ignorance of Ireland has spoken, and behold its results. What shall it be, when the intelligence of Ireland, emancipated from the shackles of a false education, shall go forth to stir the world with the watchword : Christ and Rome ?

"Once before, Irish intellect spread itself abroad over Europe, and to this day, after fourteen hundred years, the mission of these apostles bears fruit. They founded the first of the world's universities, and the greatest of the world's monasteries. Once more, the pall of an ignorance, deeper than the primeval darkness that had spread from paganism over the plains of France and the forests of Germany, lies heavily on a sick and demented civilisation. The mad world goes spinning on in its witch's dance, whipped with the scorpions of demons. Now and again, some solitary figure stands forth against it with uplifted finger, and cries : 'Go back! go back ! back to the Church, back to Christ. Lo, the precipice yawning under your feet, lo, the heavens darkening over your heads !'

"And, in answer, that mocking cry that came from scornful lips, before the thunders rolled, and the lightnings flashed on Calvary—that, 'Vah ! work a miracle and we will believe thee,' comes from men and women whose hearts are lifted up with pride, and whose necks are stiffened with the insolence of the Age-Spirit.

"The gospel of this age must be the eternal gospel of humility, a humility studied in the ranks of the outcast and poor, and practised in the *salons* of the great and wise. Stand forward, therefore, children of the Saints! It is not I that calls you, it is Christ. The ear of faith hears the clash of arms in the air above us, as it heard the voices of warning angels over the fated Holy City; the eye of faith sees the standards plunging in victory or defeat in all the battlefields of the world. From His high place at the right hand of His Father, from His bed of pain on the Cross, from the prisons of our tabernacles where He abides to watch and control the struggle and marshal His hosts for victory, the great Captain is calling to us. And it needs no great discernment, no very subtle inquirings, to interpret His invitation which is a command, for it takes articulate shape, and, echoed by the voices of His Vicar, His priests, His poor, it says to us: Come, arm for the struggle, and find your safety in the midst of it. He that is not with Me is against Me. Quit you like men—like sons of God— like heirs of immortality."

When Charlie had ceased, and, turning aside modestly, hid himself to the rear of the platform, the audience drew a long deep breath of relief. There was no vulgar applause—the theme was too sacred for that; but I saw men whispering to each other and emotional women touching their foreheads, that is their eyes, with handkerchiefs. As for my students, they were visibly impressed.

The captain stood with his back to the wall, his feet stretched out, and his hands stuck deep in his pockets. He was in a reverie. Gallwey had the

nervous look of a controversialist, as if he were
disposed to question some things that Charlie had
said. Some of the fellows pulled their moustaches
nervously, and you heard a muttered "By Jove!"
Bryce alone bent over and whispered, with a
chuckle of delight: "He didn't say a word agin
the dwink!"

As for myself, a thousand sensations shot rapidly
through me. Surprise, delight, enthusiasm on seeing
my dear old friend suddenly transformed into a
prophet and leader; and then a revulsion of shame
when I thought what a gulf separated us two, who
had been as one. He had gone beyond me, higher
than an archangel over a mere mortal; and I was
compelled to admit that he had done so, and touched
his exalted destiny by the sheer power of faith. I
probably knew twenty times as much as he: but
my knowledge weighed me down to earth, and was
a leaden burden to my feet, whilst his beautiful faith
raised and elevated him on wings of light, and lifted
him into those regions of serene and exalted thought,
where I at least could not follow. And I shuddered
when this idea struck me. If I now were to go on
that platform and tell of my experience with the
Princes of Darkness and Doubt—if I were to attempt
even to hint at such possibilities as were familiar
enough to my own sad mind, what would be the
result? I knew I should be hunted from that platform as if I were a mad dog, and the hands of the
gentlest women would be raised against me for my
profanity and blasphemy. It was an awful thought,
and a dread contrast. Charlie, an idol, a conqueror,
exulting in the noblest victory that man can attain—
the conquest of young hearts by the sheer force of
eloquence and truth, and I, a ticket-collector, at ten
shillings a week, with not one I could call friend
in that vast city—and the heavens were dark over
my head. I bent my head low on my bosom, and

covering my eyes with the battered rim of my hat, I went down into depths of darkness.and despair.

I had to take my place at the turnstile again, as the audience filtered past. I saw their faces alight with enthusiasm ; I heard their praises and acclamations. I saw old faces there, the grave, stately form of Mr. Dowling ; I heard Herr Messing chattering away volubly in his exultant enthusiasm ; I saw Alfred Bellamy, gentle and serious, and I saw Helen by his side, solemn and beautiful as ever ; and I saw myself, an outcast. I dared not speak to them. I turned my eyes away from the light, and saw the awful spectres of doom and despair before me.

When Charlie came out, I could not look at him. There was a crowd of hangers-on around him, as there is always around some great man. At last he got rid of them all except one. This person delayed him in some desultory conversation a long time. I was inside the turnstile, Charlie just without. His back was turned to me. He did not see me. But, as I placed my hand on the iron of the turnstile, in some mysterious manner his hand sought mine, and rested upon it. A thrill of delight swept through me. At the same instant, a burning pain shot through my hand, and penetrated every inch of my frame. I tried to withdraw my hand gently. I could not. I was in exquisite pain ; yet I never experienced such exultation. I felt like an exile, who has just touched his native shore, like a prisoner who has been welcomed to liberty by a friend. Then the tiresome talker departed ; and Charlie, after burying himself in a deep reverie for a moment, turned without looking at me, flung his arms around my neck, and cried, " O Goff, Goff, I knew it was you."

# CHAPTER XII

## EPHREM OF EDESSA

*" Let not thy tongue be a bridge for sounds, which letteth all words pass across it. Praise do thou send up to Him, as the tithing of thy strains. A wavesheaf of words offer unto Him from thine imagination, hymns also as first-fruits, and send up clustered hymns thy tongue hath culled."*—S. EPHREM.

"COME," said Charlie, leaving the hall after a brief interval; and I followed him as meekly as a serf would follow his master. Then I saw a wonderful sight. The street was thronged with rough labourers, coal-porters, stevedores, grimy and black most of them, and there was a strong element of ungovernable rage amongst them. They had heard of the contemplated attack upon Charlie, and they were wild with indignation. "Who were they?" "Why didn't you tell us, sir?" "Mother of God," cried a huge giant, as black as if he had come from the infernal pit, "if I was there, I'd make necklaces of their guts," all expressions very rude and unmannerly, but welling up to the rough lips from strong, brave hearts that beat and throbbed for Charlie. And women, shaggy and bare-breasted, held up their babes to see him, knowing that in some far-off time it was a thing they would gladly boast of. We broke away with some difficulty from the crowd, only to find ourselves surrounded in one of the main thoroughfares by an escort, which I had some trouble in recognising as my students. I told Charlie the history of the evening, and he was deeply touched.

When we arrived at the lodgings, he turned around and said—

"Gentlemen, Goff has told me all that you have done for me this night.  If not too late, or if you are not too numerous, I gladly invite you to my humble diggings——"

They cried, "Too late."  "Too late."

"Then," said he, "I thank you from my heart for your chivalry and devotion.  May God bless you."

And my students, with one simultaneous impulse, lifted their hats to a boy like themselves, and then walked off into the night, singing something about "Show us a man, and we'll know him."

Charlie led me upstairs to his rooms, where a very modest supper of bread and milk was laid for him, and coming over near me he drew me before the gas-jet, and laying his two hands on my shoulders he studied me long and anxiously.  Then his face relaxed into a little smile, as he said—

"And so it is you, Goff, dear old Goff, unchanged, but you look a little older and a little worn.  Something told me you were near me to-night, and I was just thinking I had been deceived when my hand fell on yours, and I knew it was all right."

He moved up and down the room, chanting in a strange soliloquy all that he had been thinking of— old times, our little chats under the limes, our separation, the wonderful ways of Divine Providence, the littleness of our planet, the strange way lives converge, &c.  Then stopping once more before me, he cried—

"But tell me yourself, Goff, how the world is using you."

"Never mind me, Charlie," I said, "you have gone so high that it surprises me that you should have remembered even my name."

"That is unkind, Goff," said Charlie meekly, "and you don't mean it.  Why, who am I but a poor student here in Dublin, trying to do a little good according to very feeble lights ? "

"No," said I, " you are Charlie Travers, the young Reformer, the pet of the priests, the idol of women, the tribune of the mob — popular, worshipped, idolised——"

" For God's sake don't, Goff," he cried in dismay, "all this is so foreign to you.   And where should I be if it were true ? "

" But it is true," I repeated, " for good or ill, and I do not presume to decide such an intricate question, for there are hundreds of good people opposed to you, you are moving men's hearts strangely; and if you are worshipped, remember, too, you are hated."

" That I know well," he said meekly.  " That does not concern me.  But you have troubled me, Goff, a good deal, by expressing a doubt if this work were from God."

" Don't mind me, Charlie," I said, touched in spite of myself, " a poor devil who has spent five years' penal servitude to doubt and denial, is hardly qualified to express an opinion on your work.  'Tis hardly fair to ask Lucifer questions about the Seven Choirs."

He saw, then, at a glance all the black despair of my soul, and he came over with infinite gentleness and said—

" Come, Goff, light a cigar, and tell me all."

My pride fought stubbornly against his humility and meekness, but I did tell him all—my callousness, my coldness, my disbelief, my insatiable curiosity after the hidden secrets of God, my pride, my anguish, the occasional upliftings under the hands of kindly men and women, my deeper depression, my dislike of religion, yet the irresistible attraction that drew me to it, my alienation from God, and the secret magnetism that dragged me to His feet, my

S

difficulty in getting near unto Christ, yet my love and devotion to the lonely watcher of our souls—in a word, all the secret mechanism that jarred and jangled within this turbulent soul of mine I laid bare to him with a kind of sullen pride, as if I half defied God to make me worse. I told him, too, from what it all sprang—irresistible pride of intellect, and an unbounded curiosity to see whether there were questions beyond human ken to know and human reason to solve. And the profound dissatisfaction that resulted from all, and sometimes amounted almost to loathing of books and teachers which still, however, maintained their wonderful attractions, and, therefore, their imperial sway over my mind—all these things I told, not with humility, but as if secretly exulting in these forbidden courses, and in my hidden worship for the idols of ancient and modern Paganism.

Charlie listened attentively, and then said—

"But, of course, Goff, you don't mean to say that you have the slightest intellectual doubt of the truths of the Church?"

"No," said I, "and there's my crime and my punishment. I have not the slightest doubts of these truths; nay, I have an irresistible attraction towards them, but what is it? Is it a lower soul or some dark slave of the intellect that prevents my embracing them as the solace and daily practice of life, and finding in them enough to quench this awful thirst for forbidden knowledge that has been my bane—and my comfort. I can now understand the craving of the drunkard for strong drink. Like him the cup must be always at my lips, though I loathe it."

"Goff," said Charlie, after a long interval of thought, "do you forget your Greek? Pardon me, you have just told me that you are always dabbling at it. Come now and get me over this curious Greek rhythm. You often lifted me in the good old days over the stiles and ditches of old Æschylus."

He took down a small volume, bound in vellum, with red edges, and he opened it, and sat down near me, in the old familiar way, his arm resting on my shoulder and his finger tracing the lines he wanted me to read. He knew the book well, and led me from passage to passage, according as he suspected it suited my malady and my moods. This is what I read :—

"To the unbelievers is he nigh akin that dares to pry : on the very edge of death the rash standeth, in that he hath left the faith in his disputations to go down and search into the ocean of hidden things. Marvel not, my child, at what I tell thee. . . . Who is there whose knowledge is great enough to feel after and mete out the sea of all wisdom ? "

"That hits me, Charlie," I exclaimed. "Who is this ? "

"Never mind," he replied, "read on."

I read :—

"The mighty nature that never was not, is spoken of by all mouths. The mouth that willeth to speak of that which is unspeakable bringeth Him to littleness, in that it sufficeth not for His greatness. Every one, then, that wisheth to magnify God exceedingly, as He is great in His own nature, himself in magnifying Him is magnified in Him. Restrain searching 'which sufficeth not to reach Him, and gain silence, which is becoming, of Him. Give me, Lord, to use them both discerningly, that I may neither search rashly nor be silent carelessly. Teach me words of edification, and make me gain the silence of discernment."

"Who is it, Charlie ? " I asked again. "There is something more than Pagan philosophy here."

"How do you discern that ? " he asked.

"Well, there is a tone of humility about it all that is quite foreign to me and my Pagans."

"Read on," he said, turning over the leaves and marking certain passages :—

"The truth above is able to increase to the east, and to spread to the west, and to lay hold on the north, and to clasp the south. Into the depth it went and conquered. Into the height it went up and abode, and ruled in all places over all."

"A curious blending of poetry and philosophy," I said. "There is nothing like it out of Plato."

"There's nothing like it in Plato," said Charlie. "Turn to these beatitudes. But what do you think of the Greek ?"

"Not quite pure, I think," I said. "There are idiotisms that I can hardly grasp."

"Read on," said Charlie.

I read :—

"Blessed be he, Lord, who in great love hath been worthy to call Thee Beloved Son, which name God Thy Father Himself hath called Thee! Blessed be he, Lord, that hath weaned his mouth from all questionings, and hath called Thee the Son of God, which name the Holy Ghost called Thee! Blessed be he, Lord, who hath been worthy to believe in simplicity and to call Thee Son, as all the prophets and apostles called Thee ! Blessed he that knoweth, Lord, that Thy majesty is unsearchable, and hath rebuked his tongue speedily, that by silence he might honour Thy generation ! Blessed he, Lord, that hath obtained a hidden eye wherewith to see how the angels turn abashed from Thee, and how that creatures cannot attain to Thee, and hath given Thee thanks because he hath been worthy of having Thee to dwell in him ! Blessed be he that knoweth, Lord, that Thou art God, the Son of God, and knoweth himself whose son he is, a mortal, the son of a mortal ! Blessed be he that hath reflected that Adonai is Thy Father, and hath also remembered his own generation, that he is a son of Adam, of the dust! Blessed he that hath reflected that the angels by silence confess Thee, and hath speedily chidden with himself because his tongue hath been so daring! Blessed he that hath understood that the heavens above were still and the earth below was moved, and hath quieted his soul whilst amongst the waves thereof! Blessed he, Lord, that hath learned that the seraph crieth, "Holy," and is still: that the seraphim search not at all, and that hath left alone what the seraphim leave, and hath chosen what the seraphim chose! Who then is not astonied that Thou art sitting at the right hand, and that dust which sitteth upon dust in the dunghill searcheth into Thee? Who, Lord, is not astonied that Thou art thé creator of all creatures, that man essayeth to search into Thee, and yet knoweth not what his own soul is? This is a wonder, that it is Thou, Lord, alone who knowest Thy Father, and yet vile dust lifteth itself up even to search into Thy Father in Thee, O Lord!"

I lifted my head. "It is wonderful, Charlie," I cried. "I did not know that there was such Christian literature in the world. Why, it is poetry, and a system of Christian agnosticism based on humility."

"You'll learn more yet," said Charlie. "We are only on the fringe of the ocean. Christian literature! Why, there's none other. What is your profane history? A drama of lies. What is your philosophy? A drama of chimeras and delusions. What is your literature? A drama of impurity. Ah, Goff," he continued, "if the masters of modern science could only know what a world of truth and grace and beauty they were hiding behind the daubed curtains on which they smeared their little caricatures of nature and its God, I think that even they would be appalled at their own conceits, and have remorse for having put before the eyes of men such poor presentments of human and divine science. Why, the very names of our greatest thinkers are unknown to modern scientists. Once in a century a George Eliot might find her recreation in Petavius ; but ask Carlyle, Spencer, Froude, Clifford, Martineau, what have Catholic philosophers written, and they will answer that they did not know that there were Catholic philosophers, and they will probably argue that the term is a misnomer, for there can be no philosophy (which is their name for doubt) where there is absolute certainty, as in the Church. They lift their hands to the star-icicles of night instead of holding them up to the warmth and light of the living sun."

I could not help admiring Charlie. He had grown so grand and solemn. The boy had gone, and here was a man in strength and solidity. But the conversation chilled me.

"Charlie," I said, "come down, like a dear fellow, from these same stars, and let us talk of something human. Why do you hold your hand over your heart in that manner ? "

"It's only a little tightness that catches me sometimes. But, Goff, you were always hankering after the human. You remember how you disliked Father Aidan ? "

"I do," I said, with a shudder, "he used to give me the chills."

"But he is a saint," said Charlie, "I never knew any one more perfect."

"Precisely," I replied, "that's just why I dislike him. We Irish never really love a priest until he shows some defects, and proves that he is human."

"I owe him everything," said Charlie, "here and hereafter. He has taught me the secret of life and death, the grave and immortality."

"And that is ? " I asked sceptically.

"Jesus Christ," he said simply.

I jumped up as if smitten. Here was that Name

flashed on me again from most unexpected quarters. I was like a man in the midst of a storm, with lightnings playing around his head from every part of the heavens and no escape.

"Yes," Charlie continued, "it is the grand secret told by God to the world. And, mind you, it is the one word that magnetises men. In the beginning of my little mission I used to talk the common platitudes of virtue and honour, &c., and sometimes I think I used to make men's hearts leap up suddenly under some stirring sentence, only to fall back again when the stimulus ceased. But once I commenced to talk about Christ—I mean the Christ of the Gospels, the Christ of the Saints, the Christ of the Martyrs—I held them in the palm of my hand. And what touched them most was what I used to call—I hope without irreverence—the *manliness* of Christ. How He held in His Hand His Father's thunders, and only touched with these awful fingers the sealed eyelids of the blind, or smoothed down the ringlets of little children; how power, and what power! went out from Him, and an atmosphere of Omnipotence floated around Him; and yet He suffered poor women to touch with their lips the hem of His garment, and with tears the very flesh of His feet; how meekly He reverenced the lowly, and how grandly He defied the strong ones and the mighty; how He never slandered or defamed, but rebuked the priests to their face and honoured them in their absence; how He chided and encouraged, rebuked and praised His poor followers, and then gave them all He possessed; the majesty of His looks, the grandeur of His silence, the sweetness and strength of His words, all, all told in the language of the Evangelists, without comment or explanation, touched some unseen chord in men's hearts, and sent them throbbing with new emotions of love and zeal. And I would never have known Him but for Father Aidan."

I was silent. How deeply his words were moving me he scarcely conjectured.

"Come, Goff," he said at last, "one more sentence and I'll let you go."

I held the volume listlessly in my fingers. I did not care what I read. I only saw "Jesus Christ" in letters of fire in the air before me, just as you see red and green shadows when you turn blinded from the sun. I handed the book to Charlie. He walked up and down the room and read or chanted thus:—

"A thousand thousand stand, ten thousand ten thousands run; thousands and ten thousands are not able to search into One; for all of them in silence stand to minister. He hath no assessor, save the Son, who is from Him; within the silence alone is there investigation into Him. If the Angels had come to search, they had met the silence, and been restrained. The First Born was conceived, and the pure Virgin suffered not. He went in and came forth in pangs, and the Fair One perceived Him. Glorious and hidden was His entering in; vile and visible His coming forth. A wonder and an astonishment to liars, Fire entered in and clothed itself with a Body and came forth! Gabriel gave the name of 'Lord' to Him, who is the Lord of Angels. He called him 'Lord' that he might teach that He was his Lord and not his fellow-servant. Michael was Gabriel's fellow-servant. The Son is the Lord of servants: high is His Nature as is His Name. The servant cannot search Him out, because how great soever the work is, greater than it is the Workman!

"Wondrous is it that the mind should gather all its forces, to break through and gaze upon Thy light. Thy Brightness came forth but a little; It scattereth it, and throws it back altogether. Who shall look upon the Son, whose rays are fearful? The whole of them, with His whole Nature, are closely blended. He is the Sun whom the Prophets proclaimed, with healing in His wings, and trouble among His examiners. Shall one feel Thee with his hands, when there is not even a mind keen enough to feel after Thee, and search Thee out, seeing Thou art a great mountain ? Shall one listen to Thee with the ears, seeing Thou art more fearful than thunder ? A stillness art Thou that cannot be heard, yea, a silence that cannot be listened to. Shall a man see Thee with his eyes, when Thou art the bright morning Light ? From all is the sight of Thee concealed !

" It is not for weak beings alone that the sight of Thee is too great, or the searching out of Thee is concealed ; for the senses of the body, since they much need other senses, which are in the inmost imagination, do not grasp even the smallest things within their search. Let us then ask the Angels that are near Thy gate. Though the Angels stand before Thee with praises, yet they know not upon what side to see Thee. They sought Thee above in the height, they saw Thee in the depth ; they searched for Thee in the heaven, they saw Thee in the deep ; they looked for Thee with the Adorable One, they found Thee amid the creatures ; they came down to Thee and gave praise. When they had begun to inquire into Thy Appearance among things created, they comprehended not how, by running up and down, to come to a stand in their search into Thee. For they saw Thee in the depth, they saw Thee above on high, they saw Thee in the sepulchre, they saw Thee in the chamber, they saw Thee dead, they found Thee a raiser of the dead ; they were amazed, they were astonished, they had no strength left.

" In every place is Thy mysterious Presence, Lord, and from every place art Thou withdrawn. Though Thy mysterious Presence be in the height, yet it feeleth not that Thou art what Thou art. Though Thy mysterious Presence be in the depth, it is not comprehended what it is. Though Thy mysterious Presence be in the sea, from the sea art Thou concealed. Though Thy mysterious Presence be on the dry land, it knoweth not that Thou art He. Blessed be the glorious hidden One, since even Thy little mystery is a fountain of mysteries ! Who is able to clear up mysteries that fail not ? If a man were to take a likeness of Thee, it would be a fountain whence all likenesses would flow, and to what should we be able to look and shadow out Thy Image upon our heart? In Thy One adorable Image ten thousand beauteous things are crowded together.

"Wondrous art Thou altogether on all sides that we seek Thee! Thou art near and far off. Who shall approach to Thee? No searching is able to extend and reach unto Thee. When it had reached itself forth to approach, it was intercepted and stopped short. It is too short to reach Thy mountain; faith doth find it, and love with prayer. Imagining is easier for us than speaking in words; the mind is able to extend itself to every place. When it cometh to walk in Thy way to seek after Thee, it loseth its path before itself; it is perplexed and halteth. And if the mind be overcome, how much more the language, whose path is amongst perplexities?

"This becometh the mouth, that it should praise and keep silence; and if it is asked to be hasty, let it betake its whole self to silence as to its stronghold. Thus only can it comprehend, if it be not hasty to comprehend; the quiet is more able to comprehend than the rash that is hasty. The weak that searcheth is as a feeble one that laboureth to measure the fearful sea.

"Lo, if the mouth refrain, Lord, from searching into Thee, no gracious act would it have done, if, able to search into Thee, it refused to search! Its weakness hindered it from that to which its audacity led it away. It had been a gracious act in it, had it decided to be still; for silence would have been a port to it, that it should not perish in perplexity in Thy sea and Thy billows.

"And if there be a mode of seeking Him out, come let us seek out the Hidden One; come let us in astonishment feel after Him if He can be comprehended. Thou art revealed, Lord, to babes, and hidden from the cunning; to him that believeth Thou art found, to him that searcheth Thou art hidden. Blessed be he that is simple in searching out Thee, and vigorous at Thy promise. Searching, Lord, is too little to glorify Thee within itself. The power that extendeth into every place is able to search for Thee, in the height to shadow Thee

forth, and in the depth to feel after Thee, but though
reaching to every place is not able to find Thee out.
Blessed be he that hath felt that only in the Bosom of
Thy Father is the inquiry into Thee fully set at rest.

" The Seraph that is winged and flieth is too weak to
search Thee out; his wing is weak in comparison of
Thee, so as not to measure out Thy Majesty. In Thy
Bosom are the worlds laid; how much soever one would
wander into it, one is hindered. The Seraph, whose
voice proclaims Thee Holy, in reverential silence keeps
from search into Thee. Woe unto him that is bold when
the Seraph before Thee with his wings covereth his face!
The Cherubs bear that Mighty One who beareth all.
Bowing downwards, do the hosts of the Cherubim in fear
beneath Thy chariot veil themselves and fear to gaze
therein, carrying yet not able to find Him, trembling when
approaching. Blessed be he that hath learnt the honour
due to Thee from them, and hath praised and been
silent in fear."

" Hath praised and been silent in fear!" Charlie
continued, " ah! here is what we want. For men,
work; for God, praise! For men, the charity that
shows itself in practical work for their amelioration,
physical and spiritual; for God, not the whimpering
and clamouring of whipped slaves around His Throne,
never lifting our voices but as ragged and leprous
mendicants; but the grand jubilations of praise,
the ' Laudates' and ' Cantates,' which make us one
with the Seraphim. And here was the glory of the
ancient monastic orders! Seven times a day in
public they vied with the angels in praising God,
and then, their hearts filled with echoes of heaven,
they stooped down to the beggars at their gates, and
made them understand, not through the intellect but
through their senses, that there was a common
brotherhood on earth, which meant a common
Fatherhood in heaven. Good God! how far away
have we drifted from these glorious times, and how

paltry and pitiful are the weak worship and cold
philanthropy of our age compared with the celestial
music and the Christian love that existed then!
Who will give us back our lost inheritance? or who
will restore to us our stolen birthright? Who will
cast light into the slums of the human heart, or who
will make sweet the foulness of the cities, that are
more pitiful in their crowded iniquity than if the fox
roamed their streets, or the night-owls built in their
walls? Who will give us back our ten thousand
monasteries, little cities of our God, and take men
out of our fetid lanes and alleys to see once more
the face of God bending over them, and the eye of
God searching them in love? Alas! not I; my
little work is done. But oh! what a vast apostolate lies before our race! The sons of the heroes,
that for seven hundred years upheld the flag of
Christ, torn into shreds, under the storm and fire of
a hell let loose, and then went out calmly, to build
out of their rags, their poverty, their ignorance, and
their disease, the Church of God in all the new
empires of the earth, surely are able at home to
revive its ancient glories, build up new shrines on
the burnt ruins of the old, and make their island
home a wonder of sanctity, as they have made their
mission abroad, a miracle of apostolic zeal!"

He woke up suddenly to the fact that I was
watching him, watching him with intense earnestness, thinking, thinking that he had been feeding
amongst the crocuses and lilies, whilst I was eating
the bread of sorrow, and drinking the waters of
bitterness. "Dust sitting on dust upon a dunghill."
I saw, too, with pain that moistened my own eyes
that all this fervour and zeal were wearing away a
constitution never very strong. All the old weariness and sadness were written on his face, and
there was a dark blue tinge upon his lips that
emphasised terribly that gesture of holding his hand

over his heart. The inner fires were burning through the sacred vessel.

" Charlie," I said at last, " once before I bade you pause and take life more easily. Now, again, in another way, you are burning up all your energies."

He said nothing for a long time. Then coming over to where I was sitting, he placed his hands on my shoulders, and whispered—

" Goff, come and live with me ! "

" Live with you," I said, " no ! It would ruin your work to have it known that a tramp, and now, in a moment of good fortune, a ticket-collector at a theatre, was living with you ! "

" I should not mind," he said ; " but Goff, have things gone so hard with you ? "

"Yes," I said bitterly ; " your Christ has been hard on me."

" There is a duel to the death, Goff," said Charlie, with strong emotion, " between you and Jesus Christ. And He will beat you down to the ground, and you shall go deeper, lower than you have gone ; and then——"

He paused : and I looked up. " Then," he continued firmly, and as if with prophetic vision, " then He will lift you up and place you by His side, and clothe you with His strength ; and the day will come when you will bless Him, because He smote you."

" But come now," he said after a pause, " we will make a trip together to the Holy Mountain. There are trials before us both, and we need strength."

" I cannot leave Dublin, Charlie," I said, "just now ; I am subpœnaed in a trial, or rather a probate case, that will come on in a few days. When that is over, I shall get a day off, and go with you wherever you please, if down to Clare all the better."

" No," said he, " it is not to Clare. I shall not

see Clare again. But send me word, and let me know when you can come."

"Certainly," I said, "it will be like Auld Lang Syne once again."

He pressed my hand warmly (we were now at the hall-door), and went back wearily, with prayers on his lips, to his room.

# CHAPTER XIII

## THE YAWNING OF HELL

Io venni in luogo d'ogni luce muto
Che muggia, come fa mar, per tempesta
Se da contrari venti é combattuto.

I came to a place, mute of all light,
Which bellows as the sea does in a tempest
If by opposing winds 'tis combated.

—DANTE.

THAT night a revelation and an awakening came. If one in love with all things beautiful was absorbed in the contemplation of some exquisite landscape, where tree and tower, river and lake, combined to form a perfect picture; and if suddenly there came a dread cataclysm of nature, rending the fair picture as you would tear a canvas from end to end; and if, in that awful, swift terror, there were made revelations of things beneath the earth which no eye should see, no mind contemplate, and the chasm was to close together with a snap, but all now was tumbled ruin where all was smiling beauty —this would be a pretty fair exemplification of the horror which overtook me when the fatal revelation was made. To understand it, let me remind the reader of one fact. With faith enervated almost unto paralysis, but not unto death, and with all my intellectual powers steeped in some opiate that made them feeble and unperceptive, I am happy to say that I still retained that which seems to be the common and glorious birthright of the men and women of our race—a reverence, timid and awesome, of whatever is pure and undefiled. It is recorded in the lives of saints that one obscene word threw them into insensibility. I can believe it. It is no legendary hypothesis. I have known those who would actually sicken at a suggestion of indelicacy. And if not quite so sensitive, I think I may lay claim to a shrinking from all suggestiveness that made it a positive torture to hear or say anything gross or impure. I knew that there was some hidden, unspeakable malice about this vice which no human mind of saint, philosopher, or theologian has ever yet fathomed ; just as there is some secret, inexplicable charm about the opposite virtue, which no soul shall see explained until it sees the face of God. Naturalists may try to explain it away by reference to secret laws of Nature ; physiologists may talk of a Nemesis dogging the steps of the irreverent ; no law of Nature, no subtle inquiries into the subterranean working of her laws, can ever give a logical insight into the traditions of our race, the instinct of loathing, or the exaltation of inspiration, which is but a lost and broken fragment of some revelation made to our unfallen father.

Let me say that this delicacy is not at all limited to children of the Church, where the white lily of purity grows in the open air, and is no tender exotic. There are hundreds who have never known the awful and sublime teachings of the Catholic Church on this subject, who have inherited the sacred virtue, and who shrink with as much pain from the slightest allusion to forbidden things, as any tender child brought up under the white saints of our Irish convents. These form, sooner or later, the ever-increasing army of converts, for it is no exaggeration of piety or faith to believe that the Holy Spirit takes for His spouses the elect and the virgins.

On my return from Charlie's rooms to my own

humble lodgings that memorable night, I soon found I could not sleep. If my words were cool, my brain was in a high state of irritation, thoughts and emotions flashing through it without consciousness or control. I took up one of the ancient classics and read it idly. Then, a little tired, and trying to understand better

> " The beauty that was Greece,
> And the grandeur that was Rome,"

I turned over the pages of a historical novel, which shall be nameless, but which was written by a distinguished classical scholar. The book was in French. It was a story of Carthage just before the time of the Scipios. Greeks, Romans, Scythians, Gauls, and Celts, civilised and uncivilised, would stand before me as if illuminated by the footlights of a theatre, and I should see them, their strange, uncouth dresses, their manners, their progress towards, or recession from, our ideas of culture ; and I should hear their words speaking the thoughts of that ancient world, whose records are hidden like the writings of a palimpsest, beneath the clear characters of Grecian and Roman literature. The first few chapters dealt with the geography of Carthage and its neighbourhood—then came groupings of discontented soldiers encamped under its walls. The colouring grew brighter; the situations more dramatic. Suddenly a festival is held, and all the barbarism that lay hid under Roman culture came out into ghastly prominence. In a midnight revel men are turned into beasts, as if Circe's wand had touched them. There is fierce bestiality and gluttony under midnight stars, blood and wine flow together, eyes glare with the insanity of intoxication, satiety is insatiable and clamours for new excitements and delights ; and the artificial lights of trees and temples reveal a hideous mass of

T

humanity, brutalised, degraded, every prostrate
figure a colossal vice, every face a revelation of
some devil incarnate within.  But these were bar-
barians—the Keltoi, and black Nubians, and wild
Scythians from the desert!  Be it so!  My Romans
at least will be discreet in their revels, as becomes a
nation of conquerors.  Yes, but the discretion shall
be the devilish one, not to exceed unto satiety, but
to reserve one's taste for pleasures yet to come.
The red lights, hung from branches of trees, flashed
luridly on prostrate figures, and on the masters of
the world, moving hither and thither amongst the
debauched revellers, turning over with their san-
dalled feet, with all the contempt of conquerors, the
poor brutes that were forgetting in their drunken
sleep that they were helots and galley-slaves.  Midnight came, and we were introduced through leafy
avenues, and long processions of nude statues, to a
lofty temple, dedicated to a Carthaginian goddess,
and placed on the summit of the hill that crowned
the famous city.  The interior of the temple,
shadowy, and dark, but for lamps that smoked
before the sacred shrines, looked large and beautiful in the dim light ; and vestal priestesses, consecrated to the worship of the Carthaginian Venus,
flitted about in white robes, and kept the sacred
lamp replenished.  Hitherto there was no suggestion of libidinous worship.  The sanctity of religion,
even though a false one, hung over all that I was
witnessing.  But now came the rude awakening.
A procession moved up towards a black bronze
statue of a goddess, the priestesses grouped themselves around, and then commenced a series of rites
which it would be indecent to describe—bestial,
lewd, abominable, yet all carried out with an affectation of religious decorum, which made the whole
thing infinitely disgusting.  I read the whole scene
deliberately over.  Then I said, this is a gross,

Gallic exaggeration! I opened Lempriere. The
thing was there clearly defined enough. I took
down Smith. The truth was confirmed — that
underlying all

> " The beauty that was Greece,
> And the grandeur that was Rome "—

under the art and gaiety and beauty of my ancient
world, was barely concealed a Satanic worship of
lewdness and defilement that surpasses any modern
imagination to conceive. All the grace and charm,
that have fascinated centuries of great artists and
thinkers, was but the thin whitening over sepulchres of rottenness ; and all my gods came tumbling
down from high Olympus, and dragging with them
such airy fabrics of hopes, and dreams of undying
art and immortal beauty, as I had been building
up during the dreary years in which I knew not
God.

What, then, was all the poetry of Greece? Immortal songs embalming corruption, and enclosing
for the centuries records of the degradation of the
race, sprung from the loins of the gods! What
was all the art of Greece, and where were Phidias
and Praxiteles? Alas! at the feet of courtesans,
and embodying in imperishable marble, to be worshipped in the temples of the gods, and then to be
handed down to an admiring posterity, the figures
and features of Lais and Phryne! Alas! for the
saints of Greece! Demosthenes at the feet of Lais
—the fathers of the Areopagus, forgetting justice in
the beauty of Phryne—Diogenes, worshipping afar
off some child of the Republic—Glycera, immortalised by the painters of Sicyon—Cotytto with her
altars and incense at Athens! And in Rome the
vestal priestesses, public courtesans, and Cicero, the
coward, declaiming virtue in the Senate, and Seneca,
the philosopher, dying with his hands gripping in

death the million and a half crowns he had wrung by usurious interest from Roman patrician and plebeian! If the ground had gaped, and I could have seen through the rent every inch of Hell, its unspeakable horrors could not have more clearly manifested to me the meaning of the words—"All flesh had corrupted its way"; and Satan had conquered the world through that vice, of which he, the incarnation of vice, is incapable.

I read the chapter over once more, then flung the book in disgust through the closed window. The crash of broken glass startled me. I stood amid the ruins of a glorious Pantheon. I saw as clear as noonday that the highest culture the human mind has ever attained was but a thin veneering of loathsome vice, and the elements of that culture, the undying languages of Greece and Rome, the theatre, the Forum, comedy and tragedy, Pindaric ode and Sapphic song, were all but the transparent veil that partly concealed, and wholly revealed, the world-old and the world-wide drama of impurity! And Satan, the uncarnal, the immaterial, the impalpable—the Coryphœus of it all!

Lizzie came in, sleepy as to her eyes, and touzled as to her hair.

"The missus wants to know, sir, if anything is broke."

"Yes," said I, "a tremendous lot of statuary."

She gaped around.

"A black bat flew in the window, and a big book went out. Pick it up in the morning, show it to no one, but bring it to me."

I sought inspiration in my old friend, the fire. Charlie's burning words came back to me—

"There is a duel to the death between you and Jesus Christ. And He'll beat you, Goff, beat you to the ground, &c."

It looked likely enough. My disillusionment, com-

menced many years ago, was reaching the end. Only
a few thin vapours were now wreathing themselves
around the sacred form of Him, whom, deep in my
heart, I had always loved. When the full revelation
came, how would it be? Degenerate as I was, the
enthusiasm of Charlie had already infected me; and I
dwelt on the gigantic issues at stake in the world, and
thought what it would be, to be a champion of Jesus
Christ. I scarcely slept that night. One thought
harassed and haunted me. If the human mind, left to
itself, as it was in Greece and Rome, could reach no
loftier perfection than the culmination of high art,
consecrated to the basest purposes; if the most
cultured races of the world could sink so low as to
become worshippers of courtesans, whilst the lofty
position of virtuous women was ignored, and everything sacred about women was polluted and despised, it is clear that there could never be a hope
for humanity outside some special revelation, or
some great gospel of light, that would be reflected not
from the reason of men, but from the luminous mind
of God. The mind of man will never touch again
the lofty heights on which Plato stood; and Plato
was an advocate of polygamy and child-murder!

Then came the reflex-thought—Whither is modern
civilisation rushing? Again we are approaching
an era of high culture. Music and the drama, the
chisel and the brush, are daily leading the minds of
men towards undreamed forms of loveliness; there
is a passion in human hearts consecrated into a
principle that education is the one thing to be desired—the one sure and certain pioneer towards
human perfectibility. Simultaneously, a great rush
is made by the masses of humanity towards a rapid
acquisition of wealth, for wealth means leisure, and
leisure means culture, and all high and holy things
—the human mind, the imperial soul, gifts of nature,
gifts of acquisition, art and its hundred handmaidens,

science and its thousand slaves, the genius of lonely
students, the recluses of the laboratory, the grandeur
of men, the holiness of women—all, all are directed
by some blind, but imperious power in one direction
—the precipice where the highest civilisations have
been shattered, as they went to their fate with the
eternal, but lying watchword on their standards—
progress and human perfectibility.    History is re-
peating itself, and on the same old lines—godless
education for the young, youth disappointed, manhood embittered, womanhood degraded, until the
painful formula appears to be universally recognised,
which says—"The upper classes of society are
materialised, the middle classes vulgarised, the lower
classes brutalised."    And the world goes singing to
its doom.    Only here and there some solitary soul
lifts a warning voice, and is hushed into silence by
the sarcasm: An idealist or a fool!    And is there
a remedy?  Yes! but the old one.  A re-incarnation
of the spirit of Christianity, through the ever old,
ever new, unchangeable doctrines of Catholicity,
which should show itself in more concrete form by
a renewal of the spirit of St. Francis Assisi, and a
revival of the dignity of woman.

Lizzie, with brighter eyes and carefully arranged
hair, brought in the book, as I sat at breakfast next
morning.    It was not much injured.

"I hope you read it, Lizzie?"

"No, sir, I couldn't.   The missus says it is
Latin."

# CHAPTER XIV

## A MOONLIGHT VISIT

> " Could I give
> One great thought to the people, that should prove
> The spring of noble action in their hour
> Of darkness, or control their headlong power
> With the firm reigns of justice and of love ;
>
> I had not feared thee. But to yield my breath
> Life's purpose unfulfilled !—this is thy sting, O Death ! "
> —Sir Noel Paton.

Was it not that master of modern pessimism, Schopenhauer, who professed to believe that life is an irremediable evil, and that that evil shall cease only when the " blunder of existence " is wiped out in the disappearance of the human race by voluntary extinction ? Did not George Eliot say something similar to her friend under the trees in Addison's Walk ? And did they not both laugh to scorn the idea that in some future age man, by his own effort, shall become " wiser, better, and happier " ? Ah me! how lightly now I treat those names that at one time magnetised me ! And why do I use them now ? Because, the evening after I had met Charlie so strangely, I had a note from him quite unexpectedly, asking me to run over and have a cup of tea with him at seven o'clock, and because I accepted his invitation, and had an opportunity of seeing that both pessimists and optimists are wrong, and that men may be lifted to something approaching to perfection, and therefore to happiness, by the magic of that Christian altruism, called charity.

"I sent for you, Goff," said Charlie, as we sat down to a very modest tea, "for, last night after you had gone, I was seized with a sudden desire to see the old house at Mayfield again. Why, I don't know; but will you come?"

"Certainly," I said, jumping at the proposal; "but you know the place is locked up, and uninhabited for ever so long, and I doubt if we can get in."

"Well, we'll try; come along."

It was a fine moonlight night, so clear, so beautiful, that we thought we saw, as in a glass or photograph, the flat disc of the moon assume its spherical shape. It threw black shadows all around us, great areas of darkness from houses, thin latticing of black bars from trees and shrubs. And the night was still as death; even the wisps of clouds that brushed the moon's face from time to time made no whisper in the breeze that floated them so softly across the night. We met numbers of people who had come out to enjoy the beautiful night, until we came into Donnybrook Road, when we were left almost to ourselves. It was delightful to find a light in the old lodge, and, peeping through the diamond panes, we saw the old lodge woman telling her beads over the fire.

She was a little alarmed on seeing us, but when we told her who we were, and the recollection of many a pennyworth of snuff came back to her grateful memory, she was delighted, and very freely gave us up the keys of the college.

"You'll find nothing but the ghosts there, gentlemen," she said; "and, according to all accounts, there's plenty of them; at least, there's plenty of one of them."

"Ah! if we meet no one worse than ourselves, it will be all right," said Charlie.

"Take this little drop of holy water with ye, whatever," she said insinuatingly.

We laughed, and went up the old circular walk to the right. "There's the gate over which Dalton fell the night of Leopardstown races," said Charlie, pointing to the iron gate that led into the garden. "The Grinder didn't seem to make much of it."

We rounded the corner of the chapel, and fitting the rusty key into the hall door, we pushed the heavy oak door open, and stood upon the pavement where I had first seen the Grinder.

"He leaned against the bagatelle-table that stood there," I said to Charlie; "and it was a revelation to me—his voice, his manner, his abruptness—what a chequered history was his!"

"Did I ever tell you," said Charlie, "what he said to me one evening—I think after we returned from Clare?"

"No," I said, with curiosity.

"He told me he often stayed up at night watching for the ghost of the old squire, who hanged himself near the small billiard-room, and that he had seen him more than once—red-coated, booted, and spurred in the library. I looked incredulous. He was positive, and he furthermore said that he often heard the click of the billiard balls at midnight, and used to wait outside the door to make sure, then plunge suddenly in—to find—no one there, but the balls resting quietly against the cushions."

I shivered, for nerves will creep at such ghostly things.

"But that's not the curious thing," said Charlie, as we passed upstairs, along the corridor, and down a back stair that led to the refectory, where the guests were smoked out by my Aunt Sally, "but his reflections. For when I expressed a doubt, and suggested mental delusions, &c., he got almost angry, and said, 'Look here, Travers, the supernatural is nearer than you think. We are touching its fringe. One might hear the garments of the dead sweep by, if our ears were not deadened and muffled by the din of daily life; and we might see the air starred with eyes gazing at us from eternity, if only we were not blinded by the vanities of life.' It was a curious saying from him, for you know we did not credit him with much faith; but I have seen it proved more than once during these five years since we left Mayfield."

"Here eyes do regard you from eternity's still-ness," said I, with a favourite quotation, "but I don't object to being watched by our friends. But why vulgarise the immortals by making them play at billiards, when they ought to be, I was going to say, in their beds?"

The door of the refectory led into a long passage, at the end of which was the lumber-room, where the dreadful deed was committed; and here were the two small billiard-rooms, side by side, where we had played many a game with the Count in days gone by. The moon was southing, so there was no light here, but the shadow cast by the lantern; and there was an eerie, lonesome feeling about the place that was indescribable. Our feet rung hollow on the flags, festoons of cobwebs hung down and brushed us like ghostly fingers in the dark, now and again a rat scampered across the floor, and I must confess there was a creepy feeling around the roots of my hair, as if it was getting ready to stand erect at some horror, according to venerable tradition.

"Charlie," said I at last, "let's get away out of this! It's an eerie place."

"Did you hear any noise?" he replied.

"None but the echoes of our voices," I replied.

"Listen!" he said, his hand to his ear. I listened, and click, click came to our ears, as clearly as the beating of our hearts or our watches.

Charlie smiled.

"I'm curious to go in there," he said.

"For God's sake," said I, thoroughly frightened, "come away, Charlie, we have had quite enough of this."

He walked over and pushed open the billiard-room door. I followed tremblingly. The yellow light shone on an empty room, into which the moonbeams were struggling through very dirty windows. Charlie walked around deliberately, throwing the light of the lantern into every corner. He then came back and said—

"I thought so."

"The supernatural has no terror for me, Goff," he said, "it's men and their ways I'm afraid of. But why are you, my philosopher, so fearful?"

"Philosophy is all right," said I, "by your fireside. But like Voltaire, in the thunderstorm, I'd have given a good deal a while ago for a drop of that holy water the old woman proffered us."

We passed along the bedroom corridor again. Charlie was quite gay.

"Here's where O'Dell gave me the fright; here's where the Grinder used to knock at the Frenchman's door, 'I'm *au naturel*, I'm *au naturel*, I cannot get up;' here's Herr Messing's room, &c."

We stood in the hall again. The chapel was on our left. We went in. On a sudden Charlie's manner changed.

"Goff," he cried, clutching me by the arm, "here were said to me the things I am saying to the world to-day. From that recess," he pointed to where the tabernacle used to stand, "came voices that penetrated every fibre of my being—not your politic voices of Goethe, but accents such as set on fire the dull heart of Peter, and broke the heart of Magdalen. Sometimes, I suppose, you were surprised at certain things I used to say to you. I only interpreted what was said to myself. And now, listen! I go to my Passion. To prepare for it we shall go up to the Holy Mountain together; for you, too, will be tried. You must be with me in my sorrow, and then, when I shall have passed away, you must take up my work. No matter," he continued, as I was about to interrupt him, "what you feel now. The light will come and shine in darkness, and the darkness will comprehend it. You don't see God now, but you will. You feel the pressure of His hands, as He conquers you, breaking down your pride; but one day He will draw aside the veil, and you will see Him as He is. Come now, let us go!"

He extinguished the light in the lantern, we passed out the porch door, and, going down the steps from which I had flung O'Dell, we were steeped in the moonlight again. By some unconscious movement we went over to the right, and began pacing up and down on our old familiar walk under the limes. Sometimes in shadow, sometimes streaked by the black bars cast by the branches, sometimes in an open sea of moonlight, we walked up and down, and, as of old, the leaves were nodding and whispering to each other in their new birth, and the scents of lilac and laburnum filled the air with perfume, and brought to our memories recollections that had long lain dormant and disused. I had often thought of that place, and that time, and these associations. Now they all came up again; but was it that dreadful thing called experience, or was it that want of imagination that leaves us so early in life? The poetry had passed away, and the glamour, and I saw only the black shadows on the dark grass, and the purple and yellow blossoms, and two fools, catching cold under night dews, instead of being warmly housed and protected. But Charlie's words had a strange effect on me: and I was beginning to feel the least spiritual pride in thinking that God was actually thinking of me. And after my humiliation I think the first indication of an awakened faith was this pleasurable emotion, that after all, humbled, defeated, shamed, conquered in the battle of life, I was yet of so much consequence that the Divine Shepherd counted me as among His flock; nay, that He condescended to wrestle with me, as the angel with Jacob, and thought me of sufficient importance to be contended with in that problem, which, perhaps, makes God less impatient of humanity, whether His love, or their pride, shall conquer in the end.

Not a word we spoke however. Charlie had his thoughts, and I mine, until some far-off clock roused us, and we woke from our reverie.

We turned homewards with some pleasant and some gloomy thoughts in our hearts, and our way lay through the city. We avoided the crowded thoroughfares, and plunged into some by-lanes that branched out occasionally into gloomy courts, where the masses of toiling and sweating humanity swarmed. Entering one of these, we were rather agreeably surprised at finding signs of comfort and cleanliness, where there had been a chronic condition of dirt and disorder. The door of a pleasant-looking cottage was open and we could see within. A number of children, conning over their lessons, were grouped around a table. Near the fire the mother sat knitting; and on the other side of the hearth, the father, an artisan, was leisurely smoking and reading. We knocked and entered. The man cast a keen glance at us, then flushed up and took off his hat respectfully.

"Everything going well?" said Charlie cheerfully.

"Everything going well, sir," replied the man.

"Plenty of employment, and enough of leisure?" said Charlie, pointing to the open book.

"Yes, sir," said the man with a smile, "plenty of both."

"Work all the week, and a trip to the seaside on Sundays, with certain baskets, which the youngsters know?" said Charlie with delight.

The children smiled at the delightful reminiscences and the still more delightful prospects revealed in that word " baskets."

" Yes, sir," said the man, " since *you* taught us, Mr. Travers, to know what life is, life has been a different thing to us."

" Ay, God bless you," said the woman, " so it has, sir, so it has !  And is this Mr. Travers ? "

" Why, look here, sir," said the man, pointing his pipe at me, " until this young gentleman came from —well—from God, I thought life was work and— porter ; I thought Death was Hell, and not a drop to wet your tongue.  I thought every penny spent on the young 'uns so many pints of porter lost.  I grudged the penny at the church door to Almighty God : because two pennies meant—porter.  God is my witness, sir, I never knew the faces of my chil- dren until you, Mr. Travers, showed them to me. Because they were in bed when I went to work in the morning, and when I came home at night, I saw only frightened white shadows, that hid under the bed and under the table from me."

The man was labouring under strong emotion.

" I never heard the birds in the spring-time, sir," he continued, " for twenty-five years since I used to go bird-nesting on the slopes of Lugnaquilla ; I had not seen the trees bursting into greenness in the spring-time, I had not seen the blue sky over our heads, nor the blue waters since I was a boy.  For why ?  Because I was blinded with the smoke of the taproom, and the poison of drink was in my eyes and ears, and my feet were clogged with the wet sawdust, and I cursed God in Heaven for making me, and my employer for not giving me more money to drink.  Of course I heard of Hell ; but what did we care for Hell when Hell was raging within us ? And we heard of Heaven, but our Heaven was within the circle of the pewter pint.  Thank God !

it's all changed. You, sir, have taught us to live. We believe now in God, for we are beginning to see all that He has made for us; and I do not envy the Queen of England, nor the Shah of Persia, when I sit on the rocks down at Bray, or up at Howth, and smoke my pipe and feel that all is good, and that life is pleasant."

"Try him with Schopenhauer," said Charlie in a whisper.

"That's all very well," said I, taking my cue from Charlie, "but, now, confess that sometimes you feel that the whole world is a mistake, and that it were better for us all to be swept aside into everlasting perdition. After all, what is life to you? Six days of work, work, work—work from dawn to darkness, work, with poor remuneration, and all your sweat and toil coining gold for your employer! And what pleasure have you in life? Poor food, a cabin in a wretched courtyard, that little square of sky obscured by dirty linen hung out to dry, and a day at the seaside, which is so dull that you are praying for evening to come to take you back to the dirty slums again. Now, be honest, and tell the truth! You know as well as I, or as well as—well as—Schopenhauer, the greatest of modern philosophers, that life is a burden to be laid down as quickly, but as easily as we can shift it off our shoulders; that we are an accursed race, living under the ban of an unforgiving, because a pitiless, because an impersonal Deity; and that there is but one hope for the world, and that is, that the wretched race of men shall die out and leave this planet a desert as speedily as possible."

I don't know whether he understood all that I had been saying, but I never saw face of actor shot through with so many conflicting emotions. He was very angry with me; but he pitied me more.

"Perhaps you're only joking, sir," he said at last,

"but if you are in airnest, God pity you! No, sir, I don't agree with you at all. I don't say it is the best possible world" ("a controverted point," I whispered to Charlie); "but I do say that life is pleasant enough to me just now. We have enough, and my old woman, and the children. I have to work for it. Yes! but my work is my greatest pleasure. I am a carpenter." (I smelt the pine aroma from his clothes.) "I go to my work at six. I don't miss the time till breakfast. Why, sir, a good tradesman loves his work and his tools. You takes up a rough board, you puts your plane on it, you sees the shavings curling over and the smooth surface coming up, you takes your chisel, cuts down corners and angles, fits your mortices, does your moulding and rabbiting; and there! you takes your pipe in your mouth, and says to yourself, 'That's a decent job.' True, my master rides in his carriage, but he must, because he cannot walk, he is so gouty. He can't ate bacon, and cabbage, and cornbeef" (the youngsters' eyes twinkled), "and, Lord bless you, sir! the doctors won't let him put a lump of sugar in his tea. He is always bandaged up like an elephant. He cannot sleep because he's never tired; he can't eat because he's never hungry. And me! I could eat horse-nails, and jump over a five-barred gate. No, sir, 'tis a grand world, if we only knew it. Look at that fellow," he cried, holding up a chubby youngster, with eyes like saucers, "isn't life worth living for him?"

"Come along, Goff," said Charlie, laughing, "Schopenhauer takes a back seat here."

"Damn Schopenhauer," I said as we passed into the street, after a cordial good-night from the carpenter. "I firmly believe that all the nonsense of modern literature, that is, all its philosophy, comes from sour-visaged dyspeptics, like Carlyle and Schopenhauer."

We were passing through a quiet street, that led into a great square, when Charlie stopped, turned back, studied one or two numbers and knocked.

"Is Mr. Weldon at home?" he asked.

"I'll see, sir," said the girl.

"Now, Goff," said Charlie, taking out his watch, "it's now exactly half-past nine. What ought a typical student be doing at this hour?"

"Let me see," said I. "A typical student is now staring with all his might from the gallery or top stall of the Gaiety at a painted Jezebel on the stage, or puffing smoke and bad compliments into the face of Mimi at the Grosvenor, or—staking his immortal soul at Dalby's that he will make a break of fifty!"

"Come," said Charlie, smiling, as the girl asked us upstairs.

We passed into a neat room, rather tastefully furnished, where a young student, in a loose dressing-gown, was smoking, whilst he sorted some papers that lay before him.

"I expected you," he said.

"Not because of any new difficulty?" replied Charlie.

"No," the student said, looking up from his papers, "there is, of course, some obstruction, and the papers refuse to print this" (pointing to a pile of manuscript), "but I should hardly mind except that the enthusiasm of some of our fellows is flagging, and—well," he said, smiling, "there is a little hankering after the flesh-pots."

"Of course," said Charlie, "that is to be expected" (but he looked despondent), "this thing is so wholly out of their ordinary groove; but we *must* go on. Will any of them quite abandon us?"

"Yes, I think so," said the other, "you can have no idea of the awful chaffing we get at the bars, in the dissecting-room, at sports, everywhere."

"I have calculated it all," said Charlie impres-

U

sively; "it's the worst evil of our time and race. But," he said, bringing down his hand with vehemence on the table, "if a dozen graduates of Oxford threw up degrees, prospects, all the pleasures and ambitions of life last year, and went out to Senegambia as missioners, what in God's name is there to prevent Catholic Irishmen from doing a little Divine work at home? What is there in Ireland to make us ashamed of doing the things that we should be proud to do in England and America? I am told that Irishmen in the Civil Service in England will serve Mass in cassock and surplice, will accompany processions, will teach at nightschools, will become good and active members of every Catholic organisation, but ask them to do those things here, and they think you are taking an unpardonable liberty!"

"Don't blame them," said the student, "they have to face an awful fire of sarcasm."

"And sarcasm is the language of the devil," said Charlie. "Carlyle is the author of that expression."

"But now, Mr. Travers," said the student, "you know I am with you heart and soul, but do you think this will do any good? In face of every kind of workmen's organisations, how can this avail?"

He pushed over a paper, or rather a thick manuscript, inscribed "Workmen's Guilds, and the French Catholic System." I turned over a few pages, and grasped the idea. It was simply a plan put into successful operation by some French Catholic capitalists of giving their men certain shares in the firm for which they worked.

"What is impracticable about it?" said Charlie.

"It makes two suppositions," replied the student. "That the monopolists can be generous, and that the workman can overcome his servility and inertia."

"But the principle is all right?" asked Charlie.

"Yes," said Weldon.

"Then keep hammering at it," said Charlie, rising. "Mr. Weldon," said he pleadingly, turning back from the door, "you won't desert me?"

"Never fear," said Weldon. "The whole thing has already done myself so much good, I am not going to give it up."

As we approached Charlie's lodgings, a young woman dressed in black passed us rapidly, then as rapidly turned back and once more faced us and stared us boldly under the flare of a gas lamp. She was well dressed, and not by any means dissipated looking; but her eyes—big, staring eyes—were the windows of Hell.

"That's the one evil we must not dare touch," said Charlie as we stood in the hall. "When a man falls, his fall is reparable, for 'tis the fall of Adam; when a woman falls, it is irreparable, for 'tis the fall of a Lucifer again. It is the breaking up of a world which the Creator only can patch together again. Let me hear from you, Goff, when you are ready for your journey south."

"All right," I replied; yet it was with a sinking heart I watched him toil heavily up the stairs, one hand clenched tightly over his heart.

As I turned homewards, the woman accosted me.

"Pardon," she said with the voice and accent of a lady, "but might I ask the name of your companion?"

"You may," I replied, "but you won't be told. There's his residence; go, ask himself."

She let out a furious oath, and I was glad to get away, and to know that Charlie was safe at home.

# CHAPTER XV

## FROM THE MOUNTAIN OF MYRRH

"Vadam ad montem myrrhæ."

"I will go to the mountain of myrrh."

—*Cant. iv.* 6.

IT was not a *cause célèbre*, as Agnes Deane supposed.
It was a minor case which attracted little attention,
for the Muse of history is now so busy that she
flings little events into the rubbish corners of newspapers, and, like the memories of men, has no room
except for a European war, or the death of a king.

I expected to be examined briefly about Leviston's
condition of mind, and no more; and I was hardly
interested about the issue of the case, for new ideas
and new sensations of a more exalted order were
rapidly pushing aside my older associations. I was
so little interested that, as I sat waiting to be called
in turn, I was busy studying a curious syllabus of
lectures which had come to me that morning by post,
sent by an unknown hand. They appeared to embrace every question of civil and ecclesiastical interest; and I could not help making the reflection
that the men who could write these must have very
little time for other reading. "The Church and
Education," "The Church and the Artisan," "The
Italian Renaissance," "Ximenes," "Pombal and the
Jesuits," "The Church and the Emperors," "The
Concordat," "The Benedictines in England"—all
these titles opened up to me a new world, in which
I, with my Kants, and Fichtes, and Schopenhauer,

was a perfect stranger. "Yet it is your own country,"
a voice whispered, and I was ashamed.

The case of *Oliver* v. *Henderson* was duly called.
It was a suit to prove the validity of a will, made by
W. H. Leviston, Q.C., on September 26, 187–, in
which testator bequeathed all his real and personal
estate to his beloved wife, Gwendoline Gascoigne
Oliver Leviston, and appointed Mrs. Oliver sole trustee. The validity of the will was contested by James
Henderson, on behalf of certain Protestant charities
in the city of Dublin, to which large legacies had
been bequeathed by the deceased Leviston by a
former will, dated July 12, 187–. I think Mrs.
Oliver was the first witness to step on the table.
After a few minutes of her examination, I began to
realise that I should be an important factor in the
case. I looked over, and saw Hubert Deane smiling
at me, and I remembered what Agnes Deane had
said. Mrs. Oliver testified that on the day on
which the will, which left her sole trustee, and her
daughter sole legatee, was perfected, she had acci-
dentally asked a hostile witness, named Mr. Austin,
as to the testamentary capacity of Mr. Leviston, and
had received the reply that Mr. Leviston had then
the perfect command of his reason—"was as rational
as ourselves." She also testified that this Mr.
Austin was particularly ill-disposed towards herself
and her daughter, had been ignominiously sent
away from her house five years ago in a workhouse
van, accompanied by her servant, who had grown
mysteriously attached to him. Since he had been
placed in charge of Mr. Leviston, he had been re-
peatedly disrespectful to her, and had crowned his
infamy by actually suggesting that she had plied
her unfortunate son-in-law with drink, and had even
gone farther, and (here came forth a spotless handkerchief, whose perfume filled the court, and made
a young solicitor sneeze), accused her of supplying

the deceased with the chloral which caused his death. The cross-examination did not shake her testimony. There was the will, signed by Leviston, witnessed by two respectable tradesmen; and they could have the evidence of a hostile witness to prove that Leviston was perfectly cognisant of what he was doing, and quite "*capax*" when the will was made. Gwennie was called, and looked pitiful enough. She could only testify that her husband had again and again declared that he intended to leave everything he possessed absolutely to her. True; he had been drinking and in delirium. Even the very day the will purported to be made, he had made a dreadful exhibition of himself, &c. Gwennie was not as good a witness as her mother. The witnesses to the will were called, testifying that they had been working at a certain public-house on the day in question, were invited to drink by the testator (which they did not refuse), were invited to sign by the testator, who was accompanied by an unknown gentleman, did sign, that was their signature, &c. Was testator drunk, or incompetent? Certainly not. He looked a little seedy, that was all.

I passed a paper on to the solicitor, who opposed probate; he read it, shook his head, and did nothing. Things looked well for Mrs. Oliver.

The opposing counsel made an elaborate statement, leaving out all the essentials. Dr. Noakes was called, testified that the deceased was suffering from delirium, produced by the excessive use of alcohol, and he would not consider that he was competent to discharge business, or had sufficient control of his mental faculties to resist undue pressure or influence at the date on which the will was made. Sister Philippa was called, and declined to give evidence, on the ground that she had been in attendance on Mrs. Leviston, and not on Mr. Leviston, and rarely, if ever, saw the latter. The day-nurse was called, deposed to the fact that Mr. Leviston was habitually delirious, and on the day in question had escaped from the house, and made a dreadful exhibition of himself, and that she had been severely reprimanded by the doctor, because Mr. Leviston had been surreptitiously supplied with drink during her hours of charge. Who supplied the drink? She did not know, but suspected. Whom? Counsel objected strenuously, and the judge allowed the objection. But Mrs. Oliver looked uncomfortable.

Geoffrey Austin was called. I mounted the witness-table unhesitatingly—I had nothing to tell but the truth. Alas! I did not know that I was standing before the modern Inquisition, which was infinitely more relentless than that of mediæval times, and which claimed the right of searching and probing into hidden depths, which no eye, but the Maker's, should see. In direct examination I testified that Mr. Leviston was quite competent to make a will, that is, he had complete control of his reason, but he had grown so weak, he had no resolution, but could be led to do anything that was suggested. He could not, I declared, have made such a will on the day in question, for subsequently, he again and again declared that he proposed to make a new will, leaving everything he had to his wife. If he did make such a will, such certainly were his intentions, but he must have been utterly incompetent when he made it, for he had forgotten all about it. My own opinion was——

"That's not evidence," shouted the opposing counsel.

"On the 26th of September, after Mr. Leviston had escaped the surveillance of the nurse, where did you find him?"

"In a public-house, called the 'Sailor's Home.'"

"In what condition was he found?"

"Hopelessly intoxicated."

"Your theory is that he was decoyed thither?"

Counsel objected.

"Mr. Austin, you were generally on night duty with Mr. Leviston?"

"Yes."

"Do you remember anything particular that occurred on the night of the 25th of September?"

"Yes. Three men entered the room where I was watching. One came over to the bedside, and after some opprobrious speeches, flung brandy into Mr. Leviston's eyes. The others remained quiet, and protested. On leaving the room, the first man turned around, and bade me keep silent, for they should be knocking around for some days, as they had business on hand."

"Did you recognise them?"

"Yes, one was Frederick Oliver, son of Mrs. Oliver —the others were the witnesses of the will to-day."

There was a flutter in court, Mrs. Oliver was startled, and whispered rapidly to her counsel. Some commotion in the gallery made me look up. There in the front seat were the two last persons in the world I should wish to see there—Agnes Deane, well-dressed, bland and smiling as usual, and Helen Bellamy, grave and solemn, her two large eyes resting dreamily on me. The judge thought the case was becoming interesting. He adjourned for luncheon.

During that half-hour the court became crowded. Detectives were summoned, and hastily exchanged notes. And in some mysterious manner, reporters began to come in, flushed and breathless, as if summoned hastily to witness a particularly interesting case. People looked furtively to where I sat, and whispered amongst themselves. Mrs. Oliver and her solicitor had gone out. The two witnesses were nowhere to be seen. I daresay some people would have been flattered at the commotion I had unconsciously caused. I was terrified. And it did not tend to soothe my nerves, when a pellet of paper was flung across the witness table to me, signed Hubert Deane, and bidding me be on my guard, for I had fallen into the hands of a particularly dangerous antagonist.

At half-past one my name was again called, as the judge ascended the bench, and counsel ranged themselves along the witness-table. As they did, a figure shot up almost beside me, and a keen, sharp, eager face looked steadily at me. I drew my nerves together for the onset. His first question upset me, though put so blandly that I had begun to reason that he must be on our side.

" Mr. Austin, what position do you hold now ? "

I flushed crimson, as I answered—

" I am gate-keeper and ticket-collector at the —— Hall."

Though I did not dare look up, I knew that Mrs. Deane and Helen started back in surprise. My examiner saw his triumph, drew up his gown over his shoulders, planted one leg on the seat, and, staring at me, said—

" You have told a pretty story about your night-watch——"

" I have told the truth," I said angrily.

" I am quite sure. Why did you let these dangerous night-marauders into a sick man's room ? Did they break in by force ? "

" No."

" How did they enter ? "

" By the door that led from the lawn into the sick chamber."

" It was open, then ? "

" No. I—I opened it."

He smiled, and looked around at judge and jury.

" They, or at least one, according to your evidence, assaulted the sick man, who was in your charge ? "

" Yes."

" You allowed it ? "

" I could not prevent it."

" You could have raised an alarm."

" There was a sick lady upstairs — Mrs. Leviston."

" It comes to this, Mr. Austin, ticket-collector at —— Hall," he shouted, changing his whole tone and manner into one of angry sarcasm, "that you —confidant, friend, warden of this poor man— betrayed your trust, opened the door at midnight to three men, whom you suspected to be his enemies, let them depart without protest, and never mentioned the incident to any one until this moment.   Is that true ? "

" It is," I stammered.

" Very good.   Have you any proof, direct or indirect, that undue influence was used towards Mr. Leviston on the day he made the will, and on the day when you declared he was quite rational and competent ? "

" I have no proof, but——"

" That will do.   Now, for a chapter of your biography.   You entered this lady's house nearly six years ago as a lodger ? "

" Yes."

" You pretended you belonged to an aristocratic family ? "

" Certainly not."

" Now, jog your memory a little.   Do you remember a conversation with these ladies about the Austins of Fermanagh ? "

" Yes."

" You protested you did not belong to that family ? "

" Yes."

" And you implied that you belonged to a more aristocratic branch in the south ? "

" Certainly not. I never cared one brass farthing for all the aristocracy of Ireland put together."

" Very good. Socialist, and, we shall see presently—freethinker. Do you remember a certain occasion when you were flung out into the street from a certain Dame Street establishment ? "

" I do."

" You appealed to the directors ? "

" Yes."

" And they said ' Serve you right' ? "

" Yes."

" Very good. You left this lady's house with a young servant girl ? "

" That's a low insinuation," I cried fiercely, but I did not know the law. The judge promptly ordered me to say yes or no.

" Allow me to repeat the question. You left Mrs. Oliver's house with a young servant, with whom you lived for some time ? "

" I was taken out——" I tried to say.

" Yes or no ! "

" I say I was suffering from pneumonia, and I——"

" Yes—or—no ? "

" Let it be ' yes ' if you like," I said in despair. I know I was flushed, hot, and angry, and I knew that Helen Bellamy's eyes were fixed on me. I expected every moment that the ladies would stand up and leave the court. Hubert Deane was playing with a paper-knife, his eyes fixed on the table.

" You abandoned the girl ? "

" I left her house : there was no abandonment."

" And then," he continued with a leer, " you joined the noble army of crossing-sweepers ? "

" It was honest, at least," I replied.

" You held horses at the theatre ? "

" Yes."

" Do you remember sleeping under the brewery walls ? "

" Yes."

" In short, you were everything disreputable ? "

" I was never a convict, like your client."

The bolt went home ; but he was prepared.

" Don't be alarmed : that pleasure is in store for you. Now, we have had a specimen of your socialistic theories. Read that. Do you recognise the handwriting ? "

" It is mine," I said in dismay, as I looked over a page of manuscript notes written six years ago.

" Thank you for the acknowledgment. It runs thus, gentlemen : ' For surely this pantheistic theory, which runs through all philosophy, pervades every literature, informs the best of the world's poetry, has attracted and held spell-bound the loftiest intellects, can be no passing chimera of philosophers, nor the watchword of contending school factions, in France, England, or Germany. The idea of an impersonal God, of nature permeated with God, of the fulfilment of the ancient prophecies, ' *Ye shall be as gods,*' is no passing whim. Where then is its reason ? On what foundations, strictly philosophical, and therefore provable, does it rest ? Plato preached it ; it passed from Egypt to Greece, from Greece to Rome ; it lay hidden in mediæval universities, it burst forth in the elaboration of Spinoza, it is whispered to ourselves in the melody of Tennyson and the rhythm of Wordsworth.' So this twaddle goes on, and you have had the hardihood to stand on that bench, to take into your hand the book whose inspiration you deny, and to swear by the God in whom you disbelieve—go down, sir."

I went down from the mountain of bitterness, crushed, withered, angry, embittered, once again in spirit a rebel and an outcast. I knew, of course, that my doom was sealed. Neither Hubert nor

Agnes Deane would condescend to look at me again, and Helen—how could I ever look at her, stamped as I was in public court as a profligate and unbeliever? I hardly heeded the low conditions of life of which I had been compelled to make manifestation. I thought their pity would cover my degradation, even though I had concealed it, perhaps dishonourably, from them. But I was not allowed to defend myself against the false insinuations of that clever dastard; and we know that, however theoretically we may affect to despise the decisions or admissions of a court of justice, it does leave behind it an indelible seal of approbation, or an equally indelible stigma of shame.

I sat for an hour, whilst this counsel was addressing the Bench, dazed, blinded by the excitement that culminated in my shame. I heard almost unconcernedly the words "Judas," "This Balaam that came to curse, and remained to bless," "This interloper," "This tramp that found his way into respectable families to purloin their secrets and sell them," and all the other invectives that are permitted under the Ægis of the British Constitution. I heard as in a dream that the verdict was given for the plaintiff, and the will was established by law. Then, amid the buzz and hum of that human hive, I passed out under God's skies, a broken-hearted and despairing mortal. I determined to push my way rapidly towards Charlie's lodgings, and fling myself once and for ever into the arms of God. And I and Charlie would go to the ends of the world together, and I would be free for ever from the good or evil report that came from these beasts of men. I passed a hairdresser's shop, and saw my reflection in a mirror. I started back frightened at my own appearance. Just then an arm was locked in mine, and Hubert Deane said, as quietly as if nothing had occurred—

"Come along, Austin, I am going to Kingstown to dine. I want a puff of air after that beastly court. Come along!"

Before I had time to protest, or explain, he hustled me into a cab, drove to Westland Row, had my ticket purchased, had plunged me into a first-class carriage, loaded me with evening papers, and then found breath to say—

"Not a word. Phew! You gave me the deuce of a run, and I am getting winded."

Without a word we glided along to Kingstown, and entered the first hotel there just in time for *table d'hôte*. Hubert was in an ever-varying mood of exhilaration, crossness, boyish fun, and masculine bitterness. He ordered the waiters around with scant respect, which rather frightened me, who had such an inborn respect for these potentates; cursed the viands, which I thought good enough for the Lord Lieutenant; asked me, with sundry profane objurations, why I was not eating; what an epicure I had become; was there anything else I would particularly like? &c. To all which I was silent, too full of emotion to eat, and not knowing what to think of my friend. At last the weary courses were ended, and we went into a private room for a cigar.

"Coffee or toddy?" he asked.

"Coffee," I replied.

"Get me some Scotch whisky and cold water. And look here, you fellow, let it be Scotch; none of your vile-smelling northern distilleries."

"I stick to the good old fashion, Austin," he said in an explanatory tone. "I don't care for these Oriental drugs of tea and coffee, that make a fellow too cautious, and watch every word he is saying. We must forget ourselves sometimes, or go mad."

I sipped my coffee and smoked in silence. I knew all this was but the prologue to some ex-

planations. I thought it was very like giving a
criminal a first-class breakfast before hanging him.
I wonder what he'll say, and how he will give me
my *congé.* Thank God! Agnes and Helen are not
here. I whispered a little litany, " *Ursula, ora pro
me,*" and went on reading and speculating. Hubert
held the usual pink paper in his hand, and appeared
to be entirely engrossed in some sporting news from
England. We were quite alone. I suppose half-an-
hour or more of this suspense elapsed, when at last,
rousing himself from his preoccupation, he stood
up, his back to the fireplace, and looked steadily at
me.

"Austin," said he at last, softening his voice,
"have I and my wife treated you badly?"

"On the contrary," I replied, "you have treated
me far better than I deserved, or could have expected."

"We admitted you freely to our house?"

"You did."

"We introduced you to our friends?"

"Yes."

"We scarcely had a domestic secret you did not
share?"

"You have been extremely kind; and I—I have
no excuse to offer."

"All this time you were starving and a beggar?"

"I was," I replied; "it was unpardonable."

"You were a penny boy on the streets?"

"Yes."

"A tramp?"

"Yes. For God's sake spare me, Deane; this is
worse than that trial to-day. I don't know what to
say, or what excuse to offer. I have treated you
shamefully, and your good wife. But for Ursula's
sake, if I may mention her name, spare me, and let
me go."

"I cannot let you go yet," he said severely.

" You owe me some satisfaction for this treatment. I dare say, now," he continued jauntily, placing his hands under his coat tails, "very often when you came to our place of an evening the very coat you wore was not your own ? "

" Quite so."

" Or, if it were your own, probably you only just had redeemed it from the pawnshop ? "

" Quite true."

" And you slept side by side with beggars and tramps ?  Is it so ? "

" It is so."

" And came to us after warming your hands at the brewery fire ? "

" Yes."

" I think I might almost condone all this squalor and lowness, but you, on your admission to-day," he said bitterly, " acted the part of a profligate and a criminal——"

" I beg your pardon, Deane," I said, " if you just allow me to——"

" Make matters worse ?  No.  Well, it comes to this, that you, a profligate, entered the society of pure women, took my sweet child into your arms, posed as a religious and virtuous man——"

" If you would only permit me, Hubert," I said pleadingly.

" Acted the part, I say," he continued, "of a noble and virtuous man ; and all the time you were a profligate, an unbeliever, a Balaam's ass, a Judas, as that learned man appropriately called you."

A few tears silently dropped on my hands as I stood up to depart.  Then I felt a stunning blow that sent me back into my chair, and Hubert Deane, casting aside the mask, said, " D——n you, Austin, do you think I am a fool ?  Or, supposing I was a fool, as I confess I may have been, do you think Agnes Deane has not eyes in her head ?  Yes, Austin,

you treated us shamefully, not, as you suppose, by
concealing your poverty, but by your infernal pride
that would not let us serve you. As for that vile story
that that vile woman invented, and that paragon of
lawyers repeated, about your profligacy, do you
think we are such idiots as not to discount it all?
Ah! and if we were, do you not know that one
thought of our little darling, who loved you, would
dispel it all? You acted meanly, Austin, in not trust-
ing us, that's all."

"I dared not speak of such things," I said humbly.
"God knows, Deane, your home was the only spot
on earth that I could reverence. I dared not run the
risk of losing it or being turned away from it."

"You are right; it was I was the fool. Agnes
saw through it all. 'Hubert,' she used to say, 'I
tell you Mr. Austin is very poor.' 'How do you
know that?' I used to ask. God help us! Women
can see, with their wonderful instinct, what we fools
cannot see with our open eyes. How mad she'll be!
She'll never forgive herself or me."

So we talked and reasoned, until about eight
o'clock a gentle tap was heard at the door, and
Agnes Deane, perfectly dressed, as usual, came in.
She walked up to where I was sitting, and leaned
over the armchair.

"Let him alone, Agnes," said her husband, "I
have abused him to my heart's content. He's a low
fellow."

She shook her head mournfully. "I told you all,"
she said to her husband. No woman could demand
or receive greater satisfaction than is contained in
these words.

"Could I have a cup of tea in this place?" she
asked. "I'm tired, thirsty, almost hungry. But I
had to see Gwennie home. Poor child, she feels
that the verdict is unjust, and wants to know from
you, Hubert, how she is going to rid herself of all

X

this encumbrance of wealth which the law gives her."

"She needn't be troubled," said Hubert, "the law and Leviston gave her but little."

"Mysterious again, Hubert," said his wife, "what income will she have?"

"About £150 a year from all sources."

"What became then of all Leviston's property?"

"Mortgaged up to the hilt. Look here, Aggie, you have a right to see this as much as I."

She took a heavy parchment from his hands, and read it eagerly. He took it back, and made a gesture as if to place it in the fire.

"We'll burn it with ceremony," she replied, "when we get home."

She had her tea, and enjoyed it, then continued looking at me curiously.

"You want to ask something?" she said.

I said "No."

"But you do. There is no use in concealing things from me. I knew all your evidence to-day before you spoke it, but I was never so tempted in my life as I was to pitch my parasol at that savage —What's his name, Hubert?"

"Warden," he said.

"I knew that lawyers can be brutal," she continued, "but I did not think that any one could reach such a climax of savagery as that wretch. Gwennie, poor child, told me all as we went home together. Mr. Austin, you must give me that girl's address."

"I haven't seen her for nearly two years," I replied.

"If she's in Dublin, I'll find her out. Katrine was her name, was it not? Why, the whole thing reads like a story. But, you were going to ask me a question, Mr. Austin?"

"I am not aware that I was, Mrs. Deane."

"But I know you were. What hypocrites you men are."

I was silent.

"Well, I may as well tell you. You need never expect to see Helen Bellamy again. I know you don't care. But, after the exhibition of to-day, of course she cannot think of ever seeing you again."

She nodded her head oracularly.

"No; never again! What's that you said that savage's name was, Hubert?"

"Warden," he replied; "what fickle memories you women have!"

"Yes, except for love or hate," she replied. "Now, Hub, if ever you give a case to that—that—that ogre again, I'll—I'll put water in all your tobacco pouches, and cut off every button from your shirts, I will."

The door was flung open, and Helen and Alfred came in. The latter walked up smiling, and held out his hand to me.

"You had a rough time, Goff," he said; "I heard to-day."

"Yes," I said wearily, "I have had quite a round of sensations."

"Never mind, old man," he cried, "but you have acted badly towards us all."

"So I've been telling him," said Hubert Deane. "I never knew such infernal pride."

"Why, my dear fellow, I had a hundred chances of pushing him on if I only knew it. And, you know, we never think of such things. Did you suspect it, now?"

"No," said Alfred, "but my sister did."

"I told you so," said Agnes significantly. "Come, it's getting late, and the wee ones must go to bed. What a lot of wisdom is outside the heads of men, Helen!"

By one of those subtle contrivances which women

alone know how to frame dexterously, it was arranged that Hubert and Agnes Deane took Alfred
under their protection, leaving Helen Bellamy to
follow with me. We went down in some unconscious way to the pier, which as yet had not become
thronged with the fashionable crowds that would
make it impassable in the summer months. A few
couples strolled up and down, or sat on the granite
boulders, and looked dreamily out to sea. One or
two yachts lolled on the roll of the tide, which
washed up with its old persistence and toyed with
the green tongues of seaweed. Far out to sea, a grey
cloud marked the passage of the evening mail-boat,
and at home, lights twinkled in drawing-room and
dining-room, and weary merchants went up the ter-
races that led to their suburban homes. For a long
time Helen and I walked on silently. My own spirit
was too full of emotion to speak. I had passed
through such a succession of bitter and pleasant
sensations that day that I hardly felt the spirit or
courage to allude to them again. And yet, what
else could we speak of ?

When we came to the end of the pier, and leaned
on the iron rail, and looked out to sea, Helen broke
silence.

" That was a bitter trial you had to-day ! "

" Yes," I said, " but I should not have minded, if
you had not been there."

" Perhaps," she replied, " we should not have
gone there. But Agnes insisted. She wanted me
to see how your evidence would break that will.
And yet I should have been sorry, for Gwennie's
sake."

" Agnes," I said, now without hesitation, " is always weaving little romances around us, Helen."

" Yes," she replied, " but, as you know well, these
things are not for me, nor for thee."

There was a long pause. I knew all this long

before, and did not for a moment hope that it should be otherwise.

"They," she said at length, in her quiet, solemn way, that put discussion aside, "they who have suffered as you have suffered, and I, must look higher for what we have to seek, or what we have to do."

"You are prophesying, like Charlie Travers," I replied, noticing, not for the first time, the strange similarity in their ideas. "He says I have a work to do also, somewhat like his own; but I am very far from that as yet."

"You have grown estranged from God," she replied, probing the innermost depths of my mind; "you placed your hopes in human wisdom, and what have you found?"

"*Poma Sodomitica, mala insana,*" I said bitterly to myself.

"Helen," said I, "have you never been human? Have you never felt all the elasticity and buoyancy and hope of youth, with its infinite promises——"

"And its very finite results?" she interrupted. "No!" she continued sadly; "I have known nothing of these things. I have read of them, and I understand them, and, of course, I have no regret for them."

"Then," said I, "you are different from all other girls that I have ever known, or heard of; but this is what I always thought."

"Not much different by nature," she said; "but you see the red-hot iron was laid rather early on my heart, and seared and scorched all the little tendrils that youth sends forth—perhaps to be more severely clipped and burned in later life."

"Then you have been deprived of all the infinite beauty and joy of your youth—all that colours and makes radiant the long vistas of life."

"True," she replied; "but what is it all worth?

Have I not seen young girls, more beautiful and fairer than I, tasting of all these sweets, and then, with a sublime disdain, turning their backs upon them for ever? Mind, I don't mean the few, who have been embittered by disappointment, and have seen and experienced all the pain and anguish that underlie the pleasures of society. There is nothing very surprising there, for we all know how sick at heart and weary is your mere worldling. But I am speaking of the young, whose blood runs warmly through the veins, and in whose eyes is the wonderful light of Hope and Love, before the disenchantment comes. These are they who see the poetry of all things, and who appreciate it. An evening like yesterday will be a luxury and a treasured memory. To us, there is a sadness and a melancholy about it all. We have torn off the veil, and have become analytic. Sadness on the sea and on the faces of the crowd, sadness in the sky and in the stars, something like hate for that well-dressed mob, something like a wish for revenge on these evening bands. We abominate these eternal waltzes, and say, ' Shall we ever hear anything new?' We are *blasés*—experienced, cynical, sarcastic, realistic; all the poetry and the bloom are rubbed off Nature, and Nature is an ugly thing in its nakedness. But for your young girl, fresh from school, all these things are surrounded by the glamour of poetry, the halo of love. To them it is evening—soft and beautiful and calm; the rustle of dainty dresses thrills them, and the subtle perfume that shakes from every movement. The sky is purple, and the stars are large, luminous moons, and the mysterious sea, ebbing and throbbing under the purple twilight, says wonderful things to them. That Strauss waltz is a divine interpretation of their young, warm feelings, and life is a gay, roseate dream of bliss. And if a word of love is whispered into their ear with all its subtle flattery, and all its delicious pain, they walk on air for days afterwards, and see a wonder and a beauty in all vulgar and common things. And here comes the miracle. That young lady in the snow-white dress, who dances to-night in the perfumed and heated ballroom, or who walks this pier with an elastic step, drinking in all the freshness and life and poetry of the world, suddenly turns her back on all these wondrous attractions, and buries herself in the depths of some far-off convent. It is not weariness or disgust or disappointment; but in the whirl of the waltz she sees a crucified figure, and in the whisper of love she hears some far-off voice that touches and thrills her; and she stands out at once from the crowd, without reluctance, without doubt. She has seen the nod of the Bridegroom's head, the beck of the Bridegroom's hand."

"I am wondering, Helen," I said timidly, for I was afraid of this girl, "that you did not follow."

"No," she said, with an unusual thrill in her voice, "that favour was not vouchsafed unto me. I am one of those who must serve the King afar off, afar off!" There was a long pause.

"Charlie is taking me on a strange journey to-morrow," I said, consulting her. "Shall I go?"

"Yes, go with him wheresoever he goes," she said, "and try to mount up to his height, that you may mount higher."

"Helen," I said, "your voice comes to me as a voice from another world. I dare not disobey. You have been unconsciously a guiding star to my life hitherto. Will you promise me one thing? Your faith, if I may speak so, in me had a rude shock to-day. If ever in the future you shall hear evil things of me, or Charlie, promise me to keep your faith in him and me!"

She looked at me curiously. I turned away my head.

"You need no promise," she said. "I did not put faith in you lightly. Nor shall I lightly cast it aside."

We went home in the twilight together. We had lost sight of our friends. Whatever had been the accidents of the day, this happy ending had removed their bitterness from my mind. The faith of this noble girl gave me strength of which I did not deem myself capable. I *would* reach her high level, I thought, come what would. The fight was coming to an end. I was beginning to see in my invisible antagonist the face of a friend, and my spirit was lifted up by the glorious vocation that was prophesied for me.

At Westland Row our friends were waiting. Agnes took occasion to say to me—

"Is it all right at last?"

"It is all right," I replied.

# CHAPTER XVI

## TO THE HILL OF INCENSE

" Come, O madman, not leaning on the thyrsus, not crowned with ivy; throw away the *mitra*, throw away the fawnskin; come to thy senses. This is no Cithæron, but the mount of God. It is not the Mænads, the sisters of Semele, who rage and revel here, but the sons of God, the fair lambs, who celebrate the holy rites of the Word. The righteous are the chorus: the music is a hymn of the King of the Universe. The Lord is the Hierophant: who illuminates and seals the initiated, and places him who has believed by His Father's side to be preserved for ever."—CLEMENT OF ALEXANDRIA.

SOUTHWARDS, once more in bright May weather, with Charlie at my side, I went, unshackled by responsibilities, and surrounded by such affectionate interest, that I felt myself softening towards all things, Nature and men; and as a consequence, towards God. After all, it is not intellect, but sympathy, that reveals Him to us. I watched with new-born interest all nature expanding and bursting into life under the soft breathing of Spring; and it was an ineffable pleasure to see the dark woods trembling into green, and the soft vesture on hills and fields made more radiant by the darkness in which were still embayed the deeper recesses of the woodlands. The ash held out its candelabra with each arm terminated in a green rich bud just bursting into life; the hawthorn hedges were white and pink with their snow blossoms, and here and there there was a flash of gold, where the laburnum hung down its tresses, or of purple, where the lilac cones lifted themselves strong and self-reliant from their heart-shaped leaves. And the whole hollow vault of heaven rang and echoed with music, and the spirit of Spring passed down into human hearts until the very porters rubbed their rough hands with delight, and the station-masters sported bunches of violets or sprays of lilies-of-the-valley, and the children had put on their summer garments, and the world woke into joyous life as at dawn in the valleys of Eden.

Charlie, looking very unwell, sat silent and preoccupied in a corner of the carriage. I had told him of my trial, my humiliation, my shame, and the kindness of friends. He understood it all, for he had foretold it.

"The duel is going on, Goff," he said, "and the Master is conquering."

Three months before I would have said something flippant. I felt an unseen hand on my lips now.

But, partly to bring Charlie out of his moodiness and mournful reverie, I drew near him, and said—

"I have often wished to ask you a question. Have you never, during all these years, thought of other things, Charlie? Have you never had a temptation to pursue your profession, and enjoy life as most men do?"

He brightened up, and said—

"Oh dear, yes! Goff, over and over again. Let me see! The drawing-room, and the soft Eastern carpet, and the easy-chair, and the books, and the open piano with *her* music lying upon it, and the humming of the gas on the winter evenings, and the laughter of children, and the sweet Good-nights —I know it all well."

He held his hand tightly over his heart for a moment, then continued—

"And if Nature had not whispered it, my own mother and sister would have supplied the defect. Such airy pictures as they used to paint—such rose-coloured Edens and gardens of delight, none but woman's fancy could picture. And, sometimes, when I was depressed and the cloud came down, perhaps the tempter became a little bolder. But one word from Father Aidan, to whom I told everything, would brace me up and send the tempter flying. You remember his voice, Goff?"

I did, ringing like the trumpet of an avenging angel, and telling me in its own metallic tones of my treason and my sin.

"'Well,' he would say, knitting his brows, when I told him of those sensuous temptations, 'but there is no perfect Eve, Charlie, and no Eden without its serpent.' And then he would draw such a picture of the world, its misery, its sin, its pettiness, that I would shrink back at once from such a tragic and poor exhibition, and thank God that I had the highways of Calvary yet to walk."

The words of Helen came back to me: "These things are not for me, nor for thee." And somehow I felt that there was this sacred and unseen bond in our three lives.

We changed trains at a southern junction, and then sped along, skirting, during the latter part of our journey, the most beautiful valley, hemmed in by hills, clothed in rich green to the summit, and bending down to look into the wide and gentle river that rolled calmly onwards to the sea. Then came another change, and we drove along the white road that mounted, steep by steep, declivity by declivity, till it was lost in the black and frowning hills. The scent of the pine was in the air, the roadsides and ditches distressed the eyes with the golden glare of the gorse; wild violets peeped out under brambles that just now were swinging under tender green leaves, whilst to our right the valley of Glenshelane wound its way amongst the hills, thick with the verdure of larch and fir, the stately lances of the pines piercing

through, and waving their pennons in the wind.
" Fit place for a hermit," I thought.   I said—

"We'll come here, Charlie, and build a hut in
that forest, and talk of nothing but poetry and
religion all the future days of our lives."

He shook his head sadly.

A turn in the road again brought us in view of
the black mountains, dreary-looking and inhospitable enough, even on this bright Spring day.
Charlie pointed with his hand to a conical hill
that drew itself up, firm and frowning, from the
black jungle of forest beneath.

" Do you see that hill, Goff ? "

" Yes," I said.

" Look a little here to the east, under that round
hillock.   Do you see anything ? "

" Yes, a black mass of fir and pine."

" Nothing else ? "

" Nothing."

" Do you see something gray poised in the air
over the pine tops ? "

" Yes, like the spire of a church."

" It is the spire of the monastery chapel.   And if
there be any place on earth where Jacob's ladder
rests, and the angels descend and ascend to heaven,
it is there."

He continued gazing at it until a dip in the road
hid it from sight.   We drove rapidly across a
bridge, mounted the hill at the other side; and
presently the savage aspect of the landscape gave
way to the mild order and decorum of civilisation.
On one side of the road were brush and gorse,
heather and scrub, wild nature bending down into
the dark glen ; on the other were well-trimmed
hedges, strong stone walls, neat plantations of larch
and spruce, and iron gates of the newest pattern,
yet they might have been dug from the catacombs,
for the sign of the Cross was over all.

We passed rapidly up the hill, swept by a neat lodge, through heavy iron gates, along a broad avenue, skirted by groves of pine, and into a large square, embayed between massive stone buildings. The one feature of the place was its neatness. Primness and precision marked grounds, trees, and buildings. It might have been the demesne of some wealthy resident landlord, who had time and money to spare in rescuing Nature from primeval barrenness, and gently arresting her steps backwards into savage wildness again. But the shouts of some lads at cricket, as the westering sun drew his glory up along the branches of the trees, dissipated the idea: and here, standing on the top of a flight of stone steps, is a figure that might have stepped out of some canvas, hidden away in the gloomy refectory of some Umbrian monastery, and engaged not in the high altitudes of mystic contemplation, but in the more prosaic, yet not less noble, avocation of dispensing doles to the poor. For this shaven, brown monk said "Welcome" with eyes and hands long before we had descended from the car. And when we came nearer, he cried "Welcome!" in more articulate language, and meant it. Clearly, Charlie was well-known here, for the old man kissed him on both cheeks, and then called on the guest-master. A stately figure, in white, came out from a recess, where he had been reading; welcomed us again profusely, looked keenly at Charlie's worn face, and with a glance at myself, took up humbly our little valises and bade us follow him. From the hall we passed into a long, narrow corridor of stone pavement and white-washed walls, along which were hung some ghostly garments, as if the shrouds of departed monks—labelled and ticketed, like the skeletons in the crypts of the Capuchins at Rome. The old chill, which always came upon me when I touched the supernatural, again seized me, and I wished myself a hundred miles away in the seething city, with the warm pulses of humanity beating around me. But on Charlie's face came a look of beatitude that made me think, for the hundredth time, that he had mistaken his vocation, and should have been a contemplative monk. We were ushered into the guest house, and served with dinner, the old monk chatting gaily with Charlie all the time. I had abundant opportunities of seeing that the characteristics of this mediæval monastery in its treatment of guests were comfort without luxury, kindness without intrusion, perfect cleanliness without artificiality, rigid rule, and absolute freedom.

After dinner we were left to ourselves, and we strolled up and down the long garden, talking of many things. The evening was beautiful, the air was clear and bright, the sun rested on spire and tree, and far down the valley on some high meadow lands; and there was peace upon all things—such peace as I had never felt before, and beautiful silence broken only by the sharp tolling of one bell, or the deep boom of the great bell that told of the hours of Office. Those wonderful bells! how the memory of them comes back to me over the chasm of twenty years! Was it the silence of the mountains, or was it the calm serenity that breathed on every human heart and conscience within these walls, that made the syllables of the bells so clear, so solemn, so distinct? One note breaks on the air and sends its waves of sound far up on the mountain; and instinctively one says, that is a call—of monk to prayer, of priest to confessional, of prior to penitent; and these other deep, solemn sounds will send the white-robed monks hurrying from garden and laundry, from library or schoolroom, into the stalls, where, before the brassbound breviaries, they will intone in the sepulchral notes of the Cistercian the praises that the "sweet harper of Israel" struck centuries ago from his golden lyre. The poetry and mysticism of the whole thing appealed to me strongly; but that unutterable chill was on my heart when I came near and touched the things that were of God.

· Charlie was jubilant and cheerful.

"We go into retreat after compline," he said, "(do you remember that compline long ago in Queenstown, Goff?) and we must not speak till the fourth day. Say now all that you have to say to me!"

Thus challenged, there on that walk betwixt the rows of peas, and sometimes picking up a leaf to crumple it, I told Charlie all that I had to tell him— all that he knew before; and the sum total was—I had not as yet touched God.

"You must see one of the priests here," he said. "How long since you have been to confession?"

"Six years ago this Easter!"

"My God!" said Charlie. "But you will see one of the priests?"

"Certainly," I said. "I shall be delighted."

"Now, good-bye," he said, as the last evening-bell tolled towards the dying sun, "and remember me!"

We went into the chapel for the last evening service, and took our places before the Virgin's altar. It was a homely statue, but with a motherly look about it, that touched me more than the radiant splendours of Raffaelle, or those ethereal visions of the Madonna which Murillo drew upon canvases, glowing with sunlit clouds, and dappled with angels' faces. And I think one of the first gentle thaws that softly melted the stubborn ice of my heart fell then and there under the outstretched arms and gentle motherhood of the Queen. The quarters chimed, the clock rang out, and instantly from the chapter-room came forth a stately procession of monks, white-robed and brown; and each with a

look of centred self-possession bowed down before
the central altar-shrine, and passed to his place in
the stalls. A few very old monks remained in the
side aisles; but the whole community, who had not
met together since two o'clock that morning, were
now assembled to sing the "Vale!" to the Queen of
the Cistercian Order, as they had chanted their
"Aves!" in the darkness of the night before. There
was something inexpressibly graceful in the movements of those monks, something that appealed very
strongly to me, who had never seen but the black
cassock of the missionary priest. Their calm, reverent
faces, slow, measured tread, their wide, white sleeves
which touched the floor as they made the profound
inclination to the altar, the graceful way in which
they drew up these sleeves and passed rapidly to
their places—the reserve, silence, dignity of the
whole scene touched me inexpressibly. And high
over their heads, the long yellow streamers of the
sinking sun struck and shed a spray of splendour
around the stained glass window over the altar, and
seemed to linger there with its soft illuminations
playing around the Divine Mother until the office
had ended. The monks chanted the evening hours
in a slow measured monotone, lingering distinctly
on every syllable, as if it were a debt, that if not
discharged here would have to be discharged in penal
fires hereafter. The voices were hoarse and deep,
as of men who had shouted themselves almost into
dumbness; and the monks stood or sat erect and
stately, with hands folded beneath their broad sleeves,
except at the doxology, when every head was bent
low over the oaken boards and brass clasps that
held the Cistercian Offices.

I daresay I was most impolite, for I could not
take my eyes away from these grand figures; but it
was all the same. They no more heeded me than
if I was hidden under the altar; they had eyes and

ears for other things. Towards the end of the Office, a choir-brother stepped up the centre, and with his hands by his sides, his sleeves touching the bare floor, advanced to the altar. With the same measured gravity he lighted two candles hidden away in the recesses of the bare altar, and went back to his place. There was a pause, and the first notes of a fine organ, hidden away under hanging curtains, floated along the air. Then for the first time I heard that marvellous "Salve Regina," that never leaves the mind or memory of those who have once listened to its solemn strains.

Since then I have heard great cathedral choirs interpreting the masterpieces of the inspired composers of Italy and France; I have heard every human invention dragged into the service of music and harnessed to her triumphal car; I have heard the silver trumpets in St. Peter's, and more wonderful still, the awful "Miserere" on the nights of Holy Week—but all have faded from my memory. Yet clear to-day as twenty years ago, the slow measured chant of those Trappists comes back to me, and is it a hyperbole to say, or a phantasm that makes me think, it is the highest attainment of Christian art? But away with that word and that thought! What has art to do here to-night as the benign Mother bends down over her white-robed children; and dearer to her than whole symphonies of angels comes up that cry of adoration, of love, of beseeching prayer from lips that are never unhallowed by human speech unless consecrated to God—from hearts that are untouched by the slightest grossness or sensuality—from bodies wrapped round by a halo of sanctity, of which the voluminous spotless choir cloaks are but the faintest type! Analyse the music as we may, and our own sensations, and our surroundings, the spell on our senses will not depart. It holds us with chains that neither reason nor incredulity can break. Science

Y

can destroy most of the magic illusions that enchain our senses under the name of poetry or art; and that terrible engine of modern science, the analysis of ideas and emotions, may unravel and explain many of those profound and awful sensations that hold our souls in bondage. But no one with a soul, that as yet had not become a mere negation, could dare penetrate behind the magic that enchained us that night, and the soft images of heaven that came down into our hearts to abide there. I confess, that hardened and critical as I was, I could not resist the pathos and sublimity that lingered over every pause and swell of that antiphon; and when organ and voices combined rose in a piteous cry at the words—

> " Eja, ergo, Advocata nostra,
>   Illos tuos misericordes oculos
>   Ad nos converte,"

I uttered the first prayer that for many a day had ascended from my heart—and it took the form of a tear.

But it was not a tear, it was an emotion of terror that burst from me, when the antiphon, having sunk down to a deep whisper at the name of Jesus, and the pleading tones,

> " *Nobis post hoc exilium ostende,*"

rose up again, piteous, sorrowful, despairful at the conclusion. If ever souls in hell could pray, surely it would be in such tones and words. If ever a soul, sunk deep down in the agonies of remorse for almost unforgivable sins, could grasp at one last hope, and put the energies of one last despairing prayer into human language, as a rift appeared on the black, frowning face of heaven, and the sweetest face that ever shone on the blackness of this world looked through—surely it would cry as these holy monks cried, there in the placid beauty of that summer

evening, "*O clemens! O pia! O dulcis Virgo Maria!*"
But what a terrible warning, threat, objurgation it
was to me! It said as plainly as words: you, the
reprobate; you, the traitor; you, the proud, inflated
fool, who would pierce behind the secrets of the
Throne and analyse the very mind of God; you, the
exile, the outcast from your Father's Home, even
you may yet find peace and mercy where the sinless
find rest and consolation! These novel feelings
were accentuated by the intense silence and peace
that wrapped us round like a garment when we
went to our rooms after compline. Some secret,
unextinguished pride revolted at the thought of
being locked in during daylight; but only for a
moment. I drew the little table near my window,
sat down, leaned my arms upon it, and looked out
on the grounds, now slowly darkening for the day's
obsequies. The silence was so profound that it
became almost terrifying. The cessation of bells,
the hushing of the organ, the very absence of all
human motion intensified it: and abroad not a
branch stirred in the calm twilight, not a bird-note
broke the dead stillness that lay as if on an entombed
world. I amused myself by examining whether the
shrubs corresponded on each side of the walk and
around the white statues that glimmered in the dusk.
Then over the tops of the pines that pierced the
clear sky, I watched the lines of yellow light fade
into gray, which gradually deepened into darker
tints, and the stars came out and looked down on a
sleeping world with their sleepless and solemn eyes.
I lit the candle and looked around the room. The
first object that met my eye was a card on which, in
large black letters, was printed *Eternity*. I shuddered and turned aside. I took up book after book of
meditations: every word was ashes in my mouth. I
drew a bronze crucifix over and gazed intently at it.
Something said to me: "There you shall find peace."

I think it was partly out of deference to Charlie's wishes, partly from curiosity to come nearer to these white monks, that I asked next day to see one of the fathers.

"Which of the fathers shall I bring you?" said the guest-master.

"You know best," I replied.

I was walking up and down, sometime after mid-day, by the north wall, that is covered with coton-caster—I was picking leisurely its waxen blossoms —when one of the monks came rapidly towards me. Now, I had some preconceived ideas about monks— that they were of necessity mediæval, reactionary, austere, ready to frown down on anything human, intolerant of everything that was not monastic. I also thought that they might possibly be well read in divinity, but that all human sciences were a sealed book to them.

"Father," I said, "I was anxious to see you, partly because Charlie Travers wished it, partly for my own satisfaction. I am a troubled soul, trying to do the impossible—that is, get along without God."

He was quite silent, walking up and down by my side, his fingers stuck in his leathern girdle.

"I don't know how to explain," I continued; "but it is this way. There is a wall of brass between me and God, and I cannot break through."

"What have you been reading?" he asked.

"Everything," I replied, "that I could lay hands on. I was a libertine amongst books, and knew no restraint."

"Did you skim them," he said, "or go right through, dragging out their marrow?"

"I went down as deep as I could," I replied. "I said to myself, 'There shall be no secrets from me.'"

"Thank God!" he answered, "that gives hope. And you found?"

" I expressed what I discovered once before, thus :
*Poma Sodomitica, mala insana !*" I replied.

" What do you think of our place here ? " he said,
suddenly changing the conversation.

" It affects me with the most startling contrasts
of feeling. Last night I was up in the clouds ; but
those low cloisters, tiled floors, whitewashed walls,
chill me to the bone. Why don't you put a little art
into your buildings, as well as into your music ? "

He looked at me and laughed. "Fretted ceilings,"
he said, laughing, "rich mosaics, lofty windows,
'richly dight, giving a dim, religious light,' 'length-
ened sweetness long drawn out,' &c., &c. What
about *pâté de foie gras* and truffles for dinner, and
down quilts, and canopied bedsteads ? "

I could not help smiling at the absurdity.

"Do you know, Mr. Austin," he said, "what
you'll do ? There is a monastery on Mount Athos ;
go there. You are a Greek to the sole of your foot.
You'll enjoy life deciphering Greek manuscripts,
eating olives and grapes, and pitching pebbles into
the Euxine."

I didn't know whether to be offended or amused.

"Come now," he said, sternly taking me by the
arm, "let's have the whole thing out. You like the
poetry of religion, but you don't like its prose. You
are a Christian on Thabor, but not on Calvary. You
exult in the power and glory of the Church, but you
don't understand handling the base things that the
Church is sent to elevate and purify. You want
a life of lofty contemplation, not a life of steady,
prosaic, thankless work. You want to live in the
altitudes, and let others work in the valleys."

"Pardon me," I said, "that is all true. You have
made a perfect diagnosis of my character. But is
not all this true, too, of you, the watchers on the
mountains ? "

"It would be," he said, "if we allowed it. But

don't think that our life is one long 'Salve Regina.'
When we stumble out of bed at two o'clock on a
winter's morning, tramp down the wet stone steps
into the chapel, where the cold cuts like a knife,
when we wear out by bleared candlelight the long
hours of the winter morning, when we work in the
schools or the confessional, or dig potatoes, or wash
shirts, or bake bread, there is not much of a poetic
stimulus to help us."

"I know, Father," I said humbly, "it is hard to
flesh and blood.   But do tell me what supports you
through all ?"

"That which was a stumbling-block to you, Gentiles," he said.   "The Cross of Jesus Christ.   And
now listen," he cried, as I was dumb under the
revelation.   "There is a great deal of what is good
and pure and holy amongst the Catholics of the day,
but we want the trumpet blast of a Tertullian to
awaken us to higher things.   For the old cry, 'Can
anything good come out of Nazareth?' is in the hearts
of worldly Catholics to-day, although it is not on
their lips.   They are prepared to admire everything,
provided it is not introduced to their notice under
the Church's sanction.   They will go hundreds of
miles to hear a Mass, but it must be sung in a public
hall by heretical or perhaps infidel artistes.   The
music of the Church is the 'barbarous jargon of
Philistines.'   In philosophy you are called upon to
admire Plato, but not St. John.   Porphyry and Plotinus we know, but who was Justin ?   The hybrid
Greek of Lucian we admire, but what of Clement or
Origen ?   We are told there are hidden beauties in
Plautus and Tibullus, Bion and Moschus, but who
ever heard of Ephrem the Syrian ?   We know all
about Giordano Bruno; what of St. Thomas ?   We
call Kant and Fichte and Spinoza the demigods of
science; what of Suarez and Vasquez ?   For one
Catholic who has heard of great apologists like the

Abbé Moigno, a hundred have heard of great iconoclasts like Spencer and Darwin. We are ashamed
of our immortals; we are proud of the *parvenus* of
science. And yet what a glorious beadroll of illus-
trious names illumines the history of the Church!
Even in modern times, what a litany one may sing
of Tycho-Brahe, Copernicus, Descartes, Galileo,
Leibniz, Pascal, Bossuet, Gerdil, Malebranche! In
oratory, what a galaxy of French and Italian geniuses!
In science, three-fourths of the world's inventions
sprang from children of the Church—from the discovery of gunpowder down to the discovery of
dynamic electricity. All the great composers were
Catholics. All the world's sacred orators were
Catholics. All the world's discoverers were Catholics. And yet your boys know nothing of names
that made the pulses of other generations beat more
quickly; and in the minds of your young girls the
heroism of a Florence Nightingale, which I do not
want to depreciate, extinguishes the tens of thousands
of brilliant deeds wrought in the ghastly *infernos* of
the world's hospitals, under the cornettes of the
daughters of St. Vincent. We conquer the world,
and bow down before its idols; we lead the world, and
then suffer ourselves to be harnessed to its triumphal
car; we give the world the example of our genius, our
zeal, our self-sacrifice, and then cry, '*Io triumphe,*'
when it parades its own little deities. Now, here
are you: you know all things but your religion.
You worship at Pagan shrines; your gods are the
gods of the Gentiles. You are stiff of knee and
neck when Christ is in question. And yet you *must*
bend before Him. He has broken stronger necks
than yours, and bowed them beneath His yoke.
Come, why do you allow the best years of your life
to run waste, like water that is poured upon a desert?
Why do you misuse, because you do not utilise for
Christ, the talents He has given you? **Do you**

think there is anything in this world worth thinking of, worth caring for, worth working for, but Jesus Christ? Come, join His glorious battalions! You do not know where you will have to serve Him, whether in the pulpit, in the study, in the hospital, in the court, in the slums, in the prison, or in the asylum. To-day you may be revelling in the treasures of libraries; to-morrow you may be teaching catechism to black and filthy aborigines. To-day you may be preaching before princes; to-morrow you may be picking your food out of scraps of leprous skin. But, wherever you go, it is Christ's work you are doing, and it is in His Face you must seek your strength and inspiration. Rise up, then, from your carnal sleep, awake with the just ones, put on the armour of Christ, and quit yourself manfully in the struggle. Take the reproach from the lips of Satan, '*Tuos tales munerarios, Christe, demonstra!*'"

We walked up and down in silence for some time, the monk almost breathless from such a long appeal, and I breathless from fear. At last I timidly asked, for I said to myself, now or never this thing must end—

"Father, must I, then, if I become what I ought to be, give up for evermore all my passionate love for the Greeks and their poetry, and all my hankering after the wandering stars of modern philosophy?"

He thought long and deeply, and then said—

"That is a question that a confessor only may decide, to whom you have shown all the secret workings of your soul. But it is a question (I am speaking objectively) that has agitated the Church from the beginning. St. Paul half decides it, yet he quotes from Pagan poets himself. Carthage and Alexandria stood at opposite poles on the subject. To Tertullian, Socrates was the 'Attic buffoon,' and he spoke of Aristotle as 'the wretched'; Clement

spoke of Plato as 'the noble and the almost inspired.'
The former believed that all Grecian philosophy was
an emanation from Satan, the latter, that it contained
the germinal truths of Christianity, inasmuch as it
was a plagiarism from the Hebrews. So, too, Jerome
saw himself in a vision flogged by an angel, because
he was too great an admirer of Cicero ; and Augustine found his greatest temptation in trying to accept
the simplicity of the Gospels after the rhetoric of the
Sophists. And, in singular alternation through the
history of the Church, we find to-day the learned
ones of the Church rifling heathenism of its treasures
and appropriating them; to-morrow casting them off
as the spawn of Satan. But I should say—yet I
speak with the diffidence of one who is not standing
on firm ground—that the truest spirit of the Church
is a spirit of eclecticism and adoption. Believing
herself the heir of all the ages, she appropriates
whatever is best in Paganism or heresy, assimilating
it, as bees suck honey from poisonous plants, and
adapting it to her own pressing wants and necessities.
Or, to change the simile, she allows her children to
use heathen writings 'by the same law which permitted the Israelites to marry a female captive, if first
they shaved her head and cut her nails.' But where
lies *your* trouble ? "

" ' I have eaten out of the drum,' I said, ' I have
drunk out of the cymbal, I have carried the *Kernos*,
I have slipped into the chamber.' In a word, I have
been initiated into all the mysteries of Paganism, and
have seen but the fætor and slime of the serpent. I
have dipped into philosophy, ay, drunk deeply from
its well; and the taste thereof in my mouth is of
aloes and myrrh. The poetry of the world is one
hopeless wail after some lost beatitude; its philosophy
a useless knocking at doors that are inexorably
closed against it. But because I have a curious
sympathy for the lost and the forlorn, I go into

trackless wastes in pursuit of them. And then, if Greek philosophy and all its modern phases are rubbish—the Greek language is Divine. A Greek text will drag me back from the gates of heaven."

"Then," he said decisively, turning towards me, "such things are no longer for you. '*Æmulare charismata meliora.*' Whatever be said in defence of a liberal education, which we most strongly advocate, its final motive is to help us to climb the heights from which we may look down upon and contemn merely human wisdom. You have reached the heights where you may rest with Christ. You have tasted the bitterness of the waters of Marah, that you may the better understand the sweetness of the honey that is distilled in the hive of Christ. Come, now, and tell the world what you have learned with much anguish of spirit—that all the ancient philosophies are but adumbrations of His teaching; that science illustrates Him, and art is valueless except to embellish His beauty and the reflected beauty of His saints; that Greek culture bowed down before His Divine simplicity, and Roman power was shattered to atoms by the might of His weakness; that all beautiful things move towards Him as the centre and source of their beauty, and that hideous things preach His loveliness by the contrast of their deformity—in a word, He is Alpha and Omega, and from His mouth hangs the sword that smites and saves, and His feet are shod with brass, to tread underfoot the grapes that make the wine of life to the nations. And, remember, that you are not called upon to frame a new system of the universe by your speculations, but to give your life as a rule of life to others. And there must be no more building of airy castles over glowing sunsets or slumbering seas. You will build your heaven of jasper and chalcedony, by making the clay of common humanity less unworthy to be the mansion of the living God!"

"One word more, Father," I said, "when and how shall I begin?"

"Await the revelation of God," he said. "There never was written a truer saying than that we are but clay in the potter's hands."

"One word more," I cried, as he departed, "stop Charlie in his mad career——"

He turned and looked at me, angry and surprised.

"What?" he cried, "mad career! You ask me to do what recreant Christians did under Nero or Caracalla—take the palm from the martyr's hands, and lift the laurels from his brow. Do you know that like the *libellatici* of old you owe your 'letter of peace' with God to his intercession?"

I did not quite understand him, but I felt that he was saying some true thing that affected me deeply. And I was not quite so stupefied as not to feel that I was learning many things, amongst the rest, that my mediæval monks were singularly well acquainted with human sciences, which, as he hinted, they had mastered but to despise; and that, at one glance, he had read the story of my life, which had been a riddle to myself.

That evening the "Salve Regina" took on a new meaning. I saw the world of philosophy and science prostrate before the Woman and Child.

Tired and weary, satisfied and dissatisfied, and with only one clear sentence ringing through my confused brain, I went to sleep. It was ten o'clock. I had scarcely dozed when the bell boomed out on the night. A few minutes after I heard the feet of a lay-brother scurrying along the corridor, picking up the boots of the visitors. I struck a light. It was ten minutes after two o'clock. The bells tolled at intervals. I do not know how long I lay awake, but just as dawn was breaking, I heard the sound of a fall, succeeded by some faint moans in the next room, which was Charlie's. I listened intently. The

moaning continued, and appeared to penetrate easily
through the wall of the room. I jumped up and
dressed hastily. "The palm from the martyr's
hand, the laurels from his brow," I repeated unconsciously. They were the last words I had uttered
the night before. I crept into the corridor gently,
and tapped at Charlie's door. No answer but a
moan. I pushed open the door gently and entered.
There in the gray dawn, lying quite prostrate on the
floor, was Charlie. He was fully dressed. He had
not thought of sleep that night. Everything round
the room was undisturbed. A black crucifix stood
on the table, and the white face of the murdered
Christ looked down pityingly on the fallen figure.
I lifted Charlie up gently, and turned his face upwards. He was quite conscious: but his face was
marble, with rivers of perspiration bathing it. His
hair was wet. His hands were clammy and wet
also. He feebly moaned.

"Let me alone for a moment, Goff. It will pass."

"What happened, in God's name, Charlie?" I
said, bending over him, and cooling his forehead
with a wet towel.

"Nothing, nothing," he moaned, "but the dread
of what is to be."

"What is to be has not come yet," I said, "sufficient for the day is its own evil."

"True," he replied, "but when the blow falls,
shall I have strength to bear it? But all this is
weakness and want of faith. I want to put the cross
aside. I fear it."

I could not dare preach to him. I was too unused to such things. I lifted his head gently and
bathed it.

"There, it is passing," he said after a while;
"what a little human companionship can do! I
suppose that is why the Master said, 'Watch with
Me.'"

"You are better, decidedly better, Charlie," I said; "come now and rest a little."

I lifted him on to his bed, and the colour came back to his cheeks and lips.

"It was dreadful, Goff, whilst it lasted," he said; "I didn't know that I could bear such an agony of dread. And my crucifix was dumb. For the first time it refused to speak to me. Go now, I shall rest!"

I went away, but not to rest. I was being surrounded on all sides by the ghostly and superhuman. I saw as yet only its sublime, and even repellent, features. I did not know of the sweetness and light that were hidden behind Golgotha.

That last day in the monastery I spent mostly in the library. I had seen and wondered at the monks at their daily toil, in the laundry, in the bakehouse, in the farmyard, in the garden, in the smithy, in the carpenter's shed. Everywhere the same order, the same neatness and regularity, the same silence. Strong athletes, clean-skinned and clear-eyed, with strong, sweet faces bending over their work, and an eternal smile beautifying their features. I thought of two things which I had seen. "Solitude is the mother-country of the strong: silence is their prayer." [1] And "Solitude is the audience-chamber of God." [2]

But it was a surprise and revelation to me, when, in the library, I had leisure to look around and examine some of the treasures of ancient and modern literature piled there. Then, for the first time, I understood that the Church possessed a literature, peculiarly its own, whilst it had adapted all the craft of ancient and modern writers to its own purposes. I saw whole shelves of philosophical literature, ranging from octavos to folios, marked by names that were quite unknown to me. And

---

[1] Ravignan.　　　　[2] W. S. Landor.

when tired from handling those heavy tomes, I sat
down, and looked up to the lofty shelves, that were
reached by a gallery, and far along the rows that
stood like sentinelled watchmen, I said, "I have
walked in darkness, and thought it was light ; and
at noonday I have stumbled, and cried for a hand to
lead me." Then I took out an old, well-worn notebook, and read these sentences which I neither
understood nor believed before this day:—

"The monasteries were the asylums of learning
and philosophy."[1]

"The Church had the monopoly of learning."[2]

"The Catholic Church was the special representative of progress."[3]

"The sure and unbroken progress of intellectual
culture had been going on within her bosom for a
series of ages, until all the vital and productive
energies of human culture were here united and
mingled."[4]

At the other end of the library, a tall monk, long-
bearded, and thin and worn, was diligently sweeping
the polished floor. Not a nook or cranny escaped
the solicitations of his brush.

"What might that Father's name be ?" I asked the
guest-master.

"Father P——s," he replied, mentioning the name
of a Libyan anchorite.

But, next day, Charlie, who knew all about the
monks, told me that he had just come from Rome,
and was the ablest opponent of the Rosminian philosophy.

"Rosminian philosophy! what is that ?" I inquired.

"There are a few things you don't know yet,
Goff," said Charlie with a smile.

[1] Guizot.   [2] Froude.   [3] Lecky.   [4] Ranke.

# CHAPTER XVII

## ARRESTED

" Sorrow gives the accolade,
    With the sharp edge of his blade,
    Whereby noblest knights are made.

Up the glory-lighted hall,
    Where the King at festival
    Meets and greets His knights withal,

They shall lead thee, stayed of none
    To the forefront of the throne,
    To the bliss of His ' Well-done.' "

NOTHING could equal the sudden revulsion of spirits that took place in Charlie the morning we left the monastery. From being moody and melancholy, he became quite gay and almost boisterous; and this continued the whole way down the mountains and road. Once, and once only, he became sad for a moment. It was just at the turn which hid mountain and monastery from our sight. He gazed steadfastly for a few moments, until the trees shut out the view; then said sadly, as he waved his hand towards the vanishing vision—

" I shall not see it again. Far-off pilgrims will wear this road on their way to our Irish Mecca. But not for me the vision again."

He lapsed for a time into silence, then said—

" It was one of my dreams, Goff, to plant a Cistercian convent on every hill in Ireland, to bring back the old days again. Did you ever hear that there were twelve hundred monasteries of one order

alone in Ireland before the Reformation. What a
garden of God it was then! And you will be interested to hear, Goff, that they were the only monks
in Western Christendom who spoke Greek. What
glorious days! And now, but one Cistercian monastery in Ireland; and—we talk of our progress!"

So he went on, chatting on every conceivable subject in car and in train until the long summer day
drew to its close, and we were glad to get out of the
dusty carriages again, and see the sun throw its
shadows across the Liffey. We had made wonderful arrangements in our journey as to our future.
We were to live together—I pursuing my own
avocations, and enjoying perfect liberty of action.
I was delighted at the prospect, and had framed all
sorts of delightful fancies of the future, in which a
club of medical students, long *conversazioni* with
the Bellamys, pleasant evenings with the Deanes,
played an important part. And Charlie, it was quite
clear, was determined to make the most of his
neophyte in carrying out his high and lofty schemes.
Altogether things were taking on a rose colour again;
and we were like two schoolboys home for vacation,
as we took up our rugs and valises, and went out
from the terminus. Charlie had slung his slender
luggage on to the seat of a side car, and I was about
to do the same, when two men, in civilian dress,
approached us.

One of the two, touching his cap, civilly inquired—

"Might I ask, sir, if you are — Mr. Charles
Travers?"

I saw Charlie's face flush crimson, and then grow
deathly pale, as he said—

"Yes, I am Charles Travers!"

"Well, sir," the man continued, "I would give a
good year's salary to avoid the job I have to do. I
hold a warrant, sir, for your arrest."

"You might not be aware," I said, interfering,

" that this is Mr. Charles Travers, a young gentleman very well known in the city."

"Know him, sir?" the man replied. "I think I
do, and every decent man in the city knows him.
And—well, there's no use in talking."

"Come," said Charlie, "there is no use in wasting
words. Let me see the warrant, and then we go
together."

He took the warrant from the unwilling hands of
the officer, and read it. I watched his face with
interest. And there I read such shame and sorrow
as I hope will never be writ on the face of a good man
again. He folded the paper, and handed it back.

"Come, Goff," he said, almost choking, "it is the
cross, and a bitter one. I should not mind it, but
oh! the shame!"

Then pulling himself together, he lifted himself
up, and threw back his head, saying—

"Come, this is human weakness; lead on, and I
follow."

The officer called a covered car, and we entered
together. I could just hear from the jarveys the
whispered remark—

"Two of the swell mob, nabbed very nicely, by
Williams!"

We drove straight to the police-office without exchanging a word.

The inspector came forward, and read out the
warrant, charging Charles Travers, law student, 24
Leston Street, Dublin, with conspiring, with one
Amelia Gifford, to obtain money under false pretences, to wit, for the purpose of founding an asylum
for Magdalens, and a home for discharged prisoners.
No bail could be accepted for his appearance before
the magistrates next morning.

"For God's sake," I whispered the officer, "take
care of him. You know he is in very delicate
health."

"Never fear, sir," he said, "as long he is with us, he will be well minded."

I saw Charlie pass in after the officer through a door that appeared to lead to a corridor of cells. Then I went out into the open-air, dazed and bewildered. " Digitus Dei est hic," was the last sentence Charlie spoke, "fear not, I have overcome the world." I saw a few officers strolling around. I accosted them.

"This is frightful ruffianism," I said. "Every one knows that my friend is incapable of such a crime. What am I to do?"

"Whatever you do," said one young fellow with a leer, "keep away from the Amelias. They're dangerous cattle."

I walked off, my brain in a whirl. On the one hand, here clearly was Charlie's trial, or passion. All the events of the last few days led up logically to it.

We should have expected it. The hand of God had fallen heavily on His chosen child. Should I then interfere? or let Providence work out His own designs? Lately, I was beginning to trace everywhere that light touch of the Omnipresent, that controls our destinies without force or fear—a touch, gentle as the fall of gossamer, but imperious and irresistible, at least where we do not dispute the wisdom of His dispensations. Yet, something should be done. It would never answer to leave Charlie under such a vile imputation. I did not advert to the ignominy of his being associated with Amelia Gifford, not knowing who Amelia Gifford might be. But, clearly, the charge was a grave one, probably to be met by remand after remand, until Charlie's delicate constitution had succumbed. The first thing, then, to do was to summon friends to come to his assistance in the morning. I ransacked my memory to discover who those friends might be. At last I remembered two city magnates, whom I had seen at the large meeting in the Leinster Hall, and who, I remembered, were particularly enthusiastic. I ascertained their addresses at a shop in Sackville Street, hailed a cab, and drove rapidly to one of their houses. The blinds were drawn, although the sun had not gone down, and I could see that all preparations were made for dinner. I pulled the bell. A footman came out; and after one supercilious glance, he slammed the door.

"Get away, we want no tramps here."

My temper was roused. I gave the bell a more violent jerk. The fellow again came out, and said with the bitterest contempt—

"Look here, you, sir, if you touch that bell again, I'll send for the nearest policeman. What the h—ll do tramps like you seek to bother respectable people for?"

"I'll forgive you your insolence," I cried, "if you just show that card and the name on the obverse to your master."

"You should have seen him at his office," the fellow replied, "master sees no one outside business hours."

"Very well," I said, turning away, "your master won't be thankful to you."

He hesitated, and in a moment changed his tone.

"Just wait and I'll see."

His master came out, gorgeous and magnificent. "Here's a splendid representative of the Catholic laity," I thought, as I then remembered some fervent oratory about the housing of the poor, and something very prophetic about the Irish proletariat.

"What does this mean?" he said, holding the card between his pink, smooth fingers, "you know I do not engage in business outside of office hours."

"Quite so," I said, "under ordinary circum-

stances ; but Mr. Charles Travers, your friend, has
been arrested on a most infamous and unfounded
charge.    He will be probably brought up before
the magistrates to-morrow morning, and some one
must be there to go bail for him."

He whistled softly to himself.   Then—

"On what charge is he arrested?"

"On the charge of obtaining money under false
pretences."

Here my merchant was called away by his wife,
who had overheard our conversation.   In a few
moments he returned.

"I shall instruct my solicitor," he said, "to—to—
make inquiries——"

"If he is remanded without bail," I persisted, "it
will kill him ; he is suffering from confirmed heart-
disease."

"My solicitor," he said, "is very prudent.   I will
give him full instructions."

He closed the door gently as the second bell rang.

Angry, disgusted, ashamed, I thought for a moment
what I should do.   Then I ordered the cabman to
drive quickly to Hubert Deane's.   I knew I was safe
there.

Alas! Hubert Deane was on the Continent.   Mrs.
Deane and her children were in Bray.   The closed
windows and drawn blinds might have told me.

Without much hope I drove to the residence of
the second city magnate.   They are all dead now ;
but we must not mention names.

He was at dinner, and when I insisted on seeing
him, and refused to go away, he came out furious,
holding his white napkin in his hand.   I told my
story simply.   He listened, hardly able to restrain
his passion.   Then in a tone of sarcasm, he said—

"I am not surprised at what you tell me.   The
thing was too good to last.   In my efforts to—a—
ameliorate the—a—condition of the working classes,

I—a—against my better judgment, associated myself with a movement that wise people viewed with suspicion. I hope I shall have my reward. I have already lost heavily by the—a—pecuniary assistance I—a—lent to this movement; but for some time I have completely dissociated myself from it. I am sorry if your young friend has got himself into trouble. It was—pardon me—anticipated. Good evening!"

I did not strike him. I only dismissed the cab, and walked home. Now, if I had only had a rightly-directed faith, I would have quietly yielded to this manifest disposition of Providence, that was evidently preparing my friend by bitter suffering for a great reward. I should have argued, by every law of the Christian dispensation, it was clear that Charles Travers, popular, applauded, flattered, honoured, was not a fit subject for the kingdom whose portals are so lowly that the lowly only can enter, and whose chief splendours are the suns that shine from the wounds of martyrs. I took a human view of the situation, for I was very human, and thought only of rescuing my dearest friend from disgrace and probable death. I was not too much surprised at the action of these great enthusiasts. Five years' bitter experience of that subtle ally of Satan, called the world, had taught me that the summer zeal of men is shortlived, or prompted by some motive that will hardly bear even the superficial and partisan glance of self-examination. There, in my lonely lodgings that summer night, I felt for the hundredth time the ground slipping from beneath my feet, and all my hopes come tumbling down. And I said, as I thought of my saint and martyr lying in some dark cell on straw, breathing hard through the long night, his forehead wet with agony, and his lips purple black, as I had so often lately seen them—What dread

Fate is pursuing us, two poor fellows who have injured no one in life, but striven for what is true and just ?   And then the old sensuous vision came back to me.   If we had only not minded high thought and principle, if we had only gone the way of the world, and sought its prizes and distinctions, we might have gained them, and then— the villa, and the garden, and the civilised Paganism, decorous and respectable, and the books and music, and summers by the seaside, where the long waves come lapping in, and under awnings we look as in a dream at the purple waters and the yellow sands, and hear the laughter of girls and the shrill cries of the sweet children, and there is no grim skeleton behind us, but wealth and peace, and the respect and esteem of all men.   *Ay de mi !*   I looked round my wretched room, smiled at the bare deal table and chairs, and the rough washstand in the corner, and the solitary photograph of Charlie on the mantelpiece, and sighed out that bitterest of all judgments—the self-condemnation of the young man—that his life was a grim failure.   I summoned my old philosophies to my aid and said : Yes, so are all human lives, for nothing can be called a success that ends so quickly : and so is all Nature a huge failure.   How many millions of lives perish every day, every hour !   How many tens of millions of creatures, each with as perfect an organisation as mine own, quite as capable of thought and feeling, are crushed every moment under the awful wheels of that idol, misnamed Mother Nature, who, like the gods of old, rears up her children only to destroy them.   A few lines jangled into my mind, that

> " Not one worm shall be destroyed,
>  Nor cast like rubbish to the void,
>  When God has made the pile complete."

I laughed at its absurdity, but grasped at the word "rubbish." Ay! there's the word. "Rubbish we all are, and not even decent rubbish—a little chemicals mixed with water, which Nature frames for her laughter, and then wantonly destroys." But it was of no use. Here was Charlie in peril, and how was he to be delivered?

Eleven o'clock next morning found me in a healthier frame of mind, as I sat, anxious enough, on the hard benches in the courthouse. We had not long to wait. A few cases of drunkenness were summarily settled, and then came the cry, "*Queen v. Travers and Gifford.*" It struck a cold chill through me. I tried to think of the martyrs of old, summoned before the grim Roman prætors; but the far-off beauty and poetry of these sublime times were not here. This was a vulgar Irish court, with an ordinary magistrate for prætor, and very ordinary policemen for lictors, and some very vulgar common drunkards in place of the eager martyrs. But something of the horror, without any of the sublimity, of the old tribunals struck me when Charlie stood up in that dock, and I saw beside him that dreadful woman who had accosted me scarcely a week before, and whose eyes, I have said, were the windows of Hell. "Good God!" I cried, "this is too much. This awful ignominy is more than man can bear!" I looked at Charlie. He was very ill. The pallor of his face was deepened by the purple congestion of two spots on his cheek, and the dark lines of his mouth. He looked straight before him, apparently not seeing any one in court, and almost unconscious of what was going on around him. His lips moved from time to time as if in silent prayer. The wretched woman beside him made several ineffectual attempts to attract his attention. It was maddening to see her affectation of intimacy and familiarity with one who had never even heard her name until last evening. She leaned against him, put her arm in his, looked affectionately into his face, to the amusement of the spectators and the police. He remained perfectly passive; the look of untold anguish on his face deepened, I thought, a little. I was almost beside myself with rage. But when the crown prosecutor had made his statement, and read the informations of Frederick Myers, who was supposed to have been victimised, and the witness stepped on the table, and I recognised my old friend, Fred Oliver, I could no longer restrain myself.

"Does your Worship know," I said, trying to level my voice, "who this man is, and what a vile plot has been concocted ? "

"I should like to know, sir," he said, "who you are that has the presumption to interrupt the business of this court ? "

"It makes very little difference," I replied; "but this witness is an ex-convict."

"I beg your pardon, your Worship," said the crown prosecutor, in a furious rage, "this is most irregular. I don't know who this fellow is, I'm sure, but the business of the court must be conducted with decorum."

"Constable," said the magistrate, "stand near this gentleman," pointing to me, "and if he opens his lips again, remove him from court."

The constable came and stood behind me. Then the travesty went on.

Fred Oliver swore that he was a gentleman of independent means; that he was engaged at a business house in Grafton Street a fortnight previously; that the female prisoner accosted him, and asked a subscription for the building and maintenance of a Magdalen asylum, presenting testimonials from some clergymen and some leading merchants in the city. She mentioned also the male prisoner's name, who, she said, was the chief promoter of this undertaking. He gave her half a sovereign. A few hours afterwards he saw the two prisoners in close conversation near a restaurant in Dame Street; and on making inquiries, he ascertained that she was a notorious profligate. (The female prisoner here laughed loudly.) He thought it his duty at once to put the matter into the hands of the police.

"Is anything known of the prisoners?" the magistrate asked.

"Yes," the inspector of police answered, "the female prisoner is an Englishwoman, I believe, of good birth, but fallen; the male prisoner is a law student, who has been giving lectures on religious topics through the city."

"A law student lecturing on religion?" said the magistrate. "We have heard of Satan quoting scripture, but a lawyer—to—be lecturing on religion! Well, well!"

The inspector asked for a remand for eight days. It was granted; and, as no bail was asked for, the prisoners were about being removed, when I braved the terrors of the bench again.

I said mildly, "Your Worship will permit me. My friend, Mr. Travers, is in exceedingly delicate health, as you may see, and cannot bear the hardships of the prison. I expected to see Mr. ——, solicitor, here to-day. In fact he was engaged to come——"

"That will do," said the magistrate incredulously. "If the prisoners cannot get bail, I must send them to prison."

"I shall go bail for Mr. Travers," I said.

"Very good. Now, for the first time, let's hear your name."

"My name is Geoffrey Austin."

"Profession?"

"I have no profession."

"Occupation, then?"

"I am gate-keeper at the L—— Hall," I replied, ashamed for the twentieth time of my menial duties.

"I see, sir," said the magistrate sternly, "that you have come here to amuse yourself——"

"I have done nothing of the kind," I said hotly. "I came here to defend an innocent man from an infamous conspiracy. You are about to remand him on the evidence of a ticket-of-leave man. There never was such a travesty of justice before——"

"You are approaching dangerously near contempt of court," he said.

"I have nothing but contempt," I said, "for this——"

"Constable!" he cried, "remove that fellow at once to the cells. I am surprised at my own patience."

I had the pleasure of going to gaol with Charlie. And it was a pleasure. I dreaded facing that hideous world again. Nay, sensuous and fond of ease as I was, I actually felt delight in the prospect of suffering along with Charlie for what I conceived to be a just cause; and I almost welcomed the spectacle of the narrow whitewashed walls, the plank bed with a mattress of straw, the rough sheets and the gray blankets that were rolled up so that the end of them looked exactly like the target of an archery club. The tin platter did not disgust me, nor the solitary comb, broken and clogged with dirt. A week before I would have shuddered at those things; this day I almost exulted in the thought that these would be my toilet and cooking apparatus for many a day.

How I spent these days I cannot now well bring up clearly before my mind. It was like an ugly dream, one long monotone of loneliness and desolation, relieved by the thought that I was innocent of any crime, and that I was in prison with Charlie. I was permitted, if I chose, to get my meals supplied from the city; but I had neither money nor friends, and I had to accept the prison fare. At first my stomach revolted at the coarse porridge and the hard, gritty bread. The second day I ate them with relish; the third day I ate them ravenously. From that forward, I picked up crumbs from the floor and devoured them, and thought of what I had heard Fred Oliver detailing of his prison experience. Of books I had none except the Bible, and a prayer-book—the "Path to Paradise." I read every line of the former from Genesis to the Amen of the Apocalypse. The historical books I read once, the Prophets I dipped into every day; and every day I chanted the Psalter, in dim, far-off imitation of my monks on the Holy Mountain; and I committed to memory the whole Gospel of St. John, especially the prayer of Christ for His disciples. But I fear my attractions there were literary rather than devotional.

One day a detective called. Very cautiously he introduced the question of the trial, of Charlie's fellow-prisoner, and of the prosecuting witness. I gave him no information. He was quite convinced, he said, of Charlie's innocence.

"Then why not release him?" I said.

"The law was circuitous; forms had to be gone through, inquiries to be made," &c., &c.

Then one day I was told Charlie was acquitted, and I could purchase my freedom.

"What had happened?"

"The chief witness had disappeared, and could not be traced. The case had broken down."

I was very glad.

"But I could also purchase freedom by making a simple apology to the magistrate."

"For what?"

"For contempt of court."

"Never!" I declared, "if you keep me here till

Doomsday. I have said nothing wrong, and I am not going to apologise."

Then one morning a letter was placed in my hands running thus :—

" Charlie dying. Come quickly."

It was unsigned, and there was no more information. I called the warder by touching my bell.

" Is the magistrate sitting to-day ? "

" Yes."

" Then bring me before him."

He had forgotten all about me. The warder explained that I had been committed for contempt of court.

" I am prepared to apologise," I said.

" Very well. Do you apologise ? "

"Yes."

" You are released. Don't come here again."

I rushed into the street, staggering as I went, the strong sunlight blinding my eyes, and the fresh, sweet air intoxicating my brain. I saw signs of something unusual in the city. I heeded them not. I had only one thought in my mind—to see Charlie alive—as I ran rapidly across the city.

# CHAPTER XVIII

## TRIUMPH AND DEATH

" Χαῖρ'. εἰ τὸ χαίρειν ἐστι του κάτω χθονός."

"Farewell! if such things be in eternity."

IT was a gala day in the Irish metropolis. From a very early hour the city was alive; and, although the shops were open as usual, and business progressed, there was a listlessness and an air of preoccupation about the faces and habits of the people, as if the usual avocations of men—the squirrel-hoarding of pine-cones and burrs,—were to-day to yield to something higher and more important. Across the main thoroughfare flags of all nations hung and drooped on lines, for the day was sultry, and the Sun-god was playing havoc with the dainty shop goods that lay exposed, and sometimes with the tempers of men. Square placards announced that certain windows in prominent places were "taken"; and young street Arabs had already climbed on every niche and coign of vantage in the street, and announced to rheumatised and portly gentlemen that these desirable localities, which might be broad enough to hold a sparrow, were to be let for proper remuneration. Here and there, at intervals, the gray white street was brightened by small detachments of schoolboys, their battalions headed by gorgeous banners; and the Dublin jarveys had pinned little flags over the green boughs that nodded on their horses' heads. Huge posters, large and

flaring as circus-bills, announced that the procession
would start sharp at one P.M.; and detailed its
route, its places of departure, of rendezvous, and
disembodiment, and the speeches and speakers at
the Rotunda.   It was to be a great Catholic demonstration ; and no one was to be neutral or indifferent
on such an occasion.

High up over a central street, that shall be nameless, Charlie Travers lay on his deathbed.   Since
his release from prison, his strength had been
gradually declining; and now, in great pain from
frequent spasms, he awaited the grand summons
He had already, even in prison, received the last
Sacraments; and every morning a Jesuit Father
from a neighbouring church brought him the viati-
cum.   I found his sister by his bedside.   Though
we had not seen each other for years, she said
nothing by way of greeting, but mutely extended
her hand.   I passed around to the other side of the
bed, and looked down at my old, old friend.   He
stretched out his hand, and grasped mine.   Then,
drawing me gently down towards him, until my face
touched his, he feebly whispered—

"You are always kind.   I'm so glad you are
here."

His voice was low and husky ; but his eyes were
stars.   One lock of fair hair lay matted and flattened
with perspiration on his forehead.   His hands were
hot and dry.   For a long time he was silent, looking
fixedly at the wall.   Then he whispered anxiously
but kindly—

" Have you seen God yet ? "

I had to say no.   I had doubts, for I thought the
awful shadow of God's Hand was upon me, and I
dreaded to look back lest I should see His Face.
But I was afraid to tell a lie to Charlie, most of all
at such a time.

"But, Charlie," I said, "best and dearest of

friends, I am seeking and striving with all my power. God knows, dear fellow, I am struggling to reach Him, if only not to be separated from you."

I let my tears fall silently on his face. And I thought, with all the bitterness of remorse, of my presumption many years ago in that lodging-house in Queenstown, when I had dared to weep for him.

"It will all come," he whispered, "it will all come. ' A la bonne heure! a la bonne heure!' as the Count used to say."

Then, after a pause—

"Mary, lift these pillows!"

She did so, ever so tenderly and lovingly, and he half sat up in bed, and stared at the opposite wall with round, gleaming eyes, as if he saw a vision.

"'A la bonne heure,'" he whispered to himself. "It must come. I used often smile at the thought that God should have chosen me for this work, and not you, nor the Count. But that is His way. 'The foolish hath He chosen to confound the wise.' But now, Goff, you will take up this work, and push it on to success. I know you will. Don't shake your head. I know it."

He coughed slightly, and his sister moistened his lips with an orange. We could hear the stirring of many men in the street below.

"Do you remember, Goff," he asked after a breathing pause, "our old evening walks under the limes? I often think of them—and the airy castles we used to build—and the long streamers of the sinking sun—and the smell of the limes—ah me!"

"You are distressing yourself, dearest," his sister gently interposed. "You know the doctor said you mustn't talk much."

"It makes very little difference now, dear," he replied, "it is but a question of minutes for me. But," he smiled, "I ought really say no more. I have talked so much. Why, Goff, old fellow, I have

spouted Niagaras of talk, or—twaddle. It makes
me laugh to think of it. I, Charlie Travers, who
couldn't say boo to a goose, actually became eloquent! What will you be, Goff, when the Divine
*afflatus* breathes on you ?"

There was a great silence in the street, as when
men hold back their breath in expectation of something wonderful.

"I wonder," Charlie cried after a moment, and
as I thought, irritably, "will the procession ever
start ?"

Then checking himself, he murmured a short
prayer, and immediately his face resumed its aspect
of divine serenity.

"I lost you for many years, Goff," he said at
length, "but you were never out of my remem-
brance. Could I dare say it, I sought you as a
shepherd might seek a sheep. Often and often, on
those great public nights, when the faces of men
surged round me like the white breakers of a sea, I
scanned them eagerly just to get a glimpse of you.
And if I had seen you, I would have been blind to
all the others; and if I had heard your voice, praising me ever so little (you know you were rather
chary of your praise, Goff), I would have heard it,
and been deaf to the applause of thousands. And
I used to say, 'Where is he ? where is he ?' and I
used to pray, 'Lord, if I have any merit before
Thee for aught I have done, send me back my friend
before I die.' And He has heard my prayer. And
again I tell you, the mantle now falls upon you.
See you take it up, and wear it! Lift me a little
more, Mary dear!"

He lay back with his eyes closed for some
minutes. I felt a great choking in my throat, and
could not speak a word. I was hoping that the
procession would start, for I felt that Charlie would
speak yet more strongly to me. But the silence in

the street was only deepening, as if the whole thoroughfare was deserted. At last he opened his eyes, and fixed them again on the wall. Then he spoke, but as if in soliloquy.

"When I am dead, Goff, men will say strange things of me for a day, and then forget me. I want you, as I said, to continue my work. I seek no other immortality here. And this also——"

He gathered his strength as if for a final effort.

"Possibly men will attribute all that I have said or done to myself. They will call it genius, talent, inspiration—or some other newspaper expression. How blind men are—yet how lovable! Because I loved them, I toiled for them, and He who loves all more than I, helped me. Many an evening did I walk with the Master and St. John on the sands of the Sea of Galilee. I see it all now. The great yellow sands, on which the tideless waters scarcely broke, but merely crept up and lapped our feet, stretching along before us; the vast tombs of famous rabbis on our right, the yellow sun sinking under the Galilean mountains, and we wrapped in a dream, for the hands of the Master were round our necks, and His voice was making music in our ears. And He spoke to us so familiarly—I thought no more of it, Goff, than when you and I used to walk together under the limes in the old happy days — and sometimes when the evenings grew chill, and the dews were falling, He would wrap His blue mantle around us, and we would talk and talk until the yellow moon came up over the tranquil lake, and made a long line of glory towards the black hills of Bashan. And it was all about men — men the toilers, the workers, red-browed, horn-handed; and when I protested, and spoke of their meanness, their sin, their small wickedness, their colossal vices, He would say, with His own ineffable sweetness, 'Hush! you do

2 A

not know Me. Try and love them, and you will
love Me !' And I told Him all about you, Goff,
and what you could do, and how brave and talented
you were: and He said nothing, but was sad. And
I appealed to John, and he said nothing, but was
sad. But every word I ever uttered came from
them—from our moonlight walks by the Sea of
Galilee."

He stopped; and his sister and I exchanged
glances. Clearly his mind was wandering.

" Hark !" he cried suddenly, with a great accession
of strength, " there goes the procession."

We could hear nothing for a few minutes. Then
the rumble of drums came from far-off and muffled
to our ears. Charlie drew himself up, and with
glistening eyes, and the flush deepening on his face,
he looked almost as well as long ago in Mayfield.
Then, as the first lines of the people came out from
the side-streets and burst into the main thoroughfares, the *fanfare* of the trumpets, and the steady
roll of drums burst suddenly on our ears; and
Charlie, kindling into excitement, could hardly be
restrained.

"I wonder might I go to the window," he said,
appealing to his sister. " I should so like to see
the poor fellows' faces again."

" Better not, dear," she whispered anxiously,
" don't you think so, Goff—Mr. Austin ? "

" I think you would gain nothing, Charlie," I said,
" you can hear everything from where you are."

For now there was a great murmur in the street,
the rhythmic pulsing of the music, the whispered
admiration of the spectators, the sweep of banners
through the air, and above all, that most solemn of
sounds—the firm, even tread of a marshalled and
disciplined army.

Suddenly, as the great mass of men swept under
the windows, the music stopped.

"What's this? what's this?" said Charlie impatiently.

I went to the window, and looked down. Every head in the vast, black multitude beneath was bared, and many a tearful eye looked up at the window. The whisper had gone abroad that the young Reformer and Martyr was dying, and the heart of the great multitude was stirred. I came back and told Charlie. A great sob burst from him, and a tear rolled silently down his face.

"The Lord was right," he feebly said. "Men with all their faults are infinitely lovable."

Then in a quiet tone, as if the sudden paroxysm of strength were exhausted, he commenced counting and naming the bands, as they passed at intervals under the window.

"That's the St. Kevin's band—I know it well—I can almost see Father Maher marching at the head of it. And the big drum—poor fellow—he would give the world for a drink just now, but he has promised me, and he will keep his promise. And the little triangle—poor little Jemmy—how proud his poor mother will be!" . . . "And now, that's the Marlborough Street Band—of course, they are *facile princeps*—isn't that good Latin, Goff?—and they have a glorious banner! . . . And here comes the Coombe fife and drum band, poor fellows! they had a hard struggle and came in last; but they said they would last the longest. Jem Fagan, and Jack Olden, and Maurice Leddon are the chief drummers. They'll do their best, I know, and Father Mac will keep them right! . . . And these must be the Confraternities, Goff; and after these come my own picked corps of the Young Men's Societies." . . .

He lay back on the pillow, as if listening in a dreamy way to the crash of the music that broke for a moment on our ears with harshness, then passed away into a soft echo. So the noise and the

steady tramp of marshalled men went on in the
street below.   In the death-chamber there was no
sound.   Charlie lay with closed eyes, as if asleep.
Then, as the music softly died away on the hot
air of the streets, he started up, and holding one
hand with extended fore-finger before him, he said
in a startled tone—

"But hark, Goff! what's this?   I did not know
we had such a band.   Listen! . . . Why, that's a
harp, and cymbals, and oh dear! the sound of far-
off silver trumpets, like echoes from distant mountains!   And they're singing, Goff, singing!   Mary,
you know everything, dear!   What *are* they singing?"

His senses appeared to be so much more acute
than ours that we bent down our foolish heads to
catch the far-off sounds—too far, alas! as yet for
us.   For there was a great pause; then a little
shriek from his sister made me raise my eyes to the
bed.   The hand was still raised to arrest our
thoughts, and the round eyes were wide open.   But
it needed but one glance to see that that hand was
just now clasped in the strong grasp of his mighty
Master, and that those eyes, blind for evermore to
all things fleeting and paltry here below, were
sweeping the vast horizons of eternity.

I do not know how long we remained stupefied
and sorrow-stricken by that glorious deathbed, the
sister's tears flowing silently, as is the wont of
women, and I thinking, thinking of many things—
of Charlie's last appeals and prophecies, most of
all, of his complete forgetfulness of the events of the
last few months, as if the dark page had been utterly
blotted from his memory.   There was silence in the
streets, only the hot sun beating down and making
quivering waves of heat from wall and pavement.
And there was silence in that chamber, neither of

us daring to speak in that awful presence. I suppose half-an-hour had passed when we heard a rapid footstep on the stairs, and Father Aidan, in his own impulsive way, burst into the room.

"Charlie, Charlie," he cried, rushing over to the bedside, "why are you not there? They are all waiting for you, I understand——"

Something in the silent and motionless figure struck him dumb, and he looked bewildered to the sister and me. He seemed to think that Charlie was speaking to us. Then, the awful truth burst upon him, and he leaned his head heavily upon the bed-rails.

Then he lifted up his ashen face, more pale than usual, and clasping his hands, he said—

"Child of my soul, and are you gone from me? Charlie, Charlie, I did not expect this. And on the very day of your triumph. Why did not the Master leave you to be vindicated before men? But, what am I, a fool, to talk thus? Surely, you needed no vindication; and if you did," he said fiercely, "it is not from men, the brutes, that you should receive it. Charlie," he cried pathetically, "you know all now, you know now if I were right or wrong. Bear me witness before your God that in all my teachings I was justified. I have to bear the opprobrium of men and their injustice—they say I drove you to ignominy and to your grave; ay, even your dearest friends rebuke me that I was your evil genius——"

"Oh no, Father," said the weeping girl, "don't say so, we know that you meant rightly."

"Ay," he said, "you know that I meant rightly. You are throwing me the alms of your charity, for giving your brother an immortality that the arch-angels might envy. True," he said, with the old irony, "he might be now a lawyer in good practice, a pretty little Pagan with his ledger filled with lies.

But would the blessings of poor women follow him like winged servitors, and would a multitude of men lift their hands to swear by his manhood and his truth? But I am only wasting words on an incredulous generation. God is my witness and His Gospel. And thou, white seraph amongst those chosen ones, who alone may look on the face of the Most High and live, thou, child of my soul, wilt vindicate me, where alone I care to be understood."

He came over to where I was sitting, and folding his arms around his dead saint, he laid the figure back gently on the pillows. Then he took the extended arm, and crossed it reverently on the other, laying both on the breast. He drew down the veined eyelids over the blue eyes, that I had looked into so often. Then drawing back, he surveyed the recumbent figure and bending down, he pressed his lips on the cold forehead. One great sob, which he instantly suppressed, burst from his iron heart: and without one word to the weeping sister or to me, he passed rapidly from the room.

In a few minutes he returned. "Mark you," he said peremptorily, "no nonsense, no demonstration, no public funeral. You will bring him by the night mail to Clare, and there he will be interred. Mr. Austin, look you to it."

I thought he had forgotten even my name. We carried out his injunctions strictly, except that Gallwey, Cal., Forrester, and two others insisted on remaining with me during the two night watches. So also did a number of workmen, belonging to the third Order of St. Francis. On the evening of the third day, a simple funeral wended its way slowly along the Dublin quays. It consisted of a bier with the coffin, and one mourning coach in which were Miss Travers and myself. It was lonely and mournful enough; and the thought would intrude itself that the work of that vanished life was over—to all human appearance, a failure. So has all the great work of the world appeared. Our impatience of results ignores the soft slowness with which God operates amongst us. We call that failure, which the hands of God are moulding into perfect form and outline. But if I had thought that Charlie's work had terminated with his death, I would have been speedily undeceived. For when we reached the outer gate of the terminus, the bier was stopped, and the casket containing poor Charlie's remains was hoisted after a friendly struggle on the shoulders of four strong men, and we passed slowly after through a long avenue of bareheaded, solemn workers—the workers whom he loved, shaggy, bearded, horn-handed, smelling of their work in wood or mineral, and whose appearance for ever belied the soft gentleness of hearts which his words of wisdom had deeply stirred. They said not a word, but their silence was eloquent. So, too, was a tear that fell now and then from a bowed head and hidden face. When we had passed on to the platform, one of them came forward and placed a superb cross of rich flowers on the coffin, and then retired. But another surprise was in store for us. For during the few minutes that elapsed till the van came around, a small knot of men, looking very like students or young professionals, gathered around the coffin, and at a signal, each in turn moved up silently, silently looked down on the dead, then placed the extended palm of his hand on the breastplate, and retired. I counted forty-six, and then gave up counting, to think that after all there are some deep unplummeted vastnesses in Irish hearts which no man yet has sounded. When the Voice shall· come, and pierce those depths, the echoes thereof shall penetrate unto the ends of the earth, carrying the old Gospel that will create once again the Kingdom of God upon earth!

# BOOK III.

" Halts by me that footfall :
Is my gloom, after all,
Shade of His hand, outstretched caressingly ?
' Ah, fondest, blindest, weakest,
I am He whom thou seekest !
Thou dravest Love from thee, who dravest Me ! ' "
—FRANCIS THOMPSON.

# BOOK III

## CHAPTER I

### SELF-QUESTIONINGS

> " Go from me ; yet I feel that I shall stand
> Henceforward in thy shadow.  Never more
> Alone upon the threshold of my door
> Of individual life, I shall command
> The uses of my life, nor lift my hand
> Serenely in the sunshine."
>
> —E. B. BROWNING.

AS I stood, with a heavy heart, and eyelids wet with
tears that came unbidden, over the open grave near
the edge of which lay Charlie's coffin, whilst the
clear voice of Father Aidan rang out the immortal
words, "*Ego sum resurrectio et vita*," the thought
would obtrude itself, "Has this life, too, fair and
beautiful in all its lineaments, been a failure?"
Everything around me preached it.  The old abbey,
picturing the decrepitude of age that sheds everything vital and beautiful, and keeps only a shell
that Time passes by in disdain.  The stones, yellow
with lichen, and with undecipherable inscriptions ;
the flaunting nettles, the thick spears of the grass
that will die one of these days, and the neglected
graves around me—all these taught the eternal
lesson of Death closing the vain little drama of Life.
And if I lifted up my eyes to where, across the sand
dunes, the black rocks stretched their blind strength
against the cruel sea, the same eternal lesson came

back, of blind forces battling with each other, and
the treadmill of Creation kept going by the ceaseless
warfare of the human and material elements of
Nature. I was rolling over unconsciously in my
mind those terrible words—

> " So careful of the type? But no !
> From scarpéd cliff and quarried stone
> She cries, ' A thousand types are gone :
> I care for nothing, all shall go !'"

when there was a pause in the reading of the
Burial Service. We all looked up. Father Aidan's
eyes were bent upon the coffin. He appeared to be
suffering from some deep emotion. Then, mastering
his feelings with his old vigour, he stretched out his
hand, and as if in prophetic defiance of all dismal
thoughts and vain regrets for the vanished life, he
rang out in trumpet tones the words in which long
ago he had foretold Charlie's high vocation—" *Et tu,
puer, propheta Altissimi vocaberis ; præibis enim
ante faciem Domini parare vias ejus.*" He stopped
for a moment, as if to challenge contradiction. The
father looked down sternly on the coffin. The sister
was weeping. A cold breeze came in from the sea,
lifted the ivy leaves of the ruined abbey, lifted the
grey curls that fell over the priest's shoulders, played
with the leaves of the superb lilied cross (the gift of
the Dublin labourers), passed on and made a little
whirlpool on the sandy hills, and after its petty
bluster and caprice, died away towards the east.
Then the priest, as if to find the apology and justifi-
cation of all his dealings with the dead boy in the
pages of Holy Writ, went back, and translated word
for word, the grand sentences of the Canticle of
Zachariah. He paused again in the middle of the
canticle, and looking Mr. Travers steadily in the
face, he said in impressive tones—

"And thou, child, shalt be called the Prophet of

the Most High; for thou shalt go before the face of
the Lord to prepare His ways.

" To give the knowledge of salvation to His
people unto the remission of sins.

" Through the bowels of the mercy of our God, in
which the Orient from on high hath visited us.

" To enlighten those who sit in darkness and the
shadow of death, to direct their feet in the way of
peace."

As he spoke these words in his own melodious
way, and threw into them the pathos and the pride
that he felt, I could see the stern muscles of the
father's face unbending, and a tear stealing silently
down his cheek. Faith had conquered human ambition and its distrust of God. And when the last
sod was placed over the grave of our beloved one,
and the people were slowly scattering, one or two
poor peasants lingered near, and covertly stole a
flower or a leaf from the wreaths that lay on the
new grave. Then a softer air came in again from
the sea and vexed the ivy-leaves of the old ruin,
and lifted up the iron-gray plumes of hair that fell
down on the priest's blue cape, and touched softly a
few ringlets of grass that hung down the side of the
grave; then passed out over the sand dunes, and
made a white gull, winging his way gravely to the
sea, poise himself motionless for a moment; and it
bent the gentle osiers by the dry brook, and lost
itself out on the mereland. And at the same time we
became conscious of a spirit form hovering over the
place, where its frail temple now rested, and a spirit
of peace came down upon us all and touched and
filled us with that serenity that is the regal reward
of the elect. I went over to say good-bye to Father
Aidan, for I had to drive to catch a morning train.
He gripped my hand fast, as if he would say, " You
at least understand me." And I read down in the
deep wells of his eyes what the veil of his austerity

cloaked from public gaze—unfathomable depths of
such love as brought tears to the eyes of Peter, and
broke the heart of the sorrowing Magdalene.   Then
Mr. Travers approached, and said, half shyly—

"Come, Father Aidan, Mrs. Travers will expect
you."

And Mary said—

"Do, Father, please come."

Father Aidan seemed to hesitate for a moment.
Then he said simply—

"Yes, I'll come."

He had not crossed the threshold of their door for
nearly twelve months.   For every account that
came from Charlie in Dublin only emphasised Mrs.
Travers' regret for what she called "this religious
Quixotism"; and then the disgrace and shame
under which Charlie passed to his reward had
broken even the father's faith in the wisdom that
had prompted such a vocation.

Mr. Travers and Mary passed humbled and
sorrowful to their home; and Father Aidan beckoned
to me.

"Can you spare me a few minutes, Mr. Austin?"

I said, "Yes."

We went out on the sands, which were now wet
with the receding tide.

"I have not asked you any details of Charlie's
last days or moments," he said.   Then, he asked
with emotion—

"How did he bear that trial, and how did he meet
God?"

"He bore the trial like a saint," I replied, "and
he met God as friend would greet friend."

Then I went into details of the trial, the imprisonment, and Charlie's last hours.   He was deeply
affected.

"Yet," he said, "when I launched him on that
perilous enterprise, I had my misgivings.   A frail,

beautiful, sensitive soul appeared to be the last that
should have been chosen for the rough work of the
apostolate. It was like sending St. Aloysius as
ambassador to some unchristian and licentious
court, or asking St. John Berchmans to be legate
at Constantinople. Perhaps it was the supreme
wisdom of Christ that selected such strong, sinewy
men as His apostles, and sent them to deal with the
masculine lustiness of the Gentiles. And yet, who
knows? 'The weak ones of the world hath God
ehosen to confound the strong.' But tell me, do
any visible fruits remain of the brief mission of our
young saint, or has it seemed otherwise?"

" I am hardly qualified to say, Father," I replied.
" He was vehemently opposed by the wise and
good——"

" Well!" he ejaculated emphatically.

" He was subjected to a good deal of ridicule," I
continued.

" Very good; go on."

" The wealthy and the powerful abandoned him
at the last moment," I said bitterly.

" Better still; go on," he cried.

" But," I continued, "the poor clung to him as to
a saviour; and young men drank in his teachings
with avidity."

" Thank God," he cried with emphasis. Then I
went into all details. The students burning the
midnight oil in work for God, the Church, charity;
young professional men snatching an hour for
prayer and the study of high things; the vesper
choirs of the city, where the old music of the
Church was sung by loving voices; the hearths
of the tradesmen made blessed by the new light
Charlie had spread; thronged churches, empty
bars, and all Satanic power leagued and concentred against a movement that was driving all evil
things into the background; and then, in the flush

of success, the apparent undoing of all this glorious work, and the apparent failure of all this high enterprise.

Father Aidan caught at the word failure.

"Failure!" he cried, with all his old enthusiasm enkindled. "There is no such thing with God! That imbecile, Carlyle, spoke one truth, 'Christ died on Calvary—that built yonder kirk.' And I say: 'Charlie spoke in Dublin: and in San Francisco and Dunedin, in Sydney and Calcutta, his words will bear fruit. You may live to see such things. I shall not. And now, good-bye!'" He looked down into the depths of my soul, whilst he held my hand tightly gripped; and for the first time, I thought I could love him. He passed away across the sands with his old quick stride. I saw him no more. I went back to the graveyard. Rover, with his nose in the air, was howling dismally; poor Rufa, the milkmaid, was praying softly, and one blind woman was crooning with the wind and the uplifted wave over Charlie's grave.

His spirit must have descended upon mine, for all along that weary journey to Dublin, amidst the jostling and jarring of machinery, the cries of children, the chatter of the young, the gossip of the old, my soul kept on saying—

"I know Thee, Alpha and Omega! the beginning and the end! I know Thee, the answer to every riddle, the key to every mystery, the term of all human knowledge, the beacon of all human hope, the fulfilling of all human desire. Thou that speakest, and all men should hear, art yet heard only in the silences and the midnight, when Thy whispers break on the bruised heart; and the thunders of Thy voice, ruling the rebellious spheres, break down into faint ripples of sound that wash on the sandy shores of deserted and desolate souls. Thou art the term of all philosophy, for Thou art the Wisdom and the

Word; Thou art the end of charity, for from Thee is the spirit of love breathed; nor is there any vindication of the daring flights of faith, except that Thou art everywhere, and wherever the reason shoots its inquisitive rays, or the imagination poises its wings, they must needs touch Thee—the Immense —the Infinite! The finger of science is guided by Thy hand; and it is Thy hand that glides over the glowing canvas, and touches the ivory keys. It is Thou who makest eloquent the dumb of speech, and makest fertile the barren of mind, weaving out of the stammering of sucklings praises that rival the melodies of Thy thrones, and out of the babbling of human speech, adoration that makes envious the courts of Thy heaven. No mind can contemplate heaven without Thee, for Thou art heaven; and earth without Thy presence were a valley of desolation, a pit and a slough of despair. The sun shines wherever Thou art; where Thou art not, are clouds and darkness, and the violence of tempests. And the magic of Thy name, and the burning of Thy words, and the strength of Thy example did not die with Thee on Calvary (though Thy Calvary too, to human eyes, spoke dismal failure), but down along the hoary centuries have extended the sweet influences of light and healing and inspiration, that have made the young leap to Thy arms, and the old crouch at Thy feet. All the sweetness and light, all the mercy and charity, the straightening of bruised reeds, and the healing of broken hearts, flow from Thy hands, which so often distilled the miracles of Thy compassion in the days of Thy pilgrimage; and as the sea lifts up its hands to the sun, and the voices of many waters beat out their lamentations to the midnight skies, so are the hands of all Thy little ones and Thy afflicted lifted up to Thee, O Christus Consolator! and the cries of humanity surge around Thee to be echoed back from the

2 B

recesses of Thy adorable heart in accents of a charity
that is boundless, and a mercy that is omnipotent.
Thou art the secret of all things—the loadstone of
human hearts—the centre of all creation, without
limit or circumference. Thou, the apex, where centre
all the circles of the just, as the circles of Hell
narrow down from abyss to abyss of wretchedness
and despair, until they terminate in the slime and
squalor of the dread Apollyon. The pens of philosophers have written Thee; the brushes of artists
have limned Thee; the voices of virgins praised
Thee; the thunder of organs hymned Thee; the
fancies of poets dreamed Thee; the lips of orators
explained Thee; and then, all have said in despair,
that Thy majesty and beauty have escaped them.
Thou alone canst understand Thyself; we best
adore Thee when we are silent before Thee. Not
that Thy wondrous attributes are fugitive and elusive,
even as some vain men imagined that Thou wert
honoured, when declared to be unknown. We know
Thee, yet bow down our eyes before Thee, for we
seek to measure none other of Thy attributes but
Thy love, and that Love, immeasurable as it is,
filleth to overflowing the broken and leaky cisterns
of our hearts, for it is a ceaseless stream flowing
from the smitten rock of Thy most holy heart. And
now, Lord, I know Thee, but I have not seen Thee
as yet. Thou hast veiled Thy face from me, whilst
Thy hands did smite me. Thou hast conquered, O
Christ! Every time I thought to soar into the high
empyrean of thought, I felt the shadow of Thy wings
hovering high above me, veiling the light, that I
might see Thee, the true Light; and threatening to
bear me wounded and bleeding to earth. And to
earth I fell—for the vain systems of my philosophy
were but the wings of Icarus, that melted away
under the fierce sunlight of Thy love. Bit by bit,
the armour which I wore in my conflict with Thee,

was hewn away by the sharp sword of Thy power, and naked and subdued I stand before Thee to receive at Thy hands the final stroke that means eternal ruin, or the accolade, that will enlist me amongst Thy knights, sworn to do battle with Thee. But I must see Thee. In the majesty of Thy power, in the strength of perennial manhood, in the lustiness of Thy great prowess and vigour, Thine eyes —flames of fire; Thy feet, shod with brass; Thy mouth, breathing the two-edged sword; Thy breast, cinctured with beaten gold—even so, Lord, as Thy saint saw Thee in Patmos, do I desire to see Thee, even if mine eyes withered at the sight, for no man could see thus and live. But I *must* see Thee. Thou hast followed me through life, chasing me with persistence, as if Thy love were hatred; Thy name has flashed across me in unexpected places, blinding me with excess of light. I have shut the windows of my soul against Thee; but Thou hast pierced them with the lightning of Thine eyes. I have hidden in dark places, and Thou hast found me. I have closed my ears against the soft breathing of Thy inspirations, only to hear the thunders of Thy threats. And now, run down, beaten, subdued, the rags of my nakedness not hiding my grievous sores, I stand before Thee, humbled and ashamed, confessing myself the least victim of Thy unwearying, Thy pitiless love. Yet let me see Thee, my Conqueror, my Master; and leave me the small meed of an all too stubborn fight—to know that I am conquered by the Prince of Ages, the Christ of the Transfiguration and the Apocalypse!"

How little as yet I knew of God! How little I understood the strength of His weakness, the richness of His poverty, the wisdom of His folly, the triumph of His failure, these poor words testify. Yet, it was some approach to Him, and the spirit that guided me was the soul of my friend.

# CHAPTER II

## AT LAST

" God hath stood in the congregation of gods ; and being in the midst of them, He judges gods."—Psalm lxxxi.

THE sun was setting behind the Four Courts as I passed along the quays that evening, feeling bereft and lonely, yet with some presentiment that my time had come, and I should see God. He, whom I had been battling against in secret during all these years, was now going to show the awful splendours of His face to me, and I was dreaming of Hermon and Thabor, and the blinding lights of the Apocalypse, with some terror and misgiving indeed, for I dreaded the face of the Son of Man. I was no longer in the least doubtful that I had been leaning, during these eventful years of my life, on the broken reeds of a false and corrupt philosophy; that I had been " whining for dead gods who could not save." In my abysmal ignorance, which I thought such sublime knowledge, I did not know that these systems of philosophy with which I was eternally dabbling, even after the beginning of my conversion, had long ago fallen into decrepitude; and that as far back as the fourth century, they had been driven in contempt from the schools of Rome and Athens and Alexandria. Nor did I clearly understand that all our modern systems of unbelief, which had for me the fatal fascination that made the angels cling to Lucifer in his fall, were but new modes of ancient errors, fresh forms of those indestructible sophisms of which

the ancient systems were the archetypes. But this
I had now ascertained after such weariness of mind
and humiliation as perhaps comes rarely to try the
soul ; and there came with it the cognate conviction
that when man leans on his own pride and seeks not
the help that has been promised to every faithful
seeker, he leans upon a weak and very frail support.
I knew now that I was but awaiting a revelation
which should for ever bind me fast to the Throne of
God. I was utterly beaten, shamed, humbled by
that invisible and mysterious pursuer, who, with
patient persistence, had been following my footsteps
through these lost years of my life, and making me
utterly disgusted with all human things, that I might
seek my rest in Him. As I made my way along the
coal-blackened quays, and looked down at the greasy
river, I shuddered to think how often the despair of
knowledge had tempted me thither ; and somehow I
felt that the compassion that might be lawfully extended to some poor frail victim of passion, who had
sought rest in the ooze and slime of that hideous
stream, would never be extended from earth or from
on high to the victim of a despair born of high knowledge and proud thoughts. A haze rose up from the
river as the sun went down, and a dark cloud came
up from the sea, and hung low over the mud and
sand wastes that the tide was leaving exposed. A
smart shower pattered out of the gloom, and I sought
shelter in the archway of a little church on the quays.
A few people gathered in the porch, and not wishing
to block the way, I passed up the dim aisle and sat
down. Then I suddenly became aware of two
piercing eyes looking calmly and terribly into my
soul—eyes brown and luminous, but with awful
questionings in every glance. These in some
strange, unconscious way I put into Latin, and my
mind went whispering, " Quare ? Quare ? " and then
" Quousque ? Quousque ? " I shook myself angrily

to set aside the delusion. But no! There were those awful eyes, penetrating my soul like arrows of flame, and my mind singing the refrain, "Quare? Quare? Quousque? Quousque?"

I felt angry with myself for being the victim of such an illusion. I felt angry with God for such a manifestation of His will. Yet my whole soul was thrilled with the thought, I am coming nearer to Him. "Now," I said, rising up, "this is a delusion caused by an empty stomach. Curious how dependent, even in a philosopher, is the mind upon the body!"

I turned to depart. But by some singular fascination, I looked again, this time analytically. Yes, there was the canvas filling up the great gold frame, partly blackened and tarnished by the years, and there in the centre was the figure of the Man-God, with the dark wounds in the hands and feet; and the fingers held open the red inner garment, to reveal a heart, crowned with thorns, dripping with blood, and bursting into flame. Realistic enough, I had seen this image a hundred times, at home, in the college chapel, in the little prints of my prayer-book; but now its eyes hold me and transfix me, and I cannot escape. But I will! And, taking up my hat from the bench, I turned to depart. I passed under the pulpit to the nave, and once more I looked back. There were those wonderful eyes, now pleading and praying to me to return, and the constant singing in mine ears, "Quousque? Quousque?" Hardly knowing what I was doing, and smiling at my own imbecility, I came back to where I had been sitting, and once more I tried by a sheer effort of the will to shake off the delusion. Then I stared back at these wonderful eyes, stared and stared and stared; and gradually the figure grew dim and disappeared, and all around me grew hazy and indistinct, and I thought I lived thousands

of years ago in far-off strange lands, amongst ancient peoples, long vanished from the earth, and I
saw without any of the incongruities of dreams
several wonderful things, and this is what I saw.

## MY DREAM IN THE CHURCH

### I

A great river rolled to the sea, and from the
bleached hills above the river a temple, glistening
in ivory and gold, sent a hundred minarets aloft to
pierce the blue sky. All the splendours of human
art were exhibited in this monument of human
worship; and I said, here is the culmination of all
that man's mind can effect when stimulated by the
twin passions that form adoration, fear, and love.
But the external glories of the temple faded into
tawdry insignificance compared with the marvels of
the interior. It was Solomon's Temple reproduced
or anticipated; but in the place that might have been
the holy of holies stood a hideous idol, all its splendid
ugliness enhanced by gold and precious stones, lav-
ished on every crevice and cranny of the figure that
could bear them. There it stood, impassive and
stupid, staring with its eyes of glittering diamonds,
as the Sphinx stares at the desert. There were
shaven priests there, moving about and muttering
incantations; and a weary people, stricken by
disease and famine, stared helplessly at the motionless idol. I thought I heard a cry of pain from the
stricken people, " Where art Thou ? " and I saw a
great look of expectation on their faces, as of people
who hoped for a deliverer and waited patiently His
coming. It was pitiful, that sad look of expectation
on old and withered faces, on faces made haggard
by disease, on the faces of the young, puckered and

distorted by pain; most of all, on the faces of little
children, that had lost all the satin bloom and soft-
ness of childhood, and put on the withered and
sallow looks of premature intelligence and premature pain.   From time to time moans would
escape from crippled creatures, from children at
the breast, from the palsied and consumptive; then
die out into a silence that was oppressive, for it
spoke so eloquently of stifled anguish.   But the
idol stared blankly forward.   There was no hope
there.   Sometimes a priest would move before the
colossal figure, and drop a pinch of fragrant incense
into a brazier; and as the soft clouds arose and
wreathed themselves around the motionless figure,
bleared eyes would lift up themselves to see some
change.   But the motionless idol stared blankly
forward, and the stricken ones bent down their
heads in despair on their naked breasts.   There
was no hope.

I do not know how long I gazed at these rueful
scenes, so like a page or picture from the *Inferno*,
when a figure, half naked but for rough clothes flung
carelessly around Him, moved down the centre,
scarcely heeded by the sufferers, but narrowly and
suspiciously watched by the priests.   It was the
figure of a leper, silvered all over with the shining
scales of the dread disease, that barely let the ruddy
flesh beneath shine forth through its hideous vesture.   But hands and feet and features were untouched, and the long hair fell in tangled masses on
His neck.   He moved slowly forward, looking to
either side.   The priests shouted at Him to retire,
and screamed out their indignation that He should
dare appear among the faithful in the temple of
their god.   He passed them by unheeding, and
stretched His hands with a pitying gesture towards
the crowds of stricken creatures that huddled close
against the walls.   Then a wonderful thing took

place. The priests folded up their parchment, and ceased to pour into the tortured ears of the poor wretches their platitudes about Buddha and Siva, and their poor philosophy from the national sage ; for at the piteous gesture of the leper a new light came into the eyes of the wretched ones, as you see a yellow dawn break on a mist-laden landscape ; and lo ! the palsied stood up in all the strength of manhood, and the blind opened the gates of long sealed eyes, and the sick children leaped from the arms of mothers and sought shelter in the bosom of the Leper. And as He came near I saw His luminous eyes resting on me for an instant, and then I knew it was Christ, and I yearned towards Him, and would have touched Him, but a mist came down on the temple and blotted it out, and I felt so sorry, and so glad, and I asked myself did He elude me on purpose, and was I abandoned ?

## II

I was standing in the midst of a vast plain, white sands under my feet, a white sky, bleached by a fierce, scorching sun over my head, and nothing to break the painful glare, but a palm tree, here and there, that drooped its glossy leaves under the intolerable heat. Suddenly I became aware of huge, uncouth figures rising out of the desert sands before me—vast, unwieldy forms, which, as they blotted out the white heavens, assumed the shape of colossal Sphinxes, moulded out of granite ; and each, with that stony stare, that has made generations wonder at the impassive immobility of the one that has survived the ravages of time, ranged itself in order until there was a broad avenue, formed by two lines of these terrible figures, as they narrowed into a perspective fully a mile away. Moved by some secret power, I walked through this avenue of

Sphinxes, afraid to look to right or left, although I felt, in some mysterious manner, the stony eyes riveted upon me.　And as almost fainting under the heat and my strange terrors I reached the end, pillars of porphyry rose in long colonnades out of the desert sands, hiding and revealing a vast temple of the Egyptian gods.　Some voice apparently from the lips of the last of the Sphinxes, cried, "Enter!" and I stood at a door, vast, and wonderfully carved in gold, which slowly opened, and I was in the temple. A large and airy structure was supported on columns of granite, around which were wreathed in fantastic forms serpents of all sizes and shapes.　Some were coiled entirely around the pillars, their heads clustered at the top, and forming a strange, foliated capital; some barely touched the pillars, and thence stretched themselves forward into the open space, forming hideous gargoyles with red mouths and forked tongues; some again lay quite flat and rigid in a perpendicular position from base to capital, making a curious kind of Doric ornament; and others, coil fastened upon coil, made a fantastic column, rigid, massive, and solid, in its appearance of vast strength.　The walls were covered with frescoes, and rude paintings in red and ochre of Egyptian deities—the cat, the stork, and the bull, Ammon, Isis, and Osiris, in their various forms; whilst certain martial scenes, and delineations of battles, in which long-forgotten emperors and princes had figured, covered the vast ceiling with a glittering mosaic of red and gold and yellow.　And scrolls, written in some obsolete language, ran around the entablatures over the square arches.　Priests, naked to the waist, each cinctured with a sleeping serpent, moved around the temple, chanting in a monotonous voice, and swinging censers, which filled the building with a strange and sleepy aroma.　And again, as in my former dream, did I behold crowds of stricken wretches cowering near the walls, or under the pillars, praying piteously for help under the fierce burning pain which twisted limbs and writhing bodies indicated. Whilst I looked on pityingly, high over the hum of the priests' voices and the shrill prayers of the stricken, there arose a Babel of cries, loud, angry, questioning—voices as of a multitude that were moving hither from some unseen quarter of the temple. Nearer and nearer they came, and I expected to see a vast multitude filing into the temple, when, in an instant, the priests stood still, and laid down their censers, and prostrated themselves, their arms stretched out before them ; the huge serpents of stone, galvanised suddenly into life, untwined themselves from corbel, capital, and pillar, and glided away noiselessly into darkness ; and as a vast crowd, now hushed into reverential awe, entered the various porticos, and with one accord prostrated themselves with the priests, I became aware of some secret, awful Presence, hidden behind a crimson veil at the farthest extremity of the temple. I held my breath, stirred by some unspeakable emotion—some vague anticipation of a vision that would destroy me, or lift me into higher regions of ecstatic thought—realms of intellectual raptures hitherto unexperienced, when lo ! the veil was slowly drawn aside by some invisible hand, and there, in the midst of the priesthood of ancient Egypt, and surrounded by the prophetic emblems, which humanity in its infancy had fashioned into its gods, was the gentle figure of Christ on His Cross, wounded and stricken by men, yet with the ever-divine expression of unalterable pity, and undimmed, inextinguishable love. I stood and gazed, filled to the lips with emotions of pride and love, whilst the lepers and the stricken stretched their pitiful hands towards Him, when a mist gathered before mine eyes, and the whole scene faded away into the dim spaces of the desert, only to be succeeded by a picture as fair and as beautiful.

### III

I was standing now at the foot of a mighty hill, along whose gentle declivities multitudes were toiling. The sun was a little more tender, less fierce; and blue waters sparkled in the distance, and gave a cooling appearance to the landscape. I, too, toiled along the height; purple grapes and pomegranates clustered on the hedges that lined the road, and the gay people gathered from the earth's abundance, and fashioned for themselves, out of Nature's prodigality, ornaments for their persons, and gifts for their gods. It was a holiday, and the people were moving onward to witness some gay spectacle— some special popular amusements devised by their archons and elders. I was borne along with them, and felt quite as full of exultation, and the buoyant anticipation of a day's pleasure as they. We came to a plateau, broad and wide, that broke the steepness of the hill; and there was a vast open-air theatre, with its tiers of seats for spectators, its statue of Bacchus in the centre now garlanded with flowers and vine-leaves; and the vast stage against the cliff, curtained and shaded, and keeping its own great secret of the play that was to be exhibited to a critical and censorious audience. The spectators were massed in the tiers of seats, the dignitaries on the lower benches; and a vast sea of wondering and expectant faces, lighted with hope and pleasure, turned towards the place where the munificence of the reigning archon was about to exhibit, with all the profuse splendour and artistic elegance of the age, some drama illustrative of Grecian glory. It was clear that something very exceptional was expected, and I shared the tense and almost painful

anxiety of the multitude around me. Then the vast
curtain was raised by some invisible hand, and
showed a scene that contrasted strangely with the
exquisite loveliness to which Nature had accustomed
her wayward and favoured children. From a bleak
and dismal sea, untouched by sunlight, and unbroken in its inky blackness by feather of foam or
gleam of sea-bird, huge rocks rose perpendicularly.
Black and jagged, as if often struck by lightning,
they lifted themselves into the clear air, their summits alone showing a little colour where sheets of
snow were hidden in clefts, or remained untouched
by the shafts of sunlight. There was an aspect
about the whole scene so inhospitable and cheerless,
so cold and forbidding, that a sensible shudder ran
through the audience; and some, to relieve the
painful feeling, turned their gaze aside and continued looking on the more gentle traits, in which
Nature showed herself habitually to them. Then
from a side wing a strange procession emerged.
Two huge unwieldy figures, made yet more uncouth
by the masks which disfigured their features, advanced on the proscenium, followed by the lame god,
Vulcan, bearing hammer and nails. And then amidst
some sighs from the audience, came a youth, clothed in
all the glory and beauty of perfect manhood. Long
familiarity with the glorious play, or some subtle instinct, had already told this quick and sensitive people
the name and nature of the drama ; but though I, in
my dream, had a dim recollection of having seen it
before, and although I could follow word for word
nearly all the remarkable passages, which were
chanted in a kind of monotone, I could not recall to
memory the name of the great Æschylean drama.
One wish was uppermost in my mind, that my old
teacher, Mr. Dowling, were with me ; for here was
the realisation of all his hopes and ideals. The
action of the drama proceeded: the brave, strong

youth, the martyr saint, was laid on the black, bare
rock, and Vulcan, at the command of Strength,
commenced the dreadful operation of nailing him
down.   I followed with acute interest the remon-
strances of the god, who was an unwilling agent in
this tragedy ; and his mournful forecast of the tortures of the future, spoken tremulously, moved me
almost to tears—

" I rivet thee against my will, with chains indis-
soluble, to this hill, remote from men, where you
shall neither hear the voice, nor see the form of
mortals ; but, parched by the bright beam of the
sun, you shall change the flower of colour ; you shall
long for night, star-mantled, to hide the light, for
sun to melt the frost of early dawn ; but evermore a
weight of present evil shall waste you, for he who
shall alleviate your pains is yet unborn."

And Strength answers—

" Let it be !   Wherefore do you delay, and show
pity in vain ?   Wherefore do you not hate the god
most odious to gods, who has betrayed to men your
honour ? "

And so the martyr is chained and nailed to the
cold rock.   The dreadful sound of the hammer
seems scarcely as harsh as the vituperations of
Strength, who orders chain after chain to be riveted
around the prostrate form, and, as a final precaution,
commands Vulcan to fix an iron bar across the
breast, so that the victim should not be able to move
in his agony or relieve his aching body.   Then, with
a parting insult, the three figures leave the stage,
and we stare at the desolate and terrible scene that
lies before us.   But not for long.   For, before the
chorus enters, or Io, a strange thing happens.   The
rock lifts itself perpendicularly ; the chained god
rises with it, and, to my consternation and horror,
discloses the features and figure of the crucified
Christ !   Yes, unmistakably !   There was the pale,

white body, exhausted of blood; there were the
gashes and rents of the scourges, the red holes made
by the nails in hands and feet, and the meek, thorn-
crowned head bent on the breast. And as the
revelation came to me, so did it come to that vast
audience, for in an instant every Greek had risen to
his feet, and echoing one to another, "It is the
Christ! it is the Christ!" the vast multitude fled
panic-stricken from the theatre, and, dreading even
to look back, swept in a hurried stream down the
hill to the city.

I was alone in the vast theatre. I felt the eyes of
my God upon me, for I was afraid to raise mine
own. Mingled feelings of compassion, fear, reverence, surged through my heart. I do not know
what I should have done, when from the left of the
proscenium issued a strange chorus—not of the
nymphs of ocean, as in the Greek play—but all the
great men of antiquity moved in slow and solemn
procession before the crucified Figure; and, as they
passed, each turned and bowed in mute adoration of
their Master, and moved out of sight beyond the
curtains of the proscenium on the other side.
Ancient sages from the Ganges and the Nile; Greek
philosophers, from Pythagoras and Plato, down to
their commentators and disciples, such as Porphyry
and Plotinus; founders of every school of mysticism;
demigods of the grove and porch; some, whose
metaphysical ravings were rejected even at their
birth as too absurd, and some whose reasonings and
dim, prophetic forecasts form the foundations of
Christian metaphysics; dreamers and logicians;
sophists and poets; rhetoricians and declaimers;
all the gods of intellect that have made the East such
hallowed ground to the student, all passed by across
the darkened stage and all did reverence, as to their
Master and Preceptor, to the dim Figure stretched
on His bed of pain, but wearing, even in His agony,

all the Divine lineaments that have prostrated the
world in a transport of adoration at His feet. "God
stood in the synagogue of gods, and, being in the
midst of them, He judgeth gods."

Once more, the vast theatre was deserted, and I
was alone with Christ. The meek, beseeching eyes
were riveted upon me, and said more plainly than
words, "Wilt thou alone despise Me ?" and I rose
to my feet, every nerve tingling with new sensations,
and hurrying across the open space, where the
fragments of the broken statue of Bacchus cut my
feet, I flung myself down, and pressed my forehead
against the cold iron that chained the feet of Christ.
At last I had found Him, found Him in the very
centre and home of that culture for which I had
abandoned Him—amongst the gods for whom I had
deserted Him—through the language for whose
beauty and associations I had contemned the sweet
simplicity of His Divine words ; and amongst the
very people who had worshipped Him as an "Unknown God" I discovered Him whom I, indeed, had
known, but had, in my pride and lust of imagination
and intellect, abandoned and despised. I had found
the Drama of Calvary in a Greek theatre, the perfection of self-sacrifice face to face with the statue
of a sensual deity, and the meek Son of a Jewish
maiden in the centre of a haughty race, who traced
their blood to the Olympian gods.

How long this vision lasted I know not ; but I
was aroused by a hand on my shoulder, and a
voice, that said, not unkindly—

"My child, you should hardly have come into
God's house in such a state."

I did not at first grasp his meaning ; but, when it
dawned upon me that he meant that I was intoxicated, I jumped up, threw his hand off my shoulder,
and looked angrily at my interlocutor.

He was a priest, dressed in a plain, black cassock ;
a young priest, not much older than myself; but he
had a white face, across his forehead were deep
lines, and his eyes were keen and kindly. He
looked into my angry face for a moment, as I stood
with blazing eyes, and all my evil pride pictured in
my face. Then suddenly he put his hand to his
forehead, and said, with pain—

" May God forgive my unworthy suspicion. Come,
I know it all ! "

But I was not so easily pacified, and I drew back
proudly. But he constrained me ever so gently,
and putting his arm around my neck, he drew me
towards him. Thus we passed through the brass
gate into the Sanctuary, and thence into the side
chapel.

I could not help looking up at the picture. The
twilight had just fallen, and the canvas was but
faintly lighted, but I saw those eyes now looking at
me, I thought kindly, and there was a singular
smile around the bearded mouth which, an hour ago,
I would have resented. But now I had no time for
reflection, for my new guide led me rapidly through
the sacristy, up a long flight of stairs, across a
narrow passage, and into a large room, which I soon
recognised as his own sitting-room and library. He
drew a table to the centre of the room, placed a chair
before it for me, and saying, "Pardon me one
moment," he left the room. The whole thing was so
sudden that I thought I was still dreaming, and I
spelled the name "Cipriani" under a picture of the
Holy Family that hung over the mantelpiece, and
then stooped down and handled the vellum-bound
books, and read, "Suarez, Opera Omnia," before I
could assure myself that this was a new experience
in my life. Then the devil whispered, "This man
is taking too great a liberty with you. You ought
to resent it." And my good angel said, "No, no ;

2 C

he is kind and thoughtful; place yourself in his hands." And my poor, weak soul panted through the anguish of wounded pride, and calmed and softened into better dispositions alternately, until again the door opened, and a servant entered, bearing an enormous tray, and my priest, following after, cheerfully wheeled a chair round for me, and knocked every bit of ceremony aside, saying, "Now, old man, say grace, and tuck in!" I blessed myself shamefacedly, and swallowed with many a gulp, but with relish, for I had tasted nothing all day, the food that was set before me. He then poured out a glass of wine, bade me drink it at one draught, then poured out another, and put a stopper in the decanter.

"Now, old man," said he, "how do you feel?"

"I feel very well, thank you," I said, "but I am quite at a loss to account for your—your—" (the devil whispered "presumption," but that would have been too mean) "your hospitality."

"Now," said the priest, turning towards me, "just drop all that nonsense. You have suffered —I have suffered—we are brothers!"

He held out his hand across the table to me; and was it the food, or my new and strange emotions, or what?—I, the stoic, the philosopher, burst into an agony of tears. I sobbed and sobbed, as a child; I drew out a very soiled and tattered handkerchief, and for many minutes could not speak. The priest kept silence, looking steadily away from me until I grew calm. When I was quite collected, I said humbly—

"You must really forgive this display of feeling, sir—Father—but I am weak."

His manner changed into infinite gentleness and pity, as he said—

"Don't speak of it. I can understand it all. Now, when you are quite yourself again, tell me on what rock you have split, because I see you have been shipwrecked in some way ? "

I told him all—my pride, my knowledge, my suffering, my agony, my shame. It was no great revelation to him. He had met, alas ! some few like myself, who had drifted, drifted away from the haven of hope and mercy, and after the delirious dreams and vain pursuits of ever-vanishing, ever-alluring phantasms of the trackless deeps of the human mind, or the storm - centres of human passion, had come at last to seek and find shelter in the Church of their childhood. He told me of the many and varied forms in which unbelief enters the soul ; how the way is paved by sensuality ; how the mind is darkened by some stray article in a magazine picked up for a penny at a bookstall ; how sometimes a professor will let fall a hint as to his own incredulity, and how the pregnant seed will sink into, and bear its ghastly fruit in the souls of the unsuspecting young. And many more things he told me, which I cannot put in print. It was all about the sadness of the world, because it knows not God.

I rose to depart as the clock chimed nine. He put out his hand. All my old pride had vanished. I was a little child again.

"Father," I said, "might I ask your name ? "

"Certainly," he said. "I am best known as Father Benedict."

The name recalled in a flash old associations.

"Father," I said, "some years ago a poor little servant mentioned your name to me and begged of me to go to confession. I rejected grace then. I must not reject it now. Would you be good enough to come back to the church with me ? "

It was late when I found myself once more upon the quays, no longer gloomy and despairful, but lighted with some strange light that shone and filled me with hopeful and buoyant thoughts. I thought I saw some beauty everywhere—in the black clouds that rolled above, in the lurid lights of the bars, in the gas lamps, whose shadows twinkled in the river; and the tramcars' bells rang merrily out on the foggy vapour—joy-bells to me.

I hurried home to my poor attic; and there by my humble bed I poured forth my soul in thanksgiving to the Lord of Life, the Giver of good things, for His mercy vouchsafed to me.

# CHAPTER III

> " Let the fancy fly
> From belt to belt of crimson sea,
> On leagues of odour streaming far
> To where in yonder orient star
> A hundred spirits whisper : ' Peace.' "

THE first fruits of my conversion were peace—
deep, solemn, divine peace, that came down and
slept over every faculty of my soul; and with it a
cheerful, optimistic spirit, that took large, hopeful
views of the future, which lay like a dreamland
before me. All things were steeped in sunshine,
except the events of the past with all their trial
and sorrow which were wrapt, as Jean Paul finely
expresses it, in the " moonlight of memory." There,
in its shadows, were the two figures that had most
deeply impressed my life, Ursula and Charlie; and,
strange to say, my imagination always linked them
together, although they had never seen each other;
and I could not think of them as spirits, moving in
the blinding whiteness of heaven, but always in the
meeker light cast by the " moonlight of memory."
Another change became daily more observable to
myself. That bitter, harsh, censorious spirit that
made me rail at all things as unsound and untrue,
and forced itself into my conversation in the shape
of unworthy cynicism, now yielded to a gentler and
more humane feeling ; and I saw what a poor thing
it is to criticise and condemn, and how charity alone
adds to our spiritual stature. For now each day I

sat at the feet of Him from whom alone sweetness
and light are breathed on the world; and I drank
in His spirit and became very gentle and meek.
After some days, Father Benedict gently suggested
to me that I must make up my mind rapidly as to
my future; and it was he first broached an idea,
that I should never have dared to originate, namely,
that I should give the remainder of my life to God
in religion. At first, I demurred very strongly, from
a deep sense of unworthiness; then the idea became
an absorbing one, and I was thrilled through and
through by the fascination of the thought.

All this time, I kept up my acquaintance with the
Bellamys, visiting them generally in the evening.
The Deanes had not yet returned to town; and
all my student-friends were scattered during the
long vacation. One letter awaited me on my return
from Clare. It was from Helston, to the effect that
he had made up his mind not to return to Dublin to
complete his studies. He would go abroad for a
year, and then decide as to his future. He cordi-
ally thanked me for all my kindness, and hoped
that we should meet again.

I had some trouble, and not a little amusement,
in breaking my new resolution to my friends. With
the Bellamys it came easy enough, yet I was very shy
in announcing to these two dear friends that I was
about to break finally with the world. Helen, as
usual, took it gravely, which made me rush to the
conclusion that she disapproved the step.

"Not by any means," she said, "but I was thinking of a saying, 'Thy way is upon the sea, and Thy
pathway on the mighty waters, and Thy footsteps
are not known.' You see the finger of an overruling Providence leans so lightly on us, that we do
not perceive it. Still less do we understand that
its pressure is irresistible. You see all Charlie
Travers's prophecies are coming true. What a

wonderful being he was — so spiritualised, so exalted, the type of a Christian idealist."

"You have said a good deal in these words, Helen," I exclaimed gratefully; "yet not too much. His was a beautiful spirit. No wonder that women worshipped him, and men obeyed him."

"And you are going to take up his work?" she said, fixing her eyes on me.

"I do not know," I replied. "It was a large vocation, and it needs great virtue and talent."

"Only the virtue of loving men," she replied, "and only the talent of making them know it."

Alfred Bellamy merely held out his hand, and grasped mine warmly.

I broke the news to Herr Messing in our old favourite place—down on the rocks at Sandy Cove. It came about thus. I proposed that we should spend a Sunday together at our old trysting-place, and he should bring Alice and Fritz. Of course, he jumped at the idea. And one of these delicious afternoons in the end of August, when the sun is veiled in clouds, as if ashamed of his too great heat, and the softened light steeps all things in gray beauty, and memory, that is so shy of sunshine, comes up and throws back the doors of the past, and lets us see down along the shaded vista of the life we have lived; and here and there forms come out of the shadows, and beckon to us, and we grow very grave and solemn and tender—well, on one of those days our little group assembled at the old spot, and the afternoon sped by rapidly in the delicious pleasures afforded by nature in sky and sea, and friendship in its warmth and security, and intellectual intercourse, at least where Herr Messing and his poets took a part.

Of course, not one of my friends, except Helen Bellamy, understood the conflict of my mind during these past years—least of all Herr Messing. For there are thoughts and struggles that men do not paint on their shields. It was, therefore, a great surprise to my dear old friend when I explained my intention to him. He at once set it down to disgust with life and my want of success. He did not attempt to dissuade me, but he was not enthusiastic.

" You know you moost gif up eferything," he said despondently.

I replied that I was aware of that.

" You moost go and goom as you are told."

" Quite so," I replied.

" Id iz bat enough to be married "—he looked around, but Alice was at a safe distance.

" Herr Messing ! " I shouted, " you of all men to speak such blasphemy ! "

" I did not mean vhat you tink," he explained. " I only did mean that you give up your liberty. And dat is joost vhat you are going to do."

" I have thought it all over," I replied, " and I am not afraid."

" But," he continued, " you moost gif up all your books and reading."

" I know," I said ; " I'm pretty tired of books. There's a tremendous amount of trash written, and it is all a wailing and wringing of hands, and a voice of despair. Look at that sea. Every line ever written about it from Sophocles down is a threnody. ' And like the moan of lions hurt to death, came the sea's hollow noise along the night ' ; and the ' Blear-eyed filmy sea did boom with his old mysterious hungering sound ' ; and ' The wayward waters, with a weeping sound, were sobbing into rest ' ; and ' The scream of a maddened beach dragged down by the wave ' ; and what touches us all most deeply, ' The tender grace of a day that is dead shall never come back to me.' All despair and gloom, and lost hope, and the sad pleasure of tears."

He looked at me incredulously. What strange language was this ?

" To tell you the truth, Herr Messing, I'm sick of it all. It's all lies, lies, lies ! "

"But, mein Gott !" he exclaimed, all the old impetuosity rising up in his veins, " you don't mean to say that our poets are all liars ?  Dot Goethe is von liar ?"

" Goethe was a bad man," I said sententiously.

He looked round again and studied me.  I looked steadily out to sea, afraid lest I should laugh, and he never forgave that.

" Und Schillare, und Novalis, und Jean Paul ? All liars ?  Mein Gott ! "

" You'll come to see me sometimes, professor," I said.  " You know how delighted I shall be."

He smoked and smoked without a word.

" And you'll bring Alice and little Fritz ? " I said. Not a word.

" And we'll have long chats over old times, and perhaps a quiet walk now and then down here, that is, if I can get permission.  Of course, I can't smoke nor talk Richter, but we'll have lots of things to say to each other——"

The professor stood up and walked away.  I thought he would not take our parting so badly.  I let him go.  I knew his big, honest heart was too full for speech.

Agnes Deane, also, threw a cold douche on my new-born vocation.

The Deanes had returned on the 1st September, and I took the earliest opportunity of calling on them.  Hubert had not returned from his office ; and, of course, after the preliminary inquiries, Mrs. Deane opened up the subject nearest to her heart.

" When is it to be ? "

" When is *what* to be, Mrs. Deane ? "

" You know very well what I mean ! "

" Well, there can be no harm in being a little more explicit."

" Well, then, I mean the great event of your life."

I said promptly, "The 24th of September."

"Oh, that is quite near! How delightful it will be! And are all arrangements made?"

"I believe so," I replied; "at least, I am not aware that anything can prevent it."

Mrs. Deane settled down to a little reverie.

"I always knew it would come to this. Not, indeed, that it needed much foresight. A blind man could have seen it. But I thought a few times it was all over, and I used to say, 'What fools!' And Hubert would laugh at all my predictions, and say, 'How badly sold you'll be, Agnes, when it is all over!' Well, my sage is out at last. Won't he be surprised and glad? And so you tell me—the 24th of September. Now, where is it to be?"

"I believe at the C—— Chapel at Mayfield."

"That stuffy little place! Who in the world selected that? Not Helen, surely? But I remember; you were at school there. Well, now, I was thinking of Clarendon Street, or the Pro-Cathedral!"

"You had always such big ideas, Mrs. Deane. You could never come down to the level of ordinary people. But tell me, have you seen Mrs. Leviston lately? Is Sister Philippa still with her?"

Mrs. Deane didn't like such a rapid change of programme; but she answered—

"Gwennie is doing well. Looking beautiful in her widow's weeds. Sister Philippa and she make quite a little picture down at Bray. I assure you people like to look at them a second time. But I should not be surprised if there were a change soon."

"You don't mean Mrs. Leviston? That would be too sudden!"

"No; I mean Sister Philippa. I shouldn't be at all surprised if your controversial friend—what's that his name is?"

"Gallwey?" I suggested.

"Well, I shouldn't be surprised if something

turned up there. He is spending his holidays with some friends at Killiney, and he seems to like the quiet, mournful society of—Mrs. Leviston."

" I see. But that will be a long engagement."

" Why ? "

" Why ? Because they have nothing to marry upon. Why, Gallwey has hardly passed his first."

" And *you* are a millionaire ! Never mind. I suppose Helen will go abroad, though she's so quiet that a trip to Killarney would suit her. I wonder what shall I wear ? I think Hubert ought to give me a new dress for such an occasion. Don't you think so, Mr. Austin ? "

" I really—don't know, Mrs. Deane," I said, trying to look puzzled, for I was getting afraid of the little comedy. " I think—there's—some mistake—somewhere ! "

" Perhaps so," she answered coldly.

" I am afraid," I stammered, " we are speaking of two different things, and I have not been sufficiently clear. The event I spoke of as likely to come off on the 24th of September is my entrance into religion as a Carmelite brother——"

Mrs. Deane looked as if she would like to leave the room.

" And now," I said, " as perhaps this is the last time I shall have an opportunity of doing so, you will allow me to thank you and Mr. Deane with all my heart for your extraordinary kindness to me during all these years. I am afraid, that in this, as in other matters, I have left you under a wrong impression : but—but——"

Mrs. Deane, from whom I had been expecting an outburst of indignation, was crying softly. I felt that I deserved to be hanged.

" You have been very cruel," she said at last. " But I don't—I will not, believe it."

" I assure you it is quite true. My only regret

now is that I have kept it concealed so long from my best friends."

"It is too ridiculous," she said. "The idea of you—a monk."

"I am quite conscious of my utter unworthiness," I said, "and probably I should have never dreamed of such a thing myself; but I have passed through some bitter experiences, and perhaps this is my best preparation."

My humility disarmed Mrs. Deane; but her surprise continued.

"You said Carmelites?"

"Yes!"

"Are these the monks who wear broken shoes, and are always exhibiting——"

I saved her modesty.

"They wear sandals, I understand."

"And get up in the middle of the night to sing?"

"I understand so."

"And never eat meat during the winter?"

"I am not quite sure on that point."

"Look here, Mr. Austin, I'm not going to stand this. There must have been some quarrel between you and Helen. Otherwise, you'd never have thought of such a thing."

I was silent.

"Then you yourself assured me that it was all arranged between you and Helen, on the very evening of that odious trial."

"I am quite sure I could not have been guilty of such a mistake."

"Do you remember," she asked, with all the emphasis of an experienced cross-examiner, "do you remember when we left you alone on the pier, and waited for you at Westland Row, and I asked you a question, and you said it was all arranged?"

"And so it was," I replied.

"Well, then?"

" It was arranged that the little romance built up by the kind ingenuity of the best of friends did not exist at all, and that neither Miss Bellamy, nor I, ever dreamt of such a thing."

" But you told me it was all arranged when I asked you."

" If I remember rightly, you asked was it all right, and I said ' yes.' "

" You know well what I meant. Oh ! it is all horrible. The idea of leaving that beautiful girl behind you, and burying yourself for life in that place ! I do *not* believe it. I'll go and ask Helen."

" Don't, please, Mrs. Deane ; I assure you that Miss Bellamy understands all ; and, in fact, it is with her high sanction I am leaving the world."

" Oh dear ! oh dear ! was there ever such perversity ? Here are two people just fit for each other ; and they go and spoil everything deliberately. I never saw anything like it. Well, Hubert is all the richer by the price of a new dress. I think I'll go into mourning."

I rose to depart.

" You know," she said, " I must have it out with Helen. I do not approve of these friendships. What's that Hubert calls them ? "

" Platonic, I believe."

" Exactly. This thing should not have gone on, and then stop abruptly. And, oh dear ! think of the coming winter. It will be dreary. All our little evening parties cut up, and you—in your cold cell, shivering, and regretting all."

Mrs. Deane's ideas of monastic life were limited. But I left it so.

" I have a suspicion that I may thank one of your own household for all this."

" No ? Who could it be ? Hubert ? "

" Guess again."

" I am sure I know no one else."

" What do you think of Ursula ? "

I did not go to the Bellamys that evening. An unpleasant surprise awaited me at my own humble lodgings. Two men had called in my absence, and would call again. They did. They were lounging about until my return. They begged pardon, but was I not engaged as witness in a will case a few weeks ago ?

I said, " Yes ! "

" There was something said about foul play ? "

" I don't remember. If there were, you're pretty slow about moving."

" The law is slow, but sure," said one of the officers.

" The law was quick, and stupid," said I, " in one case I know."

" When was that ? " said he.

" When a trumped-up case was brought against a young gentleman in the city," said I, " and you let the chief perjurer escape, and it cost that young gentleman his life."

" That was the Gifford case," he said carelessly. " The witness left the country."

" Yes," I said, " under the eyes of the city detectives."

" Well," said he, nettled, " that's all past and gone. What we want now is this. You gave evidence that there was foul play in Mr. Leviston's case."

" Indeed ? "

" Yes, we have your evidence. It isn't much : but you can give more. Now, who gave that chloral to Leviston ? "

" My dear fellow," said I, " you are too clever for your profession. If there had been criminality in the case, you should have had the delinquent under lock and key long ago."

" That won't do, my fine fellow," he said angrily ;

" perhaps when you are on the table, you'll talk more glibly.   Good-night ! "

As they went away, I couldn't help paying off an old score.   I called them back.

" You're seeking for information ? "

" Yes, and no !   We have as much as we want to start with."

" Very good.   Now, do you know Mr. Warden ? "

" Yes."

" Well, he appeared to know everything in the case, and a good deal more.   I think if you consulted him now——"

The officers said something profane, and vanished.

Next morning I was in Bray.   I did not know Mrs. Leviston's address.   I went on the chance of meeting her.   As the day wore on, and I had not seen her, I called at a hotel, and got a visitor's list. There was the address: Seaview Terrace.   I went there and inquired for Mrs. Oliver.   Mrs. Oliver didn't reside there.   Mrs. Leviston did.

She came downstairs, looking well, remarkably well, in the plain black dress of mourning.   She was so pleased to see me.

" I had heard you were here from an old friend, Mrs. Deane, and as I found myself here, I thought I would call.   I hope you are quite well."

" Very well, indeed.   There has been great peace and comfort in my life, especially since I had the good fortune to take your advice about Sister Philippa."

" Oh ! is Sister Philippa here ? "

" Oh dear, yes ! she will be delighted to see you. Will you make any stay in Bray ? "

" Not this time.   I am rather hurried.   I hope your mother is well."

" Very well, thank you."   After an embarrassing pause.   " She is not with me now."

" Indeed ? "

"No. My brother, it would appear, got some appointment at the Cape; and mother decided to go with him. She was much attached to him, you may remember."

This was the only time poor Gwennie was quite insincere and conventional. I was so glad that Mrs. Oliver was out of the country, that I easily pardoned her.

Sister Philippa came down, looking fresh and candid and beautiful as ever. I thought Gallwey's taste excellent.

She was very enthusiastic about Helen Bellamy, thought she was very beautiful and accomplished. They really were very grateful to the unknown friend who had introduced two such charming friends as Agnes Deane and Miss Bellamy.

I murmured something about my own experiences of those good ladies, and then turned the subject.

"I heard that some of my students were killing time here."

"We have met but one, Philippa, I think?"

Sister Philippa blushed furiously.

"Now," I said, "it can't be Helston. He is gone away. Nor Cal, that's Sutton. He is down South. Nor Synan, nor Forrester. It must be Gallwey."

"I think that is the name, Philippa?" said Mrs. Leviston innocently.

"It is Mr. Gallwey," said Sister Philippa, biting her lip.

"I hope he is not treating you to controversy," I said, "he is a dreadful antagonist. But he'll come around. We like those desperately earnest fellows. It is only the stupid or indifferent we despair of."

"If you mean that Mr. Gallwey will ever become a Catholic, I fear you are mistaken," said Sister Philippa, with a little pique. It made me despair of her.

"I don't know," I replied, "all depends on

sincerity. But I must go. I am starting on a long journey, and I must bid you farewell!"

The ladies looked anxious.

"I hope you are not going so far," said Mrs. Leviston, "that we may not sometimes see you."

"Well, it is hard as yet to say. But it is a strange country: and I don't think I shall return."

The ladies looked concerned, and said "Adieu!" with unfeigned regret, which was pleasant, too, even to an incipient cenobite.

# CHAPTER IV

### A WEARY QUEST

"The heart is a palimpsest, on which the older letters, however pale and effaced, will come to light again, when it has been properly handled."—Van Oosterzee.

IN an equinoctial gale of howling wind and driving rain, I made my way to the Bellamys the night before I was to bid farewell to the world. The moon was full; but it appeared to be racing like some whipped creature against the angry tumult of gray clouds that came up, numberless and resistless, from the dark caverns of the West. The rain came down, not softly and pitifully and ceaselessly; but now and again a shower of bullets burst from some dark cloud, and lashed the earth and everything upon it, rattled against windows, tried to break through the faint resistance of gas-lamps, tossed trees and shrubs about and drenched them pitilessly, and then stopped to gauge the havoc it had done, and to summon its energies for a fiercer onslaught. Very few ventured out that night. Here and there a policeman, with drenched glazed cape, stood statue-like in some recess; a few carriages rolled by; the empty tramcars jingled up and passed away into silence, and the clouds went scudding, scudding before the angry wind, and one's thoughts went out to sea, and the helpless strugglers in fishing-boats, or the steady determination of steamboats that plunged and rocked, but ever went forward in defiance of Nature and its elements and their futile rage. I thought of the quartermaster beneath the bridge, with his eye on the compass, the lookout far away in the blackness of the steamer's prow, the four silent men at the wheel, watchful, obedient, alert—it was war between Nature and science, and science was conquering. Here, on shore, Nature had the best of it; for all creatures cowered under its fury, and hid themselves from its anger.

With topcoat glazed and soaked right through, and face and hair wet and glistening, I found the cheerful drawing-room fire very pleasant; and, in the society of my dearest friends, the evening passed pleasantly by, though now and again we had to pause in our conversation, as a wilder gust, gathering all its forces far away in the sky, swept down howling and screaming, and broke itself against chimneys that moaned and rocked, and against window-panes that rattled.

It must have been about nine o'clock, when a faint, timid knock was heard at the hall-door. We were not quite sure of it, and there was a long pause until it was repeated, this time more boldly, but still timid and uncertain. It was so faint, the housemaid did not hear it. And Helen touched the bell.

"There's some one at the door, Mary; be careful that the wind doesn't force it against you."

In a few seconds the housemaid came in and whispered to Helen—

"There's an old gentleman in the hall, Miss, I think he must be a priest, and he wants to see you."

Alfred promptly rose, with some little surprise and curiosity, for priests did not visit very frequently at the house, and went out. We knew he was reproaching the visitor for venturing out on such a night, and divesting him of his hat and coat. He then ushered into the drawing-room my old guardian, Father Costelloe, whom I had not seen for six years!

"Father Costelloe wishes to see you, Helen, and perhaps——"

"Oh! it is not a matter of very urgent importance, nor so secret that you should disturb yourselves," said the old priest. "If you permit me to rest for a moment: I am really quite out of breath."

I do not know exactly what good angel put his hand over the lips of my friend, so that there was no introduction. If there had been, I don't know exactly what might have happened, for every kind of emotion was chasing, like the drifting clouds outside, through my mind. And above all, was a feeling of infinite compunction and self-anger, and sorrow and yearning towards the good old man, for I knew he was seeking me. I managed to get into the shade, whence I could see his features. He had become quite aged. There were great lines in his face, which was shrunk and pallid; and his white, wet hair streamed down and dripped on his coat. And my conscience said, "Behold your work, and all that your malevolence has wrought!" I managed to grasp Alf's arm, and squeeze it fiercely. He understood. I trusted to Helen's calmness and self-possession not to betray me.

"Before you say a single word, Father," she said, "you'll have some tea?"

"Thank you, dear," he said simply. All the old *verve* and vigour were gone. He looked absent-minded; and his gaze wandered around the room, and rested on me.

"A friend?" he said.

"Yes, a friend and visitor, Father," interposed Alfred.

Helen poured out the tea, and placed some toast and crackers on his plate. The old priest moved to the table and sat down. He took out a red hand-kerchief and rubbed his forehead and his eyes with a weary gesture. I do not know exactly what was

in the movement, but it was so humble and resigned
that it quite upset me. I put my hand to my forehead, and shaded my face from the light.

After some time, Helen said, " It was rash of you,
Father dear, to venture out on such an evening. I
fear very much you will take cold."

" I have been out on far worse nights than this,
my child," he said ; "it has been a weary, weary
quest."

Helen drew an easy chair to the fire, after he had
taken some tea, and made him sit there. Alfred and
I were in the background. I thought several times of
escaping, but it would have been cowardly ; and,
possibly, in saying "good-night," my name might
be mentioned. I determined to remain, though I
was in agony.

"After five years of fruitless labours," the old
priest said, looking meditatively at the fire, " I have
been recommended to seek you, my dear young
lady, as one who can give me some information
about a friend—a child—that I have lost."

He paused to take breath, and my heart and the
clock on the mantelpiece went running a race.

" It is a long story," he continued, "and old age is
a tedious story-teller ; but I shall try to make it brief.
Some years ago, a parishioner of mine lay on her
death-bed. She had an only son, a promising lad,
and her heart was in him. She confided him to my
care ; and I well remember the wistful look that
came into her wide eyes when she asked me to
undertake the charge, and I seemed to hesitate.
Well, she died happily, and I took the boy home,
and nursed as carefully as possible the little means
his mother left. He was a lovable lad, rather
high-spirited. I often wished that he were a little
more humble ; but then I should have been dissatisfied too. But he was for ever questioning
and inquiring, asking things that no man has ever

answered, least of all, I. It was interesting, but it made me afraid. Often on the winter nights, before he went to college, as we sat by the fireside together, he would fold his hands across his knees, and seem to find infinite sources of questioning in the bright coals or flames. He was a delightful companion to a solitary man, but it made me afraid. Well, to be brief, he went to college. I had excellent reports from his masters about him. But he came home dissatisfied, and uncertain. There was some hunger in his heart that could not be quenched. He was for ever questioning, questioning, inquiring into things which the poor short line of human reason will never fathom. At last, we made up our minds that he would try the Civil Service ; and just at that time, a circular came from a dear old college friend of mine, Father Bellamy—by the way, is not your own name Bellamy ?" he interrupted, consulting an envelope on which was written an address.

"Yes, Father," Helen replied, "that was my uncle."

"Ah, indeed," the old man continued, "that brings me nearer home. Well," he continued after a pause, "I regarded this circular as a providential message, for I am a great believer, my dear, in a Providence that, unseen itself, is for ever watching us ; and I decided to entrust my poor child to Father Bellamy's care. I took him to his mother's grave the evening before his departure for Dublin ; and he made me some little promises that I trusted to for his safety. Alas ! I, a poor country priest, what did I know of the temptations of great cities — temptations, which I have seen since ? "

He paused, as if summoning up some memories of what he had seen and heard, and wiped his forehead with the old red handkerchief.

"Well, for a time, all went right. Then, one day came a letter, without signature, which was a grave shock to me. It detailed a rather ugly practical joke, supposed to have been perpetrated by my poor boy, and the victim was the principal of the college, a nephew of my dear old friend. The consequences were sad—a hemorrhage from the lungs of this young man, who, it appears, had inherited consumption. Probably he was your first cousin, and——"

"He was my brother," said Helen simply. "He is dead."

"Perhaps, my child," said the old man, "I am speaking on a painful subject. If so——"

"No, no, Father," she said hastily, "go on."

"Well, I was awfully shocked, especially as the letter mentioned that my poor child had got in amongst a bad set in the college. I prayed for light, and, after much deliberation and a great deal of prayers, I wrote a letter as gentle and yet as admonitory, as I could compose. I suppose I let fall some hard expressions, for he never replied. Some months afterwards, the whole thing came to light. He was the victim of an ugly slander. I have never felt such remorse for my many sins as I felt for that ill-advised letter I wrote. God help us! how short-sighted we are. I wrote again, humbly and apologetically. He never replied. I sent him some money for his expenses to London, where he failed at an examination. I heard from him once more when he returned to Dublin. He wrote a short note for the remainder of the money that was due to him, and that I held. I have never seen or heard from him since."

The old man paused, as if trying to soften the pain of memory. He then went on—

"I do not know, my dear young lady, whether I was strictly bound to do any more; but that consideration never crossed my mind. His mother's eyes haunted me, and night and day I had no rest. If I spoke of repentance, of the prodigal son, of the widow's child—anything—my conscience would at once interpose, 'Yes, but where is the child that was entrusted to thee?' Then my imagination began to conjure up all kinds of dreadful things concerning him, until at last I could bear the agony no longer, and I determined to set out and seek him. It was in September of that year I first came to Dublin. I tried to put together a few pounds, and there was an annual holiday of a month allowed us, which I never before dreamed of taking, but now I had an object. And so I came to this great city. It was like searching for some lost sheep on a trackless desert. I knew no hotel. But passing along a quiet by-street I saw an Italian name over a quiet-looking place, and I took up my abode there. Only my abode. I spent my days and a good part of the night on the streets. What I saw, my dear young lady, during these dismal days and nights, it is not for me to describe to you."

What unconscious irony my poor old guardian was using! But Helen spoke not a word, but kept looking steadily at the fire.

"Alas!" continued the old man, "I never knew the wickedness of the world until then. During the day I strolled about the streets, looking in every direction for him whom I sought. Sometimes I thought he passed me by; and I would stand and stare, whilst the people wondered. Sometimes I paused before tobacconists' shops, thinking, 'now he may come here for cigarettes, and I shall surely meet him.' I used to stare at photographs in the windows, wondering if he were there, and thinking how proud I should be if I saw his photograph as of one who had succeeded in life. I spent hours in new and old bookshops, knowing how much he

loved books, and hoping he would come across me
there. And, at night, I paced the streets staring at
every young man I met, and thinking, 'now, even if
he recognises me, he, so well dressed and grand, will
not condescend to see me.' But it was all in vain.
I had to return to my little home as I left it; and it
was a very cheerless and forlorn winter for me."

He paused again, looking at the fire, and picturing
there, I suppose, the sad memories he was conjuring.

"Next year, at the same time, I was walking the
streets of Dublin again. I had not been there many
days when I got a slight clue. I entered a second-
hand bookshop one day, and turning over some
classic authors, I said, involuntarily: 'Ah, this
would be in Geoffrey's style.' The bookseller, an
old man, turned at once and said: 'Who might
Geoffrey be, sir?' I told him, and then it appeared
that Geoffrey had been employed here nearly twelve
months before, and had left, owing to some difference between himself and his employer. The
latter had lost sight of him since. I then went to
Mayfield, the college where he had been studying.
It was closed. I inquired for the rector. I heard
he was dead. For the principal, Mr. Bellamy.
Dead. I then did a poor humble thing. I employed
the little street lads to watch for me; and the very
applewomen to be on the look out for me. It was
all in vain. He was swallowed up in the mighty
city. I went home, sick at heart, and probably
should have given up the quest, but his mother's
eyes were haunting me."

He drew a great sigh, and continued—

"The following September I was in Dublin again.
I had some secret inspiration that he was in Dublin;
and that in Dublin I should find him. This time, I
advertised in the public press, and put even the
detectives on the watch. It was all in vain. And

then hope left me. Many a weary night in that raw, wet September month, did I walk the streets of the city, jostled against by, well—I shall not say. I used to peer into the public-houses, and once or twice I ventured into a billiard-room. The young men shouted at me, asked me to take a cue, what drink I should have? &c.; and then I thought better that Goff should be lost to me for ever, than that I should find him thus. But his soul! his soul! Ay, my dear child, you, in your childlike innocence, do not know, the world does not know, what we, priests, sometimes suffer. We cannot show it. But oftentimes—indeed, I might say at all times—our minds are on the rack for souls that are perishing. I suppose sin lies lightly upon the world. The sight of the world's sin, steaming up, an impure holocaust before God, lies weightily upon us. And oh! the sin of great cities, so coolly blasphemous and idolatrous, fills me with unspeakable horror. I used to yearn for home. I dared not return until my time had expired, and duty called me, for those eyes of the dying mother were for ever haunting me. Well, a fourth year, and a fifth year I returned, always without success. But, at last, God has guided me aright. In a police office yesterday, again I inquired. And a detective, taking out a file of papers, ran his eyes rapidly over them, singled out one and handed it to me. It was an account of some trial, some will case that took place some weeks ago, and in which Geoffrey Austin figured as an important witness. I took it home to my hotel, locked my door, and sat down to read it. My head swam. It transpired there that my boy, my poor child, had been a tramp, a night walker, a holder of horses for a penny; and all this I should not mind, but God help me !——"

Here he broke down utterly. Helen said firmly—

"Go on, Father, go on to the end!"

"I was about to say, my dear young lady—that he had become a profligate and an infidel; but I do not believe it. I cannot."

"Go on, Father, you did not tell us what led you here!" said Helen.

"That was simple," the old man replied. "I discovered by that paper, or rather it was pointed out to me, that the solicitor who engaged Geoffrey was a Mr. Deane. I drove to his house this afternoon, and saw his wife. I asked her did she know Geoffrey Austin? 'A little,' she said, 'but if I wanted to see one who knew a great deal, I should go to Miss Bellamy.' She kindly gave me your address. And my time is so limited, I took the extreme liberty of calling on you so late."

There was silence in the room: and I was wondering what Helen would do. She remained silent for a long time, the eyes of the old priest wistfully fixed on her. Then, as a bright idea suddenly dawned upon him, he said—

"Perhaps, Miss Bellamy, you have seen him in prison or in hospital?"

"Oh dear no, Father," she replied. "He is not a subject either for one or the other."

"Thank God!" he murmured. Then a brighter idea struck him.

"Perhaps, my dear child," he said hesitatingly, "if I am not taking too great a liberty, but could it be—I think Mrs. Deane hinted it, there may be some more—intimate——"

"Oh no, Father," said Helen, blushing.

"Things might have been worse then," said the old priest, meaning a compliment.

"Things are a great deal better with your ward, Father," she said simply.

"Thank God!" he said feebly, "but I cannot conceive it."

"You are not leaving town to-morrow, Father?"
she said.

"Not necessarily," he replied.

"Then, could you call here, say at three o'clock?"

"Certainly," he replied.

"Then you shall see Geoffrey Austin and judge
for yourself."

"God bless you," he said fervently.

Then I dreaded the parting "good night!" But
with infinite tact, Helen, by her insistence that a
car should be sent for, whilst the old priest protested, managed to get him into the hall, and I was
spared again.

When Alf and Helen returned, I had only speech
enough left to say "Good night, God bless you
both!" and I went home happy in the darkness.
The storm was still raging, but I did not heed it.

Next day, at ten o'clock, I entered on my novitiate at Mayfield. The first question the Master of
Novices put to me, after preliminaries, was this—

"I presume you have acquired a thorough
acquaintance with the Greek and Latin classics?"
the second was: "And I suppose you understand,
fairly well, the elements of mathematics and the
higher sciences?" That afternoon, I washed the
dishes after dinner, and helped to weed the garden
walks. I had come down from Olympus. At three
o'clock Alfred and Father Costelloe called.

# CHAPTER V

## FROM MY CELL

" 'Tis wicked judgment ! for the soul can grow,
 As embryos, that live and move, but blindly,
 Burst from the dark, emerge regenerate,
 And lead a life of vision, and of choice."

MANY years have rolled by since these events,
ordinary in themselves, yet of such supreme importance to many souls, took place. And I have
had no little trouble in summoning them out of the
mists of memory, and commanding them to stand
forth from the past, and be seen of all men. And I
confess, too, to a certain reluctance I had in laying
bare to the world the secret things of a troubled
soul, and the strugglings of a human conscience.
Most of the chief actors in the little drama have
passed out of life, or, at least, beyond my ken. My
dear old guardian, his last years blessed by my
happiness, has gone to his reward. To this day
his people pray and make " rounds " at his grave
in his own well-kept cemetery. His memory is a
benediction in the land. He was present at my
ordination many years ago ; for, after much striving
to escape on my part, my superiors decided that
I should be ordained priest. That was a memorable occasion. Nearly all the *dramatis personæ* of
this little history were grouped there. Alfred and
Helen, of course ; and, of course, Herr Messing and
Alice and Fritz. Agnes Deane was there also, and
Hubert, and with them Mrs. Leviston, Gallwey, and

his wife (Sister Philippa).  Gallwey looked defiant
and critical, Philippa happy, which makes me despair
of her, for it is only sorrow brings to the light,
which is God.  And there too were Forrester, and
Synan, and Cal.  How the latter turned me round
about, and criticised my white cloak and habit, and
punned on my name, and made jokes and laughter
for all, I need not now tell.  And there was my
new sponsor and father in one, dear Father Benedict, looking like one who had faced a perilous work
and had been successful.  And lastly, under the
protecting shadow of Mrs. Deane, who, true to her
word, had searched the city with lamps till she
found her, was Katrine, the happiest of the lot.
I am sure she felt that she was no small co-operator
in bringing about the events of that memorable day.
Well! nearly all have passed out of my little sphere
of existence.  Of course Alfred and Helen remain,
and often come to see me, and talk of old times.
And Fritz, now a splendid young fellow, too Irish for
his father's tastes, and too German for his mother's,
is a pupil of mine, just about to pass away from my
tutelage and face the great world.

All the others resolve themselves into shadows,
whose faces get more and more indistinct as they con-
tract and fade in the perspective of memory.  But
more real to me than when clothed in flesh and blood
are the two beings who exercised the strongest influence over my life's thoughts, and who, from the still-
ness of eternity, continue to watch over me and guide
my steps towards the home to which for ever they
are beckoning.  I am writing these memories of a
tempted soul in a little cell, facing the West.  It
is a bare cell.  It has but one ornament—the Christ
of my dream—a huge black crucifix, and the white,
stained figure of my Master.  My long white habit
sweeps the floor, and I have to gather up the voluminous white sleeves when I reach for a book or

dip my pen in ink. It is evening, such an evening
as we always loved. My window is open, and the
old familiar smell of the lindens, and the perfumed
breath of the early summer, steal in and fill the
room. The trees are nodding to each other and
whispering outside, and the setting sun catches a
few broad leaves, and slides between them to paint
circles of light on the whitewashed wall. I can
trace the long, luminous path of light back to its
source, the gateways of the West, which are now
lifted up by unseen hands to let the king of day
pass to his chamber of rest. And along that luminous path, hand in hand, I see two figures approach,
a youth and a little child. Garments whiter than
driven snow, faces brighter than the sinking glory,
feet that tread on light and make no impression,
grace as of angels, and glory as of the elect, do
not conceal their identity from me. For if my eyes
deceived me, my heart would protest and say, It is
they, they who have guided and inspired thee, the
heaven-sent, the elect of God and His apostles of
mercy—Ursula and Charlie. And as the evening
light fades away, and the sun, shorn of his dazzling
beams, goes down to his couch in the sea, I know
there are two forms whose lips are shut, because,
after the hosannas of heaven, they must not be
unhallowed; but I feel the arm of my dear friend
resting with the old familiar gesture on my shoulder,
and I feel the child-form nestling in its own old
place, and the breath of the child-saint is on my
cheek, and I lift my arm to enclose her, but something says, Not yet! not yet! And what wonderful
things have they shown me! and what new worlds
have they opened up before my eyes! Ay! so it
has been. I was dabbling in mudpools and thought
I saw the stars of heaven. I did not know of that
ocean of all knowledge and science that stretches its
illimitable vastness, and surges around the throne

of God.    Let me think, and Ursula and Charlie whisper to me when my thoughts fail.

In books of travel we are told that a wanderer in the trackless snows of the Alps, hemmed in on all sides by fearful dangers, avalanches thundering over his head, precipices yawning beneath his feet, ice-floors slippery as glass, and rocky projections that cut and maim the already bleeding hands, sees no hope but in a few scraggy palms that wave far away above his head on the dim horizon; and between him and them yawns a desert of danger, and yet a fearful fascination holds him spellbound, and he revels in the thought of his desolation, and hugs the pride of his despair.    Such was I in the days of my wantonness, and I said, This is all the world worth having, for is there not here sublimity and desolation, perils at every footstep, and certain death lurking amidst sublime crevasses, and the yawning of chasms, and over all the Spirit of the Storm, who blinds you with sifted snow, and whirls you to destruction; and with him the seven spirits who have haunted these solitudes, and painted their sublimity until half the world came at their beck, and lost themselves in the night of desolation, or hurled themselves into unknown pitfalls in all the blackness of their despair?    Sometimes a lucky traveller has stepped over slippery icefields and skirted the yawning precipice, and stepped aside from the thundering avalanche, and pushed his way, guided by friendly hands to the summit, and stood there, dazed and blinded, like the soldiers of Cortez on the peaks of Darien.    Such was I, when I emerged from my dreams of neo-paganism and stood in the vestibule of the Church.    But our traveller does not rest even on the gilded summits.    Beneath his feet, and stretching to a far horizon, bounded by a blue, limitless sea, is an empire, colossal in its vastness and power, sprinkled here and there with white cities,

whose noble buildings stand out and pierce the blue
sky ; and cornfields and vineyards, rich in the har-
vests of their abundance, make varied the stately
landscape, and broad rivers hastening to the sea
bear rich argosies on their bosoms ; and the whole
scene, from Alps to isles of Eden, is one hallowed
by sacred memories, rich in storied wealth—a land
of promise, with a glorious past.    Such appeared to
me the Church of God, at the moment that, emerg-
ing from the valleys of desolation, I stood on the
summits of faith.   The whole magnificent panorama
opened up before my wondering eyes—the past,
with its wondrous records of men and deeds ; the
present, with its triumphs and successes ; the future,
with possibilities that no man may measure or cir-
cumscribe.   But the surprise of the first moment
gave way to admiration and pride when I stepped
down from the lofty summit, and examined in detail
the wondrous attributes and endowments, the successes in every department of human knowledge,
the adaptability to every phase of human thought,
the intrinsic power of meeting each human want that
every day were unfolded to my eyes, as I stepped
from study to study, tireless because everything was
so novel, and I so interested.   I think my first great
surprise—indeed, it was almost a shock—was to
find that there was such a thing as Catholic philosophy.   Greek philosophy I had known, and the
remnants of it that survived through the Middle
Ages under the name of Neo-Platonism ; French
philosophy I had known, under the name of absolute negation ; German philosophy I had known
nebulous and transcendental ; and the schools of
Scotch and English philosophy, supposed to be
characterised by common-sense and hard-headed-
ness, but always drifting towards a common idealism ; but Catholic philosophy ?   Catholic dogma, if
you like, clear-cut, well-defined, unmistakable in its

terms, independent of argument, but a Catholic philosophy, with all the equipments of definition and axiom, and all the dread array of proposition and objection, why, this was a revelation. But still greater when I found what a firm, uniform, consistent, and spiritual system was embraced between the mysticism of the Fathers, the fiery logic of the apologists, the decrees of councils, the testimony of martyrs, until, in the writings of St. Thomas, all became crystallised in the most compact and irrefragable theses that have ever exercised the ingenuity of the human mind.   Yet, even there, it does not terminate its marvels.   For, opening out again in dissertations on the loftiest truths, and speculations on highest mysteries, as in the pages of Suarez and Petavius, it gives the human mind new empires of thought to conquer, new realms of ideas wherein to disport itself, yet all is certain and tangible and sure ; and if you are blocked by the high walls of mysteries that are impenetrable, you are taught to know, not, in the jargon of philosophers, that behind is the Unknowable and Uncognisable, but that within are the gardens of God.   It was magnificent.   Compared with this solid phalanx of mighty thinkers, marshalled and disciplined, marching under the same standard, with the same eternal watchword on their lips, and with the unbroken assurance that theirs was the cause of truth and righteousness, and therefore of ultimate victory, the scattered bands of philosophers, mutually distinguished and uniformly despairful, appeared like a ragged battalion of filibusterers, fighting for ideas that were blasphemous, and a principle of liberty, that was libertinism in thought and anarchy in action.

Their watchwords differ.   Christian thinkers cry, " Jesus Christ, yesterday, to-day, and for ever."   The philosophers write one word on their standards, " Humanity."   The former echo, " Humanity," but they mean the humanity of Christ, all-powerful to save humanity. The latter interpret the word, "Ye shall be as gods," even by your own efforts. The former declare that we are fallen, and can only rise by union with Christ. The latter admit the imperfections of the race without attempting to explain the cause, and bid us look along the interminable vistas of human evolution until we see the perfect man somewhere in the far and undetermined future.

So, too, with their professions. Ask the leading thinkers of the Church, "What are you?" and the answer of the innumerable host from the first to the nineteenth century is, "A Christian!" Ask the hybrid masses of philosophers, "What are you?" and you are confronted with Babel. Spinozists and Cartesians, Kantians and Fichteans, Hegelians of the right, Hegelians of the left, Baconians and Voltaireans, Pantheists, of the shape of Emerson, higher Pantheists, Spencerians, swearers by Schopenhauer, Idealists, Materialists, Sceptics, all mutually repellent, yet all identified by one common idea—the dethronement of God, and linked by one common ambition, the eversion of preceding theories and the erection of their own. It may be objected, "Such is the nature of philosophy, particularly of that branch of philosophy, called metaphysics. Even amongst your scholastics are found Nominalists and Realists, Thomists and Scotists. You are no better than we." True, as far as variety of modes of teaching is concerned. But these mediæval scholars exercised all the ingenuity of their keen intellects in unravelling mysteries that were accepted facts of faith. You are ingenious in devising subtleties that may take the place of faith. With them all the great truths were taken for granted before they discussed their constituent principles or ideas. You subvert all truth and try to build your own castles upon nothing. And all this would be tolerable, if you had

only speculative truths to deal with ; or if, as one of
your philosophers said when " waking from his dog-
matic slumber," life was but a bundle of sensations.
But you touch on the one hand God with the rod of
rebellion, and, on the other, man's soul, his life, his
hopes, his destinies, with a wand of despair.    In
truth, the great error of all philosophic thought
that is not guided by the Church is embraced
between the blasphemy of handling the Creator,
His existence, His attributes, as a subject for
metaphysical dissection, and the sacrilege of treating God's most perfect and delicate handiwork, the
human soul, as a piece of mechanism whose intri-
cacies are to be unravelled, and the secrets of its
organisms laid bare.    If all this concerned only the
students of the closets or the recluses of laboratories,
whose minds may have been constructed of tougher
material than ordinary, and whose experiments
might not disturb their beliefs, it would be not quite
unendurable, although even here the warning would
hold good—"*Quoiqu' elle soit très solidement montée, il
faut ne pas brutaliser la machine.*" But unfortunately
the vast majority of philosophers have aimed at being
not merely students of the unknown, but framers
and builders of systems, and have passed from
thence to the ambition of founding religions, and
establishing new codes of ethics amongst men. What
the result has been the world knows.    They have
committed the awful crime against humanity of
destroying its beliefs, and substituting wild theories
that end in despair.

But enough of this.    I have done with these
things for ever.    I stand in the light of Revelation
that shines from that breastplate of the Trinity—
the Humanity of Christ.    I see by that light a revelation of mysteries, worthy of God, honourable and
hopeful to humanity.    I see a system of philosophy
worthy of the exalted powers of the human mind ;

speculations that do not infringe on the majesty of God, or lower the dignity, or weaken the hopes of men. Curbed in its desires, but circumscribed only by the infinite, the mind of man may wander at will along the endless series of questionings that arise, one after another, and present ever new forms, each more attractive than the other. Yet all the time it does not lose itself; it is in the house of its Father, whose eye for ever rests on its wanderings, and whose hand ever guides its steps. The proud mind of the world's philosophers would shrink from that watchfulness and resent this intrusion of Providence ; but why, in the universe that is bounded everywhere by law, should the human mind alone be lawless ? Either we are gods, as the Pantheists say, or men. If the latter, why claim exemption from universal law ? Why should we be libertines in a world to which even the twilight revelations of the ancients gave the name of *Kosmos ?*

I confess that it has been a subject of ever-recurring pleasure to me to find that I might continue in the Church those metaphysical studies I had been pursuing, with such awful detriment to my soul, in the world. There is unquestionably in such high and sacred subjects a fascination that it is difficult to resist. After all, we have that within us that flies after the Infinite ; and man is never so happy as when he feels himself in the pure bright air of unrestricted Thought, and feels that he is groping after God. There is every testimony to prove that metaphysical studies have always exercised the most salutary influence on the minds and morals of men ; or, as a Protestant historian puts it: " Philosophical and metaphysical speculations had, in the absence of the more active pursuits of political life, been the chief occupation of the higher orders ; and the tone of society was characterised by a purity of manners, and a degree of charitable feeling, which probably

never have been surpassed." And it is very ques-
tionable whether all the material advantages that
have arisen from the inductive system, which
destroys itself in giving birth to modern materialism,
have not been counterbalanced by the grossness of
ideas, and the corresponding influences on the arts
and sciences which have found their lowest level in
that which we call realism.

And yet I have slowly understood that the dignity
of the Church is derived, not so much from the erudition of her sons, or the wonder-working labours
of her apostles in the domains of science and art and
literature, as from the manner in which she has
stooped down and addressed herself to meeting the
more vulgar wants of humanity. Yes, there is a
Christian realism as well as a Christian idealism; a
realism that comes down from the loftiest realms of
speculative thought to the deepest abysses of human
infirmity; a realism, that searches with no profane
curiosity into hidden places, but only seeks them to
enlighten them; a realism, that lays bare the wounds
of humanity to heal them, the sins of humanity to forgive them, the wants of humanity to relieve them.
Guided everywhere by the Divine spirit of charity, it
consults for the sinful and leprous. In its cabinets,
its thinkers frame subtle laws for its guidance, and
stoop from the highest altitudes of thought to consider and define the relations of a hind to his master,
and what little wrong to the helpless may debar from
the kingdom of heaven. Nothing escapes its vigil-
ance. However hidden under dreary platitudes, it
detects error and condemns it; and it surrounds
with inexorable and iron legislation its sacred things
and its most sacred interests—the safety of souls.
Oh! those silent confessionals from which not a
whisper breaks forth, what marvels of Christian
realism are wrought there—what wounds exposed,
what difficulties explained, what sins wiped out,

what joy imparted! Oh! these silent wards,
through which the *cornette* flashes like the nimbus
of an angel, what consolation is breathed to the
hopeless, what balm is poured on the gaping
wounds of despair! Oh! the gentle hands, the
sweet voices, the tender solicitudes, the arms of the
dying flung around the neck of the priest, the last
sigh breathed on wings of hope and peace! Oh!
the strong gospel-message, bracing the weak and
brightening the despondent! Who is this stretching his neck to the fatal blow? and this, gasping
out his last breath on Indian sands? And this,
chafing the mutilated fingers of the leper, and kiss-
ing the stricken cheeks and smoothing down the
angry spots on this awful outcast? Everywhere,
everywhere, Christ repeated—Christ, with the
strength of God, and the heart of a mother, repeated in His saints!

Ay! but one whispers, abate your enthusiasm for
a moment, and confess that, after all, your Church is
a failure. It does not meet the intellectual necessities of the age, for it will not yield one inch of its
pretensions to the demands of modern science. It
does not meet the social wants of the age, which
demand larger breadth of interpretation, and more
liberal allowances to the ever-varying exigencies of
more complex social environments. It does not
meet the moral wants of the age, for the world
needs a new morality, and your Church is not only
obsolete, but stubborn in its antiquated and futile
adhesion to law and tradition. Yes, and let the
word be spoken unhesitatingly. In the face of all
modern pretensions, as insolent as they are unfounded, the *fiat* of the Church goes forth, that it
is only in her doctrines there is truth; and only in
her charity, her poverty, her self-denial, her contempt for riches and fame, her consecration to God,
—it is only through her agency, blessed by those

sacred virtues, that any hope remains for humanity. And the world knows it. Weary souls, sick of the barrenness and gloom of heresy, seek the historic Christ of their youth in the ever-living Christ of the Church. Proud souls, exulting in all the licence of unbridled freedom, seek wisdom in the writings of the Church's doctors and teachers. Timid souls fly for security to the Ark of the living God. Pure souls, spouses of the Spirit, flutter to the foot of our altars—there to be espoused to the Lamb. Who would dare compare Spencer with Suarez? Who would prefer Ricardo and Mill to St. Francis? Who would venture to place an Act of Parliament in competition with the charity of a Vincent de Paul? And by what subtlety of reasoning can we ever determine the dismal results of the world's success in education, in legislation, in its political economy, in its hard, dry columns of statistics, in its attempts to reduce men to units, to be calculated, weighed, measured? And on the other hand, how shall we ever measure the results of that brilliant failure on Calvary, continued in the ever-varying fortunes of the Church, whose wonderful existence in face of all human opposition has extorted the unwilling tribute of the unbeliever? But she needs no such tribute. Let the leper, the lunatic, the maniac, the paralysed, the deaf, the dumb, the dying, and even the dead, speak. Was Calvary a failure? And let the world that has tasted the sweets of the Church's civilisation, and known the beneficence of its rule, and shared the exaltation of its hope, and realised the magnificence of its faith, confess that, if it may account for the limits and slowness of its success, owing to the hindrances and obstruction of human error and human obstinacy, there can be no explanation for its achievements except that behind its operations Omnipotence is veiled.

And so, running like some secret magic through all human history, inexplicable, powerful, elusive of all human efforts to analyse it, compelling an unwilling admiration, or extorting an unreasonable fear, potent for good, destructive of evil, the spiritual essence and mission of the Church unfolds itself. And whether seen in the quiet life of some such saint and apostle as Charles Travers, or exhibited on larger lines in some great evolution that touches the sympathies, or awakens the fears of men, the same uniform and unvarying issues startle the world into a momentary faith in the supernatural; for on no other grounds can it interpret or explain that which is known in Christian history and ethics as the conquest of the learned by the foolish, of the powerful by the weak, of the great ones by the little—in a word, that apparent defeat, which has marked all God's dealings with His world through His Church, which, in reality, as time develops His designs, is seen to be perfect and ultimate victory, and which, therefore, we have ventured to designate—*The Triumph of Failure.*

# CHAPTER VI

## L'ENVOI

As I lay down my pen to close this life's history, and lift my head from the desk on which I have been writing, the evening is dying away in the saffron and daffodil tints of the extreme West, and the twilight is closing around me. How shall I bid farewell to all those friends—those shades I have summoned up for the last time to meet me, and tell me their brief story? I feel very lonely parting with them. And, as I close down the window of my cell, and the two dear friends, their faces yet turned towards me yearningly, pass out into the unknown and as yet unrevealed world of spirits, and Ursula waves her little hand in farewell, I feel a darkness deepening on my soul, and a longing to break through the rigid form of dumb, irresponsive matter, and lose myself in the infinite. My cell is growing very dark. There is my little camp bed, its white coverlet glimmering in the faint light. There is my humble washstand and basin. Here is my desk and chair. That is all. But no. For here, its paleness shining through the dark, is my crucifix. I come near. There is the well-known figure—the fair hair crowned with sharp spikes, the sad eyes, the pale cheeks, and here is the great mouth of the wound, that speaks the unutterable love of my Master. I kneel down, and as in my dream in the Greek Temple, I press my forehead to the cold nails that pierce the feet of Christ:

"O Thou persistent Lover! Thou tireless Seeker after souls! Thou, Eagle of the skies, who didst drop me from Thy grasp, and let me fall plumb into the abysses, and then caught me up as my feet were touching the burning marl; and thus didst compel me to acknowledge Thy wisdom, Thy clemency, and Thy power—Behold, I see Thee now in the light of setting suns, and hear Thee in the whispers of the wind; and in the pealing of Thy organs, and the rhythmic thunders of Thy psalms, Thy voice comes to me. But most of all do I feel Thee in the sacred silence of Thy Tabernacles, and unutterable things breathe round about my soul from behind the mystic veils of Thy sacramental Presence! Dear Lord! this confession of my blindness and Thy mercy, my pride and Thy patience, my folly and Thy unspeakable wisdom, I put forth gently and diffidently into the hands of men—Thou knowest with no other object but that the wearied and broken-hearted may creep to Thy feet in the pauses of their mental anguish, and there lay down the burden of their sorrow and their pain."

## THE END

BURNS AND OATES, LIMITED, PRINTERS, LONDON